P9-DMW-632

GRAVESTONE

GRAVESTONE

A MARTY HOPKINS MYSTERY

P. M. CARLSON

POCKET BOOKS

New York   London   Toronto   Sydney   Tokyo   Singapore

This book is a work of fiction. Names, characters, places, and incidents are either products of the author's imagination or are used fictitiously. Any resemblance to actual events or locales or persons, living or dead, is entirely coincidental.

POCKET BOOKS, a division of Simon & Schuster Inc.
1230 Avenue of the Americas, New York, NY 10020

Copyright © 1993 by Patricia M. Carlson

All rights reserved, including the right to reproduce this book or portions thereof in any form whatsoever. For information address Pocket Books, 1230 Avenue of the Americas, New York, NY 10020

Carlson, P. M.
    Gravestone : a Marty Hopkins mystery / P. M. Carlson.
       p.   cm.
    ISBN 0-671-76974-X
    1. Policewomen—Indiana—Fiction.   I. Title.
PS3553.A7328G73   1993
813'.54—dc20   93-12460
                                                   CIP

First Pocket Books hardcover printing June 1993

10   9   8   7   6   5   4   3   2   1

POCKET and colophon are registered trademarks of Simon & Schuster Inc.

Printed in the U.S.A.

For Geoff, Richard, and Marvin

The author thanks Joanna Wolper,
Kay Williams, Guy Townsend, Jim McElroy,
David Linzee, Robert Knightly, and Patricia King for
sharing their expertise and insight.

1

GRAVES ARE SHALLOW IN SOUTHERN INDIANA. THE RUMPLED hills are furred with redbud, hickory, joe-pye weed, creepers. But under the skimpy layers of topsoil and red clay, the limestone stretches, hard as bone. To go deeper you need dynamite. So coffins are laid gently to bed on bedrock four feet down, and covered with earth, and tagged with headstones carved from the same mother rock.

This grave didn't have a headstone. It was marked with a homemade cross, two charred sticks lashed together. It wasn't dug down to bedrock, either. A foot and a half, maybe. The Night-Hawk leveled the last clods, kicked some leaves across, and started home. The sky was black again, the fog damp. He worried about the other one, the unwarned one. But he thought he'd done the right thing.

Royce Denton woke to the barking of coonhounds. No, it was more than that. There had been a shout, a thumping, down the hall. Now he could hear the murmur of his mother's voice. He squinted at the clock: four-twenty, still black as coal outside. His father shouted again and Royce closed his eyes. No sense in everyone getting up. But he couldn't get used to this house again. Dorothy had left him almost a year ago, so

1

when Dad got sick he'd been free to come back home, keep an eye on things. But the big square room he'd slept in as a boy seemed unfamiliar now, the house charged with alien vibrations, with something he couldn't quite identify.

Although in a way he could. It was Dad, of course. His father had been such a force in his boyhood. Now Dad was sick and old. The house felt different with the changing of the guard.

The old man bellowed again. Hell, why couldn't she shut him up? What was wrong? No hope for sleep. Royce sat up, scuffed his feet into his slippers, and strode down the hall toward his father's room.

In the hills the night was black. But the woman who emerged from the tangled bushes of the dry streambed had a glowing miner's hat, as though she wore her own moon. In her hands was a plastic container stamped with code numbers. She carried it tenderly, almost sorrowfully, as though she bore the coffin of a child. Inside the container was the body of a small fish. The fish was pale, almost white. It had no eyes.

The woman climbed to higher ground and walked toward the road. Behind her, three low shadows congealed from the night and followed her.

Martine LaForte Hopkins, twenty-nine years old and married, more or less, was trying to sleep through the jangling. But Chrissie's little hand shaking her shoulder was harder to ignore.

"Telephone, Mom."

"Uh?" Marty rolled onto her back and blinked at the window. Black sky; the sun wasn't up yet. Brad, maybe?

"It's a lady," Chrissie persisted. "Says she wants to talk to the lady sheriff."

"Shoot." Marty humped up to a sitting position and accepted the receiver from Chrissie. "Hello, Deputy Hopkins speaking."

"Miz Hopkins, there was this weird thing over on the Lawrence Road." The voice was excited. "Like a little fire, and someone dancing."

2

"A fire? Did you call the fire department?"

"No, it was real little, not even as big as a campfire. And there's no house nearby. About a mile south of the Hutchinson place, you know? Before the road starts uphill toward Dunning?"

"Yeah."

"But it was so weird. In the mist and everything."

"Okay." It was cold. Marty struggled to get the blanket around her shoulders. "Now, who are you?"

"Oh, sorry. This is Lucille Kinser. I'm a nurse. And I was driving back from my shift at the hospital, just like always. But I've never seen anything like that in fifteen years."

"Okay, we'll check it out, Miz Kinser."

"Thanks. I, uh, didn't want to call the sheriff's office. Didn't know if it was a crime or anything. I figured you'd know."

"Yeah, okay, we'll check it out."

Marty hung up and swung her legs over the edge of the bed. It was cold. She pulled her bra from the chair where she'd tossed it last night. "You get on back to bed, Chrissie, you'll freeze."

"Did that lady see a fire? Is that what you have to check out?" Chrissie was nine, curious, and impervious to cold unless she was in a mood to complain.

"No, probably no fire. Probably just somebody seeing things. Get on back to bed now." Marty pulled on her uniform shirt and dialed. "Hi, Roy. It's Marty. Grady Sims is on tonight, right? Tell him to run over to the Lawrence Road when he can, about a mile south of the Hutchinson place. Something going on there, maybe. And maybe not."

"Okay. He brought in Johnny Peters drunk tonight, guy was shooting at his wife's door. We still got paperwork to do."

"Yeah, well, whenever he can get there. Up to you guys." Marty hung up and stepped into her trousers. What the hell was she doing getting dressed now? She didn't have to go on duty for three hours, certainly not for someone's goofy hallucination in the mist. And the caller herself, what was her name, Kinser, she'd known it didn't sound like much. Hadn't even dared to call the sheriff's office, had hunted up Marty's

3

name instead. Wouldn't get laughed at by a woman, she'd figured.

Now Marty would be the one to get laughed at. Hopkins is seeing ghosts, they'd say. Marty's mirages.

She put in her earrings, simple studs for work.

The teakettle shrilled in the kitchen downstairs. Marty's mouth tightened and she popped into Chrissie's room to grab her daughter's sweatshirt before running downstairs. Sure enough, Chrissie was there, skinny and barefoot in her worn pajamas and new pink seashell earrings, her doll Polly under her arm. She'd fixed herself a cup of hot chocolate. The girl looked up warily and said, "I thought you'd want some coffee."

"Here, put this on," Marty commanded, pushing the sweatshirt at her. "You look like a war orphan. Those jammies are down to a loincloth." Chrissie grinned and pulled on the sweatshirt, then sat down at the table, perching her feet on the rung of the chair, off the cold vinyl. Marty spooned instant coffee into a mug and said, "What's got into you? Any sane person would be snug in her bed."

"I heard the phone. I thought maybe—" She shrugged. "But it was that lady. She sounded so excited."

"Yeah. She did." Marty sat down next to Chrissie and gave her daughter a hug. The kid was right—there was something in that nurse's voice, urgency and awe. "That's why I'm going, because she seemed excited. It sure doesn't sound like much otherwise."

"Maybe the fire will be bigger by now." Chrissie had Brad's dark eyes and hair and Marty's curiosity.

"Yeah. Well, I'd better check it out." Marty downed her coffee and went for her jacket in the front closet.

Aunt Vonnie was standing halfway down the steps, her pink chenille robe tight around her, her peroxided hair in curlers. "What's going on?"

"Nothing. Just got a call." Adjusting her gun belt, Marty looked up at her aunt. "Everybody can go back to bed."

"God, I don't know why you don't get a job with regular hours," Aunt Vonnie complained. Years ago her young husband had died in Korea and she'd never remarried, subsisting on an army pittance and her work at Reiner's Bakery on the Dunning town square. A few years ago she'd moved from her ancient trailer into the house to nurse her sister, Marty's mother, in her last illness. After the funeral Marty asked her to stay on to take care of Chrissie. There was friction about Marty's job, and sparks flew when Brad was in town. But she was good with Chrissie and in the end she and Marty knew they needed each other.

Marty buttoned her jacket. "Look, Aunt Vonnie, I agree with you. I'd rather be rich and live in New York City and let room service bring me a breakfast tray. With caviar, and a rose in a bud vase." And Brad, rich and famous, by her side; but she didn't say that to Aunt Vonnie.

Aunt Vonnie smiled grudgingly. "That'll be the day."

"Hey, I'm sorry I woke you up. Go on back to bed. I'll see you later." Marty clapped on her Stetson and hurried out.

The first hint of light was silvering the eastern sky, but the ground fog still hung heavy wherever the road dipped. She stopped at Straub's Service Station. Gil Newton ambled out, monosyllabic as usual, to fill up the car. Marty charged it to the sheriff's account and headed for the Lawrence Road. South of the Hutchinson place she slowed down, drove past three times. Nothing. No fire, no dancing, only the dark, the mist, and the denser shadows of trees and bushes.

On the fourth pass a car appeared. Sheriff's department. She pulled onto the shoulder and got out to meet Grady Sims. "Hi," she said.

"Hey there, Marty." Grady was tall, skinny, angular as a derrick, and didn't mind much that she was female. "Whatcha got?"

"Probably nothing. Report of someone dancing around a little fire."

"Party, huh? Over now," observed Grady, but he followed her across the ditch and through the fence.

Nothing. They checked out the field but hadn't found anything after stumping around in the misty dawn for half an hour. "UFOs," Grady concluded darkly.

"Aliens," Marty agreed. "Pretty soon we'll be in the headlines at checkout counters all over the U.S.A."

But something in the haze caught her eye as they started back. Branches a little too even, a little too dark. Among the honeysuckles and scrub maples at the edge of the field she found it, the charred cross marking the ominous rectangle of freshly turned earth.

"Somebody buried their old coonhound," Grady said hopefully.

"Then why the cross?" said Marty. "And why bury it in the middle of the night?"

Grady nodded. Sober and professional, they retraced their steps carefully, called Sheriff Cochran, and cordoned off the area.

An hour later Marty was standing guard with a couple of her fellow deputies, watching Grady Sims and Roy Adams as they spooned out the soil with trowels, cautious as archaeologists.

An engine growled behind them. Sheriff Cochran was back from talking to the county prosecuting attorney. He surged from the cruiser and stamped along the cordoned path toward the shallow hole. Cochran was a solid, silvery-haired man, his face ruddy in the morning sun. He squinted down at the diggers.

Grady's rangy frame was all angles as he brushed aside some newly troweled earth. "Christ!" he exclaimed. "Look what they've done to him! Poor fucker!"

A choked giggle escaped Roy Adams. "Wrong word for him now, Grady. Wrong word."

Marty craned her neck. A man's body, something about his face. Revulsion thickened in her throat even before her mind grasped what had been stuffed into his mouth.

"Jesus!" said Sheriff Cochran. "Well, everybody out to wait for the state evidence technicians or they'll have my ass." He moved back from the grave and eyed his deputies. "Mason!"

"Yessir?"

"You're related to this Mrs. Kinser who called in, right?"

"My daddy's her cousin."

"Okay. Get over there and get a statement. Every little thing she can remember. Hopkins!"

6

"Yessir." Marty jumped forward.

"Got a project for you too."

She nodded once, crisply, and drew herself up to her full five-seven. That wouldn't be short, except that half the sheriff's department had once been basketball stars. Including big Wes Cochran, long ago, before the years padded his belly.

He fumbled in a trousers pocket behind his holster and pulled out a rumpled yellow paper. "We got a call. Old Judge Denton thinks someone's out to kill him. I want you to check it out."

Disappointment heaved down through Marty, head to gut. "But Judge Denton isn't in his right mind!"

"His son called. Hal Junior."

"I see." Marty's shoulders sagged. Hal Denton, Jr., was one of Prosecuting Attorney Pfann's best friends. Plus, he was running for Congress. Cochran was right—he couldn't ignore this call, no matter how much off his head the old judge might be. But did it have to be Marty who went to listen to his ravings? She wasn't Mother Teresa. She made one more try. "I'm good at searches. Sir."

"Your find last night has been noted, Hopkins," Cochran said dryly. "Now, don't keep those important folks waiting."

Marty stalked across to her car. Shoot. Five years in this department and here came another kindergarten job. The token woman. The lady cop. She sighed. Get serious, Hopkins, you know what the world's like. No different from her days at Indiana University before she'd had to quit school. The guys had their Little 500 bicycle race. It was famous, Hollywood made movies about it. And then there was the girls' race. On tricycles. It was hard to get a tricycle to move fast, your knees always knocked into your elbows. It was a real athletic achievement, in fact, though everyone laughed about it. Wes Cochran had been in the stands the year she raced. He'd seen her come from behind, knees bobbing, awkward as an ostrich on the run. He'd laughed too; but when Brad hit those first setbacks trying to break into broadcasting and she'd had to ask the sheriff for work, he'd remembered that she hadn't quit till she'd won.

And shoot, much as she'd like to see New York, she did like this county, people who mostly worked hard and tried to follow the Lord, except some Saturday nights. And she liked this job. Helping people was a lot better than sitting around typing letters. People, action, Marty liked that. And she could cope, she'd proved that over and over. Highway smash-ups, robberies, lost cows. Even homicides, like that brawl when Bert Gantz had flirted with Tammy Donnelli in the bar, and John Donnelli had chased him home and bashed him with a post-hole digger. Marty and Grady Sims had taken that call, and by the time the others arrived and met Grady by poor old Gantz's remains, Marty had found Donnelli behind the silo, gentled him into handing over the post-hole digger, and was patting him on the back as he blubbered on about the cruelty of life. She was good at listening to drunks, God help her.

But Judge Denton wasn't a drunk. Batty, yes, and getting worse, they said. Excused from the bench after his first fit, six months ago. Too bad about that. She'd given evidence before him several times and he'd never let hotshot defense attorneys over from Madison or Bloomington insult the deputies' powers of observation.

She saw Sheriff Cochran's silver head swing toward her and hastily twisted the key in the ignition. Get on with it, Hopkins, she told herself. You found the grave, okay, but you don't own the case. No matter how curious you are about this poor soul, who ran into someone a whole lot meaner than John Donnelli. Besides, clear the Denton thing quick, and maybe Cochran will put you back on it. It was just a matter of holding some worried politician's hand, maybe listening to his sick old daddy's delusions.

Before pulling onto the highway she twisted the rearview mirror down and inspected her face. Yep, repairs needed before meeting a congressional candidate. She spit on a tissue and rubbed away a dark smudge on her cheek, then brushed the honeysuckle leaves out of her brown curls. Ought to shampoo tonight. She pulled her lipstick from her pocket and took a deep breath. Serenity, Hopkins. Accept the things you cannot change.

The morning fog had lifted. She readjusted the mirror and shifted into gear. The car lumbered up over the shoulder and onto the pavement like an old bear. Marty nosed it toward Judge Denton's place, floorboarded it, and screeched away.

2

IN THE NINETEENTH CENTURY THE DENTONS HAD OWNED A RAILroad, one of the lines that transported blocks of top-grade Salem limestone from the local quarries to the entire nation. The heirs had sold while there was still some profit in it and turned to banking, law, politics. But the judge still lived in the grand square limestone house his grandfather had erected. It was off the highway that led north from Dunning toward Bloomington and Indianapolis. Heavy stone lintels, like eyebrows, topped the windows that looked out on the lawn and the long driveway. The house itself was shaded by oaks and hickories.

Marty's grandfather had worked in the quarries and had left his heirs the sagging frame house on the back road where Marty lived now, trying to save up enough to get it painted. But it did have a hickory tree.

Two cars, an Oldsmobile and a Buick, were parked in the turnaround. From beyond the house the voices of coonhounds saluted her coming, deep and mellow as bells. She picked up her notebook and brushed a honeysuckle leaf from her sleeve. Her grandfather, if he'd ever been summoned there, would have used the servants' entrance. "Hey, watch this, Gramps," Marty muttered, and headed for the limestone-columned front porch.

She wondered if they were yet lifting that man from his makeshift grave. Who the hell would do that to a human being? Damn, he was the one who deserved her time, not these rich political friends of the sheriff. But she folded her resentment onto a back shelf of her mind and turned to her task.

The woman who opened the massive door was shorter than Marty, dressed in an expensive gray and white print dress. Her hair was warm brown, carefully sculpted into ripples by the beautician, and her skin glowed. "Yes?"

"I'm Marty Hopkins, from the sheriff's department."

"Oh, yes, do come in. My son called, I believe. I'm Elizabeth Denton." As the door opened wider, the brighter light showed that the glow of Elizabeth Denton's skin was all makeup, that her eyes were lifeless. "I'll go tell the boys you're here. And I have to unplug the iron, I've just been doing Hal's shirts." Elizabeth Denton moved back toward a door behind the broad staircase. "Please sit down, I'll be right back."

So she did the ironing herself. Strange, in a place this posh. Across from the living-room arch Marty saw a door into a big study. Nice old furniture, maybe antiques left by the railroad Dentons. The house smelled close, almost musty, overlaid with something sweet. She tracked it to a little bowl filled with dried petals and herbs sitting on the hall table. Potpourri. Classy. Above the table hung a large painting framed in curly gilt. A woman and a girl, life-size, both in long white gowns, holding sprays of roses. Both had an air of calm that was attractive enough on the woman but unsettling on the child, who couldn't have been much more than ten. About Chrissie's age, but Chrissie and her friends were frisky creatures of great enthusiasm, busy as a hatful of cats. Maybe in the old days ten-year-olds were quieter. The artist painted jewelry well. The woman's necklace and bracelet were flashing rubies, while the girl's were glowing gold worked in a rhythmic leaf design.

From the stairwell above Marty's head came a sudden thumping and a man's resonant voice. "Mackay! Idiot!"

"Oh, I'm sorry, I should have showed you to the living room." Elizabeth Denton reappeared at the rear of the hall.

Startled, Marty stared at her. Shoot. Could it be? "The woman in the painting," she said. "It's you?"

"Yes, it was—" Elizabeth Denton stared down and smoothed her skirt. "It was done ten years ago."

Ten unkind years ago. Not the old days after all. Marty said, "It's a lovely painting."

"Thank you. Please, come sit down." Elizabeth scurried to the double doors. "They'll be here in just a second."

Marty followed her. There were a couple of antique stuffed chairs and a sofa grouped before a carved limestone mantel. Another bowl of potpourri sat on a side table. Before they could sit down, voices sounded in the hall and two men strode in. Both wore pastel business shirts with the collars open and city shoes a lot shinier than Marty's thick-soled Oxfords.

"Ah, the lady sheriff! Thanks for coming. I'm Hal Denton." The taller of the two was all engaging grin and earnest blue eyes, familiar from posters and television. His handshake was brisk.

"I'm Marty Hopkins."

"You've met my mother. And here's my brother, Royce Denton."

She'd seen Royce before too, a popular defense lawyer. His smile was slower than Hal's, and his handshake lingered a moment on her palm. He said, "I've seen you in court. Howdy."

"Glad to meet you all," she said, opening her notebook. "Now, what can we do for you?"

"Sit down, for starters." Hal waved his hand at the sofa. Marty sat at the near end. Royce circled behind it to the other end and lounged back as if considering an after-dinner snooze. Hal and Elizabeth sat on the chairs facing them. Hal was apologizing but his blue politician's eyes were studying her shrewdly. "I'm sorry I had to call you today. Wes Cochran told me a big case just came up, but the problem is that Royce and I have to get over to Paoli to a Chamber of Commerce luncheon, and I go on to Indianapolis for a highway bill consultation."

Okay, okay, Marty thought, I know you represent our district in the state legislature, and I know you're a busy man and my boss's buddy to boot. Let's get on with this. She said patiently, "So what can we do for you?"

Hal rubbed the back of his neck. "Well now, Royce says this is nothing new, but—well, you see, I have to spend so much time in Indianapolis that I can't get down here as often as I'd like."

Marty nodded.

"So when Dad got ill, it fell mostly on Royce and Mother. Royce works nearby, and he was free to move in so he could help out a lot more. Sits with Dad, oversees the yard work—"

"Jack of all trades." Royce still sprawled lazily at the far end of the sofa. "I even run his dogs sometimes."

She said, "I see."

"We hired nurses," Hal went on, "and I get back whenever I can. But it's been a difficult thing for all of us. Dad doesn't make a lot of sense, and he has convulsions. It's multiple brain tumors," he explained earnestly. "Dr. Hendricks sent him to an Indianapolis lab for scans. He says they found all these little growths—well, you don't want to hear about all those details."

"The bottom line is, it's inoperable," Royce said. Marty became aware of a deep fatigue in his voice. Shoot, Sheriff Cochran was right, these people deserved some attention too. Even if you can afford nurses, the pain is real.

"Dr. Hendricks started him on antitumor medication right away, of course. Even so—" Hal's eyes met Royce's before he continued. "Royce sees more of Dad, of course. But it seems to me he's a lot worse than he was even two weeks ago. And I just wouldn't feel right if we didn't follow up."

"Of course," said Marty. "Follow up on what?"

"He said, 'They're killing me. Phyllis.' I was sitting right by his bed and he said it quite clearly. And I said, 'No one wants to kill you.' And he said, 'Yes. Killing. Mackay'—well, I won't repeat what he called him."

Royce's legs were stretched out before him, ankles crossed, one arm ranged across the sofa back with his fingers inches from Marty's shoulder. Her glance caught a mocking grin twitching the corner of his mouth. He said, "I bet the sheriff's department hears bad language sometimes too, Hal."

12

Marty was trying to place the name. "Mackay. There's a Mackay who works at Straub's Service with Gil Newton. He's the one who crowded someone off the road a while ago?"

"Same guy," said Hal. "Bert Mackay. Maybe ten years ago he got drunk one night and ran young Johnny Victor's motorcycle into a ditch. Killed him. Well, Dad knew the Victors, the manager of Salem National Bank, you know him?"

Marty nodded. The Victors were another of Nichols County's first families.

"So Dad threw the book at Mackay. But of course he'd been drinking so they couldn't lock him up forever. He's been out a couple of years now."

"Did he threaten your father?"

"Not that we know of." Royce turned his head toward Marty. Despite his business clothes he had an outdoorsman's skin, tanned and weathered. Not as pampered as his brother's. "And of course Dad had to sentence a lot of our local toughs, at one time or another. He does mention other names, right, Mother?"

"Yes." Elizabeth Denton spoke quietly. "Rogers, Hoadley, Phyllis—"

"Oh, hell, I thought you didn't want to—" Royce broke off.

Elizabeth looked at her lap. "Hal heard it too."

"Okay, I'm outnumbered." Royce shrugged at Marty. "Phyllis is our dear little sister, Miss Hopkins. At the ripe old age of twelve she discovered boys, except they were twenty-year-olds with motorcycles, and off she went into the sunset in a leather jacket. She wrote twice, some friend mailed them from here, then quit."

"You haven't heard anything since?"

Elizabeth Denton shook her head mutely, still staring at her lap. Hal said, "Wes helped. Your boss. He did what he could, quietly. Found some bikers in Terre Haute, but that didn't work out either."

"How long ago did this happen?"

"Eight years ago." Hal's voice too held pain. "Royce and I were a lot older than Phyl, of course, about to start high school when she was born. I was astonished when she ran away, she'd been such a sweet child. Oh, Mother, I'm sorry!"

13

Tears were sliding down Elizabeth Denton's cheeks. She turned her face from Hal and dabbed at it with a white handkerchief.

"I don't know what to do!" Hal sprang up from his chair and put a hand on her shoulder. "Mother, look, the police might be able to help if Dad really did hear from Phyl—"

"It's in his head," Royce said gently. "He's never really come to terms with her leaving."

"No, he'd accepted it, seems to me," Hal objected. "That's why mentioning her now seems so odd."

"Accepted it?" Elizabeth looked up at Hal. Under her left eye her skin was dark where tears had dissolved her makeup. "He never changed his will. Except for my trust, the estate is to be equally divided among his surviving children. All of them."

"Yeah. But I still think we should try."

Marty studied Hal as new possibilities opened before her. These guys loved their family, okay, but they also thought in terms of bottom lines. And the bottom line was, a sister who had disappeared but was still in the will could hold up settling an estate for a long time. "Mr. Denton," she said, and both sets of blue eyes turned to her. "I'm not real clear on what you want our department to do now."

"Well, there's Phyl," Hal answered. "Maybe Wes Cochran could ask about her again."

"You see, Hal Junior is running for Congress, you know," added Royce, another grin playing about his tired mouth. "It would be nice to have the family finances neatened up. And if these skeletons in the closet get dragged into the debate, he wants to be able to say he did everything possible."

"Sure, that's part of it." Hal's look was earnest and open. "But dammit, I think we owe it to Dad and to Phyl to find out if there's anything to his story."

"Can I see him?" Marty asked.

"He probably won't make any sense." Hal straightened, suddenly cautious, glancing at his watch.

Royce stood up lazily. "But all we've given Miss Hopkins so far is hearsay, Hal. You get our stuff ready. I'll take her."

Upstairs, a central hall gave access to the bedrooms. Royce

touched her elbow, indicated one of the doors, and followed her in. A color television played silently, flickering gold, rose, chartreuse. A blond woman in nurse's whites sat rocking where she could see both the screen and the dozing occupant of the mahogany double bed. Marty was shocked to see how frail Judge Denton looked, bones jutting against the wasted skin. He'd lost all his hair.

The nurse removed her earphones and stood up with a warm smile for Royce Denton. "Hello, Royce."

"Howdy, Lisa. This is Martha Hopkins from the sheriff's department."

"Marty Hopkins," she corrected. "Glad to meet you, Lisa."

"Yeah, hi." Lisa had a triangular face, smiling eyes, and a tumble of strawberry-blond hair pulled back by a bow at the nape of her neck. She added, "I think I met you once a couple years ago. At the Slam Dunk. You're Brad Hopkins's wife, right?"

The Slam Dunk. Dark oak booths, amber lights glowing in the fog of cigarette smoke, pitchers of beer, Elvis songs throbbing in the background. Brad thumping a friend on the back in greeting, pulling him and his strawberry-blond date over to the booth to meet Marty. All four of them singing along, ain't nothin' but a hound dog, Brad howling doglike in silly counterpoint. Marty had giggled like a schoolgirl. Shoot, she missed Brad.

"Old pals, huh?" Royce smiled, then turned to Lisa. "How's your patient?"

"Okay. I got the sheets changed and he took his sedative right after. It's just—well, his system isn't taking to the medication."

"Dr. Hendricks says it's his only chance. Can't operate."

"I know. Well, if anyone can beat it, he can."

"You say he's sedated. Any chance he'll wake up?" Marty had hoped to ask him about Phyllis, about Mackay.

"Hard to tell," Lisa said. "The daytime sedative isn't that strong. But he needs something."

Marty noticed that the judge's hands were tied to the bed railings. Royce followed her glance. "Mostly to protect him," he said softly. "But us, too. Maybe you noticed Mother's shiner? He has convulsions. And he's still surprisingly strong."

15

"Like a bull," said Lisa.

Marty had known since childhood how tough it was to watch over a berserk male. She turned back to Lisa with sympathy. "Has he said anything to you that would make you think there's something we should investigate?"

"Well—Mr. Denton, Hal, he thinks so."

"What kinds of things have you heard him say?"

"I don't pay much attention. He doesn't make much sense."

Especially if you're wearing earphones. But shoot, Hopkins, you can't fault Lisa for that. This is a sordid enough job without having to listen to rambling insanities. She asked, "Does he mention his daughter?"

"My daughter." The voice was rich and mellow, and for an instant Marty didn't connect it with the wasted form bound to the bed. Then she saw the judge's eyes. A fierce blue, they tugged her to him. "Phyllis," he said. "You're not Phyllis."

"I'm from the sheriff's department."

"Sheriff. Find my daughter."

"We'll try, sir."

"She's killing me."

"Yes, sir. How is she killing you?"

"Inside. Boring in." The bright eyes closed, then opened. "Wolf."

His voice held such conviction that Marty almost looked around for gray fur, even while she realized in sorrow that it was madness speaking. "I see, sir."

Royce said softly, "When Phyl ran away it almost broke him. But he got back on his feet finally, and he—"

"Royce, shut up," bellowed the old man. "Or you're off to bed without dinner."

Royce's eyebrows crawled up in a you-see-what-I-mean expression as he answered, "Yes, sir."

Marty asked, "Judge Denton. What about Mackay?"

"Mackay. Idiot."

"Sir, what did Mackay do to you?"

His lips worked for a moment but suddenly the flash of blue clouded and his lids dropped again.

Well, Hopkins, that interview won't win you any commendations. Marty stepped back from the bed. "Okay. Thanks,

16

Lisa, I guess that's all we can do here. Call the department if anything comes up, okay?" Marty scribbled the number onto a fresh page and tore it out for her.

"Sure. See you." Lisa pocketed the paper and reached for her headphones.

Marty followed Royce Denton back into the shadowy hall. He paused at the top of the stairs, blocking her. "Sorry I got your name wrong, Marty Hopkins," he murmured.

"No problem."

He was standing so close she could smell his aftershave. His hand touched her neck gently. Marty tensed. His grin reappeared and he held up the twig of honeysuckle he'd picked off her collar.

"Oh. Thanks." She hoped she wasn't blushing.

"Anytime, Mrs. Hopkins."

She swung past him and down the stairs. Hal Denton was in the hall, tying his necktie. "How is he?" he asked.

"Pretty much what you said. Did he mention a wolf to you?"

"A wolf? Don't remember." His blue eyes, milder than his father's, fixed on her. "Look, I'm sorry, we're probably sending you on a wild-goose chase. But I had to ask. Is there anything else we can do before we rush off?"

"Not now, Mr. Denton. But please keep us posted. We'll check out a couple of things and let you know if we find something."

"Thanks." He grabbed a blue jacket from the closet. "Come on, Royce, let's go."

"Hal, Royce, don't forget your clean shirts," came Elizabeth Denton's soft voice from the living-room arch.

"Damn." The two men hurried into the back of the house.

Elizabeth Denton was studying Marty, her eyes lively for the first time, flicking from her badge to her face and back. Marty asked, "Is there anything else, Mrs. Denton?"

"Not really. Unless—he said 'wolf'?"

"Yes."

"Maybe—" She stared at Marty intently. "Try the biology department."

"Biology department?"

She glanced at the door and whispered, "At Indiana University. Professor Wolfe." She stepped back into the arch as the men returned. "Goodbye."

Her eyes were glittering with tears. Hal and Royce kissed her goodbye and walked Marty out to the cars, accompanied by the mournful tune of the hounds.

3

WES COCHRAN STUDIED THE BILLFOLD ITEMS THAT THE STATE POlice evidence technician was showing him. No money; that figured. But the ID cards were still there. Indiana driver's license for a David Goldstein, five-eleven, one-fifty-two, brown and brown. Twenty-seven years old. Address out on the Lawrence Road. Next, an Indiana University student card. What the hell was an IU student doing this far south? He looked at the date—six years ago. Ex-student, then. Goldstein hung on to it, probably, to try to get special student rates on tickets. Next was a bank card, Salem National. No credit cards. A photo of a smiling black woman, young and pretty. Shit. He didn't like the feel of this case. Wes Cochran nodded thanks to the evidence technician and looked across the hills to the pale sky. It would get into the eighties today. And too much work to do. Last year Doc Hendricks had shaken his head over Cochran's blood pressure. "Take it easy, Wes. You're working too hard. Let the youngsters do the running around."

"Shit, Doc, you know it eats me up to sit in that office. That time my leg got busted up I just about died of boredom."

But every now and then something squeezed tight as a vise in his chest, and as he rested a moment, panting, waiting for it to go away, he wondered if maybe Doc was right, if maybe this job was getting to be too much for the old machine. But hell, he was only fifty-eight. A lot of good years left in him.

He didn't like the feel of this case, though. Not at all. How'd you get yourself into this kind of trouble, son? What did you stir up in these hills?

Grady Sims ambled over, his long face haggard, and handed him a plastic evidence bag. Inside was a three-by-five card. On it someone had sketched a circle, almost filled by a fat plus sign. Where the arms crossed, a diamond shape enclosed a pointed oval that might represent a blood drop. A crude, homemade Klan sign.

"Shit," said Wes Cochran, and raised his eyes to Grady Sims's.

"It was on the grave," Sims said. "Found it when we first started digging to see what was there."

"Did the state evidence cops see it?"

"No, sir. Found it before we called them."

"Keep it quiet for now."

Sims nodded and returned to the others. Watching him, Cochran heard footsteps behind him. It was Hopkins. He smiled.

He liked Marty Hopkins. He'd known her when she was little Marty LaForte, his friend Rusty LaForte's tomboy daughter. He and Rusty had taught her basketball, boys' rules, hooting and slapping each other as she outdribbled and outshot all the other nine-year-olds in the county, even his own son Billy. But after Rusty got drunk once too often and piled his pickup into a tree, Marty's mother had taken her north to Bloomington, raised her a townie. Cochran had seen her only once in ten years, that time he was up at the Little 500 weekend with some buddies, and there she was, grown up and cute as a bug on that tricycle, but scrambling for the win with the same bullheaded determination he remembered from her earlier years. He'd made a point of going down to congratulate her. "Hey, Marty LaForte. Good work!"

"Thanks." She'd glanced up at him, rosy with victory, and recognition and delight lit her face. "Coach?"

"Yep."

"Well, shoot! Coach!"

"Yep." He'd swirled the beer in his can. "Uh, how's your mom?"

"Not bad. How're things down your way?"

"Not bad."

But before they could say more, a swirl of her sorority friends had arrived and swept her off to some more youthful celebration. Later her mother had moved back to the home place, but he hadn't seen Marty again until five years ago, when that no-good husband of hers took off on one of his periodic searches for radio fame and she moved back here. She showed up in front of his desk one day holding her four-year-old and saying, "Sheriff Cochran, I need a job real bad." Turned out she'd worked security for Indiana University. Wes remembered her father, how he'd helped out Billy while they both were still alive. So he'd taken Marty on to answer phones. But she was still as pushy as ever. Nagged him into sending her out on patrol. Called him "sir" now instead of "Coach," but she still wanted to play boys' rules.

"Well, hello, Hopkins," he said. "What's the Denton story?"

"Not much, sir." She brushed a brown curl back from her forehead. "The family's all broken up about the judge being so bad. He's pretty far gone."

"You saw him?"

"Tried to talk to him. But he didn't make a whole lot of sense. Hal Junior thought he was accusing someone of trying to kill him. Maybe someone he'd sentenced. But I don't see how anyone could give him a brain tumor."

"Yeah. Someone he'd sentenced—anyone in particular?"

"The judge mentioned Mackay. Others too."

"Oh, yeah, Bert Mackay at the gas station. Ran that kid off the road when he was drunk. But he hasn't given us any trouble for a while."

"And he also mentioned his daughter, who ran off a while ago."

"Yeah. That was before you came back here."

"They want us to put out another bulletin on her."

"Shit, nothin'll come of that. She'll be grown up by now, and we don't even have a photo. Does Hal Denton truly believe his sister has anything to do with his daddy's problems?"

"The way I read it, Hal Denton has his own problems. He

20

doesn't want people thinking he's a heartless brother, a heartless son. Plus he's going to need money."

"For the campaign, you mean."

"Yeah. See, while his father was healthy he probably could have borrowed it from him. But he can't now. And if his father dies, the money'll be tied up while they look for the daughter. It's supposed to be equally divided among his surviving children."

"You'd think with three lawyers in the family they'd have written a better will after she ran off." Cochran looked off at the hills again. "But yeah, I can see that happening. Hal and Royce don't want to bother the old man about the will until he cools off about her running away. He was real upset at the beginning. Sick a lot. They gave out it was tapeworm or something but I always figured he was pining for the girl. So anyway, Hal and Royce wait to bring it up. Then *bang*, his mind goes. So now he can't make a valid change in his will. What's your opinion, Hopkins?" He looked at her sharply.

"About the will?"

"About his mind."

"I think it's gone, all right. A few things he said almost made sense but most of it was just raving. Near as I could make out, he said his daughter was killing him. He also talked about a wolf."

"Shit. A wolf?"

"His wife thought he meant Professor Wolfe. Some biologist. Didn't tell me why she thought that."

"Professor Wolfe. Can't place it." He stared at the hills, then shook his head. The sun was higher now in the hazy sky, the shadows shorter.

"Sir?"

"Yeah?"

"Do you know who was in the grave?" She gestured across the field where the state evidence technicians still worked.

"Oh. Not official yet, but the ID belongs to a David Goldstein. Address Lawrence Road. IU student a few years ago."

"Is there something I can do?"

21

Her eagerness vibrated in the air and made him angry. "Hell, no, Hopkins! You're off this case!"

Her jaw tightened and he was sorry he'd yelled. He said more mildly, "What I want you to do is, first, check out the Denton stuff. I'll send out the bulletin on the daughter myself. You check on Mackay and this Professor Wolfe."

"Yessir." Resentment simmered in her gray eyes.

"And that's an order."

"Yessir. But you don't have to protect me, sir. I can do anything they can do." She jerked her head at the men searching the shallow grave.

"I know that, Hopkins," snapped Cochran. "But the voters don't know that. Say one of the men gets hurt on the job, he's a hero, no problem. But you get hurt and I have to spend forty hours a day explaining why you were there. Reporters show up, and TV crews, and pointy-heads from IU. Ain't worth it."

Hopkins cut through his anger, and her own, to the main point. "So you think somebody's going to get hurt."

He shrugged. "We're dealing with a rough customer here."

"More than one, right?" Her voice was level, professional. "We've got a Jew killed. And a burned cross." She gestured at the evidence bag he still held. "And a drawing of a cross and blood drop. We're talking about the Klan, aren't we?"

"Hopkins, you've got your orders!"

"Yessir."

"Klan hasn't done anything serious around here since I nailed them for beating up Emmett Hines fifteen years ago! Understand?"

"Yessir. You know these folks better than I do. But—" She drew a deep breath. "You know, sir, I have to go to Bloomington to check on that Professor Wolfe for the Dentons. Wouldn't take much longer to ask about Goldstein's student days."

He glared at her, exasperated.

She said, "Of course, if it's the Klan, maybe the FBI will take over and none of us will work on it."

"FBI? We ain't calling those morons! We'll solve it here, fast! FBI don't know a damn thing about these hills!"

Her gray eyes were steady on him. She didn't have to say, "I know these hills."

Defeated, he grunted, "Okay, do the background on Goldstein while you're there. But the Denton stuff comes first, you hear?"

"Yessir." She was off to her car, quick as a deer.

Wes Cochran looked down at the blood-drop drawing and immediately regretted letting her get involved. He hadn't told her that it looked like there were some extra wounds on the body. Not just the genitals cut off, stuffed in his mouth. But nail holes, big spikes really, in the feet and in the palms.

He hoped they'd turn out to be postmortem.

4

THE INDIANA UNIVERSITY REGISTRAR SHOWED MARTY HOPKINS the short record devoted to David Goldstein. He had attended for four terms, studying English literature and Western history. His grades, Bs and Cs the first two terms, fell in the third term and dissolved into a set of "incompletes" the last term. Marty wrote down the names of his professors. Only one name, McHale, appeared twice. She was lucky; Professor McHale was in his office in Ballantine Hall.

"Goldstein. Yes, I have a vague memory of him," said McHale. Scrawny except for a little potbelly, he had a habit of nudging the center of his upper lip with his tongue as he thought. "A bright student but he cut classes, turned in papers late—ah, yes, here we are." He pulled a small green grade book from a stack of similar ones. "Here. 'The Twentieth-Century Novel.' Yes, you see, he got A– on two papers, a C on the exam, and never turned in the third paper."

"Did you get to know him at all?"

"No. You can't counsel students unless they come in and ask. I spoke to him briefly, after class, but he never came to the office."

"Do you remember if he had any special friends?"

McHale's tongue nudged his lip. "Friends. You know, I did see him once at Plum's, at a table with some people. I recognized one of them, he plays jazz there sometimes. Saxophone. Oh, what is his name? Black fellow."

Uh-huh. That fit with the Klan card. Marty was beginning to get a picture of Goldstein.

"Carter?" guessed McHale. "Or something like that. Sorry I can't remember the name."

"I'll ask at Plum's. Here, please call if you remember anything else about Goldstein." She handed him the phone number.

It was sunny midafternoon when she emerged from Ballantine Hall. A few cars rolled along the curving wooded drive in front of the tall building. She'd parked the cruiser across the street in the Memorial Union lot, which was studded with flowering trees and bordered by a tiny stream. Prettiest parking lot in the state, she thought. Should she go to Plum's next? No, right behind Ballantine was the new glass and steel wing of the biology-department building, Jordan Hall. That's why she was here, officially. The Denton case, not the Goldstein murder. Marty sighed, turned around, and hiked across a wooden bridge to Jordan Hall.

No one answered her knock on Professor Wolfe's third-floor office door, but four doors down the hall a bookshelf-lined office was open. The card by the door said RONALD HART. A bag of Fritos lay open on the desk. A broad-shouldered man in a gray ragg sweater was pulling a book from one of the shelves. "Excuse me," Marty said to his back. "I'm looking for Professor Wolfe."

He turned with a look of disgust that altered to sudden interest as the fact of her uniform registered. "Well, well! And what has our good Professor Wolfe done now? Run someone down in that old pickup? Or are the parents of one of the maidens complaining?"

"I just want to ask a few questions," said Marty levelly.

"That's what all the maidens say." The man sighed. "But I thought a sheriff-maiden might be different." His brown hair was flashed with silver, his body beginning to go to flab. Hazel eyes ran over her uniform in appraisal. Most men found it off-putting but Marty got the feeling this one could work it into his fantasies.

She said coolly, "Can you tell me where to find Professor Wolfe?"

"For once, I can. They're in class right now." He squinted at his elaborate digital watch as though trying to disentangle the time from the months, tides and phases of the moon. "They'll be out in ten minutes," he decided. "And that may be your only chance for a sighting of the elusive creature."

"Okay. You're Professor Hart?"

"Right."

"I'm Deputy Hopkins. Nichols County. Professor Hart, can you tell me anything about Professor Wolfe?"

"She *is* in trouble, then?" Hart sounded almost eager.

She. Okay. Marty said, "You expect her to be in trouble?"

"Well, they do say she killed a man once."

He was peering at her closely, and Marty made sure her voice stayed cool and distant. "When was that?"

Hart picked up the Fritos and held the bag out to her. When she shook her head he took a handful himself and said, "I don't know the details, really. Just students talking. Self-defense, they said, some guy bothered her out in the country somewhere."

"I see. What are the names of these students?"

"Oh, God, I don't remember. Must have been five years ago."

Marty decided to come back to that later. She said, "Okay. You're both biologists?"

"The resemblance ends there." Hart laughed shortly and took another handful of Fritos. Crunching on them made his voice sound staticky, like a bad radio. "I'm a hardworking professor. She's always out in the field, or flying off to do fieldwork. Never serves on committees, never in her office."

Marty glanced at the bookshelves. "Professors publish a lot, don't they? Does she publish?"

25

"Oh, sure, she publishes. Don't know why they want the damn stuff. All this new wave earth science, just speculation. She's supposed to teach about evolutionary biology but she gets into everything else." He turned back to the shelves and pulled out three books. The top one, gray, bore an illustration of a flat segmented worm with a mouth surrounded by ugly hooks. *Evolution of Parasites.* The next one had an abstract wavy design on navy blue. *Biota of the Archeon Period.* The third was something about placental mammals. Wolfe was listed as the author of all three. Hart's mouth curled down. "And right now she says she's working on cave fauna. Adaptation to darkness. No one could be an expert in all these fields. Shallow books, not much substance."

"Are you an expert in any of those fields?"

"No." He looked at her sharply, as though trying to decide if he'd been insulted. "I specialize in plant diseases, and believe me, that's more than enough. I overlap Wolfe on plant parasites, of course. And there wasn't a single original fact in her chapters on plant parasites!"

Marty looked at the bookshelves, alphabetically arranged by author. Under Hart was a single large, bright-colored book, *Introduction to Plant Diseases.* Clearly a textbook. She had the vague impression that textbooks were not as prestigious as other books among professional academics. But if professional jealousy was behind his dislike of Professor Wolfe it was best not to ask now. She wanted his cooperation. "Do the students like her?" she asked.

"A few do. Her little slaves. Always running off to the hills with her. Most students don't care about biology one way or the other. Go off to major in history as soon as they discover that biology requires tough stuff like chemistry. As for her, she comes in for her class, grabs her mail, and then she vanishes."

"Where does she go when she vanishes?"

"Doing fieldwork. No, no, don't ask, I haven't the foggiest! No one knows what fieldwork means to Professor Wolfe and her maidens. But here's the address." He scribbled it onto a pad. Didn't have to look it up, Marty noted. He went on, "But of course that's just temporary headquarters. She moves around. Probably she'll be off on some junket to the tropics before long. Out of the last ten years, she's only been here three! The rest is all grants. Fieldwork."

"Well, thank you for your help. I'd better go see if I can catch her after class. What room?"

Hart was not kind to his colleague, Marty mused as she walked downstairs to the first-floor lecture room Hart had indicated. But she'd better reserve judgment. Sometimes even unkind people were right.

The lecture room was one of those that sloped from back to front for better visibility. Marty went up the hall stairs to enter at the back of the room. Inside it was dark, the only light coming from around the edges of the window blinds, and from a bright image on a screen at the front of the room. It was a map of some kind, but Marty could not identify the location.

"Here you can see how South America and Africa fit together." A woman was speaking, a pleasant husky voice, as a lighted arrow crawled along the map. "We've already seen from the fossil record that at this period identical species thrived in these adjacent areas. Now let's jump forward, to two hundred million years ago. A rift system right along these lines broke Pangaea apart and the Atlantic Ocean began to open." A new slide with more familiar continents replaced the first map. "This event has not finished. Even today the ocean is widening. New ocean floor is forming along the rift and the American continent and the Eurasian and African continents move about two and a half centimeters farther apart each year." The little arrow switched off. "Okay. Next time we'll talk about the evolution of species on the separate continents."

The lights flashed on and Marty squinted against them. Students were closing notebooks and shuffling down the sloping aisles toward the doors. Down at the front of the lecture hall the lecturer was removing a carousel of slides. She was a tall, brown-haired woman in a white lab coat. Several young women crowded around her but she seemed rushed, almost anxious, gesturing toward the door and slamming her case closed. Marty started down the aisle but it was filled with students, so she went out the door she'd come in and ran down the stairs, dodging people, but by the time she reached the hall below it was filled with students too. She glimpsed Professor Wolfe striding ahead, rounding the corner.

Shoot. She shouldn't have been so polite, waiting at the back. But most of the professors she'd known stayed a moment or two for questions after class.

When she reached the hall, Professor Wolfe was not there. She hurried to the third floor, but Wolfe's office was dark. Professor Hart, however, was standing at his window, staring out.

"Excuse me, Professor Hart. Have you seen Professor Wolfe?"

"Oh, there you are." He glanced over his shoulder and beckoned to her. "Slipped through your fingers, did she? Look."

Marty crossed to the window. A battered black pickup truck was pulling out of the driveway below, turning west on Third Street. "Shoot," said Marty. "Well, I'll have to talk to her later. Do you have her phone number?"

"Oh, she doesn't own anything as bourgeois as a phone. Dear me, no. She says if it's really important, people will find her. If it's not really important, why should she care?"

"Logical," Marty admitted. "Well, thanks for helping."

Was her question for Professor Wolfe really important? No. A sick old man's ravings. But Hal, Jr., wanted it investigated, and he was an important man. And Elizabeth Denton's intensity still haunted Marty.

She glanced at the address Hart had given her as she returned to the cruiser. South to Plum's to check on Goldstein's friends, or west past the courthouse to chase down Professor Wolfe? She remembered Plum's from her student days. It kept late hours, the regulars not showing up till after ten. Plum's later, then.

Wolfe first.

5

MARTY DROVE PAST THE COURTHOUSE SQUARE AND OUT WHITE-hall Pike to the back roads, hitting seventy-five on the straight stretches. When she almost ran over a cat she slowed a little. Take it easy, Hopkins. Silly to burn rubber when you're not even in a hurry, just frustrated that the professor beat you out the door.

A long, rutted lane led up a hill through a tangle of trees and creepers. In a large clearing, almost a meadow, a house nestled among wildflowers and tall grasses. The black pickup and a Volks bug rested nearby. Three young women were bent over a book on the porch.

"Hi," Marty called to them as she got out. "Is Professor Wolfe around?"

"No, she isn't."

Marty glanced at the pickup. "Do you expect her back soon?"

One of them came down the steps, quick, dimpled. She was wearing a Yogi Bear T-shirt. "We never know."

"I'm from the sheriff's department and we have some important questions for her."

The young woman squinted at her badge and nodded slowly.

"Can you tell me where to find her?"

The two women on the porch laughed. They seemed to be checking code numbers on some plastic containers. The Yogi Bear shirt said, "She doesn't like to be disturbed."

"Yeah, I figured that out. This shouldn't take long."

She shrugged and waved at the hills behind the house. "Try over at the old quarry, beyond those cedars."

"Is there a road?" Marty gestured at her car.

"Bridge washed out years ago."

"Okay. I'll hike it."

Marty crossed the meadow and plunged into the woods. There was a trail of sorts, but underbrush had narrowed it and grapevines knitted the branches together overhead so that she had to duck frequently. After a ten-minute walk she heard frogs and the rasping calls of jays.

The quarry was a great scar in the earth, the blanket of soil and vegetation stripped from the pale stone. Great puffing machines and men had drilled and hammered and blasted blocks from the naked rock, leaving a gigantic pit shaped like a seven-story V. The bottom had filled with water that shone turquoise under the hot sky. Twisted cables and rails corroded in the water, dumped there long ago by the departing stone company to discourage swimmers. At the far end she could see the shadowy skeleton of an automobile, half submerged, freckled with bullet holes and oozing rust the color of old blood.

Marty scanned the stone lips of the quarry. No one was there. "Professor Wolfe?" she called. Her voice sounded frail in the vastness of pit and woods and sky. The frogs paused and then began their music again.

In a different, cleaner quarry hole, she and Brad had splashed and kissed in the midsummer moonlight.

She shook her head clear and looked at her watch. Getting on toward four. Well, enough of this wild-goose chase. She'd go to the mall. She could call Aunt Vonnie, maybe have time to find pajamas on sale for Chrissie, before it was time to grab some dinner and drive on to Plum's. Goldstein, the Klan—that was the problem she itched to work on. But first she'd better just hike around the quarry to the other side and give another holler to keep Cochran happy.

It was rough underfoot. Cottonwoods grew among the piles of giant broken limestone blocks that the quarriers had left behind. She clambered along a sort of path among the rocks. What had her grandfather called them? Spall, waste stone. The best blocks had all gone to the mills to be shaped and hauled away to become courthouses or colleges. These flawed

30

stones remained. They rested in tumbled piles, making dens for coyotes, sheltering snakes, tripping law enforcement officers.

Was that a coyote off to the left?

Probably not. You didn't see coyotes in daylight. They were shy.

She dropped her hand to her gun and unsnapped her holster.

There were red-winged blackbirds down by the water, among cattails that had found a toehold of soil along the margin.

Marty called, "Professor Wolfe?" Her words rippled back from the opposite wall. There was a hush of frogs, and then all was as before, as if she had tossed a coin into the lapping water below.

The hell with this. Time to get on with more useful projects. Like dinner. She turned back.

A burst of images: hiking boots, stone-colored shirt, a rifle, a gray coyote behind.

The rifle was pointed at her.

Marty's hand checked in midair before it could close on her gun again. She froze and looked up slowly to meet a woman's grave brown eyes. Professor Wolfe said, "Were you hunting for me?"

The rifle was held easily at waist level, unswerving, ready to do business. Professor Hart's voice echoed in Marty's ears: *They say she killed a man once.* Through dry lips Marty said, "Looks more like you're hunting me."

"Yes." The professor gave a slow nod and Marty felt that the answer had pleased her somehow. Good; keep calm, talk her down.

"You're Professor Wolfe? The biologist?"

"Yes." Beside her now were two coyotes. No, larger than coyotes, but not wolves either. They had the tight-curled tails of arctic dogs. Up close Professor Wolfe had a pleasant, serious face. Hard to guess her age. Thirties, fifties? Here she looked confident, at home, not anxious as she'd seemed in the classroom. She asked, "Who are you?"

"I'm from the Nichols County sheriff's office."

"Obviously. As they say, it's written all over you." The rifle's muzzle traced a delicate circle in the air, indicating Marty's badge and Stetson. But the voice was friendly enough. "So I know your category. But who are you?"

"Uh—Marty Hopkins."

Professor Wolfe frowned slightly. "Not Martha."

"No, not Martha. Martine."

"Good, that's much better. After the god of war and strife."

"I guess so." Marty licked her lips. "Uh, speaking of war and strife, could you point your rifle some other direction?"

The rifle held steady. Professor Wolfe said pleasantly, "You came armed, Martine."

"Yeah, but not to shoot anything. We're required to wear our guns."

"With the holster unsnapped?" Those wise brown eyes were sizing her up.

"I got nervous," Marty explained. "Thought someone might be watching."

"Someone was." Abruptly, the professor upended the rifle and hung it over her shoulder.

Relief flooded through Marty and made her realize for the first time how afraid she'd been. "Good," she said. "I don't think we want to shoot each other."

"Probably not," Professor Wolfe agreed, with the tiniest hint of amusement. "Now, you came hunting something."

They were still standing ten feet apart on the piled limestone spall, the cottonwoods whispering above, the frogs and whistling blackbirds below. A third gray dog, larger than the first two, trotted up and looked expectantly at Professor Wolfe, his tight-curled tail wagging. "Yeah, you could say I came hunting," Marty said. She focused her energy: watch the subject, be ready to lunge behind that rock if this strange woman took the question wrong. "I came to see if you can tell me anything about Judge Denton."

The ageless face remained calm. "Judge Denton. Ah, yes. How is the judge?"

"Well, not good. Pretty bad."

"What is his problem?"

"Brain tumors. Seizures, mental confusion."

Professor Wolfe nodded soberly. "I cannot cure him, you know."

"Well, shoot, I didn't expect—he's got plenty of doctors!"

There was a quick recalculation behind the dark eyes. "Sometimes people come to me with the wrong questions. A biologist is supposed to know about life, they think, so I should be able to answer anything."

"Yeah. Sheriff's deputies get some weird questions too. But the thing is, the judge talks about someone killing him. Just raving, probably, but he talks about his daughter who ran away a long time ago, and about a wolf. His wife said that probably meant you."

The brown eyes gazed thoughtfully across the quarry pit. "So Elizabeth sent you," said Professor Wolfe. "Not the judge."

"I figured he was just raving," Marty explained. "But his sons—well, they didn't mention you, but they want to find out if there's anything behind the old man's talk. And Mrs. Denton seemed to want me to see you. That's why I came, to help the Dentons," she finished lamely. "So can you fill me in? I don't really know what questions to ask."

"Elizabeth didn't say what to ask?" The grave eyes turned back to Marty, measuring her. "That's not much help, is it? Unless—well, sometimes the answer comes first, and then you know what the question was. If you're wise."

"Do you have an answer, then?"

"I have a framework, perhaps."

"Well, anything that can help the Dentons."

The professor made an impatient gesture. "You cannot rescue others, Martine. You're lucky if you can rescue your self."

It was going to be hard to keep this one on track. But there was no hurry, and good information sometimes came from odd sources. Marty pushed back a curl from her forehead and tried again. "Okay. No rescues. But maybe I can learn a little more. You're a biologist, right? I wondered if Elizabeth Denton mentioned you because she thought the judge was being poisoned somehow. Would you be able to tell us if that was happening?"

"He has doctors, you say."

"Yes." It was true, he had doctors. If Elizabeth Denton wanted a second opinion she should just get one, instead of sending Marty off into the wilderness to bother this reclusive professor. "Look, I'm sorry I disturbed you. But—"

"I'm not a doctor, Martine. I'm not a lawyer. I'm not a social worker. I'm a scientist interested in all life forms."

"But your name came up. I just hoped you might know something about it. What did you mean by a framework?"

"Okay. Come." Professor Wolfe loped down the piled spall. Mart was no slouch athletically but she had to scramble to keep up. They emerged onto one of the higher ledges of the stepped quarry wall, an eighteen-inch-wide balcony with no handrail. Below Marty was a vertical drop of ten feet to the next ledge, and on down, ledge after ledge, plunge after plunge, deep into the turquoise water. Beside her a sheer stone cliff rose ten feet to the next higher ledge, and on up to a fringe of trees and the bottomless sky.

Professor Wolfe stroked the wall beside them. "Salem limestone," she said. "Do you know about limestone, Martine?"

"Some. My grandfather worked in the quarries. Dug out the Empire State Building, he always said. I know Salem's the best."

"You know it's ancient sea bottom."

"Yeah, I think I read about that in high school. Never understood it, exactly.

"It's made of corpses."

Marty looked at the stone sharply, then at Professor Wolfe. "What do you mean, corpses?"

"From long ago. Imagine a great sea over America, Pennsylvania to Nebraska. Suppose you sail a boat out to the middle and drop anchor over Indiana. The continent's down at the equator, so it's nice tropical weather, better bring your sunglasses. There are lots of little shelled sea creatures below you. Foraminifera, brachiopods, crinoids—sea lilies, you'd say. Lots of others too. Waves, sunshine, and generation after generation of animals. Sit in that boat awhile." Professor Wolfe's eyes had darkened with enthusiasm, as though she were really seeing that ancient sea. "For five million years it'll be serene. The animals grow, make shells from dissolved minerals, reproduce, die. The waters grind and smooth their shells, and cement them into stone. Generation after generation.

34

Then underground forces push up the seabed to form land. And here we are." She slapped the wall as though it were the flank of a horse. "This stone lived, once. It's still friendly to life. You could crush it into powder and swallow it and your body would know how to use it for nerves and bones."

"Doesn't sound very tasty." Marty was intrigued, as much by the woman as by the story she was telling.

Professor Wolfe smiled. "True. Personally I prefer my calcium in oysters or milkshakes."

"Are there fossils? I don't see any," Marty said.

"It *is* fossils. The skeletons in Salem limestone are mostly from tiny single-celled organisms, and larger ones are often ground up very fine, even dissolved. Makes it smooth. But yes, there are bigger fossils too. Animals in areas that escaped grinding." She pointed at a band in the limestone wall. Marty peered at it. Tiny, exotic forms, spirals and circles and stars, were caught in the stone. They were quiet now, but once they'd been alive, struggling like herself, twisting and waving in the waters of that long-ago tropical sea, basking in the long-ago rays of the same sun that was shining on them now. Marty found that her fingertips were stroking the tiny frozen creatures in a benediction. Life and death locked together in the stone.

She became aware of Professor Wolfe's serious gaze. It seemed to penetrate her, as a moment before it had penetrated millions of years to that ancient sea. Marty jerked her hand away and blurted, "Any dinosaur bones?"

Then she wanted to kick herself. She should have asked about Judge Denton, got this interview back on track. But maybe it was a good strategy after all, because Professor Wolfe seemed pleased at the question. "No, they came much later. About the time the Atlantic Ocean began to open."

"These little fossils are older than the ocean?"

"Okay, let's be linear for a moment." Amused, Professor Wolfe pulled her rifle from her shoulder and stood it upright between them. "This is a little over four feet high. Say each foot represents a hundred million years."

"Okay."

"The top is the present. About eight inches down, the first

mammals and birds are developing. Twenty inches down from the top is the period of dinosaurs."

"I see."

"Way down there on the butt, about ankle level, is when this limestone was forming."

"God. Pretty old!"

Professor Wolfe shrugged. "There's lots older. Life began three or four ledges down. Under water."

Marty looked down the dizzying distance to the lapping water below, and quickly back up to Professor Wolfe. "When were the cavemen?"

Professor Wolfe's glance was almost pitying. She reached down for a pinch of dust and sprinkled it on the tip of the upturned rifle barrel. "You see the circle of dust there?"

"Yes."

"That's humanity. From its beginning till now."

Marty stared at the thin ring of dust. Watching her, Professor Wolfe smiled and blew a puff of air at the rifle. At her breath all humanity swirled for an instant in the sunlit air, then disappeared.

"How can you live this way?" Marty demanded. "Thinking about such long ages? It's creepy. Makes everything so unimportant."

"Yes. Living in human time, but losing your commitment to it. Sometimes you see catastrophe and think 'so what?' That's the danger." The professor's brown eyes had gone dark and faraway. "That's the attraction too, of course." She turned abruptly on silent shoes and walked farther along the ledge.

This wasn't getting the investigation anywhere. Marty hurried after. "Professor Wolfe," she called, "are you a friend of Elizabeth Denton's? Do you know why she wanted me to see you?"

Professor Wolfe stopped and looked back kindly. "No. But perhaps she wanted me to explain about cycles."

"What do cycles have to do with anything?"

"They have to do with everything. Days, months, years, human generations and animal generations. Look at the stone."

Marty looked. A fissure split the rock here, the narrowing

continuation of a deep gulley on the upper surface of the stone. "Granddad called these grikes," she remembered. "His first job was digging the mud out of them so they'd have clean stone to quarry. He used to sing that hymn, you know? 'Rock of ages, cleft for me, let me hide myself in thee.' "

Professor Wolfe smiled. "Rocks are cleft by water," she said. "Rain picks up carbon dioxide from the air and soil and becomes carbonic acid. Weak acid, but strong enough to dissolve stone. The water sinks through the joints in the limestone and enlarges them. On the surface we see grikes and sinkholes. Underground we find fissures, caves, underground rivers. Slice this countryside and it'll look like waterlogged Swiss cheese. Have you seen Mammoth Cave in Kentucky?"

"Yeah. But look, this has nothing to do with Judge Denton!"

"I can't tell you Denton secrets. I can only tell what I know."

Marty looked at her suspiciously. The professor's wise, patient gaze met hers. Could she really think that what she knew was relevant? Professors were odd, Marty knew from her IU days. They loved to lecture, and believed their own specialties were the key to the universe. Okay, Hopkins, don't blow it by rushing her too much. Plum's had to wait for a while anyway. There was time to humor her, draw her out, see if anything surfaced after all. Besides, this stuff about the stone was kind of interesting. Marty said, "I saw Mammoth Cave when I was little. You mean rain dissolved all those caverns?"

"That's right. And all that dissolved stone is carried to sea by the rivers. Little creatures make shells from it again, and die again, and form seabed rock again. Some of the seabed slides into the earth's mantle and volcanic action throws it back into the atmosphere as carbon dioxide. Mix it with rain— carbonic acid again."

"A cycle," said Marty. Could carbonic acid poison the judge? What the hell was this strange woman trying to tell her?

"A cycle, yes. Meanwhile, other seabed rock is heaved up to form new land. Did you know that the top of Mount Everest is limestone?"

"Mount Everest? Really?" said Marty. "Seashells in the sky."

"Seashells in the sky." A glint of approval in the dark eyes. "New stone, new acid, millions of years. The earth and her life-forms in a slow, precise dance. Our tiny human cycles twinkle on the surface of the great ones. Time to go, Martine."

"That's all you can tell me? What about Judge Denton?"

"That's all. If I think of something more I should tell you, I will."

Marty turned away from the fissure. What a waste of time! Yet she found herself half-disappointed to come back to the everyday world from the cosmic realm Professor Wolfe inhabited. The danger, the attraction—she could sense it too, the fascination of those ancient shells in the rock. But it sure as hell didn't have anything to do with the investigation. Marty led the way back along the narrow ledge. The three dogs waited among the spall blocks, tongues lolling in canine smiles.

Back at the trail, Professor Wolfe said matter-of-factly, "Keep your eyes open going back. People show up here every now and then for target practice. Like to shoot at that rusty car in the water, but they'll try for anything that moves unless you discourage them. It's not stupid to have your gun ready." She reached behind a block and pulled out a plastic case. Toshiba. A laptop computer. So that's how all those books got written, Marty thought. The professor added, "It was a pleasure to make your acquaintance, Martine."

"Same here." And it was true, Marty discovered with surprise. Sure, it was frustrating that the professor wouldn't focus on the question, that she wasn't very tuned in to the real world. But she was tuned in to something, something that awakened unexpected delight in Marty. Almost made her wish she were a student again. "Let me know if you think of anything more about Judge Denton. And thanks for showing me—you know, the stone."

Professor Wolfe bowed her head gravely in acknowledgment. Then she and the dogs climbed swiftly up into the rocks and disappeared.

Marty hiked back along the rough trail, her mind still sailing ancient seas. The shadows were longer now, the water below half-shaded by the limestone walls. She paused near the rim of the pit to inspect a giant limestone block. Rock of ages. Were those fossils? Yes! Sea lilies, and fora-something—what had she called them?

"Martine?"

Marty turned back. "Yes?"

Professor Wolfe was standing forty yards away, near the top of the spall. "Phyllis Denton," she called. She waved her arm toward the south. "She's down there. Below Stineburg."

"Phyllis Denton? The judge's daughter?"

But Professor Wolfe was gone again.

Damn the woman! Marty wasted thirty minutes searching through the spall before she gave up. Clearly Professor Wolfe didn't want to be found again. No matter. Stineburg was in Marty's home county. A tiny town, not much more than a crossroads. Wouldn't take all that long to search. Marty hurried back to her car, ignoring hands and elbows scraped from the rough climb. She was sweaty and excited. Maybe, just maybe, she had a case here after all.

But right now she had to get to Plum's.

6

THE HOLTZ HOUSE HAD A SAGGING PORCH, PAINT BEGINNING TO peel, a few maples, honeysuckle in the fence row. There were a thousand places like this along the county roads, but to Wes Cochran this one would always bring a taste of bile to his mouth, an ugly fifteen-year-old memory: a black man lying in those woods moaning, naked and battered, his mouth smashed, bleeding from the sockets of three teeth, one leg at an impossible angle. Wes had found him out there after Mrs. Hines, who cleaned the departmental offices, had called. She'd been cool, efficient with the directions until he'd agreed to go, then she'd broken into sobs. "My Emmett needs an ambulance, honest, Sheriff, it's real bad!"

Wes shook off the images as he got out of the car. In the side yard, a collie mix chained to a clothesline was barking furiously. Wes hitched up his trousers and walked across the scrubby grass, squinting against the late, slanting sun. The old man on the porch was watching him. Wes said, "Hey there, Lester."

Lester was sitting on a weathered wooden keg, carefully placed on the porch out of reach of the afternoon rays. He wore denim overalls and a cotton shirt. He smiled at Wes. "Hey, Wes." But his eyes were cautious.

"How you been doing?"

"Pretty good. 'Cept for the arthritis." Lester gestured vaguely at his legs.

"Yeah, that can sure get a man down." Wes paused on the porch steps, standing sideways with his right foot one step above his left, so he was facing Lester Holtz.

"Sure can." Lester smiled that careful smile again and looked at his knee. "Aspirin helps some."

"Yeah. Glad it's not one of those fancy drugs. Cost you a mint."

Lester started to nod, then his sharp blue eyes flicked up to Wes's face. "So what brings you way over here, Sheriff?"

"Yeah." Wes leaned back against the post, looking down at his shoes. "Well, it's like this, Lester. I wondered what you could tell me about those boys you used to be buddies with."

"That was a long time ago."

"Yeah, maybe." Wes glanced at the collie, still growling and pacing at the end of his chain. "See, Lester, we got a problem. Need to know about what all you fellows been doing."

"Nothing. That's what we been doing."

"Yeah. See, it's murder this time, Lester."

Lester's cautious eyes blinked.

"It was a Jew boy, Lester."

"Oh, Lordy."

"Yeah. Goldstein, over on the Lawrence Road. If we can't figure it out here ourselves, we've gotta call in the FBI."

40

Lester leaned forward, grimacing, and spat across the porch rail onto the weedy ground beyond.

Wes said, "That business fifteen years ago is all over now."

The cautious eyes flashed for an instant in blistering hatred. "All over? You hit us with a fine that broke the bank, Sheriff! Never did make back all that money."

Wes kept his voice mild. "Last time I saw Emmett Hines he was still limping."

"He was looking over Al's wife, dammit!"

"Looking ain't doing, Lester. Feds would've locked you up for what you boys did. Not let you off with a fine."

"Feds." The old man spat across the rail again.

"I sure agree with you there," Wes admitted.

"Yeah." Lester glanced at Wes and said grudgingly, "Look, Wes, I'll tell you the truth. I don't get around so good anymore. Been months since I saw anybody 'cept for Al. And he didn't say one word about a Jew boy."

"Mm." Wes nodded noncommittally. Too bad his best informant was so far on the fringes, old, left out. Well, he'd give Lester time to ask around. "You hear anything, you let me know, okay? I'll be back."

"Sure." Cockier now, Lester grinned with an edge of malice. "We don't want feds in this county, do we?"

"No. We don't." Wes looked him in the eye, unsmiling, until the old man's grin faded. Then he went back down the steps and across the ragged grass to his car. The dog yapped and danced at the end of its chain.

Back at the office there was no news from the state evidence technicians, but he hadn't expected any. Not for days. People in labs, nine-to-five jobs, couldn't have much sense of urgency. Well, in fairness, they might move faster if he told them about the Klan symbol. But he didn't want to tell them. This was just an isolated nut, he was sure. No sense calling in the federal heavy artillery unless he had to.

Mason had turned in a badly typed report on his interview with his daddy's cousin Lucille Kinser, the nurse who had reported the fire and dancing. Wes skimmed it; nothing new, really. She'd been going sixty, about the best speed you could do on that road in the fog, so she hadn't seen a whole lot.

41

Sims and Mason between them had canvassed the neighbors but most of them said they'd been asleep. Joe Matthews's dog had barked and he'd gotten up to shush him, saw a flickering light far away beyond the trees. He'd figured it was just someone out with a flashlight, coon hunting or whatever, so he'd gone on back to bed.

Marty Hopkins hadn't left a report, just a phone message. She'd interviewed the IU professor the Dentons had mentioned, had a lead on the runaway daughter. God! After all these years? Wes shook his head skeptically.

Marty had also seen Goldstein's IU records and planned to talk to a friend of his before leaving Bloomington. Wes's mouth tightened. She should've let him know, let him decide who should interview the friend, stayed out of it herself. Bullheaded woman.

On the other hand, she might have talked him into it. She was in Bloomington already, after all. He slapped the memo back into his in-box.

On the way home he stopped for gas at Straub's Service. Gil Newton came out of the office, nodded at him, and started the pump. West got out and stretched. "How's it going, Gil?"

"Fine." Gil was wiry, dark-haired, a quiet type who liked tinkering with cars better than drinking with the boys.

"Bert around?"

"He's off having dinner. Be back maybe eight o'clock."

"I'll catch him later." He wanted to ask Bert about Judge Denton, about why his name had come up in the judge's rantings. Well, no rush. He held up a hand to stop Gil. "No, don't bother with the windshield. I'll just sign and get on home."

The back room at Plum's was still large, square, and rustic-looking. In Marty's IU days she'd needed a fake ID to sneak in here. They'd caught her only once. She remembered the delicious rush that came from getting into the bar illegally, from proving that she could pass for an adult. Chrissie had cured her of that.

She turned back into the little hallway with the phone booths and fed in coins. "Hi. Chrissie?"

"Hi, Mom!"

Her words sounded blurry. Probably had her mouth full. Marty could almost see her, dark hair, bright earrings, curiosity in her eyes, and a cookie in her cheek. A smile crept into Marty's voice. "How're you doing?"

"Pretty good. Did you find that fire?"

"The fire was out. But we found a dead guy."

"A dead guy! Gross! Did he burn up?"

"No." Marty flashed on the shallow grave, the charred cross, the Klan card. "We're still figuring out what happened. So what have you been doing in school?"

"We started a new thing about Indiana history. I picked the quarries, because of Granddad."

"Good idea. Hey, did you know limestone is made of corpses?"

"Gross!"

"Tiny little creatures with shells. Like fossils. Listen, I'll tell you more later. Is Aunt Vonnie there?"

"Yeah. Aunt Vonnie!" she screeched into Marty's ear.

Marty stepped back to the end of the cord and peered into the back room. No sign of the band.

"Let me guess," Aunt Vonnie's voice squeaked. "You won't be back for dinner."

"I'm afraid not," Marty admitted, returning the receiver to her ear. "I'm in Bloomington. Back in maybe three hours." She could hear Aunt Vonnie revving up to complain and added hastily, "I'm working two cases, Aunt Vonnie. One's a murder."

"Oh, honey, be careful!" The underlying fear that made Aunt Vonnie so acid about Marty's job suddenly surfaced. "They shouldn't ask you—"

"I'm just asking questions, miles and miles from where it happened," Marty soothed her.

"They still shouldn't ask you." Suddenly her voice became distant, muffled by her hand over the mouthpiece. "Chrissie, honey, run out and play."

A brief argument at the other end ended with a door slam. Aunt Vonnie's voice came back on, quiet and urgent. "Marty, I didn't want to say this in front of Chrissie. Brad called."

"Brad?" Marty's hand clenched on the receiver. Sensations tumbled through her memory: the glow of dark eyes, the light sheen of sweat on shoulders and biceps, the tickle of his mustache. Promises of minks, of New York penthouses. And then the empty bed, the tears in Chrissie's eyes, cheery postcards in the mailbox. She breathed out slowly and kept her voice level. "From New York? What did he say?"

"Not much. Wanted to know when you'd be off work so he could call back. I told him he'd have to ask the sheriff."

"I see. And he didn't talk to Chrissie?"

"This was around noon. She was in school."

"So what did he want?" It had been two weeks since she'd heard from him. He was about to get a DJ job, he said, in the club where he was tending bar. Was this good news? Bad?

Aunt Vonnie's voice was as sour as grapefruit. "The only other thing he said was to give you his love."

Marty had to laugh. "If he knew how you say that, Aunt Vonnie, he'd never ask!"

"Honey, face it, he's no good for you! He's a charmin' man but you ought to just get a divorce and be done with him!"

Behind Marty, people were beginning to drift into the back room. She wiped a curl back from her forehead. "Aunt Vonnie, he's trying to break into a tough business, okay? And he's Chrissie's father. Like it or not." A couple of musicians carrying instrument cases passed. "Listen, Aunt Vonnie, gotta go!"

The sax player was a lean, bouncy black man, middle height, chocolatey skin, a stylish sack jacket. She called, "Mr. Cartwright!"

"*Mister* Cartwright! Who's that calling me mister?" He turned with an easy smile that stiffened when he saw her uniform.

Marty explained, "I'm Marty Hopkins. Sheriff's department, Nichols County. I've got a few questions about somebody you know. You want to talk to me now, or after the show?"

"Jesus, lady. Or sir, or whatever." He looked at his watch and sighed. "Nine-thirty. Hell, I've got a minute, might as well talk now."

Marty gestured to a table. Cartwright sat down and rocked

his chair back on its rear legs, his dark eyes wary. "So who's in trouble?" he asked.

"Guy named Goldstein. David Goldstein."

"Goldie?" Cartwright's eyebrows rose. "He's not the kind to get in trouble. Just plays piano, that's all. What'd he do?"

"When did you see him last?"

"Couple weeks ago. Lemme see. Saturday, it was. He and Kizzy turned up here, we invited them up for a guest number. Afterward he said they had an audition at a club up in Naptown. But I never heard if they got the job."

"Who's Kizzy?"

"Kizzy Horton. Sweetest black chick who ever sang jazz. Also Goldie's wife."

"His wife," Marty said flatly, but her nerves were humming. This was it, this was the key.

A shadow passed across his face. "That's not why you're hassling him, is it? You've got no call to do that!"

"No. I'm not hassling them. Was someone hassling them?"

He shrugged. "Not much. Bloomington's okay, mostly. Sometimes there are remarks, you know, or maybe some good ol' boy sitting around the courthouse square will throw a bottle at them. Course, we all know there's some bars to avoid. Not hard to do, none of them looking to hire black musicians anyway. Or Jewish."

"Yeah." Marty knew the places he meant, some on the west side of Bloomington, some in her own county. People there, old-timers mostly, talked about racial purity. There were fights, sure, but they didn't kill people. Did they? Marty said, "Goldstein lived south of here, down in Nichols County. Did he ever mention any trouble there?"

"Not to me. They only moved there a couple months ago." Cartwright was studying her thoughtfully. He blurted suddenly, "Something real bad happened to him, right? Because otherwise you'd be asking him all these questions."

Marty met his eyes and said as gently as she could, "Yeah, he was killed."

"Goddamn!" He slammed a fist onto the table, then looked at her in anguish. "Kizzy," he said. "What about Kizzy?"

"I don't know. Another deputy was checking out Goldstein's

address, maybe she was there. If not—well, where would she go?"

"If she wasn't— Her cousin's." Cartwright was on his feet, hurrying, fishing out a little address book and thumbing through it as he raced with long strides to the phone. Marty followed.

"Bernice? It's Tom Cartwright. . . .Yeah. I'm looking for Kizzy. . . . She is? Thank the Lord! I was so. . . . Yeah. Yeah, I just heard Goldie got killed. . . .Christ!" Cartwright froze. "She didn't know? . . . Jesus Christ. Well, tell her we all stand with her."

He hung up slowly. All his bounce and enthusiasm had evaporated.

"I'll need the address," she said gently.

"Yeah. Okay." He pulled out the little book again, then paused. When he spoke his voice was hard. "I give you this, what good will it do? You going to hassle her, maybe turn her over to the Kluxers that did Goldie?"

So Bernice and Kizzy knew the Klan was involved. And if Cartwright was suspicious of the police, well, she knew he had history on his side. She asked, "Did they hurt Kizzy too?"

"No, Bernice said she left for Indy last week. But God, what kind of white trash do you keep in your county?"

His question clanged within her like a deep bell tone, forcing her to face it. Somehow the unspeakable had happened in her home county. All her protests that they were basically good folks couldn't erase that fact. She said, "My job is to find that trash and clean it out."

He squinted at her, not convinced.

"Look," she said. "You know we'll find her eventually, we need her information. Of course it'll be hard on her, the whole damn situation is hard on her. But it won't go any better for her if we have to take the long way around."

Cartwright gave a brief nod. "Look, no offense, I'm not saying it's you, but you're a woman. Do the ol' boys tell you everything? Can you swear your own outfit isn't behind this?"

There was no good answer. She got along, usually, with the other deputies, but did she know enough about them to swear? Marty said, "I can't vouch for everybody. But the sheriff himself went right down the line for a black guy fifteen years ago. There's whites in the county haven't spoken to him since."

He rubbed his head unhappily. "Well, you're right, you'll find her anyway. Better you than— Can you promise to do this yourself? Not to let anyone else know the address?"

"Well, I have to tell the sheriff."

"Yeah, yeah, the righteous sheriff. But no one else."

"I promise."

He held out the book and she copied the name, Bernice Brown, and an Indianapolis address. He said angrily, "You better catch those bastards, hear? Don't let the Kluxers get Kizzy."

"I'll do my best."

He shrugged, picked up his sax, and looked at it mournfully. "Well," he said as he started across to the stage, "tonight we dedicate to Goldie."

7

ROYCE DENTON, BOURBON IN HAND, WAS LOOKING OUT HIS FAther's bedroom window at the blackness outside. The lamp there in the sickroom prevented him from seeing much more than a blurred outline where dark sky met darker hills. Even the bulk of the hickory tree near the house was more sensed than seen.

The figure in the bed stirred and Royce turned back into the room. Damned depressing, this vigil. The dynamic man who'd ruled his boyhood had seemed to him immortal. Godlike. Immune to time. His mother had always seemed frailer, and as a boy he'd worried sometimes that she might die early, leaving the three of them alone in the big house. No, four, after Phyl was born.

Where the hell was Phyl? He remembered mostly a sweet little towhead in a pink dress. Mother always dressed her in pretty dresses. She was a Denton, after all. And Dad, delighted with this child of his middle age, made her sit next to him to watch TV or asked her to sing songs for them. "Sunshine on my shoulders," she used to sing that one, he remembered.

When she was only five or six, though, Royce had followed Hal, Jr., to IU, and then came the army and law school. Home to visit, he'd tease his kid sister but basically his interests were elsewhere. He'd been in his last year of law school and had hardly thought about his little sister for months when the brusque phone call came. "You and Hal come on out tonight," his father commanded. "Phyllis is gone."

They'd held a war council: he and Hal distressed, full of questions, his mother weeping, hardly able to answer, and his father brimming with barely contained rage. Keep it quiet, they'd finally decided. She'd be back soon and there was no need to wreck her life. They'd asked around among her friends, but Phyllis had been a shy kid and no one knew anything.

Two days later they'd called in Wes Cochran and he'd put out the bulletin.

And then Mother had found the snapshot in a back corner of a drawer: Phyllis in black pants and studded leather jacket standing by a motorcycle. Incredible. His father was furious. "Why didn't I know about this? My God, she's only twelve! Elizabeth, you must have seen that jacket! Why didn't you tell me?"

"I never saw it! She must have kept it somewhere else!" There was fear in his mother's eyes, and it was true that his father looked ready to strike her, to strike out in frustration and grief.

Hal, holding the snapshot, had said, "Dad, look, we can make out part of the license plate. Will that help?" His father joined them and all three pored over the photograph. But there were few clues, and they were useless in the end. The sheriff had tried, but Phyllis had never been found.

Silly, maybe, to renew the hunt now. If Wes Cochran

couldn't find her when the trail was fresh, what could he do now, years afterward? But there was the outside chance that she'd been in touch somehow, that his father's ravings were fueled by something recent, not by remote memories. Might as well let that little gray-eyed Marty Hopkins try. She was smart, Royce remembered from the courtroom. Didn't trip up in cross-examination the way some of the deputies did. Nice voice. Pretty mouth . . .

There was a thump from the bed, and another. Royce moved quickly to the bedside, putting down his glass, checking the straps and pillows as the old man's body arced and jerked. He was so strong. Looked wasted, could hardly say two coherent words, but thrashing in a seizure he was as tough as machine steel. Royce remembered once as a teenager he'd been learning to use a chain saw and something in the control mechanism had jammed so he couldn't switch it off. He couldn't put it down because it might buck and bounce around the clearing, attacking whatever branch or human shin it encountered. He'd held it for an eternity, maybe half an hour, until the fuel ran out and it shuddered into death in his numbed hands.

His father's thrashing subsided. Royce adjusted the straps and checked his watch. Two more hours before Mother's turn.

The question prickled at the back of his mind: Was this hereditary? He knew tumors weren't passed on directly, but maybe a susceptibility of some kind? He'd thought his father was so powerful, and he'd followed in his footsteps, law school and all, with an almost superstitious belief that the power would come to him too. Like a little boy donning a Superman costume.

The fallen hero was breathing more quietly now. Royce freshened his bourbon and went to the window to gaze out at the blackness again.

On the road from Bloomington, the night was cool, a half-moon blurry behind the haze. Streamers of soft mist were forming in the dips of the road. This land was seabed once, Professor Wolfe had said, but around here the level rock had been gnawed and shaped by millions of years of rain and snow into the present rolling hills and hollows. Marty found herself humming Granddad's favorite hymn: "Rock of Ages, cleft for me." She remembered the quarry wall, the glimpse Professor Wolfe had given her into the depths of time, and shivered.

All the same, Aunt Vonnie lived in regular old human time, and she'd say snippy things tomorrow about her being late tonight.

Marty's house was two stories high, with pointed gables, peeling paint, and a double garage that used to be a big wagon shed near the rear corner of the house. The back porch light shone dully on the asphalt. In the garage, she parked next to Aunt Vonnie's car, pulled her shoulder bag from the seat beside her, climbed out, and stretched. God, a long day. Hunting for Kizzy Horton would make tomorrow long too. She headed for the porch.

There was a footstep behind her. She whirled, right hand dropping to her holster, to see a basketball smack the asphalt before her. She caught it and saw him crouching under the hoop, arms extended, guarding it. Damn the man! Anger and delight churning within her, Marty thrust out her jaw, dropped her bag, bounced the ball once and leaped high to send it to the basket. But he jumped too and batted it away. Marty caught it, feinted high, then drove under his arm for a jump shot that rolled once around the rim before dropping through. He grabbed it under the basket, and she blocked him four times before he got one in over her upstretched fingertips. He was taller, but she was quicker, and it made a good match, intense and silent except for the slap of the ball on the asphalt, the ringing thumps as it hit the backboard. Marty was leading by a couple of baskets, she figured, when she jumped high to sink another. It went through the hoop, but she didn't come down. He'd grabbed her in midair, arms circling her back and butt, nose pressed against her breast.

The ball pattered away down the side of the driveway.

Her anger had burned away. "Hey," she murmured, looking down at his dark, disheveled hair glinting in the porch light. "Personal foul."

"Yeah." He put her down gently, his arms still tight around her, his maverick grin inches away. "Hey, kid, you're panting."

"Hey, kid, so are you."

Cautiously, they kissed. He'd had a cheeseburger, she could tell, and suddenly she was giddy with joy, kissing him again, not cautiously now. Whatever had happened, this was her man.

After a few minutes she drew back and asked, "So what's new?"

"Well, I'm afraid your mink is pretty small, this time." He pressed something into her hand, tiny, silky. "But it's real mink."

She looked at its whiskery toy face. "It's wonderful!"

"We had a little setback, kitten. I don't want to talk now, but I've got a great new plan!"

"What—"

"Later, kitten."

She bit back her questions and asked instead, "How'd you get rid of Chrissie?"

"Haven't even been inside."

"Well, let's go in, then. The kid's crazy to see you."

"Yeah. Me too. But her bedroom light's off. Let's stay out here a few minutes. I need you."

Marty touched his cheek, his mustache. "Aunt Vonnie—"

His arms tightened around her. "Her light's out too. Aunt Vonnie can wait. I need you, kitten."

"Yeah, but—"

"But but but! C'mon!" He tugged her toward the garage.

"C'mon where?"

"You got a backseat, right? For old times' sake."

"Shoot, Brad!" She giggled. "That was so uncomfortable!"

"Yeah, but we managed, didn't we?" He kissed her palm. "C'mon, kitten. You don't really want to talk to Aunt Vonnie right now, do you? Right now I bet you want exactly what I want."

He was right, of course. Marty let him lead her back into the garage. She grabbed up her shoulder bag from the asphalt as he opened the door for her. For a moment they sat in the dark car listening. The house was silent, and there was only the rustle of a thousand memories. Then his fingertips began stroking her cheek, her curls. Marty shivered.

But before she even removed her gun belt, she dug into her bag. Good, still there. She handed him a condom.

"Hey. What's this supposed to mean?" he whispered. His fingers paused in her hair.

"Means I don't take the pill while you're gone." When he still hesitated, she added, "Chrissie happened in a backseat, remember? We know you don't shoot blanks, Brad."

"God. What a woman." Pacified, he took the packet and nuzzled her neck. "I've missed you, kitten. Missed you so much."

"Me too," whispered Marty, unbuckling.

The Night-Hawk had finished his shower and his workout. Sit-ups, knee-bends, push-ups, a hundred of them. All silent, that was the trick. No grunting, no harsh breathing, just air pouring cleanly in and out, quietly, efficiently, ventilation for a smooth-running engine. Afterward he'd showered again. Took a lot of washing to stay clean. Whiter than snow.

He ought to visit the saint in the cleft rock. He felt pure near the saint. Maybe tomorrow.

The sheriff had sure found that body quick. Funny, he'd thought they'd find the other one first. Must have been the fiery cross, tiny as it was. Someone had seen something. No matter, the sheriff wouldn't find anything more than he was meant to find.

He hoped he'd get a sign now, about the bodies, about the Kentucky woman. Surely now the Great Titan would give him a sign.

The Night-Hawk dressed in his painter's pants and a white shirt, sat at his scrubbed kitchen table, and opened his Bible. "And he said to me, These are they which came out of great tribulation, and have washed their robes, and made them white in the blood of the Lamb. Therefore are they before the throne of God, and serve him day and night in his temple: and he that sitteth on the throne shall dwell among them. They shall hunger no more, neither thirst any more; neither shall the sun light on them, nor any heat. For the Lamb which is in the midst of the throne shall feed them, and shall lead them unto living fountains of waters: and God shall wipe away all tears from their eyes."

The Night-Hawk never slept well. But the passage soothed him, and he lay down in his clean bed and rested for a time.

8

"OKAY, LET'S MOVE," WES COCHRAN SAID TO HIS ASSEMBLED deputies. Marty Hopkins had come in ten minutes late and he was impatient to get started. "Sims, Mason, you take Goldstein's landlord. He lives up in Monroe County, here's the address. I'll check some of the old-timers around here. Adams, man the phones today. Foley, get some sleep, you're on again tonight. Hopkins, here's a couple of photos of Phyllis Denton. The motorcycle one is the most recent. You follow up on the Stineburg tip."

He should have known. Hopkins accepted the photos but her face took on that look of calm, deceptive to people who didn't know her. She said, "Sir, I need a private word with you."

Don Foley leered at her. "Her man's back. Makes for a late breakfast. She needs some time off."

Wes frowned. "That true, Hopkins? Brad's back?"

"I don't need time off."

So he was back. Hell, that was the last straw, Hopkins distracted when they needed her cool intelligence. Wes said, "So what's there to talk about?"

"Nothing to do with my private life," she snapped. "Or Don's."

"Hoo-ee!" chortled Grady Sims. "Whatcha hiding, Don?"

"Get outta here!" Wes roared. "Hit the road, boys. Hopkins, come on in and tell me the problem." He jerked his head at the office, curious in spite of himself.

Inside, he observed, "You were late this morning, Hopkins."

"Brad's car broke down. I had to drive him to town."

"From now on he better be ready in time."

"Yessir."

"Now, what did you want to tell me?"

She took a deep breath but came right to the point. "Sir, I found out last night that Goldstein was married to a black woman. I know where she is."

"You know—" Wes remembered the snapshot in Goldstein's wallet. His fist hit the desk and the papers on it jumped. "Goddammit, Hopkins, this is supposed to be a team! Why didn't you tell me?"

"Because she's a black woman. Because the person who told me was afraid the killer might have a connection to this department."

"This department!" Wes stared at her. "Why?"

"Didn't give any special reason. I figured it was because Indiana cops used to wear sheets sometimes, and—"

"Not since I've been in charge!"

"Nobody's accusing you, sir."

Wes propped his foot on his chair and studied her. "Hopkins, what do you know about the Klan?"

Her gray eyes were troubled. "I know the Klan ran this whole state in the twenties, and they hung on in this county a long time. Daddy knew some, Al Evans and Lester Holtz— I guess most of those guys are still around. But didn't you bust this Klan back when they beat up Emmett Hines?"

"Yes and no," Wes said. "You gotta realize that these guys are mostly losers. They're trying to account for having stupid jobs and no prospects. They forget they never finished high school. They forget they drink up their paychecks Saturday night. It's easier to bear if they tell each other there's a big conspiracy of Jews and blacks keeping them down. In the old days, they'd get each other roused up on a Saturday night and go out and whip some poor black fellow. After I showed 'em that part of it was out of bounds, they backed off and made do with grumbling."

"But they still meet, to grumble?"

"Sure. They're only human. They like to think of taking over the world someday. But I'd bet good money the Goldstein killer is working alone. Maybe he's a buddy of the other Klansmen, but he probably hasn't even told them. They're losers, yeah, but I knocked some sense into their heads."

Hopkins nodded slowly. "Yes, sir. But—well, look, I know you went the whole distance for that black guy Emmett Hines. And Grady, well, I've heard that his best buddy in Vietnam was black. The others are probably okay too. But I just don't know for sure. And I promised not to turn Goldstein's wife over to the Klan."

This insubordination had to be nipped in the bud. But it was ticklish because there was a grain of truth in what she said. Grady, Bobby, Don, Roy—okay, they weren't Klan, they knew the law. But they had brothers, cousins, uncles. If the information had come to him he would have been cautious too. On the other hand, he couldn't let Marty wriggle her way into this investigation. That was no way to run a railroad.

Wes said, "Hopkins, you're on the Denton case. Period. You're to find Phyllis Denton and find out if anyone's threatening the judge."

She glanced at the floor. "Yes, sir. But what about Goldstein's wife?"

"She's not your problem. I'm the sheriff here, Hopkins."

"Yessir. You don't have to tell me that."

"I don't? You come in here offering a trade, information in exchange for being put on the Goldstein case. That's not the way this operation works."

"I know, I didn't mean that. I just want to help Goldstein's wife. I promised to watch out for her."

He could see her concern. She got so protective sometimes that she didn't realize how far out of line she was. He asked gently, "You think I won't?"

"I know *you* will. But, see, Grady and Bobby are talking to Goldstein's landlord. He'll probably tell them about the wife."

"Right. So?"

"Well, I could get there sooner, and—"

Wes shook his head firmly. "Uh-uh. No deal. You're going to Stineburg."

Marty glanced at the door, and Wes could almost hear the wheels going around: no way for her to see the wife and Stineburg at the same time; no way to head off Sims and Mason, unless— She looked back at Wes, those gray eyes cold. "Sir, her name is Kizzy Horton, and she's staying at her cousin's. Bernice Brown, Hundred and seventeenth Street in Indy."

"Okay. Now you get yourself off to check out Stineburg."

"Yes, sir. And where are you going, sir?"

"First off, I'm taking a little trip to Indy."

"Thank you, sir. See you later. Sir." She marched out, not happy but a good soldier once again. Had to keep reminding that one. Just because she was smart she thought she could run the department.

Wes glanced at his messages, told Roy he'd check in from Indianapolis, and headed north.

By three o'clock Marty was sick of Stineburg, worried about Brad, still angry at Wes Cochran, and furious at Professor Wolfe. Ought to run her in for giving false information, obstruction of justice, all the rest. It was clear that Phyllis Denton wasn't here and probably never had been.

It wasn't that you couldn't hide out around Stineburg, Marty thought as she bumped up the weathered driveway of yet another farmhouse. The countryside here was the same stony swellings and hollows as the rest of the county, and overgrown by the same sycamores and hickories, thistles and creepers. An outlaw or a recluse could easily tuck himself out of sight in some thicket or junk-filled quarry. The point was that people would know he was still there. At Padgett's general store she'd heard about two such. Crazy old Jack Cooley camped over toward White River, living on berries, possum, and the delusion that Jesus had chosen him as the second Moses and would be leading him out of the wilderness any day now. Jane Wall's son had been hiding out in one of the quarries for months now because he'd busted up a schoolroom

56

and Wes Cochran himself had come out to talk to him. The boy had bolted out the back door and hadn't been home since. Everyone at Padgett's had thought that was why Marty had come, to find the Wall boy. They told her to watch out, he'd taken a gun with him.

But when they found out she was looking for a missing person, female, twenty years old now, blue-eyed, they were puzzled. They frowned at the photos. "What's her name?"

"Phyllis Denton. But she may not be using that name. Do you know anyone of that description?"

Looked a little like Jeannette. No, not Jeannette, she had brown eyes. How about Helen? Not much resemblance. Besides, Helen and Jeannette had both lived there all their lives.

"Any newcomers?" she asked.

"Them professors north of town. Only ones left are that Drew Brewster and his wife. He's been there for years, but she's new. He teaches way up at IU. They're trying to show us how to run a farm." There were chuckles from the assembled listeners.

"What does the wife look like?" Marty asked.

"Karen? More'n twenty, I'd say." Nods from the others. "And doesn't look much like your photos."

"I better talk to her anyway. Where do they live?"

She added the Brewster farm to her list. It was farther north than the other addresses, and she'd already talked to almost everyone around Stineburg by the time she turned at a faded sign that said RIVENDELL. She was tired, sure already that it was a blind alley, sure that Professor Wolfe was wrong. And snapshots from the morning kept intruding into her thoughts: Brad sitting back against a pillow propped against her headboard, hands clasped behind his head, unconsciously showing off the muscular lines of his torso in the early morning light. Scratch that, it hadn't been unconscious at all. Moments later, Chrissie pounding on the door, bursting in almost before he'd gotten his jeans on, hurling herself into his arms. Watching them, Marty had felt hope bloom again. They adored each other. Maybe this time— But after nine years she knew love was not enough. Other things mattered, like paychecks. And he hadn't told her his great plan yet, only that the DJ job

he'd expected to get at the New York club where he worked had fallen through. The owner's cousin had gotten it instead.

She bumped up the driveway to a rambling gray house. At the foot of a long meadow the White River glinted. This was even more remote than Marty's place. God, if she and Brad had the kind of money those IU professors made, they sure wouldn't spend it here.

Karen, it turned out, was in the garden. She was a sturdy woman with brown braids, dressed in a blue calico blouse, jeans, and work boots. Marty parked near the house and walked past chickens and a couple of tethered goats to the garden. It had attracted lots of caterpillars. Karen was picking them off the leaves. "It's all organic," she informed Marty proudly in her back-East accent. "We try to replenish the earth. Plant beans in the same hills as the corn."

"Yeah, I've heard that works pretty good." Marty studied her carefully. She definitely wasn't blue-eyed, she was closer to thirty than twenty, and she had no resemblance to the photos. Still, better go through the paces. "How long have you lived here?"

"Two and a half years. I love the work. Except—well, sometimes it's pretty repetitious. Some people don't like that."

"Yeah, I never could really get into caterpillars myself. Where were you before you came here?"

"Teaching high school English in Indianapolis. And you know, once Drew and I get the commune reestablished, we're going to try to reopen our school. Maybe tie in with the history of that old village down the river." She looked happily around at the bug-eaten garden, the home-built sheds, the goats, seeing a vision that Marty couldn't quite grasp. "The trouble before was that we were trying to do everything at once, and a couple of the parents thought the children had to do too much work. Once the farm's running more smoothly it should be all right, don't you think? We'll have great books, and a natural setting, so the children can develop their minds and spirits in harmony with nature."

"I see." Marty thought of Chrissie, whose mind and spirit tended more toward the goodies she saw on TV, whose ambition was to see New York City. Brad had brought her a black

T-shirt with the Manhattan night skyline, buildings glittering against the dark. Eyes shining, Chrissie had gloated and preened all morning in this sign of her father's love. It would take a lot more than great books and caterpillars to lure her from that dream. Marty asked, "Did you attend IU, Mrs. Brewster?"

"I graduated from IU five years ago. That's where I met Drew, my last year there. Why are you asking these questions?"

"We're looking for a missing person. Phyllis Denton, but she may call herself something else now. Here's an old photo. She's about twenty now. Someone said she was around here."

"And you thought I might know her?"

Marty shrugged. "Just checking."

Karen shook her head slowly. "No. I never saw her."

"Could Phyllis have been in the school here? She was twelve when she ran away eight years ago."

"No. The Murray boy was the oldest in the school and he's only fifteen now. Besides, everyone's gone." She smiled at Marty wistfully. "If you know anybody who doesn't mind goats and caterpillars, we've got a great commune here."

"I'll remember. Thanks." Marty handed Karen her phone number. "Please get in touch with me if you or Drew think of anything that might help us find the young woman."

"Is she in some kind of trouble?" Karen asked.

"Not with us," Marty reassured her. "She ran away young, and her family hopes for a reconciliation. Her dad is dying."

"That's sad. Okay, I'll call you if I hear anything."

"Thanks. Good luck with your garden. And your school."

So. That was that. Stineburg was a big blank. Damn that Professor Wolfe. Back in the car, Marty picked up the U.S. survey map she'd been using, looking carefully at all the little black squares that indicated farmhouses. She'd hit them all. Nobody home at three of them, but their closest neighbors swore that no young women lived there. No one knew anyone who could possibly be Phyllis Denton. And in a community so small that one store served as grocery, post office, hardware store, and bar, somebody would have noticed something if Phyllis was around.

It was pointless to try any farther away. Karen's farm was

not really a Stineburg area farm; in fact, it was closer to New Concord to the west. And the same was true in the other directions. Marty had checked with everyone who could be considered to live in the Stineburg area, and then some.

Frustrated, she hit the gas and careened down Karen's driveway, raising a cloud of organic dust. But she slowed as she drove toward the Stineburg crossroads, scanning the countryside, trying to keep her mind open, trying to think if she'd missed anything. She arrived at the intersection: Padgett's store, eight houses, and the tiny church on the hill behind.

The church.

She's down there. Below Stineburg.

Grimly, Marty turned up the hill. Yes, there it was, a little cemetery on the slope behind, ragged with weeds around the edges but well mowed, plastic flowers on some of the graves. Notebook in hand, she began to read the gravestones. Corbetts, Millers, Smiths, Padgetts. Even Stines. The important thing was not the name, of course, but the date of death.

"Howdy."

"Hi." Marty turned to greet a man wearing jeans, a work shirt, and a baseball cap advertising Beechnut Chewing Tobacco. He was one of the quieter men she'd met in Padgett's.

"She ain't here either," he said.

"You know this cemetery?"

"Yeah, I'm the caretaker."

"No young women buried here recently? Or girls, she'd only be twenty now."

"Well, of course there's Annie Corbett. Got herself killed in that wreck over at Needmore." He nodded at a neat limestone marker. "But we all knew Annie."

"You're sure it was Annie you buried? Somebody saw her?"

"Oh, yeah." He shoved his cap back and glanced at her sharply, shocked at what she was implying. "It was a broken neck, see, no burns or like that. They fixed her up real pretty. Open casket, we all saw her."

"I see." Marty closed her notebook wearily. "Are there other cemeteries around her?"

"Not that anybody uses anymore. A couple of family plots, but nobody's gone into them for sixty years."

"Well, maybe you can just show me the graves here for the last few years."

There were a dozen of them: two infants, six men, three old women, and Annie. The caretaker had a story for each of them. None fit Phyllis.

Well, so much for your hot lead, Hopkins. She thanked the caretaker and he touched the visor of his Beechnut cap. She glanced at her watch as she got into the cruiser. Three-forty. She'd be off duty by the time she got back to Dunning. She'd pick up Chrissie at the bakery, soothe Aunt Vonnie, and see if she could find Brad. Time to make some sense of her private life, now that her job had come up zero.

Damn that Professor Wolfe.

She wondered enviously what Wes Cochran had learned from Kizzy.

9

BERNICE BROWN REFUSED TO LET WES IN THE DOOR.

"No, sir," she said, firmly planted before her closed door. "Nobody's seeing Kizzy unless she says yes."

"It's about her husband."

"I'm sorry, sir." Her dark eyes sparkled with determination.

"Look, ma'am, I just want to ask her some questions."

Bernice was a stocky black woman in her thirties, hair waved and glossy, with carefully applied makeup and wearing a neat coral pants suit. She looked like a front-office receptionist or office manager. She also looked downright stubborn. Damn the woman. But he couldn't go busting in. Wasn't even his jurisdiction. He was supposed to liaise with Indianapolis on something like this, but he didn't want the possible Klan involvement noised around, attracting every clumsy would-be hero in the state and nation.

He said to Bernice, "I mean, how the hell are we supposed to catch the guys who did this if nobody talks to us?"

"Sorry, sir."

Wes glanced up and down the street. It was a working-class area, the rowhouses sporting fresh paint here, a makeshift porch repair there, exuberant flowers in most of the tiny yards. A few black women and men walked past. None of them looked in the direction of the white sheriff but they knew he was there, all right.

"Okay, look," Wes said. "Tell her Sheriff Cochran wants to talk to her about her husband. Ask if she'll meet me somewhere, a restaurant maybe. Her choice. I'll wait here."

The door behind Bernice opened. "Bernice, I'll talk to him. You watch."

"Kizzy, you don't have to—"

"It'll be okay. Tom's here, and Russell."

Bernice backed into the house, shaking her head. Wes glanced at the street again, and at the windows of the house, for Tom and Russell. He didn't see anyone, but he didn't doubt her word for a minute. He said, "Look, I'm real sorry to bother you. I just have to ask a few questions."

"Yeah. Tom told me Goldie got—killed," Kizzy said with effort. She looked exhausted, her large eyes sunken, her mouth sagging. Even so she was beautiful, with fine bones, smooth brown skin, an appealing toughness in her stance. She was wearing a white blouse and silky black pants gathered at her slender waist. She held a large manila envelope. "You say you're going to catch the bastards?"

"Going to do my best." Wes pulled out his notebook. "Now, your name is Kizzy Horton?"

"Right. Kizzy Elizabeth Horton Goldstein."

"Okay. Ma'am, was this your husband?" He showed her the photo.

"Yes." The tired eyes blinked once.

"And you lived where?"

"The last couple months we lived down in your county.

Nichols County, near Dunning. Because it was cheap and musicians don't make a hell of a lot of money. Guy we knew in Bloomington owned this old farmhouse on the Lawrence Road. He rented it to us."

"Yes." He wrote it down.

"You going to tell me what they did to him?"

"He was murdered, ma'am."

"Shot? Knifed? Beat up?"

Sometimes the shock of a brutal killing would shake loose information. But Wes felt cruel as he said, "All those things."

"Yeah." She didn't seem surprised, although her lips tightened for a moment as she scrutinized him. Then she said, "I knew it would be bad. Two weeks ago we found this nailed to the front door." She handed him the manila envelope.

Wes opened it. Inside was a letter-size sheet of paper, a photocopy of a smaller paper. On the smaller one, the cross and blood-drop shape had been laboriously drawn at the top. Below, it said, "KKK sees you! Miscegenation Out!"

"This is a copy," Wes said.

"Yeah. The real thing was on a little three-by-five card. I'm afraid you can't have that."

"It would help if I could see it."

She shook her head. "Arrest somebody. You'll have it at the trial, I'm sure."

Wes decided not to pursue it for the moment. "Now, Miz Horton, what did you do when you saw this on your door?"

"I got out. Just like it said. But Goldie wouldn't leave." Her mouth trembled. "He was from back East, poor jerk. He said nobody could tell him how to run his life. Said it was a joke."

"Yeah." Wes rubbed his ear. "Wish he'd been right. He shoulda been right."

"Oh, yeah." She nodded without smiling. "The world's full of things that shoulda been."

"Sure is." He liked this tough little woman, saw why Goldie had been attracted. "So you left and your husband stayed on."

"Yeah. And nothing happened till this. We'd meet in Bloomington or talk on the phone a couple of times a day, and I was starting to think . . ." She trailed off, blinking.

"Starting to think he was right?" he prodded gently.

"No, no, I knew I was right. But I was starting to think maybe they just wanted *me* out. You know, 'Nigger, don't let the sun go down on you in this county.' "

"I see."

"I just couldn't make Goldie understand! His mama was one of those civil rights marchers in the sixties. He showed me a picture of him about seven years old walking beside her with a little We Shall Overcome sign. He said a person should stand up against injustice. I said great, you do that, you be the hero, I'm getting out, I just want to make music—" Her voice broke. Glancing up, Wes saw that she'd covered her face with her hands.

"Yeah," he murmured uncomfortably. "Uh, Miz Horton, was that card the only warning you had?"

"Yeah." The hands came down, but tears still shone on her pretty brown face. "That was it. No crosses burned on the lawn, nothing like that."

"Nobody insulted you, teased you, anything?"

"Not in your county, Sheriff. But we didn't do much in your county, because we didn't spend much time at home. We mailed letters, sure, bought a few groceries, gas, that kind of thing. But we spent a lot of time in Bloomington and here in Indy, so it was easier to do most of our shopping here. We never even met our neighbors down there. If neighbors is the word."

"What about at work? In Bloomington, or here? Did your husband have any enemies? Any feuds?"

"Nothing I thought was serious. Rick and Kurt at the Keg used to argue politics with him, until they just sort of avoided each other. But mostly he was interested in music. He got along real well with musicians."

"What about you? Or the two of you?"

Kizzy shrugged, a pretty shrug in the soft white blouse. "I know what you're asking. Yeah, some people were uncomfortable that Goldie and I were a couple. But we never paraded it around. You're saying that somebody we knew in Indy or Bloomington went all the way down there to card us?"

"Gotta look at all the possibilities."

"Yeah. Still, why'd they wait till we were so far away?"

"These people who were uncomfortable, who were they?"

"I don't know their names, Sheriff. Different people, different times, just strangers. They'd just be sitting around the courthouse square or something, yell 'nigger lover!' at Goldie. Maybe they'd go to the trouble to find out who we were, I don't know."

"Yeah. Did you or your husband respond to them?"

"No. Goldie was even-tempered, except in a political argument. These guys on the street weren't arguing, they were just making animal noises. We had better things to do than grunt back."

"Yeah. Smart." He hesitated, then asked, "What about your friends? Were any of them uncomfortable?"

"No. Not that way. Some of them said we were dumb to get married in this state. Bernice here said that." She jerked her head at the door behind her.

"No jealous rivals, anything like that?"

"Hey, wait a minute." Kizzy's dark eyes grew lustrous with anger. She put her fists on her hips, elbows cocked aggressively. "Are you trying to say this is some domestic squabble? You going to arrest some black brother and tell the world he pretended to be a Kluxer to throw us off the scent?"

"No, I'm not trying to say that, ma'am."

"Only reason I've said two words to you is, Emmett and Della Hines told me you caught the motherfuckers who beat him up fifteen years ago."

"Yeah, and I'm going to catch this one too."

"Not if you're chasing the wrong men, you won't!"

Wes put up his palm in a gesture of peace. "Look, ma'am, I've gotta ask, part of the routine."

"Well, write down the answer is no." She pointed at his notebook with angry stabbing movements.

"Okay. That's all the questions anyway, unless you can think of something else."

"No. Except—" She folded her arms. "Well, I guess with the autopsy and all, you won't let me have the body for a while."

"We'll call you when we're done. Here, at Bernice's number?"

"Yeah."

"And you call us if you think of anything." He handed her a card.

"Okay."

"The only other thing is, it would be a help if we could see that card they left. The original."

"Oh, they'll probably show it to you eventually."

"They?"

"I sent it to the FBI last night, when Tom called and said Goldie'd been killed."

"I see." Shit. That meant he only had a day or two to loosen up Lester and the others before the feds came in and everyone forgot everything they'd ever seen.

"You know who did it, Sheriff?"

"I know where to start asking," he said. "After that it's up to the good Lord."

Kizzy nodded and opened the door. Bernice drew her in protectively. Good folks. Lester would say that people should stick to their own kind. Wes figured spunky Kizzy and Bernice were more his own kind than old Klansmen who blamed everybody but themselves for their problems.

But he sure wished Kizzy hadn't called in the FBI. Now he had to report it right away, and deal with the idiots they'd send.

He drove to Arby's to pick up a late lunch and headed home, munching as he drove. South of Indianapolis the vast plain stretched in every direction, flat as a sea, so that at Martinsville the first wrinkles of the land into hills were a welcome change, like reaching shore.

Martinsville had been the home of the head Klansman until a couple of years ago. Those feelings still slept in the hills, like a snake in the sun.

He was back at headquarters before four o'clock. Foley gave him the mail and messages. No lab reports yet; state cops had a brief history of the cars Goldie had owned. Sims and Mason had finished and Bobby Mason was industriously typing the report, using both index fingers. He told Wes that the landlord had said Goldstein's wife was black.

"Yeah. I just got back from talking to her."

"Oh." Mason blinked. "That was quick. The landlord said she was some kind of singer."

They were interrupted by Marty Hopkins stalking in.

"You look like a storm about to burst, Hopkins," said Wes.

"Yes, sir." She tossed a rolled-up map onto the filing cabinet. "There wasn't a damn thing down there. Nobody's seen or heard of Phyllis Denton around Stineburg. Don't know what that crazy Professor Wolfe was thinking about. Maybe she meant some other town."

"Maybe."

"Or maybe she's got a few wires crossed."

Wes frowned. "You thought that when you were talking to her?"

He saw her mind click back into her detective mode, pondering his question. "Not really," she admitted. "I kind of went back and forth. She wouldn't stay on the subject. But at the time, yeah, I thought it was good information."

"Even if we knew for a fact she was certifiable, we had to check out a tip like that."

"I know. It was still boring as hell." She glanced at Mason, still pecking at the typewriter, then back at Wes. "How was your day?" she asked cautiously.

"Fine. I talked to her. Give you all a report tomorrow. I've got a couple more people to talk to now."

"Right. Sir, I've got nothing to report. Okay if I type it up tomorrow?"

"Sure. Your shift's over now anyway."

"Yeah. See you tomorrow, sir." She ran out, heading for Reiner's Bakery across the street to pick up her kid.

10

"CHRISSIE ISN'T HERE. BRAD PICKED HER UP ABOUT FIFTEEN MIN-utes ago." Aunt Vonnie, in her crisp apron, was rearranging the blueberry muffins in the glass case of the bakery.

"Where'd they go?"

"School playground, he said." Aunt Vonnie's tired eyes met Marty's for a moment. "He's a charmin' man. Chrissie just worships him, doesn't she?"

"Yeah."

"I remember, you worshipped your daddy, too. Another charmin' man. Your poor mama—"

"Aw, c'mon, Aunt Vonnie, we can't all be as smart as you." Marty hurried out, not wanting to fight the old fights.

A couple of blocks away at the Dunning Elementary school-yard, Chrissie was pumping industriously on a swing, talking to Brad. "Malinda said it wasn't really the New York skyscrap-ers," she said. She was wearing the Manhattan skyline T-shirt that Brad had brought her. "But she only said that because she was so jealous. Janie and Susan sided with me."

"Well, Janie and Susan are right." Brad was half-sitting, propped against the support pipe of the seesaws. "That de-sign is a totally accurate picture of the skyline. I'll tell you the names of the buildings in a minute." He looked up and grinned at Marty. "Hey, kitten, look at this Chrissie go!"

He caught Marty's hand and drew her down to the seesaw bar next to him. Chrissie grinned and pumped even harder. Watching her daughter soar back and forth, Marty said to Brad, "So, tell me your new idea."

"Well, I've been thinking." His eyes shifted to Chrissie as

68

he thought about what to say, and her heart sank. "Sometimes the best road to where you want to be is roundabout."

"Yeah."

"See, the trouble is, in a big city like New York or Indianapolis, there's so many people trying to break into broadcasting, the guys in charge don't even look at you. They just give the job to somebody they know."

"Like your boss in New York giving the job he promised you to his cousin?"

"You got it. No way to fight that unless you already have connections. So the thing to do is, break in someplace where you've got a chance. Someplace small. And then when you've got a local reputation, a gimmick, lots of tape to show people, well, they can't ignore you then."

"Daddy! Look!" Chrissie cried. She was sailing high above them, as high as the fencetop. Marty remembered doing that, the sense of swooping into space, free at last.

"Fantastic!" Brad clapped his hands. "Swear to God, you'll be a trapeze star someday!"

Marty was applauding too. "You'll be an astronaut!"

Chrissie giggled with delight. "Yeah, sure. Hey, can we go home now? I promised to show Daddy my earring collection."

"Sure, after we check on Daddy's car," Marty called. She looked back at Brad and said in a lower voice, "So you've got a lead to work somewhere smaller? Where, Bloomington?"

"Nah, the university's got Bloomington tied up. Bad as the big towns. No, kitten, the place for us is Alaska."

"Alaska!"

"The last frontier. Listen, it's perfect, Marty! Young, challenging place, just getting itself launched."

"Alaska." She rubbed her forehead.

"Yeah. See, I met these Alaskan guys in New York. Jason and Steve. They were on vacation and they told me what things were like. And it hit me, see? A gimmick. The last frontier." His face was bright with enthusiasm. "Marty, I can bounce off Alaska right to the top! Like Garrison Keillor, you know? Or Wolf Man! But even better! And Jason and Steve left their addresses with me, said to call them. Said they knew a couple of stations there that could really use me."

"Alaska. God, Brad!"

Chrissie stood before them, earthbound again, her dark eyes anxious. "Does that mean we're not going to New York?"

"No, it doesn't mean that at all, honey." Brad leaned forward and said earnestly, "It means we'll get to New York quicker in the long run. We'll go to Alaska, all of us, and I'll get established there, see. Get the gimmick I need. And then the New York broadcasters will see what I can do."

"Brad, look," said Marty. "How about Bloomington? I mean, you're right, the university has the clout there. But you could use that. Take courses in communications or whatever they call it, do a bunch of Indiana programs . . ."

"Aw, Marty, you don't know what you're talking about! In New York, they wouldn't even look at that. They'd think it was kid stuff. Hell, it *is* kid stuff. Plus, Indiana's got no image. New Yorkers can't tell it from Illinois or Iowa. Look, I've given this a lot of thought. I know what I'm doing."

What was she supposed to say? That he didn't know what he was doing? Shoot him down while he was still bleeding from his long fruitless struggle in New York? He tried so hard. Maybe he aimed too high, but dammit, that was part of him, too, that dream. Marty wished she could believe the way she used to.

Chrissie was watching them wide-eyed. Marty said, "Okay, look, let me give it some thought."

He grinned and drew her closer for a kiss on the cheek. "I know it's sudden. We'll talk about it later. Right now I'm supposed to tell Chrissie about the skyline. C'mere." He pulled Chrissie closer and carefully straightened the girl's T-shirt. "Now look. See these two square-top buildings?"

"Yeah." Chrissie's chin was tucked into her neck as she studied her shirt.

"Well, that's the World Trade Center. This one over here with the rays is the Chrysler Building."

"Chrysler Building," Chrissie repeated, like a litany.

"And this one with the beautiful spire is the best of all. The Empire State Building."

"That's the one Granddaddy worked on?"

"That's right. You tell Malinda she can look it up. It's all true." He grinned and touched Chrissie's heart-shaped ear-rings. "Now let's go see the rest of your collection."

On the way home they stopped at Straub's Service to take a look at Brad's car. Gil Newton and Bert Mackay were there, a contrast in types: dark-haired, wiry, taciturn Gil and square-built, fair Bert, his blond hair thinning and his muscular body thickening. Both were dressed in dark blue coveralls.

"News isn't real good, Brad," Bert said as he unhooked the nozzle to gas up Marty's car.

They all got out and walked into the service bay with Gil. Brad's car was a ten-year-old black Camaro. He'd bought it used the year after Chrissie was born with the money Marty had been trying to put aside for the baby's education. Brad had explained, "Look, you have to think of it as an invest-ment. We've got responsibilities now, so we need decent transportation."

Now the investment sat jacked up to eye level on the service ramp while Gil explained to Brad that it was a transmission problem. "Five or six hundred bucks."

"Shit!" Brad kicked at the cinder-block wall. "That's a hell of a lot of money!"

Gil shrugged.

"Ought to get a new car anyway," Brad said.

"That's a hell of a lot of money too," Marty protested. "Gil, how bad is it otherwise?"

Gil pondered. "Not bad," he said at last. He shoved his grimy hands into the pockets of his coveralls and thought for another moment. "Can't tell for sure. But it's been kept up good."

"Yeah, God, I put a lot of sweat into that thing," Brad said. He ran a thumb along the bottom edge of the door. Marty remembered him sanding away the chips and rust, carefully repainting. He'd worked so hard.

She said, "Brad, it's a great car, I've got something saved up to paint the house. I can help some on the bill."

"No, I don't want you doing that, Marty."

"No, really. It's a great car."

"Yeah." He slapped the fender fondly. Chrissie was running her little thumb along the edge of the door. "Well, Gil, let's go ahead with it. What exactly went wrong?"

Marty didn't wait for Gil's slow reply, but returned to her car. She wanted to talk to Bert Mackay, who was just topping off the gas. She charged it to the sheriff's department and asked, "Bert, you know anything about Judge Denton?"

Bert stowed the charge slip in his pocket and said warily, "I hear he's real sick now."

"Yeah. It's bad. You seen him recently?"

"No. Not for a couple months. Used to come in all the time for gas, but not since he's been sick."

"Yeah. Bert, he sentenced you to jail a few years ago. At the time you said some pretty nasty things about him."

"Yeah, but I—see, I'm an alcoholic," Bert explained earnestly. "Back then I didn't admit it. I kept looking for excuses for all the trouble I got into. So I blamed the judge, and my lawyer. God forgive me, I even blamed the kid. But even then I knew I was wrong, just didn't want to admit it."

"Yeah."

"Jail was terrible, a terrible time." Bert stared down at the dusty asphalt and shook his head. "But it woke me up. The reverend there, the chaplain, got some of us in AA. And he said, when we got out, that was a new chance."

"Uh-huh."

"Well, I took it to heart. Old Tom Straub gave me a break here at the gas station, and I swear I've been on the straight and narrow ever since."

"Yeah, I've never heard any different," Marty allowed.

"See, I'm born again. Like the reverend said, the Good Lord is giving me a second chance."

"Yeah." Marty didn't mention that she'd had to arrest bornagains from time to time, right alongside the unrepentant. "Bert, you say you haven't seen the judge since he got sick."

"That's right. Man, I could tell he was failing a couple months ago. He came in for gas and told me he had instructions for the mechanic. Gave me a note but all it said was, 'Not yet time,' so I threw it away. And he had a terrible time driving off, car jerking around, him shaking his fists. It was one of his fits. Never saw him again. Royce moved back in to help right after that."

"Before that, any words between you, anything like that?"

"No! Look, I've been respectful, ever since I got out. What's all this about?" Bert's pink face flushed darker.

Marty hurried to explain. "See, it's just something I have to check out. The judge thinks someone's killing him. And one of the names he mentioned was yours."

"Mine? You're kidding!" Bert stared at her in astonishment. "Hey, but listen, Royce said his dad raves sometimes. He's gotta be raving."

"Could be. He's in and out. We have to check it out."

Brad sauntered over to them, Chrissie following. "Ready to go?" he asked.

"Just a minute. I've got a couple more questions for Bert. What do you know about the judge's daughter?"

"His daughter? She ran off, didn't she? A long time ago, before—"

"Hey, kitten, you're off duty, remember?" Brad slung an arm over her shoulder.

"Yeah. We were just finishing up." Marty shrugged off his arm. "Before what, Bert?"

"Oh, you know." He nudged an oil can with the toe of his shoe. "Before I went to jail."

"Yeah. Well, listen, Bert, you think of anything, you let me know, okay? I just want to figure out why your name came up."

"Yeah, sure, Marty."

Brad clapped Bert on the shoulder. "Hey, see you around." He climbed into the car with a troubled glance at Marty, but said nothing more. They went home to admire Chrissie's earrings.

11

SATURDAY MORNING, MARTY SAT AT THE BATTERED TYPEWRITER, banging out the report on her useless trip to Stineburg. The *r* key stuck, and the *e* was filled in with black ink, but she was a hell of a lot quicker than Bobby Mason. Maybe that's why Wes Cochran wanted her on the Denton case, she thought gloomily. Hal, Jr., and Royce were lawyers, and lawyers liked lots of paperwork. So Wes had put her on it because she was the best typist.

She was answering phones at the moment too, because Don Foley had gone out for doughnuts.

Shoot, maybe Brad was right. Maybe she did belong in Alaska. Time for a fresh start. He'd do better with her help, she was sure. The first three years in Bloomington he'd done great, working up from late-night to afternoon programs, until Gary, the manager, had moved to a new job in Indianapolis. The new manager had wanted to change the format, add a newsreader. Brad had quit and followed Gary to Indy, but Gary didn't have many connections there yet and hadn't been able to help him. Marty, left behind with no rent money, had brought Chrissie to her mother's house here in Nichols County and gone to work for the sheriff.

But if the sheriff was going to slap her down because she wanted to help on the big cases, if he was turning her into a goddamn typist and phone answerer, well, Alaska looked pretty good.

Her fingers paused on the keys. Damn, what was the name of that road where Karen's organic farm was? Marty jumped up impatiently and unrolled the survey map. It would be leading north, toward—

The tiny symbol seemed to leap from the map. She'd looked right past it a dozen times, but suddenly the thin black Y seemed as bright as neon among the faded brown contour lines of the hillside: the symbol for a cave entrance.

She's down there, below Stineburg.

Slice this countryside and it'll look like waterlogged Swiss cheese.

"Shoot, shoot, shoot!" Marty snatched up the phone. What was that guy's name, the naturalist at Spring Mill State Park who'd helped them when the Moore kids were lost? Russell. Floyd Russell. She dialed quickly.

"Yeah, Floyd's coming in this morning, he's supposed to take a tour," said the naturalist on duty.

"This is the Nichols County Sheriff's Department. Tell him to meet me on Donaldson Road, two miles north of the intersection with County 860. Tell him to bring his gear."

"You got an emergency?"

"I hope not. But it sure could be."

"Okay. He'll be there."

Marty scribbled a note to Don, checked her flashlight, and ran out without pausing to pull the report from the typewriter. She burned rubber all the way to Donaldson Road, and by the time Floyd Russell's Land Rover pulled up twenty minutes later, she was searching among the redbuds and stickerbushes of the hillside. She hurried down to meet him.

"Hi, Floyd. I'm Marty Hopkins."

"Yeah, I remember." He grinned at her, a short, muscular man dressed in ancient jeans and sweatshirt, a park naturalist badge his only uniform. His pockmarked skin was partly concealed behind a short brown beard. "What's the problem?"

"Missing person. Old story, but we just got a report that she was in the Stineburg cave." Marty was still kicking herself for not catching on sooner.

"You sure?" Floyd squinted at the hillside. "It's open again, then?"

"What do you mean?"

"A few years ago the mouth of that cave collapsed. I haven't been in there for eight or ten years, and I don't know anybody else who's been in it either. So how'd she get in?"

"Shoot." Marty looked back up the hillside. "You're right, all I found was what looked like a rockslide."

"Yep. That's it, all right."

"Would you take a look anyway? Just in case?"

He shrugged. "Long as we're here, why not?" He pulled tools and rope from the Land Rover, hesitated, then slung a backpack over his shoulder and handed one to her.

Rocks had spilled down the hillside. "See, the cave used to come out to where we're standing now," Floyd explained. "Then the lip of stone over the entrance collapsed, and it blocked the opening. There's nobody in there."

"There's no other entrance to the cave?"

"Depends on what you mean by 'the cave,' " Floyd explained. He was prodding among the rocks and bushes with a crowbar. "There are long systems of interconnected tunnels and crevices. But most of them aren't large enough for people. This cave has a couple of good-sized caverns connected by a crawlway, and on beyond you can see through a crack to more cave, but it's too small to squeeze through. So in a practical sense this was the only entrance. But theoretically, every sinkhole for a couple of miles around probably leads into the system, even if you can't get there from here." Halfheartedly, he tugged at a rock with his crowbar.

"So there's no entrance now," she said.

He straightened and glanced at his Land Rover, clearly ready to quit. "Spiders and crickets get through real well. Even fish. But people? I'm afraid someone was pulling your leg."

Right now she's studying cave fauna, the jealous Professor Hart had told her back at IU. Marty said stubbornly, "The person who told me to look here probably saw her. Do you know that biologist from IU? Professor Wolfe?"

"Wolfe!" He glanced at her sharply. "I've talked to her a couple times, yeah. She sends students to me for instruction. Professor Wolfe told you someone was in here?"

"Yeah."

He stepped back, scrutinizing the rock pile with real interest for the first time. "How the hell could she—"

"You believe her, then?" Marty asked.

"Never knew her to be wrong." He climbed up to a higher point, thrust his crowbar behind a boulder, and pushed. "All right. Hardhat time." He came down again, donned a caver's helmet, and handed one to Marty. "Get that on and come help me."

Marty adjusted her chin strap and scrambled up next to him. He said, "I think this one may move."

It did. With him leaning into the crowbar and Marty shoving, the boulder pivoted a few inches on the one below.

"How 'bout that!" said Floyd.

Marty shone her flashlight inside. A steep slope of rocks led down into blackness. She felt a shiver of excitement, like the moment before a race. Floyd said, "Looks like we enter from the second floor now. You'll need your hands. Know how these carbide lamps work?"

He'd unclipped the lamp from his hardhat and held it out for her to inspect. There was a tiny nozzle in the center of a reflector, and two compartments screwed together behind it. Marty frowned at it. "Never saw one up close."

"Basically, you manufacture your own acetylene gas and burn it." He unscrewed the lower compartment and shook chunks into it from a container. "Carbide goes in the bottom section. Come on, do yours."

The lamp was clamped to her helmet with a bracket. Marty took it off and unscrewed it, then followed his example, pouring peanut-sized chunks of carbide into it. Floyd screwed his lamp back together. "Water goes in the top compartment, drips through a valve, and produces the gas. The gas comes out through the burner tip, and lo! there is light." He showed her a little tool with fine wires extending from a tube. "This is a tip reamer. Sometimes the burner tip gets clogged. You clean it out with a wire. Wires retract into the case for carrying. Now—"

"Do I have to know all this stuff?" Marty itched to get on with the hunt.

"Absolutely!" His hazel eyes flashed emphatically. "If a rock falls on my head in there, I want you to know how to keep your light on long enough to go for help. This is no tourist cave, with phones every third turn. This is the real thing."

"Okay, I see." He was right. Even if Phyllis was in there, they couldn't do much without light.

Floyd continued, "Now, this gizmo controls the drip valve, and this one is a hinged cap, where you add water. There's a water bottle in your cave pack. More carbide in there, too."

"Don't they make electric lamps?"

"Yeah. But to get this much light you need a big heavy battery. Hard on your head. Some cavers strap them to their bodies. But when you're in a tight place you can scrape the battery off or dislodge the wiring. I'm more comfortable with the old tried and true technology."

"Okay."

"Now, we start the water dripping." He filled the top compartments. "See this little wheel? Spark lighter. I usually hold my hand over the reflector a moment to trap some of the gas, then spin the wheel." He did. With a pop, the gas caught fire. He clipped the lamp back onto his helmet. "Now you."

Marty imitated him. On her third try, her light burst into flame. He helped her adjust her lamp into its bracket, then said, "Great. Everything else you need is in the pack. Let's go." He squeezed through the crack they'd opened.

Marty scrambled after him. The opening was narrow, clogged by fallen rocks, but as they descended, the space widened out. It was very cool. Soon they were in a winding cavern about ten feet wide and seven feet high, the buff stone smoothed by some long-gone river. People had been here before them—along the wall rested a few beer cans, an old belt, an oil spout, some corroded flashlight batteries. "This cave is shaped like a wiggly *H*," Floyd said when they'd gone about thirty yards. "Entrance is in the bottom of the left arm. Let's go through the crossbar to the right arm. Here, hang a right."

It didn't look like a right to Marty. It looked like a three-foot-diameter hole in the wall up at waist level. Floyd said, "You've got knee pads in your backpack if you want them. But it's only twenty feet long." He ducked into the hole. Marty glanced back. The sliver of light that marked the entrance was already out of sight. She followed Floyd.

At first it wasn't hard, although it seemed strange to be crawling like a baby through a stone tube so alien from the countryside just above it. She couldn't imagine Judge Denton's daughter in a place like this. She could smell the dank scent of clay mud somewhere. The tunnel sloped down, and gradually she realized that the sides were closing in and the ceiling was getting lower. The stone pressed in without malice, without caring at all. It seemed a long way back to the entrance. Floyd called, "Turn right here," and disappeared around a corner. When his voice died the only sounds were her own harsh breathing, the rhythmic scraping of the toes of her shoes against the limestone floor, the fainter scrape of Floyd somewhere ahead. And an odd gurgling noise. Marty's heart began to gallop. What was that noise? Where was Floyd? Was that some kind of insect scurrying away from her light?

Her backpack bumped the ceiling. She wriggled one arm out of it and let it dangle from the other shoulder, crawling after Floyd as fast as she could. The floor was getting damp now, the thin layer of dust turning to mud. Then her back scraped against the limestone overhead. Ahead she could see the tunnel ceiling easing down, ever lower, and the soles of Floyd's shoes twitching along. "Belly crawl," he called back cheerfully.

Shoot. What was she doing down here? Phyllis couldn't be here.

Then suddenly the crawl was over. Marty squeezed through the last constriction into a large limestone chamber, its tan walls lit by her lamp and Floyd's. A stream tumbled from a slit high in the right end of the chamber and disappeared into a pile of rocks at the other end. It had carved this whole rounded gallery. Marty looked at the stone ceiling and wondered how far below the redbuds they were now.

Floyd was standing beside the stream. "You ever seen a blindfish?" he asked.

Marty joined him and peered into the water. A strange white creature was moving away from their lights. "God, it's like a ghost," she marveled.

"Crickets too," he said, nodding at the wall beside them. Pale, spindly insects were huddled under a rock, antennae shivering.

Marty stepped closer but the creatures ran for the shadows. "They're like science fiction, you know?"

Floyd smiled. "Like it here?"

She looked around, frowning. "Yeah, but—not exactly. It's a wild place, isn't it? A wilderness. They've never seen light, those crickets. I feel like an invader."

His smile widened. "You'll do, Marty Hopkins."

"This is what Professor Wolfe studies?" she asked.

"Evolution," he said. "Adaptation to living in the dark."

"And fossils too."

"Yeah, she studies lots of things. I only went caving with her once, long time ago, over in Washington County. We were a couple of miles underground—difficult, wild wet cave—and we'd stopped for a snack, both of us covered with mud. She was leaning back against the cave wall with this totally blissful look on her face. Well, most of us are in this for the challenge. Overcoming obstacles, testing ourselves, going where no human has ever been. So I asked her why she liked caving and she said, very seriously, 'I'm a pervert.' She said, 'I'm in love with the earth. I want to memorize her every dimple.' Shook me up, I'll tell you."

In love with the earth. Strange woman. Had she really seen Phyllis here? Marty squinted around the chamber and asked, "There's no other way out?"

"A little tunnel up there in the boulders where the stream runs out. Pinches down too small for anyone over ten," he said. "And there's an extension of this chamber." He led her to a vertical crevice next to the rockpile where the stream disappeared. They could walk nearly upright, right then left to a dry rounded chamber with a shallow indentation at the back. An old rusty chain led from an iron ring attached to the stone floor. "Bootlegger days," Floyd explained.

It gave Marty the creeps. She said, "Well, there's nobody here. We'd better keep looking."

He smiled. "You lead. Back through the crawlway."

"Okay." Marty returned to the stream chamber, squeezed into the crawlway again, and led the way back to the main cavern, feeling almost like an old hand.

Floyd was right behind her. "Okay," he said. "*H*-shaped,

remember? We've seen all but the top part of the first arm. This section bends a little and widens out in about twenty feet."

They were walking as he spoke. A dark gleam to the right where the cavern widened. Too shiny, too regular. Her left hand caught Floyd's elbow, her right dropped to her gun.

Floyd followed her gaze. "Christ! I never saw that before!"

Steady, Hopkins, she told herself. Her jolted senses drank in the surroundings: the silence, loud after the bubbling river; the vault of blond stone walls and ceiling; the angular jumble of the fallen boulders at the end of the chamber. And the yellow-white gleam of their lamps reflected from the dark shiny rectangular shape tucked behind that rock. Was it—

She kept her voice cool, neutral. "Hold it right here a second, Floyd, okay?"

She looked around carefully. No one. There was dust, not a heavy layer, and the floor was already scuffed. Keyed up, noting her own path so she wouldn't contaminate the scene too much, Marty approached it. Yes, a coffin. On the arching stone wall behind it, someone had smoked a tall cross. There was no dust on the coffin, she noted. Nicely made of polished wood.

Should she call Wes? Not yet, Hopkins, first find out what's here.

Marty licked her dry lips. The lid had neat hinges, although it squeaked a little when she lifted it.

There'd been no need to rush, after all. The frail skeleton inside, wrapped in a moldy crocheted coverlet, was long past help. A mass of dull wavy hair lay on the satin pillow under the skull like a brown frill. The hands were crossed on a small Bible laid on the chest, and a golden bracelet mingled with the small wrist bones. The bracelet had the same pattern of leaves that she'd seen in the portrait at the Denton place.

A page from a hymnal was tucked beside the skull. "Rock of Ages."

Marty let the coffin lid down gently and raised her eyes to the cave wall behind it. Limestone. Made of corpses.

Rock of Ages, cleft for me, let me hide myself in thee . . .

Phyllis Denton was hidden no more.

12

Royce Denton sat in his father's library, paying his father's bills from his father's account. After the first two seizures the old man had given his sons power of attorney to pay certain of his bills. Hal, Jr., had been angry about the tight conditions attached. "He still thinks we're kids," he fumed. "Does he think we'll spend all his money on lollipops? Or that I'll be writing myself campaign contributions?"

"Who knows what he thinks?" Royce answered. "Probably wants to hang on to the illusion that he's in control. Wouldn't you?"

Hal gave a half-guilty shrug. "Yeah. Maybe."

In fact, in the period before the seizures became a daily occurrence, his father had consented to a couple of middle-sized contributions to Hal's campaign fund. Out of the question now; they were authorized to pay for utilities, car repairs, nursing expenses, and not much else. Royce hoped the roof would hold for a while.

From upstairs he heard the steady creak of the nurse's rocking chair. From the kitchen came the muffled drone of one of his mother's machines. She'd promised meatloaf tonight.

He put the check into the envelope. The desk where he sat, his father's, had been his grandfather's before that—a heavy oak rolltop with a scuffed work surface and myriads of slots and cubbyholes and little drawers. Everything had a place. Hal thought it was old-fashioned but Royce liked the desk, with its sense of businesslike men keeping their lives in order for long years. It smelled of furniture polish, with a hint of tobacco. Royce suspected that both his grandfather and his father had stored their cigars in one of the small drawers. His

82

father had quit smoking years ago but the old desk had not forgotten.

The coonhounds began to bay, and then there was a crunch of tires on the gravel turnaround. Royce stood to glance out the window. A sheriff's department cruiser, curly haired Marty Hopkins jumping out from the passenger side. She had a way about her, Royce thought. Serious and businesslike, yes, but he'd glimpsed tenderness and sympathy behind it, and a pleasing touch of fluster when he'd found the honeysuckle on her collar.

Right now, though, she looked grim.

Bad news, then. He didn't want his mother to have to face it first. Royce went into the hall and when the doorbell sounded he called back toward the kitchen, "I'll get it, Mother. I'm right here." He opened the door.

Marty Hopkins wasn't alone. She was standing a step behind Wes Cochran's tall bulk. Royce raised his eyebrows. "Sheriff Cochran! Well, come in! Hello, Marty." He nodded at them as they stepped solemnly into the shadowy hall.

"How are you, Royce," Wes Cochran said. He loomed over both of them, looking as grim as Marty did. "Um, I'm afraid we've got bad news about your sister." He paused. "We've found a body."

"And you think it's hers?" Royce couldn't keep the disbelief from his voice.

Wes Cochran said, "They'll run tests. But we found this on the body." He showed Royce a plastic evidence bag containing a gold bracelet with an intricate design of interlocked leaves. Royce's eyes went to the portrait. The bracelet was the same.

"Yes. It's hers," he said. It was like being punched, and he was astonished because he thought he'd prepared himself for anything. Frequently he'd had the thought that she might be dead. But it was a cold thought, intellectual, and now he realized that he'd always expected her to reestablish contact someday.

His eyes had squeezed shut. Wes was mumbling something sympathetic, but it was Marty Hopkins's hand on Royce's arm that pulled him back. "You okay?" she asked.

"Yeah." He ran a hand across his forehead and met her

gray eyes for an instant. "Just such a shock. I didn't expect— She was so young, see."

Marty nodded.

"How did she die?"

"We don't know yet," Wes said. "We know it happened years ago. Probably soon after she disappeared."

"That long ago! Was it a road accident? Or did someone . . ." He looked from Wes's face to Marty's and back again.

"We don't know yet," Wes repeated. "It'll take a while to find the answers. We're working on it."

"Yes, I know." Royce rubbed his forehead again. Anger was stirring within him.

"You can help us with some questions we have," Marty said.

"Of course. Whatever I can do."

"We found her in a cave not far from Stineburg."

"In a cave—oh, God, I know that cave! Hal and I used to play there when we were kids! Dad still owns that property. Belonged to my great-uncle before him." Both Wes and Marty were watching him closely, sympathetic but alert; Royce realized that what he was saying might be important to the case. "But that cave was sealed off a few years ago, I heard. When they were repairing the road, the dynamiting or something caused a collapse. Is that the cave you mean?"

"That's the one," said Marty.

"Did Phyllis—did she die there?"

"Hard to tell," Wes said. "We're still filling in details."

Marty added gently, "But someone laid her out real nice. Coffin and everything."

Royce remembered the photo of Phyllis in her leather jacket and shook his head. "I don't understand. She ran away with those motorcycle nuts—so it had to be an accident of some kind, right? Why would they put her in that cave? In a coffin?"

Marty Hopkins said, "Maybe they just didn't want to get involved with the police."

"Well, dammit, they're going to get involved now!" Royce slammed his fist into his palm. "We'll pull out all the stops! Damn! How could this happen to her?"

Marty asked, "Did Phyllis know that cave too?"

Royce took a deep breath and tried to remember. "I don't know. Probably. We used to go there for picnics. Dad liked to fish on the river near there. But Hal and I were a lot older. I went off to college before Phyllis was old enough to do much exploring."

"So she didn't talk about the cave later, when you came back to visit?"

"Not that I remember. But when I came back, Phyl and I usually talked about TV shows, things like that."

"Well—" Marty glanced at Wes. "We'd better break the news to your mother."

"Yes, of course." His mother. Damn. He didn't know if he could face his mother right now, see her tears. "She's in the kitchen fixing dinner."

Wes gestured toward the rear of the hall, and reluctantly Royce led the way into the kitchen, a big square room with two walls of counters and a maple-topped work island. On the island, the grinder was whirring as his mother fed red chunks of beef into it. A mass of ground meat oozed from its nozzle into a glass bowl. His mother looked up, glancing from one face to another, and turned away hastily to rinse her hands at the sink. She asked, "What happened?"

Wes said, "I'm afraid we have bad news about your daughter, Mrs. Denton."

She turned slowly to face him.

"We think she's dead. I'm sorry."

Two slow tears squeezed from her eyes. She covered her face with her hands. Marty moved toward her but paused when Royce hurried to his mother. "Mother. God, this is rotten!"

She let him put his arms around her, but she remained stiff, rejecting comfort. After a moment he moved back a pace and asked gently, "Are you all right? I know it's a shock."

She lowered her hands and peered at him with glistening eyes. "No. I knew."

"Yeah. In a way I knew too. It's still a shock when it's confirmed."

Wes Cochran cleared his throat and asked gruffly, "Mrs. Denton, how did you know?"

She looked at him vacantly, as though she didn't understand.

"Did someone tell you?" Marty asked.

"Tell me—?" There was a thump from upstairs. She looked at Marty but seemed to be listening fearfully to the creak of the nurse's rocking chair. "No," Elizabeth said. "I just knew."

"She wrote twice and quit," Royce said. "I worried that she was kidnapped, or hurt. But no ransom demands came. I figured she was just a kid who ran off, and kids forget to write."

"Uh, Mrs. Denton," the sheriff rumbled, "may we ask you a few questions about the time right before Phyllis disappeared?"

"Yes." Her voice was flat, lackluster.

"Now, as I remember it, you had no idea she was involved with this motorcycle group?"

"No. None." She gave a quick, fearful glance at Royce.

He patted her shoulder reassuringly. "None of us had any idea, Sheriff. Not until the photo turned up."

"Yeah, I remember. You showed that to me a few weeks later. Well now, Mrs. Denton, there's a cave down near Stineburg. Your son says it's on your property."

"Yes." His mother frowned and drew a shaky breath.

"Do you remember your daughter ever saying anything about that cave?"

"Yes. She liked that cave. All the children did. You remember, Royce, you and Hal Junior used to play in it."

"Yeah, I remember. Phyl explored it too?"

"Yes. Of course her father and I only went in a few steps, but she enjoyed playing there. Of course she didn't go far because it's hard to carry a flashlight in those small places. And we used to get upset. Once when she was nine she took the flashlight and was gone for close to an hour. I was terrified. But she always found her way—" The tears brimmed over again. Marty found a paper napkin and handed it to her.

"I'm sorry to trouble you, Mrs. Denton," the sheriff said uncomfortably. "But did Phyllis say anything about the cave? I mean around the time she disappeared?"

"No." She shook her head. "I don't think so."

"Okay. Now, you people own that land. Did other people visit the cave?"

She looked at Royce, and he answered, "A few times there were trespassers. We found beer cans near the mouth every now and then. Or graffiti. Hal Junior and I cleaned it off."

"Can you think of any connection between these trespassers and your sister?"

"No. Never knew who they were. But that's an interesting idea," Royce added. "Maybe if we could find out— Mother, do you have any idea who they were?"

"No. Except for the Packer boy who left his name there," she answered. "We didn't know him. The boys cleaned it off."

"What about Professor Wolfe?" Marty asked.

"I don't know."

"Who's Professor Wolfe?" Royce asked.

"A professor at IU," Marty said. "Works in caves. Told me Phyllis was there. What did she tell you, Mrs. Denton?"

"She said she'd seen Phyllis in the cave."

"She'd seen her?" Royce exclaimed. "When?"

"I don't know. She told me years ago."

"Why didn't you tell me?" Royce kicked angrily at the island counter. "Dammit, Mother, we've been wasting time!"

"But, Royce—we heard so many reports. All false, don't you remember? And your father got so upset every time— Sheriff, you remember!"

"Yeah." Wes nodded. "You weren't around much, Royce. But she's right. Even keeping things low-key, avoiding publicity, we got all kinds of nuts thinking they'd spotted the kid. One guy visited his granny in Indianapolis and thought he saw her there, another one was down at French Lick—we checked out dozens of reports." He looked at Royce's mother. "When did the professor tell you this?"

"I don't remember exactly. Maybe a year after Phyllis had disappeared."

Royce burst out, "Mother, you should have told us! This report was true!"

She was crying again, her face hidden behind the napkin Marty had given her. "There were a dozen reports I didn't tell you about! They weren't true!"

Wes Cochran said, "Don't be too hard on her, Royce."

Marty Hopkins's sympathetic hand was on his arm, gentling him. "Besides, she told us to check with Wolfe this time."

"Yeah, but all that time gone!" Royce ran a hand over his face. They were right, this anger was a waste of energy. Cool off, get to work. He looked across at the sheriff. "Hell, it's just so frustrating. But now we know. And it's time to pull out all the stops, right?" He looked the sheriff in the eyes. "We're going to get the bastards who did this. They're going to pay."

His mother's eyes glittered with tears, but his words had awakened something like rage in her too. "Yes!" she said, with an intensity that surprised him. "Yes, they'll pay!"

Marty touched his mother's shoulder. "We'll do our best, Mrs. Denton. Now, Royce, your mother remembered Professor Wolfe because your father had said something."

"That's right!" Royce exclaimed. He could hear his father, almost, babbling about idiots, about Phyllis, about being eaten, about wolves.

"I think we ought to talk to him," Wes Cochran said.

Royce said, "He's not very clear about things, Sheriff."

"Yeah, Hopkins here told me. Still, we oughta try." Wes cleared his throat. "Hopkins, you stay with Mrs. Denton, okay?"

Marty nodded. But his mother said, "I'd rather be alone a few minutes."

"Sure, ma'am." The sheriff's gentle voice surprised Royce. In the courtroom he'd always seen quite a different man, with a matter-of-fact steeliness that seemed to go clear through. He held the door for Wes and Marty and they went back into the hall. Behind them, the grinder still whirred.

As Royce started up the stairs, he saw Marty glance up at the portrait. He looked at it too, really seeing it for the first time in years. Phyllis's sad, quiet, painted gaze met his and kindled tears. He didn't let them out, of course, but they burned behind his eyes all the way upstairs.

He'd get those bastards somehow, the ones that killed his little sister.

His father was sleeping. Royce touched Lisa's blond head

and she scrambled up from her chair, removing her earphones. "Oh, hi, Royce!"

"Sheriff Cochran, this is Lisa."

"Howdy, Lisa." But the sheriff, unable to hide his shock completely, was staring at the gaunt sleeping figure in the bed.

"Should we wake him up?" Royce asked Lisa.

"Oh, dear, I only got him settled down half an hour ago."

"Yeah, I heard him thrashing around earlier." He looked at Wes Cochran, who was shaking his head sorrowfully. "Sheriff, if it's okay with you, I'd rather wait and tell him when he's awake."

"He doesn't get much peace," Lisa explained.

"Yeah." The sheriff hitched up his belt. "I didn't know he was so poorly."

"What did you want to tell him?" Lisa asked.

"My sister. They just found her. She's dead," Royce said bluntly.

"Oh, I'm sorry!" Lisa's hand flew to her mouth.

"Yeah. Anyway, if he wakes up clearheaded, let me know."

"The news will be hard on him," Lisa said. "Maybe we should wait until he gets some strength back."

Wes turned to Lisa. "We're trying to get a line on a Professor Wolfe. I hear he's mentioned the name?"

She looked doubtful. Royce saw Marty glance at the earphones, then at Wes, and saw Wes register the message. Lisa said, "Maybe. But he usually doesn't make much sense."

"Well, let us know if he says anything. Thanks."

"Okay, we will." Royce rubbed his forehead. "God, I want to get those bastards!"

Marty Hopkins's serious gray eyes met his. "We'll do our best, Mr. Denton."

Somehow Royce knew he'd heard a pledge.

13

WES COCHRAN BANGED DOWN THE TELEPHONE RECEIVER IN HIS office. They'd driven to Monroe County but no one was at Professor Wolfe's farmhouse, and although Hopkins had warned him that she didn't have a phone, he hadn't believed she was that primitive. Turned out she was. He rolled his chair to the door of the main room and glared at Hopkins. "Shit, the woman is impossible!"

She cranked the paper from the typewriter and added it to the other pages of her report. "No listing, huh? Well, there's no law says people have to have phones. We might call Professor Hart. He'd maybe have an idea where she is." She gave a sidelong glance at Wes's glowering face and added, "Sir."

Wes thumped the arm of his chair with his fist while he thought it over. "I hate to wait for, what is it, Tuesday next week when she lectures? Hell, there's so much yet to do on the Goldstein case." Thump, thump. "Tell you what, Hopkins, no sense keeping two of us tied up. You take over finding this Wolfe character. See if you can track her down before Tuesday." He stood and shoved his chair angrily, sending it skittering back to his desk. "I'll go see what the state evidence boys found in the cave. Then I gotta get back to Goldstein."

"Okay."

Wes began to gather his things. Notebook, sunglasses. Shouldn't need his jacket. Well, better take it, he might be late. He could hear Hopkins on the phone out in the main room. "Professor Hart? I'm calling to find out if you can tell us where Professor Wolfe is. . . . Yeah, we'd like to talk to her again. . . . Yeah. I wondered if you knew where we could

90

find her before that. . . . We tried her house, yeah. No one was home. . . . Where would she go on a field trip?"

Field trip! That was for little kids, wasn't it? Wes didn't like this evasive woman he'd never met. He wondered darkly if she'd killed the Denton kid herself. Pretty late to be confessing now, but maybe her conscience had bothered her all these years and she finally wanted to own up.

Hopkins replaced the receiver. Wes grabbed his hat and strode out into the room. "Any luck?"

"Maybe. He said she was off in the wilderness somewhere on a field trip. He seems to know when she goes, but not where. She's usually back before dawn, but after that she might be off again."

"So how do you reach her?"

Hopkins shrugged. "Be at her house before dawn."

"Shit. Before dawn!" He saw Grady Sims drive into the parking lot and looked at the clock. "Well, look, Hopkins, play it by ear. Remember, this gal might be the killer. I'll do backup if you need it. Give me a ring."

"Probably won't need that, sir. But you'll know where I am."

"Yeah. Be careful. Right now, your shift is over. You can go home."

"I could check the cave with you on my way home."

Wes sighed. "Hopkins, you're a deputy. I'm a duly elected official of this great county and the buck stops with me. I'll authorize your sunrise safari but not this. You want to work a lot of unpaid overtime, you have to beat me in the next election."

"Yessir."

"Brad's okay?" he added.

"He's fine. Thinking over his next move."

That didn't sound very promising. Well, it was her problem. He said, "See you tomorrow," and shoved the door open, meeting Grady Sims coming in. "Sims, how ya doing?"

"Fine. Anything going on?"

"Same old things. You're still following up Goldstein's landlord, right?"

"Yessir. Nothing's turned up yet."

"Klan boys say they've been little saints. You heard any different?"

Sims shrugged. "Few months ago, Uncle Mel says Al went off to some rally down in Kentucky. Nothing much since."

"Well, keep your ears open." Wes hurried to his car. He'd better ask Lester about that rally. Would the aging Klansmen around here encourage outsiders to come in to do their dirty work? Strangers who struck and disappeared were tough, even when you put out bulletins to other departments. Well, when the feds arrived he'd give them the Kentucky connection, and maybe they'd go away for a while. He wondered how much longer he had before they showed up on their white horses. To cover his ass, he'd sent them the information about the Klan card in Goldstein's grave after he'd talked to Kizzy Horton. But he hoped they wouldn't get it for another day or two. He'd get chewed out for the delay, but what the hell, the voters didn't much like the FBI nosing around. They'd understand. Anyway, Kizzy's letter would get there soon, maybe Monday.

His fists clenched on the steering wheel. Damn feds. In his bones he knew that this case had a local stink about it.

And the damn Denton thing cracking open right now too. Well, that's how it went, weeks of boredom and then suddenly the sky fell in. So this week, speeders in the county would just have to go on speeding, and if a cow fell down a sinkhole that was tough.

The tenseness he'd been feeling across his chest was condensing behind his breastbone, squeezing tighter. Damn, he didn't have time for this foolishness! But the pain spread, running toward his left shoulder. He pulled over to the side of the highway, panting, and fumbled for his tablets. There they were, in his right pocket. Wes got one under his tongue, then pulled out his notebook and sat for a minute pretending to look at it, waiting for the nitroglycerin to work. He hadn't been doing anything strenuous. Worrying, that was all. Of course Doc had said he shouldn't fret about things, but with two bodies and one of them probably a Klan thing, who wouldn't? Doc had said he should exercise too. Hell, he got plenty of exercise. Although it wasn't very regular. He tried, sure, but it was hard to find time, and it was depressing, reminding him of all the things he couldn't do anymore. Fast dribbling, hard drives up the court, feints and leaps. He remembered the splendor of his teenaged body, the crowd roaring encouragement, the glow of victory, of going to All-State. Shirl's bright eyes. And even after the army and driving a truck for a couple of years, the basketball triumphs were still fresh in people's minds and he'd been elected sheriff without much trouble, especially since old Sheriff Cowgill had been seen in Indy with a fancy woman. Wes had been sheriff ever since. He'd come close to losing that year when he'd run in Lester and Al for beating up poor Emmett Hines. But that was also the year he'd caught that Kentucky ex-con who raped the Fiske woman, and he'd gotten the message across to the voters: Sheriff Cochran solves county problems in the county. Sends outside troublemakers packing, whether they're ex-cons or feds.

Couldn't keep them out this time, though. All he could do was get the information before they arrived to muddy things up.

He was feeling a lot better. He put the notebook aside and pulled back onto the highway and started for Stineburg again. But the Lord didn't mean him to check that cave today, because he'd only gone a few miles when the radio crackled.

Foley's voice was very faint. "Ten-fifty-five. Six-o-two Maple."

That meant another body. "Got an ID?" Wes asked.

"Old black man name of Willie Sears. And sir, there's another one of them cards."

Wes U-turned back toward town and stomped the accelerator to the floor, siren screaming.

At the Dairy Sweet, Chrissie was bouncing her doll impatiently on her knee. "So are we going to Alaska?"

Brad and Marty answered at the same time. She said, "No, not right away," and he said, "We're still talking about it."

"Well, I'm only the kid," Chrissie said, "but I think we should get enough money to go to New York."

"You're right." Brad grinned at her. "That's the goal, Chrissie. The end of the old rainbow. And Alaska's how we get there. Hey, Marty, let's order. What do you want?"

He was right, Chrissie complicated the situation. Better talk later. She said, "Chocolate swirl."

The glass doors opened for Eddie Bronson in his paint-spattered overalls. "Brad! Son of a gun! Thought you were in New York!"

"Hey, Eddie!" Brad clapped him on the shoulder.

"Son of a gun! What happened? You sell someone the Brooklyn Bridge and retire on the profits? Hi, Marty."

Her mouth full of ice cream, Marty nodded at Eddie.

Brad said, "Man, that old Brooklyn Bridge story hides a real truth, Eddie."

"What's that?" Eddie was grinning in anticipation.

"See, it came to me one day. I was walking around the Upper East Side, you know, where all the millionaires live. And I passed this bakery. Didn't call it a bakery, it had some la-dee-da French name. And right there in the window next to the fancy cakes and pies, damned if they weren't selling bugs."

"Bugs?" Eddie's round face was as eager as Chrissie's.

Brad hunched over, elbows angled out, wrists in, fingers spread and curved. "Chocolate grasshoppers! Candy ants!" They were all three laughing. Brad grinned, leaned back again, and waggled his index fingers above his head like antennae. "Even this huge caramel cockroach. Swear to God, it was big as my finger. Think of biting into that thing! Man, it turned my stomach! But see, that guy knew the secret of New York."

"What's that?" Eddie asked.

"A gimmick." Brad's eyes flicked to Marty's, just an instant, to be sure she was getting the message too. "That guy doesn't have to worry about his candy tasting any better than the next guy's. All those New Yorkers, see, they've seen it all. So you give them something new and they fall all over themselves paying you for it. That cockroach cost five bucks."

"You're kidding!"

"Swear to God, Eddie."

"You got time for a drink? Man, we got a lot of catching up to do!" Eddie's grin hadn't left his face.

Brad shrugged. "It'll have to wait. My car's over at Gil Newton's. Transmission trouble."

"Yeah, that can be a bitch," Eddie sympathized. "But c'mon, I can run you home afterwards. You'll let him off this once, won't you, Marty?"

It wasn't a real question. Even Chrissie knew it, sitting with legs swinging from the plastic seat of the booth, licking methodically at her ice cream cone. Marty just shrugged.

Brad was back before midnight. He came to bed scrubbed and minty-breathed, and woke her with kisses on her ear, murmuring how much he needed her. She rolled into his arms with a kind of despair. His hunger made her feel so good. Chrissie wasn't the only thing that complicated the situation.

Wes Cochran headed home about midnight too.

Before he left, he gave one last look around Willie Sears's kitchen. Willie was a high-school custodian and he'd lived alone, his brother from Evanston said. The wife had died of heart disease several years before. The house was small, full of makeshift but functional repairs: tin-can lids nailed over knotholes in the floor, plastic storm windows still tacked on some of the windows, tape wrapped around a fraying electric cord. The worn linoleum in front of the back door had been patched with a different pattern. In the next room a pine bed had been dismantled, the mattress askew on the floor. Still, the fraying house seemed well cared for, except for the stain of Willie Sears's blood on the floor near the kitchen wall. The dishes had been done except for one pot that had been soaking for three days.

Not surprising. Willie Sears had been dead for three days when the brother from Evanston had finally checked on him.

"Looks a lot like Goldstein," Wes had said as soon as Grady Sims showed him the body.

"Yessir. But not quite." They were both holding handkerchiefs over their noses.

"I bet Goldstein had been nailed to a cross too."

"An upside-down cross like that?"

95

"We'll ask the state boys if there's any medical evidence that Goldstein was upside down. You can check his place again for something that could have been a cross."

"Okay."

"Looks like this one was made out of side pieces of a bed."

"Yessir. There's a bed all taken apart in the next room. I'll check Goldstein's outbuildings for anything like that."

"Wonder why the killer buried that one, and not this one?"

"Don't know, sir. Goldstein hadn't been dead this long."

That was true. Willie Sears was getting real smelly. There was another difference, too. Both bodies had been mutilated. But Goldstein had been castrated, his genitals jammed into his mouth. Willie Sears was intact except for the blood-crusted, maggoty pits where his eyes had been.

The hand-drawn Klan card was the same. Wes let the state evidence technicians take it this time.

He sent Sims home, and waited for the crime scene technicians to leave. But even with the distractions gone, no solution came to him.

He knew the killers were sending a message. Goldstein had fucked the wrong woman. Willie Sears had seen the wrong thing.

But what? What the hell had he seen?

14

THE ALARM WENT OFF AT 4:00 A.M. MARTY SWATTED IT INTO silence. Brad muttered drunkenly in his sleep. Half-sympathetic, half-annoyed, she patted his shoulder before she slipped from bed and pulled on her uniform. She didn't bother to call headquarters. Wes Cochran knew where she would be.

The cool night air was pleasant and she almost enjoyed the long drive to the farmhouse near the old quarry. She parked in the grass behind a Volks bug. There was no sign of the pickup truck, and no lights on anywhere. Once she'd switched off the headlights she needed her flashlight to get to the door.

She rang the bell repeatedly, hollered, pounded on the door.

Nothing.

Shoot. Professor Hart must have been wrong. But Marty didn't have any other leads.

Marty sat on the porch steps, switched off her flashlight, and leaned her shoulder against the post. Hart had said to be here before dawn. It was still some time till sunup. She'd wait a few minutes, just in case.

In the west, a blurry moon was setting behind thin clouds. Even the brightest stars were hazy and faint, without personality, in the black sky. The woods were even blacker, but formless too. Impossible to tell how near or far the trees were. Only the house had shape and solidity in the blackness.

She wished she were in her own house. Sound asleep.

Watch it, Hopkins, don't doze off.

It was so dark, black as Chrissie's New York T-shirt. Night in the city was sure different, a setting for the sparkle of humanity, the bright glow of friendship, rivalry, music, laughter. God, she wanted to see New York! Brad belonged in that kind of place. Seeing him with Eddie today made her remember all those times with their friends in Bloomington, Brad telling the stories, leading the laughter. He was a city man. Maybe a New York man.

Not an Alaska man. Gimmick or no gimmick.

God, she was sleepy. She leaned her head against the post beside her and closed her eyes.

What the hell was the answer? What was best for Brad, for Chrissie? For people who needed her, like the Dentons or Kizzy Horton? She knew how to help people here. But in New York? In Alaska?

In Alaska, she'd heard, sometimes it was light for most of the night. And sometimes as dark as this for most of the day . . .

A rumbling snarl.

Marty's eyes flared open. Fangs, fur, charging at her.

A husky voice called, "Luna, Ursula. Enough!"

The dogs skidded to a stop. Three of them, curled tails wagging now. Marty breathed again and discovered herself crouched in combat stance on the steps, revolver drawn, blood racing. She twisted her head to look at the woman approaching from the pickup truck. Tall, light blazing from her helmet. Behind her, four more helmets spread a bobbing puddle of light. Marty saw mud streaked on the woman's clothes, hands, and—yes, holster, as she slid a gun back in.

Marty put her own gun away, took a deep breath, and said, "You've been caving."

"Yes, Martine. Have you?"

Marty looked at the others, who had paused at the foot of the steps. They were muddy too. Professor Wolfe said to them, "Go on in. Take your showers. I have to ask Martine a few questions."

They trooped up the steps, dropping their cave packs on the porch. The dogs sniffed at the packs and flopped down nearby. One student switched on the porch light, and they all turned off their head lamps before they went in.

"So you found her." Professor Wolfe removed her hard hat, extinguished the flame, and settled lightly on the same step, across from Marty. The porch light above and behind them cast the planes of her face into sharp relief.

Marty leaned back against the post. Her pulse was still pounding. "You didn't make it real easy."

"It's not an easy situation. Someone intelligent was needed."

"Did you kill Phyllis Denton?" Marty wasn't feeling very kind.

The answer came evenly, unperturbed. "No, Martine, I didn't."

"But you've known where she was for years!"

"Tell me, how did the family react?"

"Mrs. Denton cried, what do you expect? Royce, the brother, he got mad and swore to catch the guys who killed his sister. Judge Denton was too sick to understand. Under sedation, usually crazy when he wakes up. He may never be able to understand." She watched Professor Wolfe carefully and returned stubbornly to the question. "You've known for years! Why didn't you tell us?"

But the professor's answering gaze was flat, unreadable. "Why would you need to know?"

"Why would— God, to catch the guys who did it! They let a kid die, maybe killed her, and then disappeared!"

"To catch them. For revenge?"

Marty closed her eyes for an instant. Watch it, Hopkins. This woman has information, might even be the killer. And exasperation isn't a very useful emotion in detective work. She said, "Yeah, revenge, whatever. To stop it from happening again."

"Stopping it is a difficult goal, Martine. But revenge—yes, I can understand revenge."

"The thing is, you should have told us."

"Martine, please don't make the mistake of thinking I'm a good citizen. I'm a scientist. I have other concerns. I told Elizabeth Denton because it was Elizabeth's business. Not mine. Not even yours."

Marty held on to her patience. "I didn't mean me especially. I'm in law enforcement, that's all I meant. Any law enforcement officer would do."

"And yet it seems personal for you."

"Now it is. I've met the Dentons." She glanced across to gauge the other woman's reaction. "Those people are full of pain, Professor Wolfe."

The professor was studying her with that soul-stripping gaze of hers. "I'm sure they are. I don't want to increase it. But it's more than that for you, isn't it, Martine? Do you have a daughter?"

"Yeah, but that's beside the point!" Marty slammed her fist on the porch step, realized she was about to lose it, and took a deep breath. "Look, I do what I do for everybody's daughters. Or sons."

"Of course." Professor Wolfe looked away, toward the east. Almost imperceptibly the black sky was easing toward inky blue.

Marty said, "It would help a lot if you'd explain how you came to find the body."

"Didn't Elizabeth tell you?"

Marty said automatically, "Yeah, but it's better if we hear it in your own words."

The dark eyes flicked back to Marty, a glint of mischief in them now. "That won't work, Martine. I killed a man in Pennsylvania. And some of the best interrogators in the state demonstrated their techniques for me."

It gave her goose bumps, not so much the confirmation of Professor Hart's malicious tale as the offhand way Professor Wolfe referred to it. Marty tried to sound offhand too. "Yeah, I heard something about that. What was it all about?"

"He was hunting, out of season," Professor Wolfe said readily enough. "Drinking, too. He shot a doe. I was working on my placental-mammals project nearby. The doe came stumbling almost to my feet, in great pain. Coughing blood, intestines spilling out. I only had my knife but I killed her. I've carried morphine ever since." At Marty's glance she added, "I'm a licensed vet. Well, the hunter came crashing after her. He got belligerent, pointed his rifle at me. The logic seemed to be that I'd robbed him of his prey, so I must become his prey. He told me to take off my clothes." She fell silent, looking again at the east. The horizon was taking form in murky silhouette, shaggy tips of cedars, rounder cottonwoods and maples, a distant firetower.

"So what happened?" Marty prompted.

The dark eyes came back from some faraway place. "Oh. Well, a rifle isn't much use at close range, is it? A knife is. Besides, he seemed very distracted once I'd unbuttoned my shirt."

"I see." Marty shivered.

"It turned out the fellow had been arrested a couple of times for sexual assault but never got to trial."

"I see. Uh, where in Pennsylvania did this happen?"

The mischievous twinkle was back. "Let me save you some time, Deputy Hopkins. The man you want to contact is Joseph Cooper, district attorney of Haughton County. He directed the investigation."

"Thanks." Marty made a note.

"After all the interrogations, Cooper decided I'd done it in self-defense."

"Sounds right, self-defense."

"Sometimes your laws are not far from the mark, Martine. Selves should be defended."

Marty met the serious gaze square-on. "Yeah. I agree. But so should daughters."

"So they should. Defended, or revenged. Now, Elizabeth told you I found the body. What else?"

Marty hesitated. Professor Wolfe had just admitted to knifing a man. Wes would probably whoop with delight. But to Marty it now seemed less likely that the professor had killed Phyllis Denton. Marty could see herself reacting the same way to a drunken hunter. Hell, just minutes ago she'd almost shot the professor's dogs. She decided that she'd get more from Wolfe if she dropped the games, and said, "Mrs. Denton didn't say much more. She said you'd told her, but she hadn't passed it on to us because they'd already had a lot of false alarms. That's all she told us. She was so shaken up, crying, I couldn't comfort her. Her son couldn't either."

Professor Wolfe frowned. "Do you think revenge would comfort her, Martine?"

"Comfort?" Marty gazed out at the horizon while she thought about it. The sky was silvering now, and the first glints of light reflected from the firetower. "Not comfort, exactly. Nothing could possibly comfort me if I lost Chrissie. But revenge might at least make me feel that pain has been balanced by pain."

The professor nodded slowly. "A good and honest answer, Martine. Let me tell you, then. My work here is a twenty-year study of the evolution of cave fauna. One of the sites I considered studying was the Stineburg cave. Six years ago I checked to see if it would be suitable for my study."

"How'd you get in?" According to Floyd, the cave mouth had collapsed before that.

Professor Wolfe said, "The easiest way. A boulder near the top of the entrance pivots open."

"Yeah. Go on."

"I saw Phyllis there, in her coffin. I spoke to her mother, and left it to her judgment."

"But she thought it was a false alarm. Didn't you give her any proof?"

"You mean, a lock of hair, a shoe? Of course not. I didn't want to disturb anything. All I took was the card, to find the family."

"What card?"

"There was a card. Her name, birth and death dates."

"How did that help you find the family?"

"I don't have your resources, Martine, so I had to go to the courthouse myself and look up birth records. Luckily she'd been born in Nichols County." The dark eyes fastened on Marty again. "Birth records can be very useful sometimes."

"Okay, so you found the Dentons and spoke to Elizabeth. Did you speak to the judge too?"

"No. I know it was Judge Denton who mentioned my name. All I can suggest is that Elizabeth told him, and he remembered."

Marty nodded, frowning. If Elizabeth had told him about this so-called false alarm, and he had connected it to something else—but then why hadn't he followed it up? Had he made the connection only recently? "Have you talked to any of the Dentons since that time?"

"No."

"And you didn't urge Mrs. Denton to call the sheriff?"

"That was her decision to make, Martine. Maybe you would have chosen differently."

"Damn right!" Marty sighed. Civilians sure messed up investigations. Well, at least she'd learned the reason why Professor Wolfe hadn't called the cops. Stupid reason, but it fit with everything else she'd learned about the professor. And she could sure see why Elizabeth Denton would figure that this weird woman's story was just another false lead. Time to move on. Marty said, "Okay, back to the cave. When did you find her?"

"May, six years ago."

"Had she— Well, I know you're not a medical examiner, but you are a scientist. Could you tell how she was killed?"

"No, there was nothing obvious."

"No guesses? I mean, are we supposed to think Phyllis lugged a coffin into that cave, lay down in it, and starved herself to death?"

"When I saw the body, decomposition was well under way," the professor said gently. "The reason for death was not obvious."

"Well, can you guess how long she'd been there?"

"Not with any accuracy. In a cave there are fewer insects and other species to decompose the body, and the cool temperature slows the organisms. I'd say more than a month, less than a year. The death date seemed reasonable."

"You didn't do any tests?"

A smile twitched at the corner of Professor Wolfe's mouth. "Ah, you're beginning to know me, Martine. Of course I considered it. Part of my study involves how cave creatures exploit the food sources that come in from the surface. But in fact, such studies have been done already with animal carcasses, and not much new would have been learned from analyzing this one."

"I see." Marty was revolted at the thought of a dead person as a food source for cave creatures, and was caught off guard by the professor's next remark:

"I didn't touch the body. I replaced the boulder at the entrance, and never went back to that part of the cave, because it seemed to be a kind of shrine. Like you, Martine, I grieve that it was the death of a child."

Startled, Marty met the professor's dark eyes and saw that it was true. They both grieved for young Phyllis Denton. Professor Wolfe added, "That surprises you?"

Marty shifted on the step. "Well, you usually seem so distant. Saying it's not your problem. Talking about millions of years, and about doing studies, and about a dead child as a food source for cave creatures."

"That's a truth too, Martine. Other deaths are necessary to our life. We kill fish and vegetables to feed on, we kill bacteria and tapeworms to maintain our health. And when we in turn die, bacteria and insects and plants feed on us. Death is at the heart of life."

"That seems horrible!"

"Yes. But there's beauty in it too, in the diversity. Blindfish, deer, tapeworm, human—a tweak of the DNA and new forms unfurl. Life has infinite possibilities. But that makes each actual creature infinitely unlikely, infinitely precious. Just as the vast depths of time underline the miracle of this passing instant." The professor's hypnotic voice seemed to caress the world. Marty suddenly understood the students who followed this woman into caves, into the microcosm, into deep time. "This instant. The scent of cedars, the faint light, the bustle of birds awakening, two human minds touching. I grieve that Phyllis Denton had so little time to know the rapture of it."

Marty's throat was tight and she could only nod. It took her a moment to remember that she was supposed to be asking questions. Snap to, Hopkins! She tried to think. They'd covered finding the body, telling Elizabeth Denton, even that killing in Pennsylvania. What else? Marty ran her fingers through her hair and said, "Uh, let's see. Oh, do you have that card you took from the body?"

"No. It was thrown away."

"Shoot! There might have been handwriting, something—"

"That's all I can tell you." Professor Wolfe stood up abruptly. The rosy glow of dawn brought out the russet shade of the cave mud smeared from forehead to boots. "Brother Sun is up, and I want a shower. Martine, talk to Elizabeth privately, when things are quieter. And give my best to your Chrissie."

"Okay." Marty got to her feet too. "Uh—Professor Wolfe, if I type up what you just told me, would you sign the statement?"

"Probably not. But bring me news, and we'll talk again someday before I leave."

"Before you leave?"

"I have other studies in other places." The professor stepped onto the porch. "Goodbye, Martine. Go on defending everyone's daughters."

"I'm doing my best."

"And defend your self."

"Myself?"

104

"There are many demands on you, I think. Your job, your daughter, perhaps a husband."

"Boy, you said it!" Marty admitted with more vehemence than she'd planned.

"Defend your self. For your daughter's sake too."

Those dark eyes held hers with surprising urgency. "Okay," Marty promised.

Professor Wolfe disappeared into the house. The door slammed behind her.

Marty walked slowly to the car, pondering what she'd heard. They'd hit the points she came for. Wes would be especially pleased to hear about the killing in Pennsylvania. Have to call that D.A., but it would check out, Marty was sure.

So they'd covered what she came to find out, and then some. And yet Marty felt uneasy. Something was missing. Professor Wolfe could have told her more, if she'd only known how to ask.

Behind her the four women students came out, their clothes clean, their hair damp. They waved, piled into the Volks bug, and pulled out around Marty's car. Marty turned the ignition and followed them down the rutted lane. She drove home through the slanting light of daybreak.

15

"GOOD MORNING, BRIGHT EYES!" SHIRLEY COCHRAN WAS WEAR-ing a bib apron over her pink Sunday dress. "No hugs. My hands are all over flour."

"Hi, sweetie." Wes, in business shirt and suit pants, leaned down to kiss her. There was a full twelve inches between their heights but it had taken him only two dates, back in his senior year of high school, to decide that finding pretty Shirl's lips was worth any contortion. He straightened and grinned down at her, a perky smiling woman holding her floury hands carefully away from her skirt. She was a few pounds heavier now, with blond hair showing gray roots instead of brown, but just as sweet and energetic as in her cheerleader days. The only time her eyes lost their sparkle was when she remembered their Billy. Wes nodded toward the rose-and-white kitchen behind her. "What're you fixing?"

"Just biscuits. And don't go slathering them with butter, you know what Doc Hendricks says." She bustled back to the rose-pink countertop where she was cutting out circles of dough.

"Okay." He stopped at the sink to scrub his hands.

"You didn't sleep real well last night." She put the biscuits into the oven. A puff of warm air stroked the side of his neck as she closed the oven door. Shirl joined him by the sink and began to wash the flour from her hands, then her wise eyes turned to him again. "Nasty one, huh."

"Ahh, killings are never nice," he said evasively.

Shirl took the towel from him to rub her hands dry. "Go get yourself a cup of coffee, Champ, and show up at that table in eight minutes. You need a good breakfast, 'cause I've got a feeling you're going to want to work today."

"Marty! Time to go!" Aunt Vonnie's voice from downstairs was sharp as a saw.

"Almost ready!" Marty yelled. Brad winced, and with a pang of compassion as well as annoyance she added more quietly, "Chrissie, run tell her we're just getting our shoes on."

Chrissie ran out. Brad touched his temples and said, "Oh, man. Feels like a watermelon instead of a head."

Marty had changed the uniform she'd worn to Professor Wolfe's for her blue chambray dress with a little edge of lace at the collar and yoke. She glanced at her watch as she pulled on her white sling-back heels. Good, they'd be a few minutes late, and he wouldn't have to talk to anybody for an hour.

Cedars of Lebanon Methodist Church was a foursquare stone building erected early in the century by the local stone-

106

cutters. There wasn't much fancy carving on it. Cedars of Lebanon was straightforward and Protestant, its lintels square, its windows plain, its beauty arising from the exquisitely cut buff limestone blocks. Inside, the golden oak pews were straight-backed and the cross was simple.

They slipped into a pew near the back just as the second hymn began. Aunt Vonnie looked thunderous, her brow low and tight under her piled golden curls. Chrissie, wearing her red-and-white print dress and a pair of red-and-white earrings that looked like little exclamation points, went in next. She was clinging to Brad's hand as though fearful that he'd fly away. More likely to slide under the pew, Marty thought grumpily, bringing up the rear. She nodded to Shirley Cochran, who was smiling at them from across the aisle. Next to Shirley, tall, silver-haired Wes stared gloomily at the front of the church. Marty followed his gaze to the big oak cross. Damn, that must have been ugly, that poor black guy nailed upside down. She'd had a restless night herself and not just because of her talk with Professor Wolfe. That little skeleton in the cave had awakened her more than once in its hideous sadness. But Marty wasn't sure she'd want to trade dreams with Wes just now. What was going on in this county?

She found the hymn they were singing, handed the book to Brad, and opened another hymnal for herself. "Our shelter from the stormy blast, and our eternal home," she sang, and began to relax a little as the familiar words surrounded her with memories of easier days.

Familiar people surrounded her too. How could such ugly things happen among these people? Home folks, her friends, her co-workers. The Cochrans, of course. Bobby Mason and his family. The Johnsons, the Tippetts, the Russells. Eddie Bronson, as bleary-eyed as Brad. No Grady Sims today. And no Dentons or Pfanns, of course. They wouldn't come here for an ordinary Sunday service like this because they were Presbyterians, like most of the rich folks around here. But if she could get away, Elizabeth Denton might go to the Presbyterian church up the road. Hal, Jr., might be with her, if he had no political stops to make. And certainly Royce, with his lazy smile and his grieving blue eyes. Marty hoped he'd find comfort at his church.

A few rows ahead of her, Bert Mackay from Straub's Service stood next to his pretty little wife and three fidgety kids. Why had Judge Denton said he was an idiot? Of course, he'd said everyone was an idiot. Just raving, probably. Bert's partner Gil Newton sang all alone, three rows over. Behind him, old Lester Holtz stood next to Al Evans and pudgy Laurie Evans. Al was tall, a head above the rest of the congregation, like Wes. He'd been a basketball star long ago, same year as Wes and her own dad, someone had told her. Of course after that mess with Emmett Hines, Al wouldn't speak to Wes. Wouldn't even let him on his farm, Grady had told her. Hard to believe that those old fellows in their tight suits were behind that. Or behind the mutilations and killings of David Goldstein and Willie Sears. After all these years, why start lashing out now?

But if not Al or Lester, who?

These were good people who tried to raise decent kids, who tried to follow the Commandments, or so Marty had always believed. Aunt Vonnie might think you were asking for trouble if you went out with a black fellow, but she'd treat him with compassion if he was sick or hungry. Marty had thought everyone was like Aunt Vonnie, had thought her law enforcement job was basically to help with accidents or calm down high-spirited teenagers and drunks. But now, leaving Phyllis Denton aside, they'd had two horrible killings in just a few days. Probably one crazy guy, she told herself. That's what Wes thought. But even so, the guy could be feeding on the bitter emotions that swam under the surface of the good, decent people in this very room. It was scary. *What kind of white trash do you keep in your county?* Well, best to leave the Klansmen to Wes. He knew those guys.

"They fly forgotten, as a dream dies at the opening day," sang Brad next to her. He must be feeling better because his voice was getting stronger. It was a nice voice. He'd thought about being a singer before he discovered that announcing songs was even more fun. Not that it paid any better. Dammit, if he'd just take her advice, straighten out, quit making up beery dreams about fame and fortune, things could be really great. . . .

But he did love the music. She listened to him beside her, his voice lifted despite his aching head, praising the Lord. He wanted to do what he loved to do. She could sympathize with that. Shoot, she wanted to work at the job that suited her, too. But what suited Brad was harder to find. Of course he got frustrated when doors were slammed in his face. She wanted to help him, dammit. If she only knew how!

Brad had his own idea of how she could help. Claimed he'd tied one on last night because she was dragging her feet about his great plan, his gimmick. "That hurts, Marty. That really hurts," he'd said, and she'd felt like a selfish worm. But shoot, wasn't he being selfish too? Why should she give up the work she loved for Alaska? For a fifty-fifty chance that he'd finally find what he wanted there?

At least there weren't any Klan killers in Alaska. None she'd heard about, anyway.

And Chrissie. What was best for Chrissie? Maybe Brad was right, they should get her out of this murderous place. But something in her balked. She didn't want to turn tail and run, not till they'd caught this guy. And when he was caught it would be a good place for her daughter again. Wouldn't it?

The hymn ended. They sat down and Marty found her four A.M. start catching up with her. Her eyelids were drooping during the Bible readings, and toward the end of the sermon she almost drifted off, until she felt a sharp pinch on her bottom. Marty almost jumped, her eyes jerking toward Brad. But he was gazing serenely toward the preacher.

Had it really happened? Had she dozed off and just dreamed it? But then his laughing eyes flicked toward her for an instant, dark as an imp's, and Marty had to gulp down the wild giggles that bubbled up in her right there in church.

Dammit, he sure kept life interesting.

After the service, Wes and Shirley came over while Chrissie skipped off to see Janie Tippett and Malinda Russell. "Hi, Marty. And Brad Hopkins! It's great to see you back!" Shirley exclaimed.

"It's good to be back." Brad was better, all right, his smile charming again. He looked dashing in his jacket and tie.

"You here for a while now?" Wes asked him.

"Yeah, a little while, anyway. I'm working on a couple of things but I have to wait to hear. Meanwhile, I'm helping Eddie Bronson paint the Wilson house."

"Well, it's sure good to see you," Shirley said. "Vonnie, how're you doing? Are you going to the circle meeting Friday?"

"Of course. It's at Joy Ann's now, isn't it?" Aunt Vonnie and Shirley bent their blond heads close as they talked. Wes was frowning. Marty followed his gaze and saw old Lester Holtz talking to Al Evans. Al's glance at Wes was murderous.

Chrissie came galloping back, her red-and-white earrings bobbing. "Daddy! Malinda says— Oh." She spotted Wes and stopped short.

"Hey, Chrissie, how you doing?" Wes asked.

"Fine, thank you."

"Go on!" Wes grinned at the girl. "Tell your daddy what you wanted to say."

"Well, see, Malinda says her parents are going to take her to visit New York!"

Brad dropped to one knee to look Chrissie straight in the eyes. Sunlight glinted on his dark hair and neat mustache as he said earnestly, "I'm going to take you too, Chrissie. As soon as I can. And that's a promise."

"Okay," she said dubiously.

"And we're going all the way to the top of the Empire State Building." His fingers wiggled, stair-climbing to a point high above her head. "After all, it's your granddaddy's building, right? He cut the stone for it. We'll go all the way to the top and we'll look down on the other tall buildings, we'll look down on the people and the cars and the churches. We'll see everything for miles and miles. You'll be the princess of the world!"

Marty could see the vision grabbing Chrissie, delight blooming deep in her eyes. Memories of broken promises and dreams betrayed swam into her mind. Dammit, Brad, quit! she screamed silently.

110

Wes had been watching Chrissie with amusement and turned now to Marty with an approving grin. But something must have shown in her expression. "You okay?" he asked softly.

Her eyes met his, then slid away. "Just, you know, thinking about my dad."

"Yeah. I miss the guy too." When he looked back at Brad and Chrissie he seemed thoughtful.

"Let's go say hi to Malinda and get this straightened out," Brad said, standing up again. He gave Chrissie his hand. They headed for the side lawn of the church, where the Russells were talking to the Tippetts and the Mackays.

"Anything more on the black guy, what's his name?" Marty asked Wes.

"Willie Sears. Grady drove over today to talk to his brother. Aside from that, we're waiting for the lab work."

"Neighbors didn't say anything?"

"Nobody noticed anything. Our perp must look pretty ordinary, drive an ordinary car. They said they hadn't seen Willie Sears for a few days. The houses are pretty far apart in that section so nobody thought to check on him. Figured they'd just missed him." He glanced at Marty. "How about you? Did you find that Professor Wolfe last night?"

"Yeah. Got up about four A.M."

"Thought you looked a little ragged. What did she say?"

"Can't arrest her yet. She said she was exploring caves, saw the body in its coffin. She found a card that gave Phyllis's name and birth date, looked up her family in the county birth records, and told Elizabeth Denton where the body was. Then . . ." Marty paused. She didn't know how to explain to Wes about that magical moment when she'd glimpsed the rapture of creation through Professor Wolfe's eyes. Two human minds touching. She said, "Then she told me she went off to think deep thoughts."

"And she thinks that clears her? Goddamn pointy-head."

"Yeah. She could be lying. Except that she told me she killed a guy in Pennsylvania. Self-defense, she said."

"Shit, Marty! This could be a break! Why the hell didn't you call it in?"

"Here you are. Sir." She felt silly, unprofessional, in her blue dress with the lace. Like Debbie Boone pretending to be a cop. She handed him the note about the DA in Pennsylvania. "She said this guy handled the case."

"You're not very excited about this," Wes said accusingly.

"The woman is weird, all right." Marty frowned, trying to explain. "It's just—well, just a feeling. I think she was telling the truth. She was attacked, she fought back."

Wes snorted.

She said, "Look, check with that DA, okay? My point is just that I can't see her putting a kid like Phyllis Denton in the same category as an armed attacker."

Wes squinted toward the parking lot. In his dark suit, his height and silvery hair made him look almost regal. "Look, you say the professor thinks it's okay to waste armed muggers. Okay." His blue eyes shifted to glare at Marty. "How do you know Phyllis wasn't attacking her? The kid was running with a rough crowd, according to the Dentons."

Marty shrugged. "Sure. It's possible. Sir."

He studied her for a minute, and she knew he was adding her cop's intuition that the professor hadn't killed Phyllis to the complicated balance sheet on this case. In a minute he said, "So the professor didn't give you anything more?"

"Well, she told me what the scene looked like when she saw it six years ago. But see, she says she hasn't been back since. Says she took the card with Phyllis's name on it, nothing else. That's all she could tell me. I asked her if she'd talked to Elizabeth Denton, how come the judge was the one who mentioned her name? She said she didn't know, go ask the Dentons."

"Christ." Wes glanced down at the paper with the DA's name.

"Well, I figured we could check out these things. You're calling Pennsylvania?"

"Yeah. Tomorrow."

"I'll ask the Dentons how the judge found out, maybe today, and catch the professor again Tuesday, when we've got more."

Wes hitched up his suit trousers. "Yeah. Go with that. Me, I'm going to find out what Al Evans told Lester Holtz."

16

IT WAS MIDAFTERNOON WHEN MARTY DROPPED BRAD AND CHRISSIE at the ice-cream store and drove on to the judge's big limestone house. As she got out of the car, she heard the dogs in the distance. The hazy afternoon air was laden with the breath of cedar and wild cherry from the woods beyond the lawn. In the shade of taller trees, a couple of dogwoods bloomed, white as ghosts. As she walked up the stone steps, Marty realized that this time she felt more worthy of the Denton house because today she was in her Sunday dress.

Yeah, big deal, Hopkins, next you'll be wanting diamonds.

Elizabeth Denton answered the door. "Please come in. Royce should be back soon. He's exercising the dogs." Her dress was navy silk with a spattering of tiny cream flowers.

"Well, I can talk to him later." Marty shifted her shoulder bag to a more comfortable position. "But maybe you'd answer some questions. And maybe, if the judge wakes up . . ."

Elizabeth shook her head sadly. "He doesn't make much sense. It's worse every day. Is there anything special you want to ask?"

"Well, you see, I spoke to Professor Wolfe again."

Elizabeth Denton remained motionless, yet Marty thought the older woman seemed suddenly tense. "Did she—well, did she explain what happened?"

"Yeah, she described the scene and how she came upon it." Marty spoke gently, seeing the shine of tears on Elizabeth's face. "She said she'd told you what she found in the cave."

"Yes, we talked."

"But you didn't tell us. Did you tell your husband?"

"Not right away."

113

"Well, see, I was wondering how he found out. He was the one who mentioned her first. Did Professor Wolfe speak to him too?"

"Maybe. But I don't think so. It was just a little while ago that I told him what she'd said."

"A little while. You mean after he got sick?"

"Yes. About two weeks ago. He had a clear time, and we got to talking about Phyllis."

"Mrs. Denton, Professor Wolfe told you six years ago. In all that time, you didn't tell your husband?"

"No, because—you see, it was more than a year after Phyllis left, but he still got so angry at all the false stories."

"You wanted to spare him?"

"I didn't want him upset." Elizabeth Denton glanced up the stairs. "I should check on him now."

"Oh, of course," Marty agreed. She followed Elizabeth up the stairs and added, "It must be hard on you, all this nursing."

"Oh, no! Not at all!" Elizabeth turned, one worn hand resting on the banister. "I'm happy to do it. Royce helps out, and Lisa on weekdays. But I'd be happy to do it all myself."

Marty nodded. Sometimes she felt like that too, so happy to be able to help, to lose herself in kindness. But people often didn't appreciate it, wouldn't take her advice. She ended up feeling like a doormat instead of a saint. She hoped the Dentons were more appreciative of Elizabeth's efforts.

When they entered the sickroom, the gaunt old man was clearly asleep, his raspy breaths coming with machinelike regularity. "He seems to be sleeping all right," Marty said in an encouraging tone.

Elizabeth Denton fussed with his blanket. "Yes. He sleeps a lot now. It's hard." She turned abruptly to Marty. "Please, tell me something. Did Professor Wolfe mention Alma?"

"No. Alma who?"

"She didn't? I thought she might— Well, I guess not."

"Idiots!"

Elizabeth whirled to look at her patient. The judge's eyes sparked blue. Marty stepped past Elizabeth and confronted the old man. "Judge Denton, sir. You know we found your daughter's grave?" Shoot, she had no idea how much to say. She should have asked first off what they'd told him.

"Phyllis is dead," he said. The bright eyes were fixed on her. She was sure he wanted to tell her something.

And this could be her last chance. She said, "Phyllis was in a coffin. In a cave, where Professor Wolfe said she was."

"I'm dying," he said. "Eaten up." His voice was strong but came haltingly, in bursts. "Phyllis. My daughter. My baby."

Eaten up. Food for cave creatures. Marty swallowed bile and said encouragingly, "Yes. Do you know how Phyllis died, Judge Denton?"

His pained eyes darkened to gunmetal blue. The thin lips opened, closed, opened again. Then, to Marty's horror, the judge's frail body arced up, held by the armstraps. "Pillow his head!" Elizabeth barked, suddenly taking command. Marty dropped her bag and sprang forward to grab the thrashing skull. He was so thin it was as though she held the bone itself. She managed to bend the pillow around it and pressed it there, trying to soften the pistonlike thrustings of his tortured frame. Strings of saliva landed on her hands and wrists. Elizabeth was gripping his feet as they jerked in their straps. The gaunt body arced and recoiled, again and again, and it seemed like aeons before it subsided.

Elizabeth came to Marty's end of the bed with a washcloth. Marty said shakily, "God! Did my questions set him off?"

"Maybe." Grimly, Elizabeth wiped her husband's mouth.

"I'm sorry."

Elizabeth raised her eyes and noticed Marty's distress. "Oh, no, no. Don't feel bad. Anything might have set him off."

"Yeah. I see." Great little public servant today, aren't you, Hopkins? You're supposed to comfort the victims, not the other way around. She asked, "Will he be all right now?"

"For a while." Elizabeth nodded to the door. "Royce is back. Do you want to talk to him?"

Marty turned to see Royce hurrying from the stairs. "Well! Deputy Hopkins! What are— Oh." His eyes rested on the washcloth in his mother's hands, and the enthusiasm left his voice. "I take it my father is not yet up to explaining himself."

"He just had another fit," Elizabeth said calmly.

Royce looked at the old man and said almost under his breath, "I don't know how he hangs on. He's so strong."

Marty nodded, awed too by the power in that wasted body. "He's amazing, all right. I hope I can figure out what he's trying to tell us." When she glanced up she found Royce studying her, a kind crinkle at the corner of his eyes. He was wearing jeans, hunter's boots, a navy corduroy shirt open at the throat. That's the way he should look, she thought, a man comfortable in the country, not crowded into a city suit like his brother.

"Dad's trying to tell you something?" he asked.

"I just have the feeling he knows something more about it. Maybe just lying here he's thought of something."

Royce frowned, then nodded slowly. "Yeah, he's been talking more and more about Phyllis. When he first got sick he talked about paying bills, about his friends, and so forth. Didn't he, Mother?"

"Yes. He doesn't talk much about them anymore."

Royce said, "Maybe he thinks he's dying, focuses on his family."

"He doesn't mention you or me, Royce," Elizabeth pointed out gently. "Except sometimes to yell at us."

Marty caught the glint of pain in Royce's eyes and wanted to reach out to him. But he said lightly, "Ah, well, it's the prodigal child who always gets the attention, right?"

She wished she could comfort Royce, but she was also eager to follow up the new possibility. She asked, "Suppose we're right, he's trying to tell us something. See, he only just heard about Professor Wolfe. Now, you didn't realize Professor Wolfe's story was true. But he did, somehow. Maybe it fit with something else he knew. We should find out what. Maybe start by checking his cases."

"Good idea. I can help with that. And how about his appointment calendar?" Royce suggested. "To tell you who he talked to, what he might know."

"Do you have that?" Marty asked eagerly.

"In his desk downstairs."

"Let's look." She grabbed up her shoulder bag.

Marty hadn't been in the book-lined study before. A big

table in the middle of the room held a couple of ledgers and sportsmen's magazines. There was an immense golden-oak rolltop desk against the wall, a comfortable red-cushioned desk chair before it, and a pair of red leather wing chairs. Aunt Vonnie had tuned in *Masterpiece Theater* a few times, and this room reminded Marty of the room in the introductory shots, the sense of history, prosperity, complex human beings with complex stories, all made melancholy by the tragedies of illness and a lost daughter. These sorrows were far from the petty bar brawls and domestic spats she usually dealt with, far from the ugly Klan murders.

And far from motorcycle gangs. That didn't fit. What was Phyllis's problem? Had she found this place oppressive? Marty looked down at her white shoes treading the oriental carpet. Hey, not oppressive at all. She could get used to this pretty damn quick.

The image of that slender skeleton in the cave came into her mind again. Shape up, Hopkins, she scolded herself. Find out what the judge is trying to tell you about his daughter's death.

Royce had gone straight to the big rolltop and unlocked it. He pulled a desk calendar from a cubbyhole and said, "Here's the one he was using when he took sick last fall. The earlier ones are in the bottom drawer."

"We'll need everything, but let's start with the most recent," Marty said. She joined him at the desk and looked on eagerly while he turned the pages.

The appointment calendar was thorough. "He's even written down the court cases he was hearing," Marty said with approval.

"Yeah, he was pretty well organized," said Royce. He flipped the pages and they studied them in silence for a moment. The judge's former life took on a shadowy reality for Marty as she read of lunches with businessmen she knew, of trials for the burglars and drunken brawlers she and the other deputies brought in. Here was the judge at the dentist, here in Indianapolis for a bar meeting, here picking up some dry-cleaning.

"This is one of Hal's campaign meetings." Royce flicked a

page with his fingernail. The scent of his aftershave was mingled with a hint of sweat and a whiff of the woods where he'd been running the dogs. He was shouldering a lot these days.

"He must have had more campaign meetings than that one."

"Oh, sure, but Dad only went when bigger politicos were going to be there too." He turned the page.

"Dr. Storey," Marty said, pointing. "Who's that?"

"The vet. Maybe one of the dogs was sick. And here's a note on picking up the car at the garage."

"Where?"

"Next page." He picked up her pointing hand and moved it gently to the facing page. *Car at Straub's,* said the scribbled words now at the tip of her finger. His hand was warm on hers.

She pulled back and said hastily, "Is it okay if I take his calendars to the office? Wes might see things I can't. I'll give you a receipt. Is that okay?"

"That's okay." There was amusement in his glance as he bent to pull out the old calendars from a lower drawer. "Here you are. You know, you're a very unusual deputy, Marty Hopkins."

"How do you mean?"

His grin was teasing. "Well, for example, very few deputies win tricycle races."

"Yeah." She scrabbled in her bag for a receipt. Why did he make her feel so off balance? She was just trying to help him, to figure out what the hell happened to his sister.

He said, "And very few look so good in lace collars."

Oh boy, watch it, Hopkins. She didn't answer, just wrote out the receipt in silence. "Here you are."

"Thank you, Mrs. H." He took the paper. "I see that Mr. H. is back in town. Saw him at the Slam Dunk last night."

Shoot! And Brad busy tying one on!

Royce added gently, "Forgive me for thinking that he's one lucky son of a bitch."

Marty flicked a glance at him, just enough to tell that he wasn't teasing after all. She dropped the calendars into her bag and snapped it closed. "Let me know if your father mentions anything useful," she said as coolly as she could. "I'll be back in touch if we get any news."

She tried to look dignified as she returned to her car. Dammit, Hopkins, from now on you talk to the Dentons in your uniform.

Wes Cochran followed the sound of a chain saw to the fencerow behind Lester Holtz's barn. The earsplitting whine drowned out the frantic barking of the aging collie that greeted him, silver-muzzled but ready for battle. Lester, guiding the chain saw in a cloud of blue smoke, couldn't hear the barking but after a moment he noticed the dog's furious posturing and carefully lifted the saw from the four-inch maple log he was cutting up. He looked around at Wes and switched off the saw. In the sudden silence the dog's barking sounded puny and shrill.

"Quit your yapping, Cutter!" Lester shouted. The dog subsided, skulking through the scattered logs and brush that surrounded his master. Wes spotted a shotgun leaning against a honeysuckle bush. Lester put down the saw and wiped his forehead with a blue bandanna. He said to Wes, "Nothing to report."

That's the way conversations with Lester usually started. Wes said mildly, "You talk to Al?"

"Yeah. He never heard of any Jew boy."

"How about the high school custodian? Willie Sears?"

"Was he the nigger got killed?"

"What'd he do, Lester?"

The old man shrugged elaborately. "You didn't tell me to ask about him."

"Did Al say anything about him?"

"He wondered too. It wasn't us."

"You're sure? Who, then?"

Another shrug.

Wes put one foot on the biggest of the stumps in the fencerow, ignoring the old collie's renewed growls. Chain-saw smells of gasoline and exhaust hung in the air. "You're saying Al didn't know the white guy was a Jew? And he didn't know why Willie Sears died? Come on, Lester, you can't tell me the Invisible Empire is that bad off."

"We ain't had a meeting for six months, so it's hard to keep track of everything."

"Yeah, I bet it is." He looked narrowly at Lester. Talking to this guy was like walking a tightrope. One sign of weakness and he'd shut up. But push too hard and he'd shut up too. Or worse. Lester was the smartest of the old Klansmen, the only one who seemed to understand that Wes had done them a favor when the Emmett Hines case was prosecuted, getting them off with fines instead of jail sentences. The others had felt betrayed that it was prosecuted at all in a county that had ignored racial crimes for a century. Wes reminded him, "We're trying to keep the FBI out of this, Lester. I don't want 'em here, and you and Al sure as hell don't want 'em poking through your records. Now, six months ago at the meeting, what'd you talk about?"

Lester answered sulkily, "About a rally they was having in Kentucky. Al went, but my arthritis was kicking up so I didn't."

"The rally? That's all they talked about?"

"Yeah." The old man spat into the brush. "Nothing else new around here."

Wes didn't believe him. "You sure they haven't had any meetings since?"

"You trying to say they wouldn't tell me about a meeting? Listen, they'd tell me!" Lester stepped toward the shotgun and glared at Wes, like a kid brandishing his secret club membership.

"Yeah, you've earned your stripes, Lester," Wes said soothingly. He leaned forward, keeping his eye on the shotgun and his hand ready to snap his handgun from his holster if he had to. "See, the thing is, we've got two killings. Let's say you and Al don't know anything. I'm not asking who's running things, I know you ain't supposed to tell. But I need a name, somebody to talk to, so I can straighten this out before the feds come in."

"How come you're so sure it was us? Al didn't know anything either."

"Guy was carded, Lester." Wes was sickened by the blaze of triumph in Lester's eyes at this news. He added, "Maybe they figure you and Al are too old to be in on it."

"The hell we are!" Wes was pleased to see the triumph ooze away, replaced by hurt.

"So let's have it, Lester. Who do I talk to?"

"Can't tell you."

"You can tell him to contact me, and we'll keep it in the family."

"Can't do that either." A smug defiance came into Lester's face. "See, the boys know you ain't on the right side. So we wear hoods. That way we don't know each other, can't tell you anything."

"Jesus, Lester, you expect me to believe that? You're no idiot. You recognize voices, you recognize cars."

"We're careful nowadays. We leave the cars behind the bar along with everyone else's."

"The voices, then. Don't be an asshole, Lester!"

"Look, I tell you true, Al and Sam I recognize, but the new guys, I swear I don't know who they are. They're the ones started the hood business, so we can't hurt each other if somebody changes sides."

"Can't help each other either." Wes waited a second, squinting, to try to read Lester's expression. "Look, Lester, you telling me an old fox like you's got no idea who the head man is? The whatchamacallit, the Great Titan?"

"No idea."

"Well, don't blame me when the FBI comes knocking."

"Can't tell them anything either." But he looked uneasy, maybe realizing at last that he was the one with a record, he was the one who'd take the fall for the guys he was protecting.

"You saying I should go ask Al?"

"Sheriff, he'd shoot the minute you set foot on his land!"

"The hell he would. *I'd* shoot the minute he reached for a gun. And you know that, Lester."

"Yeah."

"That's why I'm asking you, to save everybody a lot of trouble."

"I just don't know about a Jew. Or a janitor."

"Well, how about out-of-towners? What did Al tell you about the rally in Kentucky?"

Lester shrugged. "Speeches, cross-burning, hymns. Usual stuff."

"How many people from this county?"

"Maybe half a dozen, Al thought. He wasn't sure, because like I say, we wear hoods at meetings here."

"Yeah."

"And everybody was saying let's cooperate," Lester added proudly. "Indiana and Kentucky and Illinois and some others. Let's cooperate."

God, these guys were pitiful. But Wes couldn't afford to tell the old man how pitiful he was. Lester was his only frail link to the Klansmen around here. Wes said, "Okay, Lester, that's all for now. But the feds are going to come nosing around in a couple of days, and if I don't have the answer on a platter, you and Al are going to get a lot of flak."

"Yeah." But then the old man's head went up. "They're poisoning our country, Jews and niggers. Had to be done."

"The hell it did! In the old days you guys got your way with warnings, right? And this time, the woman cleared out. Gone two weeks when the guy got hit. And a school custodian, for chrissake! That's a stupid way to play the game. You want to take the fall for that kind of asshole?" He sighed, straightened up. The old collie growled. "Think about it, Lester. And you can tell your dog if he comes any closer I'll kick him."

Lester grabbed at the dog's collar and Wes walked back past the barn and house to his car. Made his shoulders prickle, turning his back on these old boys and their shotguns. But Lester had almost convinced him that he didn't know anything. Maybe he really was out of it. Too old.

On the other hand, a chain saw was no kid's toy. Lots of power yet in those old arms. Wes wondered if the arthritis was put on for the sheriff's benefit alone.

17

THEY CAME SOONER THAN WES EXPECTED, EARLY MONDAY morning. He was still briefing the deputies on Willie Sears's death, on the necessity of reconstructing the old black man's last days since there were no immediate clues pointing to his killer. The door swung open and a scowling Prosecuting Attorney Pfann chugged in, two strangers flanking him, stiff as honor guards.

Ah, shit. Feds. Might as well throw in the towel on the Goldstein-Sears investigation. Wes felt his shoulders tighten but kept his voice peaceable. "Hey there, Art. What can we do for you?"

"Howdy, Wes. Got a little bone to pick and a lot of work to get at." Young Art Pfann, elected prosecuting attorney just last year, had a booming voice that served him well in the courtroom and on the stump at election time.

"Sure thing. Mason and Foley, you get on those interviews now," Wes said smoothly, just to underline who was in charge in this office. "Adams, you're on dispatch. Hopkins, stick around until I'm finished with these gentlemen."

"Yessir." The troops split up briskly and Wes gave them all points for loyalty. Marty Hopkins began to type a report while the door was swinging closed behind Mason and Foley's exit.

"Come on in." Wes led the way into his inner office and stood behind his battered gray-painted desk. There was only one other chair in the office so he didn't sit down. That was okay. Standing he had a good six inches on everyone else in the room, eight on the short spiffy guy. Pfann closed the door behind them.

123

"Wes, meet Special Agents John Jessup and L. D. Manning. FBI. This is Sheriff Wes Cochran."

"Mr. Jessup." Wes stuck out his hand and the shorter of the two agents took it crisply. Jessup had fair skin with dark intense eyes, dark thick brows, and dark hair so smooth that it seemed painted on. His movements were quick, almost mechanical. Wes was reminded of a present his son Billy had given to little Marty LaForte for her fourth birthday, a wind-up metal dog that moved jerkily this way and that for a few seconds and then paused for two tinny yaps before repeating the motions.

"Sheriff Cochran. How d'you do, how d'you do." Sure enough, Jessup's voice was tinny too. His dark eyes rested on Wes only a moment before shifting away to scan the office— the report forms strewn on the desk, the chipped paint, the gold-framed portrait photo of Shirl and teenaged Billy with their sweet grins, the snapshots of Wes and the mayor and a lot of balloons on election night, of Wes holding a fifteen-inch bass he'd caught.

Wes said, "Pleased to meet you. And Mr. Manning." He turned to shake hands with the second agent, a lumpy-faced youngster who was clearly junior to Jessup in status and age. Manning mumbled something and Wes turned to Art Pfann.

"You want to pick bones first?" he asked mildly.

Art said, "Well, Wes, we were just wondering. You found this Goldstein on Thursday morning. Didn't report it to the FBI until late Friday. Didn't report the Klan aspect to me until Saturday, when the Sears body turned up too. I called right away, of course, and these gentlemen got here as fast as they could, but with the weekend and all, we've lost four days."

Wes nodded and propped a foot on his desk chair. "It wasn't real clear what was happening at first," he said.

"How, how d'you mean?" Jessup asked.

"Well, we can't go calling you fellows every time some high-school kid yells 'nigger' at somebody," Wes explained. "Here we had a white victim and a hand-drawn card, nothing that looked official. I started checking, of course, but—"

"Next time let us check," Jessup snapped, his tinny voice

impatient. "But let's get on with it. Here now, we're here now. We received a communication from Mrs. Goldstein."

"Yes. She told me she'd sent you the hand-drawn card that was nailed to their door," said Wes. "I spoke to her Friday. Black jazz singer. Art has my report on that interview, and we'll get you copies."

Jessup asked sharply, "Why'd she report it to us instead of you?"

Wes smiled at him benignly. "She was in Indianapolis visiting her cousin when her husband was killed. Maybe she didn't trust the cops there."

Jessup opened his mouth, then thought better of it. Art Pfann said, "Okay now, why don't we work out a way to attack this."

"Fine, fine." Jessup pulled out a sheet of paper. "We have the names of some people here we'd like to interview. Tell us if these addresses are right. Al Evans on Monroe Road?"

"Right."

"Lester Holtz on Maple Valley Road?"

"Yep."

"Mitch Carney on North Quarry Road?"

"No. He moved."

"What's his address?"

"No idea. Somewhere in Florida."

"I see. How long ago did he move?"

"Maybe seven years ago."

"I see. Well, how about Melvin Sims on Bald Hill Road?"

Damn. Mel was Grady's uncle. Wes had visions of long afternoons without Grady Sims, of working shorthanded while Jessup interrogated Grady about possible Klan ties. Just as well Grady was off today. Wes said, "Yeah, Mel Sims is still there. Of course, Tom Straub isn't."

"Tom Straub?"

"Well, he's dead now. But he used to be Great Titan, until the Klan was dissolved in this county."

"But it was active in the sixties."

"Sure. But these days there's no official organization," Wes said. "Now, I know Al Evans went to a rally in Kentucky back in February. Others may have gone too, I don't know."

125

"A rally? How do you know that?" Jessup demanded.

"Like I said, I started checking when I saw that handmade card. First step is obviously looking at the boys who used to be in the Klan."

"Uh, yes. What did they tell you?"

"Not much. They'd heard of a white guy living with a black woman. They didn't know he was Jewish."

"Are you sure?" Art Pfann asked.

"Nope."

"Why not?"

"Didn't have time to double-check. Right after I heard it we found the Denton girl's body, and then the Sears body."

"Who's this Denton girl?" Jessup asked sharply.

"Old case, nothing to do with this," Art Pfann explained. "She's from a good family hereabouts, disappeared when she was twelve or thirteen, seven years ago. Deputy just found the bones in a cave near here. Damnedest thing." Art seemed genuinely sad. Well, he'd been a buddy of Hal Junior's since high school and had known the kid sister. Wes remembered interviewing him seven years ago, when he was just out of law school, about motorcyclists who might have known Phyllis. Art hadn't been much help then either.

"Back to this, this case," Jessup said. He talked so fast that he stuttered sometimes, as though his little wind-up gears were missing a tooth and slipped occasionally. "Are there other Klan sympathizers you know about?"

"About ninety percent of this county sympathizes with some of their ideas," Wes said. "Close to a hundred percent of us are opposed to murder, all the same."

"Close to?" Art Pfann asked.

Wes looked him in the eye. "Wednesday I would've said a hundred percent, period. Wouldn't you?"

"Yeah. This isn't a bad county, really. But now—" He shook his head.

"Art, I've been wondering," Wes said. "That rally in Kentucky. You suppose Al stirred up someone down there? Talking about those two shacked up?"

Art leaped on the idea. "That's gotta be it! No trouble around here for years, then out of the blue—"

"There've been plenty of rallies over the years," Jessup said. Wes beamed at him. "Yeah! I knew you'd have the big picture. If this is a national thing—mind, I'm not saying it is— we don't have the manpower. We go out of the county every now and then to ask a question, but you're the fellas with the computers."

"We'll check, of course. But we have to check here too," Jessup said coolly, and Wes realized he wouldn't be easily deflected. "National conspiracies have to have local headquarters. Did this Al Evans tell you he talked to, talked to someone there?"

"Al Evans doesn't exactly confide in me," Wes said. Understatement of the year. "Maybe you'll do better. I should probably tell you, he's armed."

"So, so are we. Okay, let's summarize. No overt Klan activity in this county since the sixties. Still have a number of members around—sorry, ex-members. A few go to rallies. Including the one in Kentucky in February. No connections to the Martinsville Klan?"

"Possible. I don't know of any," Wes said. "There are pockets of what you call sympathizers all over the state. Fellows who blame every little slump in the economy on black folks or Jews. Here." He picked up his reports from the desk. "I can copy these for you. Look them over and see if you have any more questions."

Jessup glanced at them and handed them to Manning. "Okay. Let's take a quick look, then get moving."

The phone buzzed and Wes grabbed the receiver. Adams's voice said, "Press is here. *Indianapolis Star*, about the Goldstein murder."

"Be right out," Wes said. He replaced the receiver and hitched up his trousers. "Press is here," he repeated to the others. "What are we telling them?"

Art Pfann looked at Jessup, who frowned. "Just that the investigation is, is proceeding well. The FBI is investigating possible civil rights violations. Don't mention the Klan yet." He nodded at Art. "Pfann, you be spokesman. We'll all refer comments to you."

"Fine with me. You talk better'n I do, Art," Wes said. He

wasn't unhappy. The case was down the tubes for the time being, with little metallic-voiced Jessup trying to get information out of the old boys. A few days from now he might give Lester another visit, see how the wind was blowing. But for now he predicted massive silence. And Art Pfann could use his fine booming voice to report lack of progress.

Art opened the door and Jessup and Manning started out. Wes said, "Just a minute," and put a hand on Manning's shoulder.

"What is it?" Jessup asked. Art closed the door again.

"We haven't made copies yet," Wes explained.

"We prefer to work from, from the originals."

"Fine. No problem. But I need a copy of the thing too."

"We'll get it back soon as we've gone over it."

Wes took a step toward them so that Jessup had to cock his head back to look up at him. "This case is an open murder investigation," he said mildly. "No proof yet that it really is the Klan or anything else that might require federal lawmen."

Behind Jessup's back, Art Pfann was gesturing for Wes to shut up. Wes didn't care. So the hostility came out in the open, so what? This investigation was dead until the outsiders went away again.

Jessup was glaring up at him, but he took the papers from Manning and handed them to Wes. Wes smiled at Pfann and motioned him out. Pfann took a deep breath, opened the door, and went forth to fend off the man from the *Star*. Wes took the report to the copier and ran off a copy. He showed them both to Jessup and spoke loud enough for the reporter to hear. "There you go. The report and a copy. Exact copy. Take your choice."

"Thanks," said Jessup shortly, taking the original. "Let's move, Manning." They headed for the exit, skirting Pfann and the *Star* reporter.

"Hopkins," said Wes, motioning toward the inner office. "Time to chew over the Denton case." As she came through the door, he added quietly, "You remember that little wind-up tin dog we gave you when you were little?"

"The little yappy one?" she asked, puzzled.

"Yeah." He jerked his head toward Jessup's back. She glanced back, then followed him into the office with a chuckle.

18

WHEN YOU CROSS THE OHIO RIVER SOUTH INTO KENTUCKY, THE landscape doesn't change a lot. It's still limestone country, but the bands of stone below the russet soil are not as thick and flawless as the fine-grained belt that surfaces in southern Indiana. So there are fewer quarries blasted into the earth, fewer men pounding and sawing at the bedrock. But the rains fall in Kentucky too, and the water sculpts the limestone as it does in Indiana, carving rounded hills and valleys and sinkholes, tunneling out caves as magnificent as Mammoth, and decomposing the top layer of rock into soil suitable for growing a pelt of maples and redbuds and wild grapevines. Indiana is known for the frost on its punkins and for its persimmon pudding, but pumpkins and persimmons grow in Kentucky too. And in southern Indiana, as in Kentucky, the soil sprouts mint for juleps and makes the bluegrass green.

It makes gardens green too. On the outskirts of Louisville, where the yards are wide and edged by hedges and fences, a woman and a little girl were weeding their backyard vegetable patch. The woman was in her fifties, sturdy and pleasant-faced, her eyes hazel and her hair streaked brown and silver. She wore old khaki twill trousers, a green-striped cotton blouse, and a green-billed baseball cap to shade her eyes. The little blue-eyed girl, kindergarten age, had a ponytail, worn jeans, and a blue knit polo shirt. "Grandma, what are these?" she asked.

A couple of cars passed on the street in front, and the mailman ambled past on his way to the end of the block. The woman inspected the plant that the grubby little finger was nudging. "Carrots," she said. "See the lacy leaves?"

129

"Looks like little hairs." The girl squinted at the tiny plants. She had a smudge of mud on her cheek.

"You're right, it does, Milly."

"What about this one? Do I pull it?"

"No. That's going to be a pepper. But we better pull this one. It's a wild grape, and it'll wind around the other plants and choke them."

"Choke? Like this?" Milly put her hands around her own neck, rolled her eyes, and stuck out her tongue. "Ga-a-a-ah!"

The woman laughed. The kid was smart as a whip, but such a clown sometimes. "Not exactly like that, but the plants are just as dead when it's done. So it's best to pull out wild grapes when we can."

"It's strong, Grandma." Milly tugged industriously at the vine.

"Has to be, to choke other plants. Here, dig around the roots a little bit, and it'll come out easier." She handed Milly her little gardening fork, then squatted back on her heels and looked around. A pleasant day, quiet except for the hum of insects, occasional birdcalls, and passing cars. Most of the women in this middle-class neighborhood worked days, and except for Jan at the end of the block with her preschoolers, there were few human sounds. An aging black sports car rolled by on the street, sputtering, and pulled up to the curb next door. The driver got out and she heard the creak of a hood opening. He pushed back his white baseball cap and peered through his sunglasses at something. The motor, no doubt, although it was hard for her to see what he was looking at because the hedge between the yards ran all the way to the road and masked the front of the car. She saw him shake his head. Poor fellow. Should she offer to call a service station for him? He walked around to the back of the car and opened his trunk. He tossed a blanket out next to the hedge, took out a metal toolbox, and a moment later she heard him tapping at the car. So maybe he could fix it himself.

The bees were buzzing, and she could hear Jan's four-year-old, Timmy, shouting in his backyard at the end of the block. Milly was industriously digging up the grapevines, but that wouldn't last long. Sure enough, in a moment the little girl said, "I want to do dandelions."

"We worked on them yesterday, honey. We'll probably have to do them again next week, but not yet. Tell you what, I bet the mail's here. Why don't you go see if there's any in the box?"

"I can put it on the table too."

"Okay, but wash your hands first. Make sure they're really clean. And then come tell me if there's anything special in the mail."

"What's special?"

"If the envelope has handwriting on it instead of just typing."

"Okay." Milly trotted toward the house and the screen door slammed behind her.

The woman retrieved the gardening fork and bent to her weeding again. She didn't see that the driver of the black sports car had slipped along the hedge that bordered her side yard. She didn't hear his quiet approach across the grass behind her. She was aware for an instant that he'd clapped a cloth across her nose and mouth, but she was unconscious too soon to know that he was folding her into the blanket, dragging her swiftly along the hedgerow, pausing an instant to check for passersby, and then shoving her into the backseat.

The black car pulled away smoothly, not sputtering at all.

Milly, her hands almost clean but her cheek still smudged, bounced out of the house a moment later. "Grandma?" she called. She looked around the silent garden for a moment, ran to check both side yards, looked inside the house, upstairs and down and on the front porch, and went out back again with a puzzled frown. But then her face cleared. When Grandma needed something she generally went down to Timmy's house to ask Jan. She was probably there now. Milly skipped along the roadside, serious because of the importance of her mission. She had to tell Grandma that one of the letters she'd brought in had handwriting on it.

19

"SEE, I'M SORT OF SCARED BECAUSE NEW YORK IS SO BIG AND I don't know where things are," Chrissie said.

She was wearing her Manhattan T-shirt yet again. It'd be nothing but rags by the Fourth of July, Marty thought, stroking her daughter's dark hair as she said, "Yeah, it's scary to go to a big place you've never been to before."

"But there's nothing to worry about, angel! A smart kid like you?" Brad patted Chrissie's shoulder encouragingly.

They were sitting at one of the outside tables at McDonald's. Wes had told Marty to take a long lunch hour because at four o'clock he wanted her back to go with him to the cave where Phyllis Denton's body had been found. So Marty had had her hair shampooed and then, still in uniform, she'd picked up Chrissie after school. Brad was helping Eddie Bronson paint the Wilson house but was willing to knock off and come with them for Cokes.

Chrissie had taken her doll Polly out of her school satchel and was bouncing her on her knee, always a sign that she was worried. "But there's so many people in New York," she said. "I won't know anybody. And also, I won't know anybody in Alaska, and then when I get to know somebody we'll be going to New York!"

Marty said, "Yeah, I know how—"

"Hey, look, you two!" Brad held up a hand in protest. They were sitting in the shade of an awning, but the bouncelight from the cement sidewalk outlined his cheekbone and jaw, picked out the smear of yellow paint on his work shirt, and emphasized the gestures of his lively hands. "Look, I was there quite awhile, okay? And first of all, I'll be there to show

132

you around. Second, you'll figure out how to get around real quick. I mean, sure, it's big, but you don't have to go everywhere the first week, right?"

"Yeah, one step at a time," Marty agreed.

"That's right. Plus, it's not that hard to meet people. It'll be fun, angel!"

"I'm still scared." Chrissie bounced Polly even faster.

"No, you're not. You're not scared," Brad insisted. "Because New York is wonderful. Unbelievable." He leaned toward Chrissie earnestly and she steadied in the glow of his enthusiasm. "It's like the pinnacle of everything, you know? Just think of something, anything, and it'll be the pinnacle."

"Like what?"

"Oh—music. Buildings. Kites."

"Kites?" Chrissie pulled a disbelieving face and glanced at Marty.

Brad laughed. "You think I'm kidding? No way. See, I was walking by Central Park one Saturday and I saw this kite in the sky. It looked strange, like a bird or something. So I walked into the park to see what it was."

"What was it?"

"It was a kite, all right. An American eagle kite. Amazing thing. When the guy brought it down you could see every feather painted on."

"Yeah, sounds nice," Chrissie said politely.

"And that wasn't all. See, there was this whole kite club. Big bunch of people. And they had every kind of kite you could think of. Some were real slick, aerodynamic things. You know, scientifically engineered. Real strange-looking. And others were fancy designs, like the American eagle. One looked like a shark." His hand, fingertips together, swam and plunged through the air. "Mean shark, too. Big teeth. Really something. And there was this duck. A brown duck, and instead of bows on the kite tail, there was this bunch of little fuzzy ducklings. All swimming. Swimming through the air. And there was this real pretty kite, some kind of see-through plastic in different colors, and it looked like one of those church windows. Amazing! And there it was, up in the skies, floating over the people, over the park, over the tall buildings."

Marty could almost see them, marvelous kites over the marvelous city. Brad was leaning across the table, his voice confidential, one hand on Chrissie's shoulder and one in the air describing the soaring kites. He ought to be on TV, Marty thought, not just radio. He made life seem like a poem. He said, "And you know what else?"

"What?" Chrissie too was bewitched with the vision. The doll had stopped bouncing and lay limp and forgotten in her lap.

"There was one kite, all sequins and sparkles. And it was Elvis."

"Elvis?" gasped Chrissie.

"Swear to God, Chrissie. Old Elvis, sparkling up there in the sky. Looking down from the blue heavens on all the rest of us. I mean, I saw those kites and I thought, this city is not just a big city. This city is magical!"

"I want to go there," Chrissie whispered.

"So do I," Marty admitted. Soaring kites, soaring buildings, soaring dreams. A city where kites looked like Elvis, and candy looked like cockroaches, and Brad was rich because he held the key to it all.

"Of course you do. And I'm taking you, as soon as I get my foot in the door. Nothing's stopping this family!" His hand still rested on Chrissie's shoulder but his magnetic eyes were full on Marty.

She pulled her gaze away, looking at the scuffed table, the dusty roadside plantings, the big numbers on the signs at the gas station next door, the hills and dips of the limestone countryside beyond. Her grandfather had dug out this stone, her mother had gardened in this earth, and her dad had died on these highways.

But she was drawn by the big city too. The pinnacle of everything.

Brad asked, "So what do you say?"

"This place doesn't have but one little mall," Marty said.

"Man, don't I know it!" Laughter glinted in his dark eyes.

Marty took a deep breath. "Brad, I don't want to go to Alaska."

"It's not Alaska! We're talking about New York! Look, I

explained all that." He ticked it off on his fingers. "You need a gimmick to impress people in New York. And Alaska's the perfect gimmick. And so we go to Alaska. It's just temporary. A goddamn stepping-stone!"

She shook her head. "Maybe we can find some other stepping-stone. See, my family lived here. I own the house. I've got a good job. Chrissie's got friends—"

She trailed off as he slapped the table angrily and leaned back. "Can you hear yourself, Marty?" he demanded. "*I* this, *I* that! What about the rest of us? Don't you care about us?"

"God, Brad, of course I care!"

"Hell of a way you've got of showing it."

"Okay, just tell me one thing. Can we get to Alaska without selling the house here?"

His eyes slipped away, just an instant, and she had her answer. He said, "Hell, I don't know. We've got to decide what we want out of life, and then figure out the details. Go for it."

"Yeah." Marty felt tears stinging behind her lashes. "That's what we've got to decide."

"God, you are so stubborn! Don't you even—" He stood and slammed his chair against the table. "I'll see you later." He stalked away toward the half-painted Wilson house.

"Daddy!" Chrissie hurled herself after him. Polly dropped unnoticed to the ground. "Daddy, wait!"

He looked down at her sadly. "I'll be back soon, angel."

"Daddy, we'll find a way!" She spoke in a rush. "We all want to go. I wasn't really scared, don't worry. I really want to go."

"I know, angel." He hugged her.

"We'll figure out a way."

"Yeah. Your mom just needs a little time to figure it out." He kissed her forehead. "I'll see you back home in a little bit."

"Okay."

She stood watching him walk away, and Marty suddenly remembered across the years another nine-year-old girl watching her father storm away. "No, Rusty, I'm not swapping the home place for that beat-up bar," her mother had insisted. And young Marty had withered inside, hating her mother's

135

stubbornness, fearing her father's betrayal. When she was grown up, she'd promised herself, things would never be like that.

It was like staring into an abyss.

Chrissie came back slowly, spotted Polly on the cement, and picked her up. Marty cleared her throat and said, "Chrissie, things'll work out somehow. I know it's scary."

"I'm *not* scared!"

She curled up silently in the far corner of the car seat and hugged Polly all the way home.

20

WES COCHRAN FLIPPED TO THE NEXT PAGE OF HIS NOTEPAD. "Okay, now the next victim. Willie Sears," he said. "Mason, what've we got on him?"

Bobby Mason shifted uncomfortably in the corner. They were all crowded into Wes's inner office, six of them—Wes, Mason, Foley, Prosecuting Attorney Pfann, and the two FBI agents, Jessup and Manning. The outer office was full of reporters from the *Star*, the *Herald-Telephone*, the *Courier Journal*, and some wire service or other. So, Wes had crammed the lawmen into his office for the briefing.

Mason said, "Sears worked at the high school. Custodian, grounds work, and so forth. Wednesday night they had a baseball game and he was there late, cleaning up. They were going to have some kind of schoolwide athletic field day all day Thursday so it couldn't wait till then."

"Why didn't any, anyone call in that he was missing Thursday?" Jessup asked in his metallic voice.

"He had Thursday off. Supposed to make it up Saturday night when they were having a dance. And Friday his supervisor called his home two or three times. Wrote a reprimand in his file. Didn't expect anything like this, of course."

"Okay," Wes said. "What time did he leave the high school Wednesday night?"

"The guy who was working with him said it was a little after eleven. And we have a report that about a quarter to twelve he stopped at Gus's Mini-Mart for a six-pack."

"Good work." Wes paused and glanced at the opening door. Marty Hopkins was squeezing her way in. He'd told her to take a long lunch hour. Was it four o'clock already? He looked at the clock. God, it was. He was surprised at how ravaged Marty looked. What the hell had she been up to? Well, this wasn't the time to ask. He said, "Hopkins, good. Will you grab that county map out there and bring it in?"

"Yessir." She was back in two seconds with the map. Wes unrolled it on his desk, letting Mason and Hopkins hold down the corners on their side of the desk.

Wes pointed to a spot south of the center of town. "Okay, here's the high school. Willie Sears leaves here after eleven." He saw that Jessup was peering avidly over Hopkins's shoulder. They were almost of a height, those two. He went on, "And here's Gus's place on the city limits, where Sears got his beer. Quarter to twelve. Would it take twenty minutes to get there?"

"More like ten," said Bobby Mason. "But those times I gave you were approximate."

Wes nodded. "And out here is Sears's house. So, yeah, Gus's is where he'd stop if he wanted a six-pack to take home."

"Something else too," said Hopkins, squinting at the map. "The place Goldstein lived is on that road."

"No, it's the next road over. The Lawrence Road." Jessup reached around her and pointed.

"Yessir." Hopkins glanced at the little FBI man. "But the back of the property goes all the way down to this road, and you can see the back of the Goldstein place from down here."

"Foley, make a note," Wes said. "Check the roadside there where the Goldstein place is visible."

"Check for tire marks," Jessup explained. "See if they match Sears's tires."

Jesus, did he think they were in kindergarten? Wes beamed at him too broadly. "Good idea. Now, it so happens our next report is on tire prints. The state lab reports a match—they got a clear impression at the front of Willie Sears's driveway."

"What's the match?" Jessup looked sullen.

"Matches the tire print at the Goldstein driveway, that partial we picked up along the right-hand edge."

"Great!" Art Pfann said enthusiastically.

"Long as it's not the mail truck," Wes said. "Now, how about the interviews with the ex-Klansmen?"

Jessup looked surprised. "I'll write the report tonight."

"I see." Wes kept all emotion out of his voice. "You think the deal is, we tell you everything as soon as we find it, and you tell us what you find when you get around to writing a report."

Art Pfann frowned. Jessup, his shiny face just a tad pinker, said, "There's not, not much to report yet."

"Not even from Lester Holtz?" Wes asked.

"He didn't know anything. And his damn dog kept barking."

"How about old man Sims?"

"Told us about that same, same rally in Kentucky. We've called up the reports on that rally."

"You mean you know who all was there?"

"Uh, not all. The main speakers."

"Good to have the list anyway," Wes said kindly. "How about Al Evans?"

Jessup smoothed back his smooth hair. "Claimed he didn't know anything. Said we'd better have a warrant if we came back."

Yep, that's what Al would yell between shotgun blasts, all right. Wes said, "Evans has pretty strong feelings about law enforcement officers. Okay, let's see. Only other thing here is Grady Sims's report. He hasn't typed it up yet either. Two reports, really. First, an interview with Willie Sears's brother Jimmy, the one who drove over from Evansville to check on him. This brother said Sears had lost touch with a lot of his friends since his wife died two years ago. No special problems, just occasional complaints about his supervisor at the high school, like always. Now, the second report. Sims checked the Goldstein outbuildings and there were a couple of boards that could have been pieces of a cross. State lab is working on them now. Any thoughts?" He looked at Pfann.

"Looks like a long slog," Pfann said soberly. "Is the neighborhood canvass complete?"

Mason said, "We talked to everybody except two. We'll get them tomorrow, at work if we have to."

"Fine, do that, Mason. Now, the Denton case. The state police say they've finished with the Stineburg cave and want to release the crime scene, so I have to take time out to go out there. Art, with all the excitement about Sears, you never got to that cave either, did you?"

"No. Guess I'd better have a look too."

"Hopkins, you're on the Denton case, you come too. Rest of you write your reports and go on home. Mr. Jessup, I'm looking forward to seeing what you get on that Kentucky rally." He smiled at Jessup and nodded to Don Foley, who opened the door.

The reporters sprang up from where they'd been waiting and began shouting questions. Wes said to Art, "You'll have to give them something. I'll meet you at the cave."

Art Pfann nodded in resignation and stepped through the door from the inner office. "Gentlemen and ladies," he boomed, "I have a short statement about . . ." His voice rolled on.

Wes grabbed Marty Hopkins's elbow and steered her out the door to the car. "Good point about Goldstein's backyard," he said.

She climbed into the passenger seat. "I remembered what you said about that poor guy's eyes being cut out. Do you think—"

"Too soon to know." He turned the ignition.

"Coach, I thought this was a good county. Good people. How come all of a sudden we've got this ugly Klan stuff?"

"Our folks are no better and no worse than most. There's always losers who want to blame their problems on other people."

139

"You think they feel like losers? How come?"

Wes snorted. "Who knows? Maybe they never got picked for the sixth-grade team, or their daddy whipped them too much, or they failed algebra in school. So they decide to blame niggers and Jew-boys. And I don't care who they blame, long as they don't hurt the other people. Then it's my business." He glanced sideways at her. "Most folks in the county are okay, Marty—they stop at grumbling. This is just a nutcase we've got here. Now, back to Phyllis Denton. Let's run through it from the beginning."

"Okay." She pushed her hair back from her forehead. She looked exhausted. "What we know is that Phyllis ran away at thirteen, no signs of trouble before that. Or none we've heard about."

"What does that mean?" Wes asked sharply.

"Nothing. Not relevant." She sounded embarrassed. "I was thinking about my own kid."

"She's run away?"

"No, no. It's nothing to do with this case. Sorry. Sir."

Wes glanced at her. She was trying to look professional, jaw firm, shoulders straight, trying to hide the ache in her eyes. He stared at the highway, turning over her words for a moment. The idiot husband, he decided, wishing he could help. But he remembered Shirl's advice when he'd fretted over Marty before. "She wants to be on the team, Wes. You remember that from when she was real little. If you pamper her, she'll hate it, and the guys will resent it and make things even harder for her."

He turned into Donaldson Road toward the cave and said, "Okay, Hopkins, let me know if I can help. Right now, let's get on with the Denton thing. Kid runs away."

"Yessir," she said gratefully. "Now, next thing was finding that photo you showed me. Phyllis in the motorcycle outfit. Where was it, exactly?"

"In a drawer where Phyllis kept her shirts and things. Pushed way to the back. Most of her books and papers were gone, so she must have just missed that one."

"I didn't know her. Could you tell when it was taken?"

"Not long before she disappeared. Kids change fast at that

GRAVESTONE

age, but she looked about the way she did last time I saw her. Except for the leather get-up." Wes shook his head, remembering. He'd never seen little Phyllis in anything but ruffles before that photo.

"She wasn't wearing leather in her coffin," Hopkins said.

"No, she wasn't."

"Okay. So you hunt all over, send out bulletins, but nothing turns up. Lots of rumors, but no facts." She was getting into it, animated again. Shirl knew how to call them, all right. "The next real news is over a year later. Professor Wolfe gets into the Stineburg cave, finds the body, and tells Elizabeth Denton."

"Yeah. Right."

"But Mrs. Denton thinks it's another false rumor. Her husband is sick anyway and she doesn't want to upset him. And the professor doesn't tell anyone else. Doesn't want to get mixed up with the law again, maybe. Have we heard from Pennsylvania yet about that hunter she says she killed?"

"The D.A. there remembered the case. He's sending the details. On the phone he pretty much confirmed her story. Said she's a strange woman, but it was self-defense, all right."

"Yeah. Okay. So anyway, nobody else knows about the cave and nothing happens for years. Then the judge gets these tumors, and his wife happens to tell him what the professor said, and he starts trying to tell us something. I figure the professor's story fit in with something else he knew."

"How're you coming on those appointment calendars?"

"About half done. It's slow work. I've gone through the two years after she disappeared and there's nothing obvious yet."

"Okay. After we look over the cave, we'll decide what you should ask Professor Wolfe tomorrow. Here we are." He pulled to the side of the road. They climbed the rock-strewn hillside to the cave opening, where a bored state trooper sat tapping his toe to a rock radio station. He switched it off and jumped up as Wes and Marty approached.

"Howdy," said Wes.

141

"Hello, Sheriff. Sergeant Weaver is in there already. He's got the reports."

"Fine, we'll join him. Mr. Pfann will be here soon. The prosecuting attorney."

"I see you've got lights," said Hopkins, looking at a generator by the entrance.

"Yeah, they got temporaries in there," said the trooper.

"Okay." Wes stepped over the police tape, looked dubiously at the dark opening between the boulders, and motioned to Hopkins. She slipped through and he ducked his head and grunted his way after her. Have to do something about this damn paunch.

Hopkins's comment didn't help. "They widened this opening," she said. "Probably to get the coffin out."

Inside, a pile of boulders led down to the smooth cave floor. The tunnel was more than ten feet wide, and he could straighten up under the seven-foot ceiling. Work lights had been strung along one wall and splashed brightness every thirty feet against the tan stone. In between, it was dim, even black wherever an unevenness in the cave wall cast a shadow. "Spooky place," Wes said.

"Try it without work lights," Hopkins said.

"Hey, Sheriff!" A figure appeared at the end of the cavern.

"Sergeant Weaver?"

"Right. Glad to see you. Let's get this show on the road."

"Okay. Pfann will be here any minute. But we can get started."

"Fine," said Weaver. "I'll tell you, my men are sick of this place. It'll be good to release the scene and get out of here. Would have done it sooner but somebody high up said to play it by the book. Politics."

"Yeah. The Dentons are connected."

"Yeah. But all this happened a hell of a long time ago."

"Right, no chance of smoking guns here," Wes agreed.

There were more lights in the chamber where Weaver stood. Wes studied the dusty floor marked with dozens of footprints. Mostly cops'. "Any useful footprints?" he asked.

"We got photos. We'll need elimination prints from your deputy's shoes, and that park naturalist's. But it'll be uphill to prove anything. There's been plenty of traffic but it's hard to tell when. No rain to wash out the old ones."

Wes grunted. "Well, work on it. This where the coffin was at?" He was standing by the wall where most of the lights were concentrated. Two low, flat boulders sat five feet apart, and centered above them was a cross smoked onto the wall.

"Yeah. Here's the cave inventory from the technicians. Just got it an hour ago." He handed Wes a typed sheet.

Marty Hopkins was peering into a black crevice at one side of the chamber. "You checked these side passages too?" she asked.

"Yeah, Sunday. That one's only three feet deep. There's a crawl tunnel nearer the entrance that leads to a stream cavern, and that's it. All they found was a few bugs and fish."

"They didn't kill them, did they?" Hopkins asked sternly. Wes looked at her, surprised at her sharpness.

"I doubt it," Weaver said. "My impression was that the bugs and the men went opposite directions."

Wes grinned. "Let's look at your list."

The three of them huddled by a yellow work light and inspected the inventory. Near the entrance, the searchers had found and removed for analysis a short list of items: an old belt, several beer cans, sandwich wrappers, a broken penknife, an oil spout, two old-style Coke bottles, and something listed as "possible dried human feces." In the chamber where they stood the state cops had found two more beer cans and the coffin, nothing else. The coffin's contents were listed also—the skeleton, the fragments of rotten clothing, the bracelet, pads and pillows, "Rock of Ages" torn from a hymnal, a Bible with a leather marker, and a—

"Shit!" said Marty Hopkins. "Oh, shit!"

Wes's eyes, lagging an instant behind hers, saw it then. "Shit!" he echoed, and kicked the cave wall.

Art Pfann, his dark business suit streaked with cave dust, was approaching, rounding the turn. He looked around the room. "What's wrong?" His big courtroom voice echoed in the chamber.

Wes took a deep breath. "We can't release this crime scene. The feds will want to see it. We've got complications."

"What kind of complications?"

"Damn corpse was holding a Bible," Wes explained. "And there was a card tucked in it, with a hand-drawn cross and blood drop."

"Shit!" boomed Art Pfann, and kicked the cave wall too.

21

THE NIGHT-HAWK'S RIGHT NAME WAS BLOTTED OUT.

That was good. That was as it should be. His name was worthless, no account, made of smoke, gone like smoke. A shadow. No one except his mother had ever called him by his right name anyway. She read him Bible stories about sweet Jesus, and sang songs about Christian soldiers, and kissed his forehead, and called him by his right name, and then one day ran off somewhere. When he asked about her, his father had whupped him. Shhh, his big brother Chip had said, don't worry, she's a no-account tramp anyhow. We'll do better without her.

Chip used to call him Shadow because he hung around all the time and because even then he could silently slide around corners and into tiny spaces. Everybody else, his father and his biggest brother and everybody else, called him Pip. Here they come, Chip and Pip, they said. Pip for Pipsqueak. Worthless, no-account Pipsqueak. The baby brother, the no-account baby brother.

But not now. Now, nobody could say the Night-Hawk was no-account. He that overcometh, that was the Night-Hawk.

The Night-Hawk was part of a great, holy, historic war. A war against the mud-people, Cain's people, Satan's people.

He'd learned about the mud-people from Chip, home on leave, and from his papers, the *Vanguard*, the *Crusader*, the *National Alliance Bulletin*. The mud-people ruled the earth. They controlled international banking, and business, and money, and almost everything else. But when the war came they'd be wiped out, in fire and flood. They'd see then. They wouldn't call him Pipsqueak then!

And things were starting to move. He was doing the Great Titan's will now. The Great Titan didn't always give clear instructions, but that was as it should be. The Night-Hawk always understood in the end. He didn't understand this last one yet, but a message would come at last, he was sure. He just needed patience—patience and skill. Rest yet for a little season. He could wait for the message.

Right now, he waited silently in the blackness. The water gurgled beside him but he was focused on the low cross-tunnel, listening for sounds of activity. No one was there yet. He'd been surprised when the second batch of police scientists had arrived earlier tonight. He'd thought they were finished because the last two days the guards had been sporadic. Maybe now they really were finished, but caution was always important in war.

Everything seemed to be as it should be. He knew the pattern: on the hour, the state trooper on guard duty roused himself from a near-snooze in his patrol car, entered the cave, flashed his light into the cross-tunnel as he walked through the main cavern to the chamber where the body of the saint used to lie in state. The cop then turned around, walked back through the cave and up the pile of rocks at the entrance, and sat down outside for a cigarette. The trick was to slip out while the cop was looking at the chamber, deep in the cave, before he turned back.

The Night-Hawk was waiting in the stream cavern. He'd discovered this cave when he was ten, exploring with his brother. He knew it by heart. It was shaped like an H—a main cavern running parallel to this stream cavern, and a low cross-tunnel connecting them. There was more cave beyond a tiny V-shaped passage behind the breakdown pile of rocks where the stream disappeared, but of course he couldn't fit through that anymore. The Night-Hawk was strong now, a powerful engine of the Lord, a far cry from little Pipsqueak who had explored this cave long ago.

There were still no noises coming from the main entrance cavern. The Night-Hawk folded back his black cuff to look at the glow of his watch. Two more minutes; time to start. He covered his watch again, then moved toward the horizontal slit leading to the crawlway to the entry cavern, surefooted in the dark familiar surroundings. A shadow among shadows. *They need no candle, neither the light of the sun; for the Lord God giveth them light, and they shall reign for ever and ever.* When he was small he'd been frightened of the pale fish and crickets in these parts, but he knew now that they moved away from him, exquisitely sensitive to his presence, and he could travel the cave without fear. They were pale, maybe the Lord's white creatures, he thought. Whiter than snow. Not like the muddy-colored insects and fish of the outside.

Someday his raiment would be white too, washed white in the blood of the Lamb, and he would taste the glory of the Lord. But for now he must walk in darkness. *The people that walk in darkness shall see a great light.*

He felt his way to the connecting tunnel, slithered silently through the belly-crawl to the bend, and waited. The gurgling of the stream was a whisper from here; and fainter yet, a shout sounded far behind him, puny against the immense thicknesses of stone. No problem.

Then it came: clumsy cop footsteps, and the flashlight beamed into the side tunnel, splashing carelessly over the passage walls before him, unsuspecting of the shadows just around the bend. The footstep sounds retreated toward the saint's chamber, and the Night-Hawk, restored to his friendly darkness, moved out in a crawl so smooth he might have been on wheels, a well-tuned engine of the night, sharp and silent, the black sword of the Lord.

The dangerous part was next. The lights were strung across the far wall, and he would be exposed, black against pale stone, as he crossed from this tunnel to the giant boulders that had tumbled into the entrance. Once there, he'd blend into their shadows.

He extended his head slowly to sight back into the cave. The cop was invisible around the bend, but his footsteps still sounded, retreating in an unhurried manner. The Night-Hawk coiled himself back into the shadows, then shot from the tunnel, silent on rubber treads, reaching the shadows of the boulders in an instant. There he sighted back again, coiled, and launched himself again. He ricocheted skillfully from shadow to shadow up to the cave entrance.

For an instant he crouched in the blackness beside it.

Was someone there, waiting for the cop?

The night was moonlit. He hated moonlight. It invaded his world, cold uncaring moonlight, illuminating great spaces where the light-lovers might be.

But no one was there tonight.

The Night-Hawk slid away from the cave mouth, into the woods, and down the well-known trails.

After a moment, back at the cave mouth, the cop emerged, yawning and patting at his pockets to find his cigarettes. He was wondering what kind of rear-echelon asshole had decided it was necessary to keep watch on an empty hole in the ground.

22

MARTY HOPKINS, ICY ANGER TINGLING IN HER VEINS, STOOD still and attentive outside the door of the lecture room in Jordan Hall. She was mad at Professor Wolfe, mad at the FBI. Mad at Brad.

Don't think about that.

Channel your anger, Wes had said. Use it if you can, lock it away if it's distracting. Don't think about it. Just do the job.

A few people, blue-jeaned students mostly, wandered

through the halls. From inside the double doors she heard voices. There was some kind of final exam scheduled for Thursday, and students were asking about the material to be covered. Professor Wolfe's answers, pitched low in her husky, pleasant voice, had an edge of impatience today. Well, so much the better. Marty flexed her fingers. Today she wasn't going to be put off. And it might help to have the professor a little off balance. Wolfe had danced around this long enough, with all that damn talk about limestone and cycles. Bad enough when Phyllis Denton's death was a melancholy domestic tragedy. But now they knew the Klan was involved, and the FBI was breathing down Marty's neck. Wes had helped her slip away to this interview while he entertained yappy little Jessup with the files on Judge Denton and the work they'd done seven years ago. But the agents would probably be here soon with their computer links and their ironed socks. So she had only this one chance to get the professor to give her the rest. And she knew the rest, Marty could feel it in her bones.

This morning, raw from a sleepless, loveless night, she'd tossed around a few ideas with Wes before Jessup interrupted them. Wes still thought they were dealing with one nutcase, but Marty was convinced that Judge Denton was trying to tell them about the Klan connection. The problem was, there was more than one possible connection. For one thing, Judge Denton had presided when Al Evans and Lester Holtz got fined in the long-ago Emmett Hines case. Of course they'd behaved themselves, more or less, for fifteen years now, but grudges died slowly with those two. For another, there was Bert Mackay. Tom Straub had been Great Titan of the Klan before he died five years ago, and Tom Straub had hired Bert. Unfortunately, Bert was still in jail seven years ago. And like Al and Lester, pure as the driven snow these last few years. There were also the shadowy figures of the motorcycle gang. Wes had run into repeated dead ends seven years ago, but looking back he realized that there could have been gang members who were Jewish, even black. A judge's daughter in such a group might be enough to tip some Klansman over the edge.

Wes stuck to his theory of one guy, although he allowed that the guy had clearly been around awhile. But panic nagged at Marty. It was bad enough when the victims had been Jewish or black, the usual targets of the haters. But Phyllis was white, Christian, a girl like Chrissie. Wes pointed out that Phyllis hadn't been treated like the others. Her coffin was like a shrine. But it made Marty scared, and angry at every stumbling block they encountered.

The FBI had come in just as Wes had decided to send her off to Indiana University to talk to Professor Wolfe while she could. Jessup had heard the news about the Klan involvement and pounced on the case like a spring-loaded rat trap. She'd slipped out and left Wes to handle him with his usual blend of big smiles and one-upmanship. So he was counting on her, and she'd better not muff this interview today.

Inside the lecture hall, the shuffling increased suddenly. Chairs creaked, voices murmured. Marty shifted her weight to the balls of her feet. The first students flung the doors open, and only steps behind them came Professor Wolfe in her white lab coat, carrying a briefcase across her chest like a shield.

"Professor Wolfe!" Marty leaped between two students and confronted her.

"Martine." Professor Wolfe sidestepped and started down the hall. "I'm leaving now."

Marty stayed with her, dancing sideways, arms out like a guard in a basketball game, bumping a student or two out of the way. "We have to talk."

Wolfe didn't slow her long, loping steps. She looked frazzled, grim. "Some other place, Martine."

"Now, Professor Wolfe. Maybe it's not convenient, but it's important."

"Not here!" They had left most of the others behind, Wolfe's long strides sweeping them around the corner into the next hall. Marty kept pace beside her, turning when she turned, stuck tight as a shadow. Only one student had stayed with them, on the trot like Marty. Marty recognized the young woman who'd been wearing the Yogi Bear shirt out at the farmhouse.

"It's important," Marty repeated. "How about your office? The stairs are right here. Just a few minutes."

"No." Professor Wolfe strode past the staircase, headed for the exit to the parking lot.

Angry, Marty jumped ahead and spread-eagled herself across the double doors. "I'm sorry, Professor Wolfe. It has to be now."

Wolfe and her student halted and the professor's dark eyes looked down into Marty's. "Martine, you are upset," she observed. "I said not *here*. I didn't say not *now*."

"You mean we talk now, but not here?" Careful, Hopkins, this isn't victory yet. "Where, then?"

"You have a car here?"

"Yeah."

Professor Wolfe shifted the briefcase to her left hand and reached into her right pocket. Under the lab coat Marty glimpsed khakis, a photographer's vest crowded with pockets, and a gun belt. Marty reached toward her own holster. But the professor's hand came up with nothing but a car key. She handed it to her student. "Here, Callie, take the pickup and I'll meet you at the house."

"Sure." Callie grinned at Marty. "Have a good talk."

They exited and Callie trotted off to the pickup. Marty escorted her prize to the brown-and-tan department cruiser across the lot, tempted to put the professor in the back behind the prisoner's screen, where there were no inside handles on the doors. But Professor Wolfe seemed cooperative enough, even anxious. She stripped off her lab coat and got in the instant Marty unlocked the passenger door. Marty started the car quickly and was rolling out of the lot before the pickup had even backed out of its slot. She was still half-afraid of losing the professor, and had vague visions of the pickup racing past them, Wolfe leaping aboard, a high-speed chase across the limestone hills.

Okay, Hopkins, calm down. Do the job. She's more or less cooperating, after all. "You're in a big hurry to get back to your place," Marty said as they moved down Third Street.

"I don't like towns."

"Don't you get bored out where nothing's going on?"

"You mean out where there aren't many people. No, I'm not bored."

Marty stopped for a light and glanced at her passenger. Professor Wolfe was sitting calmly, her long frame composed, only the hands gripping the briefcase tense. Marty took a deep breath and made sure her voice stayed cool and neutral. "Look, Professor Wolfe, there's been a nasty turn in the Denton case. And I don't think you've been leveling with me." The light changed and she headed toward Whitehall Pike.

Professor Wolfe said edgily, "I've answered your questions, Martine. But ask more if you want."

"Okay. You opened Phyllis's coffin, right? Six years ago when you found it?"

"Yes. And closed it before I left."

"Okay. Tell me what was in it."

"A nearly skeletonized body of a girl of around twelve years of age. Signs of previous insect action."

"Yeah, yeah. What else?"

"Clothing? It appeared to be a dress, rapidly decomposing. There was a gold bracelet on the wrist. Pillow and pad under the body, standard casket type, less deteriorated than the dress. A coverlet. I suspect that the pillow and coverlet were synthetic, the clothing natural cotton. Biodegradable, as we say."

"Yeah, okay. What else?"

"There was a Bible under the child's hand. And a card in the Bible."

"Goddammit!" Marty thumped the heel of her hand against the steering wheel. "Why didn't you tell me about the damn card? It was a Klan card! We've had two other Klan killings, did you know that?" Probably not, Hopkins, a little voice told her; Wes hasn't told the papers. But Marty held on to her anger. Use it, Wes had said, especially if you're interrogating someone who's already edgy. You may rattle them into telling the truth. "Two other killings, Professor Wolfe. And you could have told us this one was connected. Helped in the investigation of all three. Professor Wolfe, this looks an awful lot like obstruction of justice."

"The Klan? How strange." The professor was studying her

151

with real interest. "So that's why you're so angry. But no, I don't believe I'm obstructing justice. Tell me, Martine, what sort of justice am I supposed to be obstructing?"

"You're obstructing enforcement of the law. What else? You're slowing down our investigation. Three investigations!"

"Turn here, Martine."

Marty glanced at the highway signs, saw that Professor Wolfe was right, and jerked the steering wheel abruptly. The car careened around the corner, tires squealing, but the professor seemed unperturbed. Marty straightened out onto the county highway and accelerated again. Professor Wolfe stretched lazily, flexed her arms and shoulders. She said, "So you want to enforce the laws, Martine. And you think I'm obstructing them. But true laws don't need enforcing."

"Are you crazy? We've got three dead people!"

Professor Wolfe rolled her window down another notch and sniffed the May breeze with satisfaction. She seemed more relaxed, more powerful. The anxiety Marty had seen back in Jordan Hall had evaporated, as though her strength flowed from these wilder surroundings. There was even a twinkle of mischief as she glanced at Marty. "I am a mere scientist, Martine. Not a law enforcement officer. But the laws I respect need no enforcement. The laws of gravity, the laws of chemistry, the laws of physics."

"Quit playing word games! That's not what I mean!"

"Martine, if you'd been going just a little faster when you turned onto this highway, the laws of physics would have rolled us into the ditch. Even you obey the laws of physics. No enforcement needed."

"So what? I'm talking about the laws we make so we can live with each other."

"Such as?"

"Things like 'thou shalt not kill.' Ever hear of that one?"

"Frequently. Especially from the district attorney in Pennsylvania." Professor Wolfe didn't seem upset by the memory. "I hear there are exceptions, for self-defense, or war, or if you kill a nonhuman creature."

"And how about 'thou shalt not bear false witness'? That

152

kind of thing. Our state laws and county laws and federal laws are based on those ideas. With reasonable exceptions."

"Yes. There's a wilderness within us, Martine. Your laws try to control that wilderness. 'Thou shalt not kill; thou shalt not bear false witness; honor thy father and mother.' Your daughter—does she honor her father?"

Startled by the question, Marty heard herself answer, "Yeah, too much," before she caught herself.

The professor frowned. "Too much? Yes, I thought there was another problem. Martine, you will defend your self?"

"Don't change the subject!"

"You promised you'd defend your self."

"Okay, okay! Dammit, let's get back to the point!"

Professor Wolfe nodded. "The point is that your laws are mutable, Martine. Different societies, different times, different laws. And different people. We say, 'honor thy father and mother,' but fathers and mothers may not all deserve equal honor. In the end your laws can't always cope with our individuality, our inner wilderness."

"But they're all we've got. So I enforce them."

"Yes. I'm not saying it isn't worthwhile. They're better than nothing, sometimes."

"And they say I can arrest you for obstruction of justice."

"Point taken, Martine." The professor's dark eyes were on her, searching her. "But I hope you take mine too. You are good at your work. You've chosen it well. But I have a different calling. Suppose you are deep in a wild cave, where no human has ever been, where no sunshine has hit since the stone was living sea creatures, three hundred and fifty million years ago. Or suppose you are high up on a mountain, above the trees, above all human habitation, climbing the jagged edge of a collision of continents. At undistracted times like that you know you are alone. All you have is yourself. And you know you will die. Your own mortality becomes a fact, like gravity."

" 'You gotta walk that lonesome valley,' " Marty murmured.

" 'You gotta walk it all by yourself.' Yes, gospel songs have a lot of truth in them," Professor Wolfe said. "They tap in to the wise, frightening wilderness within us and tell us yes,

153

we're alone. Yes, we'll die. And they try to tell us the rest too. The exhilaration that comes from knowing that our life and our loneliness and our death are part of something grander, wilder, more beautiful."

Marty remembered the fossils at the quarry pit, those little crystallizations of life and death and aeons. She ran a hand through her hair. Watch it, Hopkins, don't let this damn woman distract you again. Do the job. She said, "Okay, you're probably right. Now let's talk about the Klan."

"I can't help with the Klan."

"Professor Wolfe, you just said you found the Klan card in the Bible!"

"No, Martine. I already told you about the card I found. It was near the front of the Bible. It had Phyllis Denton's name and birth and death dates."

Shoot. She'd forgotten about that one. Marty said, "You didn't see the Klan card?"

"No. I didn't." She was frowning. "It was in the Bible too, you say? Was it easily visible? No, it couldn't have been, because you saw her Saturday and you didn't mention it when we talked Sunday."

"Yeah." Marty was frowning too. "I didn't open the Bible at all. The lab found the Klan card inside."

"I didn't see it."

"Okay, tell me what you did see. Was there anything that seemed like the Klan?"

"No. But I don't know about the Klan."

"Try, Professor Wolfe. Elizabeth Denton told Judge Denton your story very recently. And I think he's been trying to tell us something ever since. Maybe about the Klan."

The professor shook her head. "I can't help."

"We've had three killings. A Jewish guy, a black guy, a white schoolgirl. We have to find out what's happening!"

"Yes. Martine, is the Klan threatening you? Your family?"

"No." Marty's hands clenched on the steering wheel. If they'd killed Phyllis, of course they threatened her too. They threatened every woman, every girl. "Not specifically."

"But you feel such urgency."

154

"Someone evil did these things, Professor Wolfe. Deeply evil. I want to stop them."

"That is your goal in life, Martine?"

"Yeah! Yeah, I mean, I want to help people to be happy. My daughter, my husband, as many people as I can. Stopping these guys is a good first step. Don't you agree? Isn't it your goal too?"

"My goal is different, Martine, and surer than yours."

"What is it?"

"Someday, to merge with the earth. Her seas, her stones, her mountains. Perhaps even to become seashells in the sky."

"Wow. Great goal, all right." Marty snorted. "I'll probably join you. But meanwhile, maybe you could pause to help us with some bad guys? Even the FBI is interested in these."

"The FBI. Yes, they'll be there too now, won't they?" The professor looked troubled, gazing out at the woods and fields. "Well, Martine, you're right to defend your work. But I can't help with the Klan."

"Yeah, okay. But I've got a problem here, Professor Wolfe. Judge Denton says your name. Okay, I talk to you out at the quarry. And I learn a lot of stuff about fossils and cycles and limestone and Mount Everest. And oh, by the way, you say, Phyllis Denton is below Stineburg. I waste a whole day hunting around Stineburg. A whole day!"

"But you found her at last. And you were glad."

"Of course! I mean—I was horrified. Before that we didn't even know for sure that she was dead. But—"

"But your intelligence, your toughness, had found her at last. It was a triumph. You know that."

"Look, I don't need anybody to set little tasks so I can triumph. I need straight talk so I can find out who's behind these ugly murders. And I wasted a day. You're the one who talks about cosmic time and how little of it we have before we—you know, become food for other creatures. And I wasted a day of it!"

"Martine, you are a teacher's delight."

"No. I'm a law enforcement officer," Marty said stubbornly. They had reached the rutted drive that led to the farmhouse near the quarry. Reluctantly, she turned in.

"But let the teacher reply briefly. First, your wasted day would have been wasted anyway if we hadn't spoken. And I'm glad that you now frame the waste in terms of cycles and deep time."

"Okay, fine." Marty slowed because the three dogs had materialized and were escorting them up the last stretch of the driveway. "Now how about telling me what you know about Phyllis?"

"I never met Phyllis alive, Martine."

"Dammit, the Klan is involved!"

The professor shook her head. "All I know is that Klansmen are frightened, puny men who catch a glimpse of the wilderness within them and are so terrified that they project it onto others and try to kill it. Truly, I cannot help with the Klan."

Hell, she might be right. Professors didn't have many dealings with the Klan. Marty switched off the motor. "You've told me all you can?"

"I think so. Tell me, how is the judge doing?"

"Worse and worse. Royce and Elizabeth Denton have their hands full." Marty shook her head, remembering. "He had a seizure the last time I was there. He's still so strong. Amazingly strong. His mind's gone, mostly, but I really think he's trying to say something, about his illness, about his daughter, maybe about the Klan—I can't tell."

"Of course you've asked Elizabeth if she has any ideas."

"Yeah, and Royce, and the day nurse. Nothing. Elizabeth did confirm that she didn't tell your story to Judge Denton until just a little while ago, so that's where he heard your name."

"Yes, that makes sense. Did she say anything else?"

"No. Wait, she did mention something about you. Wanted to know if you'd told me about—not Anna. Started with an A, though. Alma. That's it, Alma."

"Alma. You know, that's a good idea. You'll want to talk to Alma. She can tell you much more than I can. Ask her about the girl's birthday." Professor Wolfe was out of the car suddenly, briefcase and lab coat in her left hand. She leaned down to talk through the window. "It's Alma Willison. She lives on the Madison Road, outskirts of Louisville. Goodbye, Martine."

"Louisville? Wait!" Marty jumped out. "Who's Alma?"

156

The professor was already halfway up the porch steps. "Talk to her. She knew Phyllis."

"What do you mean? How did she know her?" Marty ran after, but halted at the foot of the steps when Professor Wolfe swung around to face her. A friendly sun lit the clearing but the porch was shadowed, and the tall woman above her, raising her right palm in warning, seemed to speak from a kind of dusk.

"Ask her, Martine. I've told you all I can. If you don't want to waste time, talk to Alma."

"Yeah, okay." Sobered by the professor's firmness, Marty nodded. But when Professor Wolfe inclined her head kindly and turned back to the door, Marty couldn't help adding, "Can't you at least tell me how you know Alma?"

"I don't. Goodbye, Martine." She disappeared into the house.

Shoot! Marty kicked the porch step. Ought to call out a SWAT team, storm the place, lock her up until she gives with the rest. But hell, there was no evidence that she knew any more about Phyllis. Or the Klan, or even Alma, for that matter. Maybe Wolfe had really done nothing more than find the body and tell the family, just as she'd said.

But who the hell was this Alma? Alma, who knew Phyllis, and could tell her much more? Maybe she'd tell them something that would allow them to arrest Professor Wolfe. Marty muttered, "Damn bitch," and got back into the car.

The pickup truck rumbled into the driveway in a cloud of dust. Marty backed around it and headed south, thinking. It would be no favor to Wes to tell him now about this interview, she knew. He'd just have to pass it on to the FBI. She'd like to talk to the Dentons about it, too, but by now the agents were probably already there hassling them.

Watch it, Hopkins, crossing state lines is real tricky.

But shoot, it's about time to talk to someone who knew Phyllis.

Marty decided she'd phone Wes later. "You gotta walk it all by yourself," she hummed, and headed for Louisville.

23

THE WORLD WAS BLACK. AND COLD.

And she didn't know why.

He'd given her some kind of a pad and a blanket, but she was still cold. And her head hurt, at first a roaring kind of ache that wiped out rational thinking. Moving made it worse.

But sitting here shivering wasn't much fun either.

How long had it been? Had she been asleep or awake?

She was awake now. Maybe. It was so dark. Only dreams were this dark, right?

And quiet. There was something, or was it just a ringing in her ears? She covered her ears, took away her hands, covered them again. Yes, there was a noise outside, a small steady low-pitched hiss, like tires on pavement or water from a faucet.

After a while it seemed that maybe her head wasn't quite as bad as before. Maybe she should try again to get out. She had a dim memory of looking for an exit before, back when the headache was worse. Maybe she'd missed something.

Her joints were creaky too. She was too old for this. There had to be a mistake. Grandmas didn't get kidnapped, kids got kidnapped. She'd told Milly never to talk to strangers and all the rest. She'd never dreamed it would happen this way. Was it Milly they'd really been after? Maybe the little girl had been caught too, maybe—

Her mind was spinning off into a nightmare land of horrible thoughts. She dragged it back. Worrying wouldn't help Milly. Surviving might. Getting out of here definitely would. Time to do something, focus on the present. She managed to stand up again and rolled her head around a couple of times to

158

loosen up. She wriggled her shoulders and pulled the blanket up to warm her chest again. Then she moved one foot forward. Her leg was a block of ice, no feeling. And there was an unexpected jangle. She tried the other leg. Same thing. A dim memory stirred, colored by headache. Something on her legs. She squatted and felt her ankles.

Shackles.

She was chained.

She ran her fingers along the cold metal links. They were fastened to the metal cuffs around her ankles. Some kind of fastener was on the cuffs, but her fingers couldn't make out the construction. A second chain was attached halfway along the ankle bond, and she followed it, shuffling along in a half-squat, fingers on the chain where it lay on the floor. Then her head hit something, and waves of pain rolled through her again.

But she'd found the place where the tether ended, a big metal ring that was sunk into stone.

The floor was stone too. And the walls. She patted the wall around the ring, and up to the point where she'd bumped her head. Slowly, leading with her hands, she followed the shape of the wall on up. As it rose it curved inward. A few feet above the metal ring it arched out of reach over her head.

Be methodical now. Figure out what kind of space this is, see if maybe there's a door of some kind. She was standing by the ring, her only landmark so far. Okay, move left from the ring, see what's there. Except *see* was a silly word to use here. She stepped cautiously to the left, trailing her right hand on the wall, her chains clinking and sliding. A few feet along, the wall stopped abruptly. Cautiously, she ran her hands along the edge. Around the corner the wall continued. But when she stepped toward it, her left hand hit the wall again and her toe stubbed against something. Not a door, then. Just a narrow opening, maybe ten inches wide. Narrower at the top. And it didn't reach all the way to the floor. There seemed to be rocks piled in it. She couldn't feel a back wall. It was a deep crack, black as the rest of the world. But there had to be a bigger opening somewhere or she wouldn't be here, right? She continued on to the left, still following the cold bumpy wall, until a painful jerk on her ankle reminded her of the chain. It was pulled taut.

Okay. Other direction.

She shuffled back past the crack in the wall, and almost tripped. Something soft. She gasped and reached trembling fingers down to touch it.

The blanket. It had fallen off. She'd been so intent on exploring that she hadn't even thought about the cold.

She pulled it around her shoulders again. Moving was good, warmed up the blood a little. She found two corners of the blanket and knotted them clumsily. Then she continued her investigation.

There was the ring again.

This time she should go to the right. She explored carefully, hands patting the wall, chains clinking. Something scraped her shin. Something round, and hard. It felt like a boulder. The wall still curved in above her, was still solid behind the boulder. She moved around it and followed the wall. It stayed cold, solid, curving, all the way to the end of the chain.

Now what? She sat down for a moment to think, leaning back against the wall.

And with her chains quiet, she heard something else. A faint bump, a pause, another bump. Maybe that's why she was awake. The hiss was always there but the bump was different.

And light. Suddenly there was light ahead. She squinted. Maybe just a trick of her straining eyes. But it got brighter slowly, funny yellowish shape in the blackness. The bumps were getting louder too. And a sort of scraping noise.

Suddenly there was a glare on the yellowish shape, and she saw her own hands and legs before her in the reflected light. And then a painful blazing circle of brightness appeared. She gasped and averted her blinded eyes. She could see her arm, the brown floor, the blond wall. Through her eyelashes she squinted back toward the glare. A person—that man, she thought—pushing something toward her. She could see sturdy hands, black work shoes, black jeans in the light. The light was on the person's hat and she couldn't see his face or anything else behind the light.

"Here," he whispered. He always whispered.

Blinking, she looked down at the box he was shoving at her. "What is it?"

There was a brief pause. He said, "Egg McMuffin."

She made her cold fingers open the box. Foam box. He was right, inside there was an Egg McMuffin. She gulped it down. There was coffee too. She drank some and said, "Thanks. Uh, can I go soon?"

He seemed to be thinking over the answer. Finally he said, "When I get word."

"What kind of word? What do you mean?"

He didn't answer.

She asked, "Why am I here?"

He said nothing, just turned away.

She said, "We're not rich, you know. I hope you know that. We can't give you much money. There's only the bit we were saving for— Oh, God, please listen! Don't go away!"

But he was gone, and the light went with him.

She scrambled to her feet and hurried after, but the shackles tripped her and she fell, spilling the rest of the coffee. "Please! Please, come back!" she cried, trying to crawl toward him, jerking her ankles until the pain stopped her.

He didn't come back. She watched the light fade and disappear, heard the bump of his steps becoming fainter and fainter. Soon it was black and quiet again. She lay sobbing in the dark for a long time.

24

WES SHIFTED IN HIS OLD DESK CHAIR AS GRADY SIMS, ACROSS from him, licked his lips. "No, sir. Uncle Mel never said anything about going with them to Kentucky."

"It was a major Klan rally," snapped Special Agent Jessup. "Not that long ago, November last year. You would have noticed if, if your uncle was gone for two days."

"No, sir. I go weeks sometimes without talking to him."

"But you said you were on good terms with him."

"Yes, sir. We don't fight. We more leave each other alone."

Wes asked, "How d'you get along with your uncles, Mr. Jessup?"

Jessup looked at him coldly. He had avoided the third chair to go for the extra height of perching on the corner of Wes's desk, his shoulder to Wes and more or less facing poor Grady, who had folded himself like an extension lamp into the visitor's chair. Beforehand Wes had warned Grady, "This won't be man to man, now. Our little special agent wants to interrogate you."

Grady had shrugged. "Let's get it over with, then."

But right now he looked mighty uncomfortable. Wes was glad when the intercom buzzed and Foley said, "Royce Denton here to talk to you, sir."

Wes looked politely at Jessup. "Do you want to talk to the congressional candidate's brother?"

"Of course!" Jessup flipped his hand impatiently.

"Send him in," Wes told Foley, then looked at Grady. "Sims, go check the reports from the neighbors on Goldstein and Sears. Especially cars. See if anything looks odd."

"Yessir." Grady unfolded his long limbs and escaped grate-

162

fully, pausing only to hold the door for Royce Denton as he came in.

"Sheriff! Glad to see you!" Royce Denton strode in, hand extended.

Wes shook it and said, "This is Special Agent Jessup."

"Yes, we've met," Royce said. "Is it true? There's some connection with the Klan?"

"Looks that way," Jessup said.

"You want to sit down?" Wes asked.

"No, no, this'll just take a minute. But I— Well, it's just so unbelievable! I mean, in the sixties there were plenty of Klan members around, a lot of Dad's political supporters, like Tom Straub. But everyone quit after the Hines thing, I thought." To Wes, Royce looked strung tight. There was a tenseness around his eyes and his easy smile was nowhere to be seen. Not surprising. Learning that your kid sister had died at the hands of the Klan was a shocker, and this guy already had a lot to contend with. Wes remembered the glazed gauntness of the once-powerful judge. Royce had a tough row to hoe right now.

Jessup was standing too, drawn up to his full height, such as it was. The fluorescent light gleamed blue on his slick hair. He said, "We're checking on a number of possibilities. Goldstein and Sears aren't in the national computer, but we have some information on the Klan members in this county."

Wes said, "The ones who used to be active. He's also checking the ones who attended a recent Klan rally in Kentucky."

"Yes, yes, of course." Jessup had been reluctant to admit that there were possibilities other than incompetence in Wes's department, and Wes was pleased to see that Royce's presence had improved the little agent's attitude. He decided to stay quiet and let Jessup continue. "We talked to Goldstein's wife, investigating possible connections with the black man who was killed. We're checking everything we can. But this, this sad discovery about your sister makes it look as though we have a long-standing problem. So I've asked for all the information we can get from those days, too."

Royce said, "That ought to eliminate some of the possibilities, right? Has to be someone who's been around awhile. But of course most of the old boys aren't recent arrivals anyway."

He was right on the button there, Wes reflected. Al Evans, Mel Sims, Lester Holtz—they'd all been around a long time. Tom Straub had died a few years ago, leaving his service station to Gil Newton and Bert Mackay. But with secret societies and invisible empires, it was hard to know who was in and who wasn't.

Jessup asked, "Do you have any ideas about how your sister might have tied in to the Klan?" Royce was already shaking his head, but Jessup went on, "For example, I'm told she was interested in motorcycles. Could there be some connection there?"

"Wes, what do you think?" Royce asked. "You went over this stuff with a fine-tooth comb."

"Yeah." Wes hitched up his trousers. "We never did get ahold of those bikers, except to talk to them. We figured out who they must've been, a bunch that ran between Bloomington and Terre Haute, probably drug runs and stuff like that. Main guy was a Charlie Hatchet, he called himself. We pulled him in, talked to him, heard all about his philosophy of life and what he thought oughta be done to all sheriffs and their deputies. Nothing that had to do with young Phyllis. One of his pals cracked a little, gave me the names of girls they hung out with in Terre Haute."

"You didn't tell me about that!" Royce exclaimed.

"I ran the names by you," Wes said. "Asked if you'd heard of them. But see, the girls' names were Puma, Rocket, and Karly King."

"Oh, I remember. I didn't know what you were talking about."

"Nobody did. Wasn't much of a lead, we thought then. We looked, but couldn't find any other organized bikers."

Jessup said, "The report listed other names for those girls."

"Not last names," Wes said. "Terre Haute tracked them down. Lori, Michelle, and Karla was all they could get. Terre Haute said they liked drugs and leather and chains, and they were about fifteen years old."

Royce Denton said in a tight voice, "Phyllis was only twelve when she disappeared."

"Yeah. That's why I didn't tell you more details then. Terre Haute couldn't get any of the bikers or the girls to admit to knowing Phyllis, or anybody else from here. None of her family or school friends had ever heard of any of the bikers. Seemed more useful to look for some other explanation of that leather-jacket photo. But we couldn't find any."

Jessup said, "In our experience, white supremacists and bikers don't always agree politically."

"In our experience too," said Wes.

"But you've checked with Terre Haute again?" Royce asked.

Wes nodded. "Called them as soon as Hopkins found the body, told them to reclassify as suspicious death and get us an update on all the bikers and their gals. No word yet. Maybe Special Agent Jessup could speed them up."

Jessup nodded curtly and made a note.

Wes said, "Any word from the judge? Hopkins thinks he may be trying to tell us something about the Klan connection."

Royce shook his head. "No. He's in real bad shape. He was coherent for a few minutes yesterday. But he was more interested in having his dinner taken away. Didn't suit him. Maybe his appetite's gone too. But Mother and I are trying to stay alert."

"The nurse?" Wes asked.

Royce shrugged. "We asked her but she hasn't reported much. How's Deputy Hopkins doing on his calendar?"

"She's working on it," Wes said, "going over the appointments. And she went up to Bloomington today to talk to that professor who found the body. Something in the professor's story may have triggered the connection your dad is trying to tell us."

"Yeah, I'm interested in that professor," Royce said. "Deputy Hopkins said she was strange. My mother agrees—she didn't believe her story at first. Dad was the one who thought we should check it out."

Wes nodded. "Yeah, Hopkins is hoping that he'll be able to make us understand whatever he knows. Or guesses."

"It's a real uphill fight," Royce said soberly. Jessup nodded wisely, and Wes felt irritated again. Jessup came clanking in from outside, hadn't even known the judge, and here he was nodding and pulling a long face as if he knew what Royce meant.

Royce said, "Deputy Hopkins hasn't called back?"

"Not yet." Wes glanced at his watch. "Shouldn't be much longer." In fact, she should have reported quite a while ago. She'd learned something, probably, and was tracking it down before she checked in. Ordinarily he'd chew her out, but he took a secret pleasure now in realizing that the home team had a chance to score a point without outside meddling.

But why the hell hadn't Professor Wolfe told her whatever it was before? This was the third goddamned time Marty had interviewed her.

Jessup was saying to Royce, "We have the full resources of the Bureau working on the Klan and other white supremacy groups in the area. We'll see what we can add on the bikers. We're checking background on both Goldstein and Sears too. But of course your sister was so young, it's more difficult. If you can develop any information, it could be very helpful."

Royce nodded. "So the best thing we can do is go home and listen to the old man."

"I'm afraid so, sir," Jessup said. "Let's talk again tomorrow. I may have a report by then."

"Thanks." They shook hands and Royce Denton left.

When the door closed, Jessup jerked around to face Wes, his dark brows looking like a painted frown on his smooth pale face. "Professor Wolfe," he snapped. "You haven't said anything about interviewing this professor again."

"Can't tell you everything at once," Wes said mildly. Now that Marty Hopkins had been there, Jessup could mess around to his heart's content. So he added, "The professor killed a man in Pennsylvania. Self-defense. Just got the report this morning." He tapped District Attorney Cooper's packet.

"Why the hell didn't you mention that?" Jessup grabbed the papers and began to flip through them.

"I was getting to it," Wes said. "But we got sidetracked into talking to Deputy Sims."

Jessup glared at him. "Where can I find, find this Professor Wolfe?"

"Biology department, Indiana University," Wes said helpfully. "Jordan Hall. I forget the office number."

"See you later." Jessup clattered briskly out the door.

Wes sat down and began to pull things from his in-box. He was smiling to himself. The idea of the FBI up against Professor Wolfe kind of appealed to him. Serve them both right.

25

IT WAS DUSK BY THE TIME MARTY FOUND THE MADISON ROAD outside Louisville, and she decided she'd better call Aunt Vonnie. But Brad answered. "Kitten! Where the hell are you?"

"Working late. Just wanted to see how things were going."

"We gotta talk, kitten."

"Yeah. I know. But this is a major case, Brad."

"Let Wes handle it, okay? You're a wife. A mother."

It was like a knife in her side. She said hotly, "I'm also a—"

"You're also the sexiest lady in fifty states." His voice was low and earnest and she could almost see the hunger in his dark eyes. "I need you, kitten! Don't you understand? I love you!"

"Shoot, Brad." Marty slumped against the side of the phone booth and combed her fingers through her hair. She wanted him too, dammit, wanted his hands on her skin, his voice in her ear instead of sixty miles away on the phone. "I'll come back as soon as I can. You know that."

"Where are you? Sheriff said Bloomington."

"No, I'm—" Marty caught herself. She had no business telling Brad she was in Louisville before she even told Wes. She said, "I'm south of Bloomington now. It's still the same job. Take me a couple more hours. Is Aunt Vonnie around?"

"She went out in a huff half an hour ago."

"Shoot, Brad, what did— Oh, never mind." No time now for her to referee that complex, ongoing battle. She asked instead, "Is Chrissie there?"

"Come on home, kitten."

"In a couple of hours. Let me talk to Chrissie, Brad."

He muffled the receiver but she heard him calling, "Chrissie, angel! It's your long-lost mama!"

Then her daughter's voice said, "Mom?"

"Hi, kiddo. Just wanted to tell you I'd be back in a couple of hours."

"You have to work?" Chrissie's tone was accusatory.

"Hey, don't make it sound like I'm clubbing baby seals. I'm the good guy, remember?"

"Mm."

"Okay, listen." Marty sighed. "You know that lady who called real early, about the fire?"

"Yeah." Grudging curiosity crept into her daughter's voice.

"And remember that skeleton I found in the cave?"

"Yeah! That was—yucky."

"Sure was. Well, it turns out they're connected, but we don't know how yet. So the sheriff and I and all the others are working on it. Even the FBI is helping. It's a really big case."

"Mmm." There was a brief silence. "Well, Daddy and I want you to come home."

"I know, honey, I want to come home too. I will, soon as I finish this part of the job."

"Daddy says girls shouldn't be interested in that kind of stuff."

"Well, we can talk about it later." Marty didn't want to fight. But she saw her knuckles whitening as she clenched the receiver. When she saw that in someone she was questioning, it was a signal to follow up, the point was important. And somewhere in the back of her mind, words chimed: *You've chosen well. Defend your self. For your daughter's sake too.* She said, "Chrissie, the thing is, your daddy's in the entertainment business, so his job is to keep people cheered up. But sometimes bad things happen, and somebody has to catch the bad guys, even if it's not very cheerful."

"Mm."

"Maybe he's right that girls shouldn't be sheriffs, but it's okay for grown-up women to be sheriffs. Law enforcement is really important, because we want to stop the bad people who do bad things to other people. It's really important. And if a woman is good at it, that's what she should do."

"Mm." Another dubious pause. Chrissie said, "But don't you want to take care of Daddy and me?"

"Honey, of course I do. But this is the kind of job where I have to take care of other people too. Some of them are in bad trouble. And you and Daddy are strong and smart, you know how to take care of yourself while I'm helping people with really bad problems. Then afterward we can take care of each other. Okay?"

"Mm. Okay."

"I'll be back as soon as I can. Okay?"

"Okay."

" 'Bye for now."

" 'Bye, Mommy."

As she hung up Marty realized she'd forgotten to ask if Chrissie had finished her homework. Dammit, Brad and Aunt Vonnie were right, she was a pretty poor excuse for a mother.

But she had to work, dammit, when she never knew what Brad would be earning. Or spending. If she could just get him to buckle down and work here in Indiana instead of aiming for that elusive star, then—

Then what? Then she'd want to sit around all day, dusting vases and waiting for Chrissie to come home from school?

Face it, Hopkins, you told Chrissie the honest truth. You're doing important work, helping with bad problems, and you love it. And you're curious as hell to find out about Phyllis Denton, about what the dead girl's friend might tell you.

She got her jacket from the trunk of the cruiser. Floyd's cave pack was still in there—ought to return that soon. She drove out the Madison Road. The number she'd found in the directory was out where the sidewalks ended. In the dusk it was hard to see a lot of details but she had an impression of middle-class houses, kept up with care but not fanaticism. Lawns were mowed but not always edged, hedges were un-clipped but well weeded. When she reached the Willison num-ber she was pleased to see lights downstairs. The broad front porch had a swing and terra-cotta pots of flowering plants, young petunias and marigolds. Marty pushed the doorbell.

The porch light flashed on and the inner door swung open immediately. A graying man in his late fifties stood on the other side of the screen. He wore a plaid work shirt, twill trousers, and hornrimmed glasses on his lumpy nose. His eyes were blue and anxious behind them. Like the yards, he seemed clean but unfussy, his short gray hair uncombed and spiky. "Hello, Officer."

"Hello. I'm Deputy Hopkins, from the Nichols County Sher-iff's Department. Indiana."

"Indiana!" He nodded vigorously and shoved the screen door wide for her. "Please come in. What have you heard?"

A girl, younger than Chrissie, was shyly holding on to the man's belt. Marty smiled at her, than glanced around the room. Beige wall-to-wall carpeting, a brick fireplace, a coloring book and crayons on a flowered print sofa, a big TV in the corner silently showing Archie Bunker's mobile face. She asked, "Is this Alma Willison's house?"

"Yes. You have news of her? In Indiana?"

"News?" She swung her gaze back to the man. He was staring at her anxiously, blinking behind the hornrims. The little girl was watching them both, her blue eyes worried too. Marty asked, "Who are you, sir?"

"Oh. I'm Wayne Willison. I'm Alma's husband. And this is Milly." He patted the little girl on her head.

"See, I'm working on a case in our county, and someone said Alma had some information about it. So I'd like to talk to her."

"But she's not here!" Agitated, he ran his hand across his head the wrong way, and she saw why his hair was spiky.

Marty asked, "Will she be back soon?"

"I don't know! I'd hoped that you— See, I was at work. And I don't know where she is, or when she's coming back, or—" He glanced down at the little girl and closed his mouth firmly.

A silent rumble of dread filled Marty, like the vibration of a bass note too far away to hear. She said, "Your wife doesn't often go off alone, then?"

He shook his head vigorously. "Never. We've got Milly, you see."

The little girl looked up at Marty and said, "We were digging. And Grandma went away."

Marty crouched down to Milly's level and asked, "Did she tell you where she went, honey?"

"No." Milly had a brown ponytail that flicked back and forth as she shook her head. "Grandma was digging. And I was pulling up a grapevine that chokes things. And then I got the mail, I washed my hands first. And then I went out again. See, one of the envelopes had writing on it."

"Okay," Marty said encouragingly. "And then?"

"And then Grandma was gone. And I went to Timmy's house, and she wasn't there either."

"And that was the last time you saw Grandma?"

"Yeah. She shouldn't go away without telling us."

"Yeah." Marty stood up and looked at Willison. "When did all this happen?"

"Yesterday afternoon," he said. "And Alma never did anything like that. I called the police last night when she didn't come back. Louisville police. But they said they couldn't do much when an adult left. They didn't understand! She doesn't do things like this! They said they'd keep their eyes open but they couldn't force her to come back." He shook his head in wonder. "Force her! They said that."

Marty nodded slowly. People ran off sometimes, husbands and occasionally wives, and generally they didn't want to be found. Running off was cheaper than divorce. And sometimes after a week or two they decided life in the big world was even worse than what they'd run away from, and they came back. The Louisville cops were right, you couldn't force people back together. Better to make sympathetic noises at the family, note down the name just in case, and then get on with solving the solvable crimes.

But still that low note of dread thrummed in her soul.

She asked Wayne Willison, "Did she leave any note? Any messages with neighbors?"

"No, and believe me, I asked everybody! Jan—she's the neighbor who had Milly—she hadn't heard anything. Alma's garden tools and her hat were out where Milly left her. And she didn't take the car. So I've been searching all over, anyplace we can walk, but I haven't found—anything."

"She must have gotten a lift, then."

"She would have left word!"

"Yes, sir. Now, I don't mean to alarm you, but I have to ask. Have you received any kind of call or note for ransom?"

He shook his head. "Nothing. The Louisville police asked that too. I just don't understand it." His voice was thick with fear for his wife.

"Yes, sir. It's hard to understand."

"There was only one odd thing. I told the police on the phone and he said he'd come take a look as soon as he had time. So I saved it."

"What is it?"

"Came in yesterday's mail. Milly brought it in, she says, about the time that Alma—left. But it's not a note, or a threat, or anything. And it was mailed a long time ago." Willison took an envelope from the mantel. "This thing," he said apologetically. "Probably nothing. I can't figure it out." He held it out to Marty.

The outside of the envelope was scuffed, postmarked Louisville, Alma's name and address in neatly penciled letters. The postmark was a month old. "This came yesterday, you said?" Marty asked.

He bent to Milly. "Was this in the mailbox yesterday, sweetie?"

"Yeah. It has writing on it, see? Not typing. Grandma said letters were special if they had writing. But when I went to tell her, she was gone already. She wasn't at Timmy's house either. I looked."

"You did the right thing, sweetie," Willison told her.

The envelope had been slit open and Marty tapped the contents into her hand. A three-by-five card. Nothing on it, no message, except for the too-familiar sketch of a cross and blood drop.

Marty drew a deep shuddering breath. She had to tell Wes. And the Louisville cops. She was way the hell out of her jurisdiction. She said, "Mr. Willison, this may be important evidence. I'd like to make a phone call. And then, if you and Milly will come with me to your local police station, I think I can persuade them to step up their efforts to find your wife."

Willison licked his lips. "Thank you," he said. But Marty saw that he knew it wasn't good news.

26

"SHE WON'T TALK TO YOU," SAID CALLIE.

Marty saw Wolfe's pickup parked by the moonlit drive. She pushed a curl out of her eyes. It had already been a long night. She'd taken Wayne Willison and little Milly to the Louisville police, explained that Alma might be in trouble with the Klan, and put them in touch with Wes. After they'd talked to him they'd told her grumpily to get back to her own jurisdiction. "This thing'll get the feds in. That's enough outsiders," they'd said. "We'll take care of the Willisons and keep in touch." And she hadn't learned much from Wayne Willison anyway. He'd said that Alma's interests were Milly, her church activities, and her garden, but he hadn't recognized Phyllis Denton's name. Alma had so many friends, he explained, and he didn't keep track. So Marty and Wes had decided to tackle the professor again.

Not that it was doing any good. Callie just stood there in her jeans and green T-shirt with a bear cub design, polite but unhelpful. Marty said impatiently, "Look, it's really important."

Callie nodded. "I'm sorry. But Laurel got back from campus

173

P. M. CARLSON

and said the FBI was asking about Professor Wolfe. She
doesn't want to talk to them."

"So she's hiding from me too? Like I said, it's important."

Callie shrugged. "Yeah, I'm sorry."

Marty hadn't expected such a firm refusal from the young
woman who'd casually waved her on to the quarry the first
time she'd come. A pleasant-looking young woman, with dim-
ples, thin lips, intelligent eyes. What made her tick? How
could Marty win her over? What made her so loyal to Wolfe,
anyway? "What do people study with her, Callie?" Marty
asked.

"Biology. Some want to be veterinarians—she's licensed, you
know. Others are more theoretical. I'm studying adaptation."

"Adaptation."

"Evolutionary adaptation in cave crayfish. *Orconectes pellu-
cidus*. How the species evolved to fit its ecological niche—you
know, the particular places they live."

"You mean like caves are dark, so they don't need eyes?
That kind of thing?"

"Yeah. Of course, not needing them is only half the story.
The other half is that eyes are bad for them."

"Bad for them?" Marty was curious despite herself. "How
come? Why can't they just have eyes, and not use them?"

Callie nodded. "That's the question behind my thesis. Not
just eyes, of course. Actually there are lots of differences between *Orconectes* and surface crayfish. The darkness causes the
differences only indirectly, because plants can't grow and
make food in darkness. So the big problem in a cave is lack
of food. The bottom of the food chain is kaput."

"What do they do?"

"Well, start with the smallest. The microorganisms and
worms and so forth feed on things that wash in from the
surface during the spring floods. Like CARE packages coming
from the surface. There's not much food, and it only comes
occasionally. So cave creatures have evolved to be ultra-
sensitive to the nearness of food." Callie was gesturing enthusiastically now. "Also, they time their reproductive cycles to
take advantage of the flood season. So, farther up the food
chain, predators like *Orconectes* have evolved to be energy-

174

efficient, and to withstand long periods of fasting, and to reproduce in phase with their prey. On the surface, *Orconectes* can't compete with larger crayfish that have eyes and are dark enough to be camouflaged from predators. But in the dark, they win hands down."

"Okay, but I still don't see why they don't have eyes."

"Because it takes energy to grow eyes. And in the dark, it's a waste of resources to grow them. So the individuals with small or no eyes are more energy-efficient in the dark."

"You mean, not having eyes gives them more miles to the gallon."

Callie laughed. "Yeah. In species after species, eyes are lost when animals evolve in a totally dark environment. Parasitic worms that live in mammalian guts have become eyeless too."

Time to try again. Marty said, "Look, I've got a kid at home I haven't seen all day. Please tell Professor Wolfe I'm here."

"She knows. She won't talk to you."

Damn the woman. "I thought it was the FBI she was avoiding!"

"She said she'd told you all she could, and you'd know how much to tell them. And she went off to the woods. I mean, I'm sorry about your kid. But the truth is, she won't talk to you."

"The best way to get rid of the FBI is to solve this damn case! But everything she's told me just complicates things!"

Callie nodded soberly. "She does that to all her students. Leaves us with new questions to solve for ourselves."

"I'm not her student!"

Callie smiled gently. "Don't be too sure."

Marty kicked the porch post. "Look," she said. "Tell her Alma Willison has gone missing. And a Klan card was sent to her house. And I want to hear from her!" She turned away abruptly, gave one despairing look at the black and tangled woods, and stomped back to her cruiser. Damn the woman! She careened down the driveway too fast and screeched onto the highway.

The sax player's question still rang in her head: *What kind of white trash do you keep in your county?* And her own earnest reply: *My job is to find that trash and clean it out.* Sure, Hopkins, and a great job you're doing, too.

Well, try again tomorrow. Right now it was time to get home to her disintegrating family.

27

WEDNESDAY MORNING WAS DEPRESSING.

Wes Cochran arrived at headquarters to find a TV van parked in front, and a heavily made-up, earnest, curly haired brunette talking into a camera. She broke off as he approached the door and turned to him. "Sheriff Cocker, have you caught the murderer?"

He gave her a goofy Sheriff Cocker grin and said into her mike, "We sure are trying. And we're asking for the full cooperation of the public."

"What's next in the . . ." she began, but Wes turned away and chugged up the steps into the office. Where the hell was Pfann? He smiled and nodded at the reporters inside without slowing down to answer their questions, beelining back to his own haven. Except that's where he found Pfann, taking refuge there with Jessup.

"Hey, Art, you're missing your big chance to be on TV," he said mildly, nodding to them both.

"I didn't miss anything. She asked me fourteen questions and I gave her the same answer fourteen times. Got tired of it. Then she started in on Jessup and we decided to hide out."

Wes gave up any hopes he'd had of private reflection and stuck his head back into the main office. "Hopkins! Sims! Mason! Time for a meeting!"

Gratefully, the three abandoned the noisy front desks and joined the others in Wes's office. Wes said, "Let's compare notes and then get this thing solved. We've had a new development. Art, you called Mr. Jessup last night about the Willison woman?"

"Yeah. Left him a message."

"But I don't see what this has to do with the rest," Jessup said.

"Hopkins, tell us about it, from the beginning."

Hopkins looked tired. He could tell from the slump of her shoulders, the shadows around her eyes. Wes felt a qualm. Was this case too much for her? She was good, damn good, but she'd never been involved in a situation this ugly. Not that he had either, not since the war. Well, hell, he'd tried his best to keep her out of it, even though she'd wanted in so bad. He knew she didn't know what she was asking for. But then the damn Klan card turned up in the dead girl's Bible and she was in the thick of it too. All he could do now was try to protect her from the worst of the mess.

Not that she'd thank him for it.

She was summarizing her trip to Kentucky in self-consciously official language. "I informed Mr. Willison that we should bring this to the attention of the Louisville police immediately. I called Sheriff Cochran to inform him of the situation, then proceeded with Mr. Willison and Milly to the—"

"Who's Milly?" Jessup asked.

"The little girl I mentioned earlier. Willison's granddaughter."

"Go on."

"I took them to the nearest police station and explained the situation to Sergeant Ellmann there. He contacted Sheriff Cochran."

"This was at nine-o-eight P.M.," Wes said. "Sergeant Ellmann and I agreed to keep in touch. I informed him that federal agents were assisting on the case, and he agreed to coordinate his investigation with ours."

"Did you find out anything about this missing woman?" Jessup asked Hopkins.

"Yes, sir. On the way to the Louisville police, I questioned Wayne Willison about his wife. She's fifty-eight years old, five

177

foot five, one hundred thirty-five, hazel eyes, graying brown hair. The little girl's mother is dead so she's living with her grandparents, the Willisons. Alma Willison used to be a book-keeper with Kentucky Textile Products but is a full-time home-maker now. Active in church groups, PTA, neighborhood activities."

"Are any of those activities of a nature to upset the Klan?"

"Not that I could tell, except maybe for local mission work for her church. Maybe they get into helping black families or something. I didn't have time to ask. Willison mentioned church suppers, overseas medical relief, garden club. That kind of thing. Still, I only had time to hear a brief description. Sergeant Ellmann will send a photo and more details soon."

"Or you can talk to Willison yourself," Wes put in. "Hop-kins, after you left you returned to Professor Wolfe and asked her for more information, right?"

"I tried, sir. It was too late to see the Dentons again, but Professor Wolfe keeps late hours and I hoped to talk to her. But she wasn't there."

"Where the hell does she keep herself?" Jessup broke in. "I looked for her most of the day. At her house, at her office. But at least I found a colleague of hers, a Professor Hart, who promised to help us."

Hopkins nodded at him soberly, but Wes thought he saw a hint of amusement in her gray eyes. He said, "Soon as we finish here, we'll go see Royce Denton. He'll maybe know if there's some connection between the Denton girl and Mrs. Willison. Besides the Klan card, I mean. Now, we've got two other murders too. Hopkins, did you ask if the Willison woman knew Goldstein or Sears?"

"Yes, sir. Mr. Willison didn't recognize the names. He didn't recognize Phyllis Denton's name either. All we have is Professor Wolfe's statement that Mrs. Willison knew Phyllis. But Professor Wolfe says she doesn't know Mrs. Willison."

"Are we really sure they're connected?" asked Wes. "What did Wolfe know about the Klan cards?"

"Nothing, she says. But that's one of the things I wanted to ask her about."

Wes looked at her, uneasy again about the strange and elusive professor. Some bad 'uns beat the law once and figured they were untouchable. Was Professor Wolfe in that category? Teasing them, making a game of a crime she herself had committed? There was no fear in Marty's tired gray eyes. All the same, he'd make sure she had backup from now on when she spoke to this Wolfe character.

Art Pfann said, "The Klan is so splintered these days. It could be separate groups."

"It was the same kind of drawing," Hopkins said firmly. "Goldstein's and Willison's card were done by the same guy. I haven't seen the other two."

"Three," said Wes. "The Goldsteins were carded before the murder. That one even had a message on it. There was no message on the Willison card?"

"No, sir. Just the drawing, just like Goldstein's. I guess that's a bad sign."

Wes nodded. It was a bad sign, all right. "Mr. Jessup, have your people come up with any connections yet?"

"We've only been here two days!"

"Yessir, I know. Hard to get the feel of a place in two days."

"We're putting it into the computer. I'll send in the information on the Willison woman as we get it. And I'll talk to this Wolfe woman soon."

"Good. Sims, Mason, what's new on Goldstein?"

Grady Sims cleared his throat. "Well, sir, we interviewed all Goldstein's neighbors again. We think Marty's idea was right. One neighbor, it was Joe Matthews, he saw a car similar to Willie Sears's car. It was that same night that Goldstein was killed, and it was parked downhill from Goldstein's. Matthews can't see Goldstein's from his place because of a hedge. But if Sears was parked where Matthews says, he coulda seen something."

"Good work. Did the two know each other? Goldstein and Sears?"

"Not that we could find out. We asked everybody, and lots of people knew who Willie Sears was when we reminded them he was a high-school custodian. But nobody knew Goldstein, except his landlord and Reba at the post office. And all those Bloomington people."

"Did you ask folks if either Goldstein or Sears could have known Phyllis Denton?"

"Yeah, I mean yessir, but it's not real clear. Willie's worked about twenty years at the high school, but see, Phyllis never did get old enough to go to high school. The guys who knew Sears were pretty sure he'd remember Hal Junior and Royce. But the little sister probably didn't get to the high school often."

"And Goldstein, no connection with Phyllis there, I suppose."

"We didn't find anything, no, sir."

Hopkins said, "Wonder if Goldstein ever rode a motor-cycle."

"A motorcycle?" Wes nodded slowly. Goldstein had been an IU student in the process of dropping out at about the time the Denton kid had disappeared. If they could connect Goldstein to Phyllis Denton, and figure out why Wolfe had connected her to the Willison woman, that left only Willie Sears. And Sears was black, maybe connected somehow to Goldstein's wife, Kizzy, or maybe a witness to some part of the Goldstein killing. Plenty of reasons for murder in the eyes of some Klansmen.

But why the white Christian woman? And the white Christian girl? Klansmen were supposed to protect white Christian women and girls.

But if the white Christian girls were running around with Jews on motorcycles—

They needed more facts. No sense running ahead of the facts. Wes said, "Royce Denton oughta be in his office today. Let's go."

28

ROYCE DENTON CHECKED THE TITLE SEARCH ON THE BRAUNER property and made a note to have Annie schedule the closing. Everything was in order. Good to have something in his life in order. He'd reached the point of almost enjoying the run-of-the-mill wills and ordinary land transactions that had bored him when he first joined his brother and began practicing law. Back then he'd sometimes been jealous of Hal, who had taken most of the interesting trials that came their way, letting his little brother handle everyday paperwork. But Hal soon began itching for wider horizons, especially in politics, and he'd moved to Bloomington almost eagerly when it became clear that there wasn't enough work in Nichols County for two lawyers who had to disqualify themselves every time the trial was assigned to their father. Royce had enjoyed the extra work after Hal left, the competitive excitement of cases that had to be won, not merely recorded properly. But these days, exciting cases just meant more stress.

He put his pen back in its onyx holder. His brother's selection, of course—the whole office was Hal's taste, or rather Hal's decorator's taste: the old-gold walls, the chestnut-colored leather chairs, the pale almond carpet and furniture. Pleasant enough, not worth changing, although if it had been his own choice he would have preferred a stately wooden desk to the sleek metal one where he sat now. He ought to do something about it. He'd had hand-me-downs all his life, it seemed. Quality things—jackets, bikes, guns, offices—but mostly used, by his brother or by his father. Even his ex-wife, Dorothy, had been Hal's girlfriend first. One of these days, Royce decided, he ought to try something on his own.

He was too tired right now, though. Ever since Dorothy had left he'd been tired, and after he'd moved back to the old place to take care of his father, the edge was really gone. Before that, he'd been absorbed in his work, so absorbed that the divorce had come as a shock. He'd thought everything was okay. Sure, they argued sometimes, but didn't everybody? And of course sometimes he had to work long hours, researching some case or other. His father had done the same. But Dorothy hadn't understood.

Well, water under the bridge.

But the divorce had thrown him off stride. And then when his father had fallen ill, he'd felt that the fixed points in his life had collapsed, that suddenly he was no longer rolling along a solid, well-marked highway but was floundering in sand. Mother was too upset to be of any help now—quite the opposite; he was the one who had to keep her from losing her balance. And Hal was upset by Dad's illness too, and too wrapped up in his own political hopes to notice Royce's problems.

So, ordinary work had become a solace, an orderly center to the turmoil of his life.

He put the Brauner papers into the box for Annie but hadn't yet opened the next folder when Hal knocked and then strode in without waiting. "Well, hello!" said Royce.

"Hi." Hal closed the door and flopped back into the client's chair, legs outflung. He loosened his necktie and closed his eyes. "God, I'm tired."

"Me too. What brings you here?"

"I'm on my way to see Dad. Channel 6 canceled so I'm just detouring on my way to lunch in Paoli. How's Dad?"

"Pretty rotten, Hal."

"Worse?" His brother's sad eyes clicked open to meet his.

"Yeah." Royce nodded. "They can't increase the sedative any more. But every time it starts wearing off, he has a seizure. I don't think he's been fully asleep for two days. Or fully awake."

"God." Hal rubbed a hand over his face. "He's not going to make it, is he?"

There was no way to say it gently. "No."

"Hell." Hand still over his face, Hal drew a long breath. Then he asked, "How's Mother?"

"Distraught. Won't leave him. Even when Lisa's on duty."

"What a mess." Hal rolled his head back. "And all this stuff about Phyllis. God, I can't believe it! Had two reporters snag me already today, asking about my sister's tragic death and about the Klan. What the hell am I supposed to say? But my campaign manager says if I come out too strong against it, I'm insulting the values of half the voters Dad's age. He's right. But if I don't— See, he's developing this family-man image for me with Penny and the kids, while the press is busy asking about motorcycles and night riders. God!"

"Well, he went along with calling in the cops again."

"None of us ever dreamed they'd find this Klan connection!"

"I know. That little deputy of Cochran's opened a real can of worms. Still—I for one want to know what happened to my sister."

"Yeah. Yeah, me too. God, that poor kid!"

"I know. I want to smash the guys that did it, too. And maybe —" The intercom sounded. Royce said, "Yes?"

"Mr. Denton, the sheriff and some other people are out here," came Annie's voice.

Royce raised his eyebrows in inquiry. Hal nodded and adjusted his necktie. "Send them in," Royce said into the box.

Wes Cochran opened the door and held it for Marty Hopkins, all business today in her crisp khaki uniform, and for the smooth little FBI agent, what was his name, Jessup. They shook hands all around. Cochran said, "Glad we caught you both here. We've got a new development and need to know how your sister fits in."

"A new development?" Hal said warily.

"You found out who did it?" Royce tried not to sound too eager. He wanted to hear—for his sister's sake, for his parents' sake, for his own sake. Whoever had killed Phyllis—or caused the accident that killed her, he reminded himself, trying to be fair in the midst of his rage—whoever it was, he must pay.

"No, sir, we don't know, not yet," Wes Cochran said. "This may or may not lead somewhere. Hopkins, run it by them."

"I went back to talk to that biology professor," Marty Hopkins said. She looked tired today, Royce thought, but there was still intelligence in her eyes, and warm sympathy. "The one who told us that your sister was in that cave."

"You asked her about the Klan card they found with Phyllis?" Royce asked.

"Yes, sir, and she said she didn't know anything about the Klan. But she said I should see Alma Willison, in Louisville." She paused, watching them closely.

Special Agent Jessup asked, "Do you know Mrs. Willison?"

Hal frowned. "No. I don't know her."

"I'm a blank too," Royce said.

Hal added, "Though there's something. Louisville?" He closed his eyes for a moment, then shook his head again. "Sorry. Whatever it is, I can't remember. Maybe it'll come to me."

"So what about this Alma Willison?" Royce asked.

"In her late fifties. Five-five, one-thirty-five, graying hair," Wes said. "Used to be a bookkeeper for Kentucky Textile. Any of that ring bells?"

Hal shook his head. The sheriff said, "Hopkins, go on, tell the rest."

"Yeah, what did she say?" Royce asked. "This Mrs. Willison?"

Marty Hopkins pushed aside a drooping curl. "She wasn't there," she said. "She went missing Monday afternoon. And the thing is, a Klan card was mailed to her house."

"A Klan card? And she's missing?" Hal looked at Royce in consternation. "What the hell is going on here?"

Wes Cochran said, "We're all trying to find out. We're working with Louisville too, of course."

Royce said, "This professor must know something! What does she say?"

"Special Agent Jessup will be talking to her soon. We came here first, hoping you could help. Did Phyllis have friends in Louisville? Or go there for some reason? What I can't figure is, this Willison woman is a lot older than Phyllis."

Marty Hopkins said, "Teacher? Scout leader, maybe?"

"I don't remember!" Hal's fists were clenching and unclenching. "And I just don't understand this Klan stuff! Phyllis was just a kid, for God's sake! She was—"

Royce laid a hand on his brother's arm. "Hal," he said. "Calm down. The press doesn't have any of this, right, Sheriff Cochran?"

"That's right." Cochran's eyes were on Hal, sympathetic but alert. "We don't even know for sure that the professor's right about Phyllis knowing the Willison woman. We're looking for confirmation, that's all. That's why we're asking you. Another question." The sheriff hitched up his trousers. "We wondered if this motorcycle photo could be connected to Goldstein. Do you remember if Phyllis ever mentioned his name?"

"Goldstein?" Royce shook his head. "I don't remember anything like that. Hal?"

"No."

"We weren't around much at that time," Royce continued. "But Mother was. Look, why don't I knock off and we'll all go talk to Mother? Okay, Hal?"

"Yeah." Hal rubbed his face. "She'll know, won't she?"

But his mother didn't turn out to be a lot of help. She came partway downstairs when she heard the door open and watched them all file in. Hal ran up a few steps and she embraced him with one arm, looking at the others, her worried eyes moving from him to Sheriff Cochran to Special Agent Jessup and resting at last on Marty Hopkins.

"Mother, how's Dad?" Hal asked.

She glanced upstairs. Her lips tightened and she shook her head. Royce heard steady thumping from his father's bedroom. Sounded bad. Where did the old man get his strength? His mother asked, "Is there news? About Phyllis?" She was looking at Marty Hopkins.

"Not news, Mrs. Denton. More questions."

"Goldstein," said Royce. "Did Phyllis know someone named Goldstein?"

"No. I don't think so. She never mentioned a Goldstein." Her eyes strayed upstairs again.

"Maybe a motorcyclist? A biker?" Royce pressed.

She shook her head, puzzled. "No. The sheriff asked about motorcycles before, but I don't remember. I didn't—" Her voice broke. "God help me, I didn't pay enough attention to her."

Tears slid down his mother's cheeks. Royce took a step up toward her but Hal was already hugging her so he changed the subject instead. "Mother, this Professor Wolfe. The one who told Deputy Hopkins where Phyllis was? She also told her to talk to a Kentucky woman named Alma Willison. She said this Mrs. Willison had known Phyllis."

His mother turned her head from Hal's shirt, a handkerchief still lifted to her eyes. She looked hopefully at Marty Hopkins. "What did she say? Did you talk to her?"

Marty's curly head shook somberly, and Royce said, "We're trying, Mother. The trouble is, this Mrs. Willison seems to be missing."

"Missing?" She looked at him blankly. "What do you mean, missing?"

Hal said, "Don't upset her, Royce."

Wes Cochran cleared his throat. "Excuse me, Mr. Denton. But it'd be real helpful if Mrs. Denton could try to remember. She's said she doesn't know how her daughter might be involved with the Klan. But the Klan card connects her and the Willison woman."

"The Klan? I don't understand." Her eyes slid fearfully from Wes to Royce to Marty.

Marty said gently, "When I went to talk to Mrs. Willison she'd gone missing. Her husband didn't know where she was, she hadn't left any messages. But there was a Klan card that arrived the same day. Her little granddaughter told me it had come with the mail the day Mrs. Willison disappeared. Mrs. Denton, you told me to ask about Alma. Why? Who is she?"

His mother shuddered and Hal patted her shoulder. She said, "A Klan card? Why? I don't— Are the Willisons— There was a card with my Phyllis!" The thumping upstairs was louder now, more irregular. She looked up fearfully, then back at Marty. "I don't know Alma Willison. Professor Wolfe can tell you, I don't know her. I don't know about the Klan. I'm sorry."

"Professor Wolfe told you something about Alma? What?"

"Please, he's having a fit! I can't think, I'm sorry. I don't understand. I don't know who they're after."

Marty's voice was soft but insistent. "We thought if Phyllis was involved somehow with Goldstein or one of his friends, it would help explain the card. You don't remember anything like that?"

"I'm sorry, I just can't help." Her gaze slid back upstairs. "The Klan— Maybe Professor Wolfe knows. I don't understand all this."

Upstairs, the thumps suddenly became even louder. Hal looked up, then bounded upstairs two steps at a time, his mother close behind. Marty Hopkins started up too, but Royce touched her forearm as she passed him. "We can't help," he said. "Two is enough. Even Hal is one too many."

She looked at him, her gray eyes filled with the sympathy he hungered for. "Yeah," she said after a beat, and stepped back down to Wes Cochran's side.

They listened in silence to the thumping, Hal's increasingly frantic questions, the soft quick answers from his mother and Lisa. After a long moment Hal reappeared at the head of the stairs, hair tousled. "Damn! How is she supposed to stand this?" he cried. "How are any of us—"

Marty was up the stairs, quick as a cat. "Mr. Denton, sir," she said.

"How can—" He looked around, wild-eyed, and noticed Marty at his side. "How can she stand it?" he asked brokenly.

"She'll do okay, sir, if you help. You have to stay strong."

"He's so— It's like a collision, like two locomotives crashing in one body. All that power against itself."

"I know. Come downstairs, Mr. Denton, let's go sit down."

Wes Cochran watched her help Hal down the stairs and said, "We'd better be getting on."

Royce nodded. "Right. Sorry she didn't remember anything. I guess Phyllis was pretty secretive about whatever it was."

"Yeah, kids get that way," the sheriff said. "Well, we'll follow up. Let us know if any of you think of anything. We'll do our best." He turned to the door and put his hand on the knob. "Come on when you're finished, Hopkins."

She had settled Hal into a big chair with a gentleness that disconcerted Royce. "Be right there, sir."

"We'll keep you posted," Wes said. He shook Royce's hand and went out, followed by Jessup. Royce heard their shoes crunch on the driveway gravel. He looked back into the living

187

room, where Hal sprawled in the chair, jacketless, tie loosened again, eyes closed in weariness. Marty draped his jacket over the sofa back and started out.

As she passed him Royce said softly, "Thanks for calming him down, Marty. He's upset."

"It's no problem," Marty said. "You guys have a lot on your plates right now."

"So do you."

Up close, he could see that the crisp uniform disguised deep weariness, that her gray eyes were bruised by sorrow. But that gentle mouth still held a secret promise of comfort. Royce touched her lips with his fingertip, then made himself step back.

She had stepped back too. Slowly. "Goodbye, uh, Mr. Denton." She fumbled for the doorknob.

He grinned. "Goodbye, Mrs. Hopkins."

He watched her run out to the cruiser, athletic and graceful. Then, reluctantly, he turned back to his family.

29

CLINT EASTWOOD WAS ON TV TONIGHT, AND THE NIGHT-HAWK watched for a few minutes after he'd showered, sitting in his clean white shirt and white painter's pants. He didn't watch television often, never the news or those talk shows with the pretty faces, glib and kike-controlled. He got angry watching them. They lied but they were cunning lies, and he could never think of the right answers. Later, reading his *Vanguards,* he found the answers. But his tongue wasn't quick, and even though he daydreamed about telling them off, he knew that the real way to win was the way he had chosen.

Chip had come home from Nam on leave and introduced his little brother to the *Vanguards* and to the new Klan. They both remembered the old days, when their father went night-riding with his buddies. They weren't supposed to know, but anytime his father moved around at night it was best to stay alert even if he was pretending to sleep. The Night-Hawk couldn't remember why it was best. There were walls in his memory, and he couldn't get through. His father was a good God-fearing man, that's what the preacher said, and the other grown-ups. So the Night-Hawk didn't know why the walls that hid those memories seemed to glow, to glow with fear.

He preferred the unglowing dark.

Anyway, it was the little no-account Pipsqueak who was afraid. Not the Night-Hawk, who was strong in the Lord, and in the power of his might.

And he could remember some things. He could remember the nights his father went out. The house was dark, and Chip would nudge him in the ribs and they'd creep silently to the window. It was a thrill to see the robes, pale and almost fluorescent in the moonlight, as the riders rolled silently away to leave provisions for a poor Christian widow, or to card some nigger or kike.

"They shall walk with me in white, for they are worthy," his father read to them. "He that overcometh, the same shall be clothed in white raiment, and I will not blot . . . I will not blot . . ."

The Night-Hawk couldn't remember the rest. Anyway, the important part was about overcoming. About winning. But these days you needed new ways to win. Chip, on leave before he went back to Nam and got killed by the mud-people, had explained it to him. The mud-people were taking over the world, he said. Gooks in Nam, niggers in the United States—they were all led by the commie Zionists. They'd taken over other countries, and even infiltrated the American government. You could tell because the American government sent money to Israel, and encouraged civil rights marchers, and bused niggers to white schools. But it didn't send any money to help the working man, the hardworking white man. A good white man trying to clean up America could even get himself arrested by the puppet cops.

Wes Cochran was a puppet, he'd learned. So were his pipsqueak deputies. He'd seen them this last week, talked to them even, and heard them ask all the wrong questions.

On TV Clint Eastwood had reached the showdown scene, blasting away at some mud-people. The Night-Hawk watched carefully for a moment but it was an amateur effort, not realistic. The other side was a lot more cunning than this movie showed. But at least Eastwood was no pipsqueak.

The Night-Hawk was no pipsqueak either. Not anymore.

He opened his Bible. "And lo, a great multitude, which no man could number, of all . . ." No, that wasn't right, that was the wrong verse. That verse didn't soothe him at all. Here was the right one, a little farther along: "These are they which came out of great tribulation, and have washed their robes, and made them white in the blood of the Lamb."

The Bible could beat Clint Eastwood any day.

30

MARTY FLOATED IN A SUMMER-WARM QUARRY HOLE. SOMEwhere there were troubles but she was at peace, naked, tickled by the lapping waters and the warm mint-scented breezes. The sunlit quarry walls stepped up and up to the trees, and beyond that the Empire State Building reared all the way to the sky. The waves stroked her sides, her belly, her breasts, her chin. When they reached her nose she opened her eyes and blinked. Brad was there. She said, "What—"

"Shh." He stopped her with a kiss and whispered, "It's only five o'clock, kitten. You don't have to wake up. But you're so gorgeous. I just wanted you so much."

She twisted her head to squint at the clock. He was right, it said 5:05. The only light came from the bedside lamp, and he'd draped a towel around it to keep it low. The lapping waves tickled her cheek and chin. No, she was confused, couldn't be waves. She looked and saw that it was the little stuffed mink. Brad trailed it down her neck.

Oughta get some sleep, Hopkins, be ready to solve some crimes in the morning.

But the mink's silky fur on her nipples was too much to resist. Marty said, "Mmm," and reached for Brad.

By six-fifteen she'd dozed off again. When the alarm buzzed she slapped it quiet. She felt good, really good, inside and out. Brad, in jeans, was sitting in the armchair watching her, his dark eyes warm. "Hi, hunk," she said groggily and sat up.

He smiled. "You know what?"

"What?"

"You're the sexiest lady in fifty states."

She stood, stretched, and walked over to him, pushing the curls away from her eyes. "I get a little help from you."

"Yeah." He caught her hand, still warm, still serious. "Kitten, we're good together. So damn good."

"Yeah, we sure are."

"But we've got to get out of here. If I'm going to do anything with my rotten life, we've got to get out."

Her stomach knotted, wringing all the well-being from her body with one squeeze. She shook her head. She felt like a worm. "Brad, I can't—"

"Kitten, I know it's hard, believe me. And you've done so much already. But we've got to take risks sometimes to get ahead."

He was so warm, so earnest, so talented. He needed help, and she could give it. It was wrong to put her own selfish needs ahead of his.

Wasn't it?

Marty walked to the closet and put on her robe. She picked up clean underclothes and a uniform shirt and started for the door. Brad, his eyes full of entreaty, said, "Marty?"

"Brad, let's save up some money, okay? Stay here, save some money, and when we've got enough we can—"

"Stay here?" He was out of the chair, holding her arm tightly and gesturing with his other hand. "Dammit, Marty,

I'm thirty years old! Thirty! If I don't get my break soon I'm washed up! And I know how to do it now. God, it's so close I can taste it! And we can do it together. You're my hope, kitten. My good angel."

"Yeah." She could feel his pain, his desperation. She could save him. Merge her strength with his, dissolve into his bright future, saintly, selfless—

Defend your self. For your daughter's sake too.

Marty ducked her head toward the clothes she held to try to push aside a curl that had fallen down again. She failed, straightened, and met Brad's eyes. "Brad, I want to help. You know that. But I won't sell the house, and I won't quit my job. That's the—"

"Christ, are you made of ice?" Brad flung her arm back so hard that she stumbled and almost dropped her clothes. "Haven't you been listening? Don't you even care?"

"You know I care! Dammit, I've been—"

"Well, give me a hand then! We're a family, for chrissake! We're supposed to help each other out! But you come in trying to run things, telling me to stay in this dumb town, telling me my business— Marty, look, I know what I'm doing. Don't you believe in me anymore?"

"Of course I believe in you! It's just—" She looked up at him, surprised. "I guess I don't believe in us."

That stopped him. He searched her face. "You're kidding! You gotta be! You—you've been cheating?"

"No! Of course not! I meant, your job and my job—" But she remembered the touch of Royce Denton's finger on her lips and a shiver of guilt ran down her spine.

Brad pointed at the bed. "All that was a lie?"

"No!"

"Have you turned into some kind of tramp? Carrying around those— God, I should have guessed, you carry around those goddamn condoms!"

"Brad, I didn't know when you were coming back!"

"What a sucker I've been! Thinking you'd hang in there for me—God! You don't want to leave. You've got other plans for that money. I see. Oh, I see now!"

Blinking, Marty ran from the room and locked herself in the bathroom.

She scrubbed herself hard, trying to wash off the confusion, the sting of his accusations. Dammit, what was wrong with her, that she couldn't make him understand? He needed help to get started, and she could help him, but surely gambling away their last bit of security was not the answer. Other plans for the money—yeah, okay, she did have other plans for the money. A home, college for Chrissie—she wouldn't give that up. And saying she was a tramp! "Please, God," she prayed to the water spraying over her, "don't let him think that. Please, help me rescue Brad. Help me rescue my marriage."

But God didn't answer. She heard only the echo of Professor Wolfe's voice at the quarry: *You're lucky if you can rescue your self.*

Chrissie met her at the bathroom door. She was wearing her Manhattan T-shirt and clutching Polly to her chest. "Where's Daddy?" she asked.

"I don't know, honey."

"He's not upstairs."

"I'll look while you use the bathroom."

She was right, he was nowhere in the house. His duffel bag was still in the corner of the bedroom. But his work shirt was gone. Probably he'd called Eddie. Marty pulled on her trousers, fixed some toast and coffee and a cup of hot chocolate for Chrissie.

Chrissie drank it in silence, except to ask, "Did you make him go away?"

"No. But he's mad because he wants to go to Alaska and I don't."

"We could go for a little while. Then New York. That's what he says."

"Yeah. But see, honey, if we all go to Alaska I have to quit my job and sell the house. And we'd have nothing to come back to if it didn't work out. And it might not work out. He was supposed to send for us from New York, too."

"Yeah." Chrissie pushed away her toast and stood up. "I'm not very hungry."

"Me either." Marty went to her daughter, dropped to one

193

knee, and hugged the rigid little body. "Honey, I love him too. He's a wonderful, magical man. And it's really, really rotten that it's not working out."

Chrissie pushed her away. "It *will* work out! You'll see! We'll go for a little while, and then New York! You'll see!"

"Honey—"

"Isn't it about time to go to school?" Chrissie said stiffly.

Marty nodded, even though it was still early. "I'll drive you to Janie's to wait." She got her gun belt from the top shelf, buckled it on, then picked up her checkbook and dropped it into her shoulder bag. Chrissie stuffed Polly into her satchel and sat in the passenger seat in silence to Janie's, near the school-bus stop. "See you this afternoon," Marty said. "At the bakery, okay?"

The girl nodded curtly and stalked up Janie's walk.

Marty drove on to Straub's Service Station. Gil Newton was replacing an engine, and pivoted the mass of steel out of the way as easily as swinging a gate to come fill the cruiser's tank. She asked, "Gil, how much does Brad still owe on his car?"

"I'll have to check."

"It's ready to go, right? Soon as he finishes paying you?"

"Yeah. Parts came in Monday morning and we got it done right away. I tested her. She's ready to roll." He hooked the nozzle back onto the pump and pulled out the charge slip for her. She followed him into the small office. He and Bert Mackay kept a surprisingly clean place for a garage. There was a scrubbed orange countertop over the storage bins and a calendar that featured a blond, blue-eyed Jesus who was suffering little children to come unto him. Nice change from the naked Dolly Parton lookalike who adorned Foley's locker door at the sheriff's office. Marty waited while Gil checked the account book and told her, "He still owes us two hundred and sixty-two."

"Shoot. Well, maybe next year we can paint the house." She wrote out a check and handed it to him.

He placed it in the cash register and made a note in the account book. "You want the keys?"

"No, give them to him when he comes in. I'm not sure I'll see him before he needs it. Gil, I've got another question."

"Yeah?"

"About Tom Straub. He headed up the Klan around here until it dissolved fifteen years ago. Did he ever try to get you or Bert involved in that kind of thing?"

"No." Gil stared at the orange counter, brow wrinkled. "Tom worked long hours here, didn't do much else. He was real old when he hired me six years ago. He talked about the old days, yeah, about how he and the boys took care of their own kind. Helping poor white families, giving to the church. He told Bert and me to join the church."

"He didn't talk about beating up Emmett Hines?"

Gil's dark eyes met hers briefly and he shrugged. "No. Tom tried to be a good man. Good to me, good to Bert. Tom tried to help folks. Thought folks should help their own kind."

"And you don't think Bert followed in Tom's footsteps?"

"How? Bert's a good churchgoing man, if that's what you mean."

"Yeah. Well, thanks, Gil."

Gil nodded and she walked back out to the car, glancing at her watch. Time for one more quick stop before work. She felt as if she'd been up for hours and hours and fought a couple of wars already. One more to go. She drove out to the trailer park and stopped at a battered one near the back.

Aunt Vonnie was already dressed for work and came to the door with a hairbrush in her hand. "Well. Come in," she said coolly.

"Shoot, Aunt Vonnie, you too? I don't have a single relative who's glad to see me." Marty straddled a straight chair and sat down, elbows on its back.

"What do you mean?" Aunt Vonnie was teasing her blond hair into a heap of curls. She glanced from the mirror to Marty.

"For one, Brad's probably leaving."

Aunt Vonnie snorted. "No surprise there. How come?"

"The usual. I want to save up instead of throwing everything we've got at his Alaska project. So he says I'm selfish, and a tramp besides. I can't figure out how to explain to him."

Aunt Vonnie thawed out some. "It's not your explaining,

girl. It's his understanding. You know what he wanted me to do?"

"What?"

"He wanted me to talk you into selling the house. Can you believe it? Sell your mama's house, after all she went through to keep it?"

Marty didn't feel like hashing over her mother's problems. She said, "She was real fussy about the house. I mean, when she was real sick she called me in and made me promise never to put Brad's name on the deed. She never liked him much."

"Oh, no. She had her reasons, but she liked him all right. Brad's a real charmin' man. Just like your daddy." Aunt Vonnie flipped the last golden curl into place high above her scalp and turned to Marty. "So Chrissie's mad at you too. Blaming you for her daddy's problems. Is that it?"

"That's it. She's real broken up about it. I came to ask you to give her a hug. She sure didn't want my hugs this morning."

"That happens. Well, I'll be there when she comes in," Aunt Vonnie promised, and held out her arms. "C'mere, girl, looks like you could use a hug too."

31

WES COCHRAN GRUNTED AS HE TUGGED ON HIS BOOTS. DAMN, soon as all this blew over he really would do something about this belly. It'd be worth it, once he had an hour to spare. He could work out, maybe get into the pickup games in the park. Might even enjoy it. But not now. He stood and scooped his wallet, keys, notebook, and comb from the top of the dresser and put them into his uniform pockets. Then he patted his pockets and ran his fingers over the top of the dresser again, frowning.

GRAVESTONE

"Here they are." Shirley, in pink cotton, came up beside him, holding out the pills. "Wes, listen, take it easy today."
"Sure thing." He reached for the packet.
She didn't release it. "I mean it, Champ. I can count."
He looked at her then, at the worry in her blue eyes. "Ahh, hell, Shirl, this thing is too big. But when it blows over, I promise."
She pursed her lips, unconvinced.
"Look," he said gruffly, "this turkey is hurting women and kids too. After we lock him up I can relax. Not before."
She let him have the nitroglycerin and hugged him, belly and all, her sturdy arms holding him fiercely. He stroked her blond hair. In a minute she released him with a sigh and said matter-of-factly, "The Thermos and sandwiches are on the kitchen counter."
"Okay." He put on his gun belt, buckling it as he walked into the kitchen. He kissed Shirley goodbye, grabbed the brown bag and the Thermos, and went out to the car. His mind was already grinding away at the case. Easy to tell Shirl it would blow over. But with Jessup to babysit, and the damn reporters, and even the citizens full of questions, it was hard to get hold of any train of thought without being interrupted.
So what did they really have? Klan cards. For Goldstein, Sears, little Phyllis, and the Willison woman. What the hell was the connection? They hadn't made much headway on the possible link between Phyllis Denton and Goldstein, but the motorcycle thing was still worth chasing down. As for Willie Sears, they hadn't found a link with Goldstein or his wife. The most likely thing was that the black custodian had simply been in the wrong place at the wrong time. He'd stopped to take a leak or whatever, noticed something up the hill at Goldstein's, and then somebody had noticed him noticing. He was followed home, killed, and crucified—Wes prayed it had been in that order.
The Willison woman was a whole different puzzle. Had she seen something too? If so, what? Goldstein and Sears had been killed, what was it now, one week ago. Today was Thursday again. The Willison woman hadn't disappeared till Monday. She lived in another state—but people drove around.

197

Suppose she'd seen something, and it had taken the guy that long to track her down— No. No, that didn't make much sense, he'd know she would have told someone else by then.

Hal, Jr., had said there was something familiar about her name. Maybe the connection was with Phyllis, then. He should give Hal, Jr., a call today, see if he'd remembered any more. Louisville would probably have more about her today too. He'd ask them to double-check times and destinations of any driving she'd done out of town.

And he'd send Hopkins to Bloomington again. She said she could probably catch Professor Wolfe after her lecture. He'd give her a choice: promise not to go off into the country alone with the woman, or take Bobby Mason along as backup. Jessup was trying to find Wolfe too. Might be pissed if Marty reached her first, but that was Jessup's problem.

Wes pulled into Straub's Service Station. Gil Newton was on morning duty, as usual, lean and bashful in his dark coveralls. Wes got out, bought a candy bar from the machine, and asked him to fill 'er up. He chewed slowly, staring at the looped gas hoses and the stacked oil cans and wondering what a Louisville woman could have to do with a crucified man or with a young girl's skeleton in a cave. He looked up when Gil asked, "How's it going?" and handed him the charge slip to sign.

"Okay." He picked up the pen.

Gil managed to overcome his shyness enough to say, "Sheriff, they say you, uh, you got some bad murders."

"We'll handle it. But this is a mean one, all right."

"Yeah. Grady was asking some questions, and Brad Hopkins's wife, about Bert. And I been reading the paper."

"Well, don't believe everything those asshole reporters say. But if they're saying the guy's mean, it's true." He should check with Marty Hopkins and Grady Sims, find out their take on Bert Mackay. A lot of strands to keep straight.

Gil asked, "You think he'll, uh, go after more people?"

Shit, couldn't even buy gas anymore without getting grilled. Wes said, "Not if I can help it," and handed the signed bill through the window. "Bert Mackay'll be here later, right?"

198

"Yes, sir." Gil tore off the receipt for him. "See you around."

"Okay, Gil." Wes poured himself some coffee in the top of the Thermos, put the cup on the dashboard, and turned the ignition.

As he rolled away, he had the nagging sense that he'd forgotten something. Something odd, about the cave, maybe. Something that had flitted past, not quite seen. Or not quite heard. He worried at it for a moment, then gave up. The thought would work its way to the surface on its own. If it even was a thought. Meanwhile, there were calls to make, an investigation to organize.

He picked up the coffee and managed to finish it before he reached the office.

For the third time in a week, Marty drove north to Bloomington. For the third time in a week, she pulled open the door to Jordan Hall, hoping to find Professor Wolfe. The lecture was over a little before three, she knew, fifteen or twenty minutes from now. She walked upstairs to check Wolfe's office and was surprised when Professor Hart's head popped out four doors down.

"It's the sheriff-maiden! Deputy—Hopkins, is it?"

Marty paused. "That's right."

He was wearing the same ragg sweater she remembered from before. He smiled and asked, "Now, are we looking for Professor Wolfe again?"

"That's right. Her lecture's over soon."

"Oh, but I have something important for you. Do come in a moment."

Marty glanced at her watch. "Well, just for a moment. Or I could come back later."

"No, no, a moment is enough. You'll want to see this. Come in, come in!" He held the door until she entered, then closed it behind her and went around his computer to his desk. He opened a drawer. "Now, where did I put it?" He rummaged in the drawer. "Are you making progress on your investigation, Deputy Hopkins?"

"Some."

"Our Professor Wolfe is a witness, I hear. But she's elusive, isn't she? A wild animal, timid until cornered, then a sudden flash of fangs."

"She seems pretty smart to me," Marty said.

"Wild things can be intelligent too. Would you like some corn chips?" He held out the bag.

"No, thanks."

He took a handful himself and opened another drawer. "The FBI is asking about her too."

"Yeah, I saw their car in the lot out there. They're cooperating on the case."

"Cooperating. An interesting phrase. Here it is!" He pounced on a paper. "Oh, sorry, that's not it." His bright eyes looked up from the drawer to inspect her. "You aren't annoyed that they're going over the same ground?"

"They have different resources. Look at things a different way. We're glad to have them," she said stiffly.

"I see. Now, where did I put that paper?"

"Look, Professor Hart, why don't I come back for it later? Is it so important to see it right now?" She reached for the doorknob.

"Oh, yes, it's relevant right now. It's a schedule of Professor Wolfe's semester. You do know the semester's almost over?"

"Yeah, I guess it is. Hadn't thought about it much. Yeah, a schedule would be useful. But I do have to catch her today."

"Of course. But you know, the FBI is much more generous than your sheriff's department."

"Generous?"

"To citizens like myself." He glanced out the window and smiled. "Of course, a federal agency has more resources, I imagine. But even so—"

Marty was thoroughly annoyed. "Look, Professor Hart, I don't give bribes, okay? Quit wasting my time!"

"Pray forgive me, sheriff-maiden." He took another handful of corn chips. "Oh, look, it was here all along." He picked up a paper from his desk and smiled at her.

"Thanks, Professor Hart." Marty took it from him and glanced at it as she reached for the doorknob. Could be useful, she saw. The last date on the list was tomorrow: graded exams available in departmental office after 4:00 P.M. Was today exam day, then? Sure enough, there it was: "Professor Wolfe will present slides for identification until 2:30. Exam papers must be turned in to Callie Burnham by 3:00 P.M."

Marty checked her watch. "Shoot! She may already be—" She looked at Professor Hart's smile and suddenly understood. She leaped to the window. Sure enough, Jessup and Manning were there, pushing Wolfe into the FBI car. "Stop!" Marty yelled, struggling to pull the window higher. "Wait!"

They ignored her, except that Professor Wolfe glanced up briefly just before Manning shoved her into the backseat. Marty slammed the window closed. Goddammit! If Wolfe decided to tell Jessup anything, it could be days before he condescended to pass it on to Wes and her. If he even realized what she meant. But if Professor Wolfe decided not to talk to him, she'd end up permanently cured of talking to any cop at all.

Hart was still smiling at her. Asshole. Marty smiled back. "Thank you for your kind help, Professor Hart," she said. She picked up the bag of corn chips, emptied it onto his computer keyboard, and stomped out of the office.

32

ALMA WILLISON HAD MEMORIZED EVERY LINK IN HER CHAINS. The fifth and sixth from the wall were roughened by thick rust, the seventh, eighth, and ninth less so. The eighteenth was twisted. And at her end, the link that connected the chain to the leg cuffs had a nick, a small sharp-edged notch. She imagined some former prisoner sawing away at it in the dark, hour after hour, sustained by ever-fading hope.

She didn't have a lot of hope left.

She didn't even have anything to saw with.

She knew her surroundings now. The first full day—Tuesday, she told herself, not wanting to lose track—she'd spent exploring, hunting for a way out. And crying, lots of crying. Crying for Wayne, for motherless Milly, for herself, for each new hope of escape as it was dashed. By Wednesday morning she'd lapsed into a deep depression. He'd left her breakfast— her fourth meal—and disappeared silently once more. By then she'd realized that the easy ways were not going to happen. He wasn't going to take pity on her tears and release her, explaining that it was all a mistake. Wayne wasn't going to appear at the head of some underground posse, having tracked her with police bloodhounds or whatever. A secret door in the rock was not going to groan open the way it did in the movies. She wasn't going to slip her feet from the steel cuffs, lull her captor into leaving as usual, and follow him out of the cave, where she would turn him over to the law and they'd reinstitute the rack and thumbscrews for him alone. None of those things would happen.

But after a few hours in a state of mind that matched her black surroundings, she'd pulled herself together, after a fashion. Alma Willison believed in God, and she told Him straight out that she didn't understand why all this had to happen, but since it had, how about giving her a little strength? She calmed down and listed her few pluses.

First and most important, he hadn't killed her. She had to hope that some sort of ransom negotiation was going on.

Second, she was no dummy. She was a bookkeeper, after all, capable of cool, logical thinking and organization. So, she'd get herself organized, make some plans for escape on her own.

She set up housekeeping. A place for everything and everything in its place. That was twice as important in the dark. She picked a place near the wall for the McDonald's containers. He never took them away. One corner of the cavern became her latrine. She wished there was some way to cover it up. Well, at least here it didn't attract flies. At the other side, as far away as her chain allowed, she moved the pad he'd brought her to sleep on. No place to wash up, of course. Some of her meals had napkins, and she wiped her face and hands as best she could.

Escape plans were harder. She didn't know where she was, and she didn't know much about her captor, except that he bought meals at McDonald's. That didn't exactly qualify as unusual. But she studied his every move. For example, he always lit his headlamp in the last stretch of tunnel before he reached her, and switched it off in that same stretch after he left. She'd paid careful attention to confirm that he wasn't just rounding a corner. He wasn't; he really was extinguishing the light. So, that meant he didn't want light beyond that turn. Maybe it could be seen. Maybe he was just very cautious, but maybe, just maybe, there were people out there sometimes. People who could see her if she got that far. So she drew a little hope from that.

She also drew another conclusion. The faint thumps she heard when he came and went were steady and confident, even when the light was off. He knew his way around very well. He traveled in darkness, this man, and was at home in this strange dark place. In fact, she had the feeling that he'd prefer not to have the light on when he visited her, except that she herself was unpredictable, and he wanted to see what she was doing. He never came close to her. Even when he gave her food, he stretched to set the container just barely within her reach.

So Alma came up with one ingredient for a plan. She'd always crawled forward to meet him when she saw the light, stretching the tether to its fullest extent. It might surprise him, give her an edge, if she sat back just a little. Not far back, just enough to make him think she was in her usual place, but where she could lunge at him if that ever seemed useful.

But she needed a plan before she started lunging. And for that she needed to know more about him. Her tears on the first day hadn't moved him. But if she ever wanted to see Wayne and Milly again, she had to find out his weak points. So she prepared to meet him, tucking a few feet of the chain back around the ring, straightening the rest so it looked stretched out.

Finally the light appeared. She crouched, alert, and said a prayer.

His light appeared, dazzling her, and lit the cavern. His shadowed shape behind it moved forward cautiously, his arm stretched out, and he put down the container.

"Thanks," she said. She was hoarse, and had to clear her throat. "What'd you bring?"

"Big Mac." He didn't seem to mind talking about food.

"Good," she said. "They're good. Did you have one too?"

"Yeah."

"Good. Do you know yet why I'm here?"

"He still didn't let me know."

"Soon, maybe," she said brightly, casually. "Will you be seeing him today, d'you think?"

He made a harsh noise that might have been a laugh. "Never see the Titan. He'll send me a message."

"Oh, I see. He sent you the message to pick me up, right?"

"Yeah."

"Guess he wants to see me."

He was silent. She ate her Big Mac and said, "This is good."

He asked, "You a kike?"

"What?"

"You a kike? A Jew?"

"Goodness, no! I'm a Methodist! Ladies' Circle at Riverside Methodist, three blocks from where you found me!"

He was silent again, and she was too, trying to figure out what it meant. Why would he think she was Jewish? Had there been a mistake? Was there some way to convince him it was a mistake? But if so, this might be the guy who'd made the mistake. She decided she'd better not ask him. Accusing him might rattle him into doing something terrible. She drank some coffee, carefully. After spilling it that first time, she was careful.

His hands were clenching and unclenching. Finally he put them in his pockets. He asked, "You ever sleep with a nigger?"

"No!" For an instant she panicked at the thought of what might lie ahead. What horrible sports did this Titan have in mind for her? But she thought of Milly and got herself back under control. Nigger. Kike. She knew people who talked about niggers and kikes. They also talked about white Christian womanhood. Maybe she could get herself into a more favorable category. *Think!* She said, "You know, there's Amy Wilson. I'm Alma Willison, and people are always confusing me with Amy Wilson." She prayed there was no such person.

"You're lying," he said firmly. "The Titan said, find Alma Willison."

"Yeah. But I bet he wants me to tell him about Amy Wilson. See, I never slept with anyone except my husband. I'm a faithful, white, Christian woman."

His hands still moved nervously in his pockets. She wished she could see his face but the glare of light from his headlamp was too bright. Clearly, she had him off balance now; but she wasn't sure if that was good or dangerous. Who was this Titan? Someone real? A figment of this guy's sick imagination? Either way, best to treat him as real.

"That must be it, he wants to hear about Amy Wilson," she said. "Tell him I'll be glad to cooperate." She leaned forward confidentially. "Besides sleeping with a black guy, you know what some people say? They say her real name is Kahn. She's a kike."

He jerked his hands from his pockets with a little chinking sound and lunged out through the cleft in the rock. This time Alma didn't call after him. Maybe he'd believe her fiction, maybe convince his sick mind that he really wanted Amy Wilson and let her go.

What had that little sound meant? It occurred to her suddenly that he might have dropped something. Something useful. She wriggled forward, chains dragging, and felt her way toward the place where he'd been standing. She lay down so she could reach further and patted her hands on the stone floor. She didn't have much hope, but what else was there to do?

So it was a shock when her fingers touched something. Small, hard, jointed—keys! Keys, on a ring! She snatched it up, holding it tightly in her palm. Keys, keys!

Thank you, God!

What was on this ring? Her anxious fingertips fondled each

one, trying to identify it. Here was a house key, probably.
Two more similar ones. Next a small one, luggage or cash
register, something like that. A pair of car keys—

Car keys.

He'd notice they were gone. He'd notice right away.

What did the lock on her shackles take? Something very
small, to judge from the circular keyhole on the cuffs. Frantically, her fingers tested each key.

Nothing. No key that would fit the shackles.

And far away, yes, she heard the thumping of his return.
Getting louder.

She picked a key. Not car keys, not the largest or smallest,
but one of the house keys. She heard him coming closer. Heart
thudding, she found the split in the key ring and worked her
chosen key off it. Then she tossed the ring of keys carefully
toward where she thought the cleft in the rock might be. She
coughed at the same time, hoping to disguise the sound of its
fall. She heard a hesitation in the rhythm of his approach,
then he came closer.

Alma retreated a few steps and pulled her blanket around
her. The entrance cleft brightened as he lit his lamp, then
came the blinding circle of the light.

Her lips were dry. "You're back soon," she said as casually
as she could.

Thank God, he spotted the keys right away. Her aim hadn't
been true in the dark, but they'd bounced off the rock beside
the entrance toward the place where he'd been standing. He
said curtly, "Dropped my keys." He pocketed them, turned
around, and started away again.

Alma waited cautiously until the light was gone, and the
thump of his footsteps. If he came back she'd have to throw
this one too, as though it had fallen off the ring somehow.
But he didn't return. She took the key in her right hand and
felt along the chain with her left. There it was, the notch that
the earlier prisoner had started.

Alma began to saw.

33

By nightfall Brad still hadn't shown up. His duffel bag lay in the corner of the bedroom, and Aunt Vonnie was hesitant about staying the night. But since Marty felt too raw to deal with Chrissie, Aunt Vonnie sighed, unpacked her hair-rollers, and settled back into the room she'd left Monday, for the kid's sake, she said. Marty was relieved. She sat down to watch TV with Aunt Vonnie that night, trying to get herself interested in the show. But her mind kept gnawing at her problems. Phyllis Denton. Goldstein. Brad. Professor Wolfe. Professor Hart. Jessup. And Alma Willison. There had actually been a small breakthrough on the Willison front. When Marty had returned from her aborted attempt to see Professor Wolfe after class, Wes had told her that a neighbor of the Willisons remembered seeing a black sports car with Indiana plates, maybe a Chevrolet, parked on the street at about the time Alma Willison disappeared. Little Milly confirmed the color, and added a hazy description: a guy with a cap like Johnny Baker's, putting something in the mailbox. The Louisville cops had traced down Johnny Baker, a Sunday-school playmate of Milly's. His favored cap was a white baseball cap. Not much to go on, but more than they'd had before. Wes said also that the feds had finished looking over the cavern where Phyllis had been found and released the troopers guarding the crime scene.

"Aunt Vonnie?" Chrissie asked, her dark head bent over her homework in the next room.

"Yeah?"

"Ask Mommy what sea-lily fossils look like."

"I will not!" Aunt Vonnie snapped, half-rising to glare at

Chrissie. "Your mother is right here, young lady! Fight with her if you want, or ask her about sea lilies if you want, I don't care. But don't drag me into the middle!"

"Sheesh!" Chrissie rolled her eyes. "I was just asking!"

"The fossils look like circles or stars, usually," Marty said. No sense rubbing Chrissie's nose in it—Aunt Vonnie had made the point. "See, the original thing has a stem that looks like a stack of little spools, and a kind of flower with fat, pointy things for petals. So when the stone is cut, it looks like circles if you slice across the stem, or stars if you slice across the top."

Chrissie was squinting at vacancy, visualizing slices of rock. "Could you dig out the whole thing? Like a dinosaur skeleton?"

"I guess so. Except these are pretty small, so it'd be hard to keep from breaking them."

A little later they sent Chrissie up to get ready for bed. Aunt Vonnie kicked off her shoes and rubbed her feet, then said, "Oh, shoot. I meant to water the garden. It's been days since there was any rain."

"I'll do it." Marty jumped up.

"Oh, I can do it in the morning. It's dark now."

"There's a moon. And I'd like some fresh air. I'll be back in half an hour."

She unrolled the hose from the back wall of the house and pulled it to the garden in the back corner of the yard, wedging the nozzle against the upper fence rail to let the water rain gently over the baby tomatoes and beans. The soft rush of the water was soothing to hear, and the cricket song. Far off, she heard the baying of coonhounds. She wondered if it was Royce Denton, out with his father's dogs.

Royce. What was it about him? He wasn't flirting with her, exactly. Royce stuck to business. But then suddenly something in him would crack, and a flash of sadness and need called out to her. But how could somebody like Royce need her? She shook her head. He was rich, he was educated. He had all that property, an important family, a brother who might get elected to Congress.

And after those flashes, before she could figure out how to respond, his defenses would roll back into place like a security door, and he'd give her an amused grin and call her Mrs. Hopkins, totally in control again.

Was that the sound of tires in the driveway out front? No, probably just the whoosh of the water. She walked to the bottom of the garden to make sure that the plants there were getting sprinkled too.

Maybe she was making it all up. Maybe she was hurting so much because of Brad that she was grabbing for the first prince charming she saw. Somebody who was in control, who already made money, who wouldn't ask her to sell her house and her daughter's future.

Who'd never tell her about a glorious skyful of kites, or bring her a toy mink.

Tears stung her eyes. Dammit, Brad, why can't we work things out? We look at the same world and see two different visions.

And I love you for your vision, dammit, I do.

She was leaning against the fence post, hugging it with one arm, lips pressed together to keep the sobs inside. Then a soft voice spoke behind her. "You're unhappy, Martine."

Marty whirled but she'd already recognized the voice and was no longer surprised. She cleared her throat. "Yeah. My husband's leaving, I guess. And I'll miss him. And my kid loves him."

"A husband, a father. A heavy loss."

"Yeah." Marty swiped at her nose with the back of her hand. "I could go with him. Quit my job and go. What would you do, Professor Wolfe?"

"It doesn't matter what I'd do. Don't try to choose my way, Martine. Choose your self."

"Shouldn't I care about other people? My husband, my daughter? The people I try to help at work?"

"Of course." The professor's voice was concerned, almost warm. "But care for your self too, Martine, or you'll lose the true roots of your strength. What will you have left to share?"

The true roots of her strength. Marty looked at the moonlit garden, at the house her mother had bought, at the limestone hills behind. Were these the roots of her strength? Not exactly.

But her roots were sure as hell not in Alaska. "God, it's confusing," she said.

"Yes."

"Hey, listen." Marty turned back to the professor. "You didn't come out here to be Ann Landers."

"No."

"Listen, I'm, uh, I'm sorry about the FBI. I would have helped if I could."

"Don't worry, I didn't let them violate me. But they took so much time, and kept asking about the Klan. I know nothing about that. They had no understanding. You have understanding, Martine."

"Not enough. Uh, you know it was Professor Hart who set you up?"

"Yes." In the moonlight, Marty wasn't sure whether Professor Wolfe smiled. "Professor Hart is a foolish man. I hear he got corn chips in his computer. But, Martine, I'm troubled by Alma Willison's disappearance, and by the Klan card. I'd hoped to look at the cave again."

"It's under guard now. You have to go with one of us."

"Or else the back way."

"The back way?"

"Through the breakdown pile in the blindfish cavern. But it doesn't matter, I won't have time now because Agent Jessup took up so much of the afternoon. Martine, tell me. What would you do if someone raped your daughter? Killed her?"

"What?" The sudden change of subject was like a punch in the gut.

"What would you do?"

"I'd, uh, I'd try to catch him." Was that the sound of tires again? "I'd track him down."

"If he killed her?"

"Yeah, okay, I'd want to kill him too," Marty admitted. "I'd maybe try to arrange to shoot him."

"Martine, Martine, use your imagination! You'd want revenge. Real revenge. You'd want to see his body invaded as he invaded hers, his flesh destroyed as he destroyed hers."

"His flesh?" Marty whispered. The vision of Goldstein's

corpse swam into her mind: mutilated, torn, castrated, dumped in that shallow grave. And Willie Sears, and—

"Mommy! Mommy!" Shrieking, Chrissie raced across the moonlit grass. "Stop him!"

"Honey, what is it?" Marty stretched out her arms and the pajama-clad girl flung herself into them, sobbing and pounding her fists and her doll against Marty's shoulders. Was she hurt? Raped? Was this the rape Professor Wolfe was warning her about? Marty gripped Chrissie's arms and fearfully inspected her daughter's clothes, her face.

"Stop him! You've got to stop him!" Chrissie cried.

Behind her, Marty heard clicking, the bolt of Professor Wolfe's rifle as she chambered a round. Marty asked urgently, "Stop who, Chrissie? What happened?"

"Daddy! I tried—I said, wait a few days—but he went away anyway."

"Oh, honey . . ." Half-relieved, half-furious at Brad, Marty tried to hug her.

But the girl was pounding at her again, short useless punches. "Why can't we go to Alaska? Why? Why?"

"Chrissie, we talked about it. It's not—"

"I told him I wasn't really scared! I told him! Mommy, make him wait! Make him!"

Marty shook her head helplessly. "I can't make him do anything. When he comes back, it's because he wants to."

"Mommy, did I hurt his feelings? When I said I was scared to go to Alaska? Later I said I wasn't, but maybe his feelings were hurt."

"No, honey, it's nothing you said or did. It's not your fault. It's a grown-up problem."

"Were you scared to go to Alaska?" Professor Wolfe asked gently. She had stepped through the rails and was squatting near them, leaning back against the fence, her rifle beside her. The three dogs lurked behind, in the shadows.

Chrissie looked at the professor seriously. "I was scared. But he said I wasn't, so I said I wasn't. I didn't want to hurt his feelings. And he said after Alaska we'd go to New York. And I really do want to go to New York. Really! And I want to be with him."

211

"I see. What's your name?" There was real warmth in her voice.

"Christine Hopkins."

"Christine. Yes, I was sad too when my father left. It made me wonder if my mother would leave too."

"I won't leave her!" Marty protested. "Don't put awful ideas in her head!"

But Chrissie was tuned in to Professor Wolfe. She said, "Yeah. I used to wonder that all the time. What if Mommy goes away too?"

"But I didn't! I won't!" Marty was astonished. She'd never realized that her daughter was worried about that.

The professor said to Chrissie, "When my father left it was like a betrayal. Parents are supposed to stay with their kids and stay together."

"Yeah."

"It's important not to betray other people. Don't you agree, Martine?"

"Yeah. Yeah, but . . ."

"But?"

"Okay, dammit, it's also important not to betray yourself!"

The professor nodded gravely and turned back to Chrissie. "Growing up is full of changes. You separate from your family, you learn how people think things are supposed to be, you try to learn how things really are in the wilderness inside us. You become a woman. You become your self."

Chrissie hugged her doll. "I don't want changes."

"I know, Christine. I didn't either. But everything on earth is always changing. Bugs, plants, rocks, oceans. People too. We lose people. But you see, in a way we don't. They become part of ourselves, our changing selves."

"But I want to be with him!"

"Yes. But maybe you don't want to betray your self for him."

Chrissie drew a deep breath. Marty was quiet, wondering at the depth of the professor's sympathy, at the strange communion between the two. The girl said, "I won't lose him. He's like a fossil in my heart."

"Yes, Christine. My heart has fossils too."

"It's still not fair."

Professor Wolfe nodded agreement. "No. It's not fair. Martine is trying to make the world more fair. That's her job, and she's good at it. She's brave and curious. It's a good way to be on this changing earth. But a lot of things are still unfair."

"So what can I do?"

"I can't tell what's best for you. For me, it's best to look at things respectfully and truthfully. I like science because scientists try to see things as they are. And then I decide how to be fair to myself and to other people."

Chrissie kicked at a clump of grass, then looked up. "I'm going to be sad."

"Yes. That's true. Respect it."

"I'm mad at Mommy."

"Martine will probably be sad and angry sometimes too."

"Yeah, I know. Last time we yelled at each other a lot." Chrissie hugged her doll, then suddenly handed it to Professor Wolfe. "Here. You know about changes. I want you to have Polly."

Professor Wolfe accepted the doll gravely. "Thank you, Christine. I'm honored."

Marty said, "Chrissie, are you sure? Polly's such a comfort to you!"

Chrissie said, "Things change."

She started for the house, small and slim and dignified. Marty thought she looked an inch taller. She ran a few steps to catch up and said, "Chrissie, one thing won't change. I'll always stick with you."

"Maybe I'll still be mad at you."

"Doesn't make any difference. I'll stick with you anyway."

Chrissie looked up at her gravely. "Yeah. I kind of know that."

"Good. Is Aunt Vonnie okay?"

"Yeah. She didn't say much to Daddy. She didn't even tell him you were out back. I told him, but he said he knew. He left anyway."

"It's hard on him too, honey."

"Yeah."

213

"Okay. I'll be in as soon as I finish talking to Professor Wolfe."

"But she's gone."

Marty looked back. Chrissie was right. Wolfe had disappeared again. She called, "Professor Wolfe?"

There was no answer. She said, "Shoot. I thought she might tell me something more." She had so many questions, about Phyllis Denton, about the mutilated murder victims, about Professor Wolfe's own involvement. But right now she'd better stick with grieving little Chrissie. She said, "I'll be there in a minute. I'll just roll up the hose."

Marty turned off the water and listened for Professor Wolfe, but there was nothing. The coonhounds were silent now too, although the crickets still sang. She curled the hose next to the house and followed Chrissie inside.

34

WES COCHRAN ROCKED BACK IN HIS DESK CHAIR AND LOOKED at his gangly deputy. "Okay, Sims, whatcha got on the high-school custodian?"

"Willie Sears didn't do anything unusual that week." Grady Sims scratched the bony wrist protruding from his uniform sleeve before he went on. "He just went to work every day. Some high-school kids got in a little parking-lot scuffle Tuesday afternoon. Willie called the vice principal and helped him break it up. 'Cept for that, he just mopped floors and collected his paycheck."

"After hours?" Jessup asked. The little agent was taking notes too, his hair slicked back flawlessly, his pale fingers moving the pen jerkily across the page.

"Nothing there either, sir. Went to his church on Sunday,

church supper Wednesday night. Didn't say anything unusual to anybody. Watched TV, drank a few beers, gassed up his car, joined in a couple of pickup basketball games."

"Who else was in those games?" Wes asked.

Grady Sims flipped a page in his notebook and read off a dozen names. Wes recognized them. No troublemakers, just working stiffs. "Any fuss at these pickup games, Sims?" Wes asked.

The deputy shrugged. "Just the usual. Insults to the other side, you know, all in fun. And they all say Willie stayed out of arguments. Knew his place."

"Any evidence, evidence that he knew Kizzy Horton? The black singer, Goldstein's wife?" asked Jessup.

"No, sir. I asked special."

"She says the same thing," Jessup admitted. "We interviewed her for two hours trying to establish a connection. No go."

"We're back where we were," Wes said. "Willie Sears saw something Thursday night. That's the most likely. Saw something going on at Goldstein's, and somebody noticed him seeing it."

"We don't know for sure," Jessup said pompously.

"No, we don't," Wes admitted blandly. "Why do *you* think his eyes were dug out?"

"Well, yes, but we need more, need more proof."

Wes beamed at the little FBI agent. "Hey, good idea! Now, Mr. Jessup, did you all talk to that Professor Wolfe?"

Jessup tried to look deadpan but Wes spotted a triumphant sparkle in his eye. "She gave us something to check out, yes. I'll get back to you tomorrow."

Wes felt his jaw tighten. Damn woman. He said mildly, "Good going. Deputy Hopkins couldn't get much from her." Not strictly true, he admitted to himself. Wolfe had told Marty about the Denton kid's body, and Alma Willison's address. But before he'd sent Marty out this morning, she'd told him about Wolfe's nighttime visit, her hints about rape and murder and revenge, and her claim that she hadn't said anything to the FBI. But now here was Jessup acting as though he held the key to the case. Wes asked, "What did Wolfe tell you?"

215

"Just mentioned a place to look for evidence," Jessup said smugly. "We'll check it out, see if it's worth anybody's time."

Interagency cooperation. Ain't it wonderful. Wes paused just long enough to be sure that Jessup wasn't about to come across with more information, then said, "All right, we go our own ways for now. Meet here again tomorrow morning, is that okay?"

"Sure," said Jessup.

"I sent Hopkins to talk to the Dentons this morning. Sims, when Mason gets back from that accident call, you and he contact Louisville about the Willison woman, see if there's any news. I'm going to Bloomington myself."

"Bloomington? Why?" Jessup asked.

"Just to check something out. See if it's worth anybody's time." Wes winked at the little man.

Jessup snapped his book shut and walked out. The others followed.

Wes glanced at the paperwork in his box. Better get it out of the way first. Then he'd go to Bloomington. See that damn Wolfe character and get the whole story. He wouldn't be surprised to learn that she'd done it herself, loony as she was. Looked like she'd just been jerking Marty around if she had a lead to give Jessup. Well, maybe she was one of those women who preferred talking to a man. He'd been so damn busy. Hadn't been able to help Marty Hopkins much. But maybe now it was time for him to take over.

35

MARTY GOT OUT ONTO THE GRAVEL DRIVEWAY AND CRUNCHED her way toward the limestone-columned porch. Wes had been skeptical, but she thought maybe Wolfe had been telling her something last night, hinting that Phyllis had been raped, that Judge Denton would want revenge. But how, from a sickbed? And who was the rapist? Goldstein? Were the Klan symbols a smokescreen? Or could the Klan be guilty, and Goldstein, like Willie Sears, perhaps an unfortunate witness? She wished she knew what the judge had been trying to communicate to them ever since his wife told him that Phyllis's body had been found in the cave. Marty's gut feeling was that the judge had only then figured out what had happened to Phyllis. Maybe something about the cave rang a bell. His children had played there, and he probably knew it from his childhood too.

In any case, Marty was ready to sit in the sickroom today for as long as it took for him to reach a lucid moment.

Royce opened the door for her. As he stepped back into the hall light, she saw that his skin seemed more weathered than before, his fit body more slumped, his eyes duller. "Marty," he said. No mocking "Mrs. Hopkins" to greet her today, no teasing grin.

"Hi, Mr. Denton. I wanted to ask some—"

"He's dead, Marty." Royce cleared his throat. "He— I can't believe it. Damn."

"Oh, I'm sorry! I'm so sorry!" Marty put a hand on his arm and studied his face. "What happened?"

Royce shrugged. "Went into one of his fits. It lasted a long time. He never came out of it."

Marty remembered the wiry body bucking in its restraints,

217

the flecks of saliva spattering about. She suppressed a shudder. "God. I'm so sorry, Royce."

He managed a nod and patted her hand.

She asked, "What can I do? Do you want me to call people?"

"No, I did that. The doctor's on his way, the funeral home, all that. Lisa's helping Mother now."

He seemed all right, shocked but all right. The cop side of Marty kicked in. "When did it happen?"

"Half an hour ago."

"Who was here? You, your mother?"

"Yes. And Lisa."

"Not your brother?"

"No. He's out campaigning. I haven't called him yet."

"Yeah. We'll need an autopsy, you know."

Royce made a face but nodded. "Yeah. But we know what happened."

"Yeah. Can I see him?"

"But he's—" His eyes dropped to her badge. "Sorry. Sometimes I forget you're a deputy, and I'm not supposed to protect you. Yeah, of course, go on up." He closed the front door behind her and gestured to the staircase. He followed her up but stayed in the doorway when she entered the sickroom.

Elizabeth Denton and Lisa were straightening the room, collecting the medicines, stacking pads and towels. Marty said, "I'm so sorry, Mrs. Denton."

Elizabeth Denton looked at her with stunned eyes.

Marty said awkwardly, "Maybe he's out of pain now."

"Maybe." Elizabeth looked at the bed, puzzled. "He's so stiff and hard."

Marty forced herself to look at the body. The judge, gaunt and almost skeletal, lay with arms and legs extended, back arched, head back. They'd released the restraining straps, but the position made the body look as though he were still heaving himself against the bonds. Marty stepped to the bedside and touched an arm. Elizabeth was right; the body was totally rigid. Marty looked at Lisa. "When did he die?"

Lisa looked at her watch. "Twenty-five minutes ago."

Same thing Royce had said. Marty touched the body under the arm. He was warm as life. She frowned at Lisa.

Lisa said, "I never saw it set in so fast either. Maybe it has to do with the convulsions."

"Doctor will tell us," Marty said. She looked back at the tensed body, the sunken, vacant face. Judge Denton, she asked silently, what was it? What did you want to tell us? Well, it's over now, poor man. She straightened his pajama collar and turned to the others. "Let me get some facts down before the ambulance gets here."

The three of them gave her the information. Judge Denton's convulsions had become more frequent in recent days, and last night, sometime before 3:00 A.M., Elizabeth said, another attack had come. Royce got up to help his mother, and they'd battled it as usual, checking the restraints, positioning pillows near the old man's pitching, jerking head, waiting for the seizure to spend itself. But this time it hadn't. They'd called Dr. Hendricks after a while, and he'd said they couldn't move him until the seizure ran its course, but they should take him to the hospital the minute it was over. After forty-five minutes they'd called the doctor again. He'd sent Lisa with anticonvulsants, and in a rigid phase she'd managed to inject him, but it hadn't helped. By that time the judge had been in convulsions for five hours. The next time he'd gone still and rigid, Lisa had started to put the needle in again but suddenly realized it was all over.

"What set it off this time? Anything special?" Marty asked.

"No. Things were just as usual," Royce said. "I mean, usual since he got ill. Same medicine, everything."

"He didn't want any dinner last night," said Elizabeth Denton.

"He hasn't been eating well for days now," Lisa said. "Most sick people aren't real hungry. But some days he'd refuse everything."

"Almost as if he wanted to rush it along," Royce said, and suddenly kicked the doorjamb and turned away from the three women.

Elizabeth said softly, "I think he was in pain. The seizures.

The last few weeks, he complained sometimes when he had a clear moment about how his muscles were sore."

Lisa nodded. "He was a brave man. I'm surprised he hung on as long as he did."

There was a sound of sirens outside. Marty closed her notebook and followed Royce downstairs and onto the porch. "Hi, Ricky," she greeted the medic. "No rush, I'm afraid."

"Oh," Ricky said. "I'm sorry, sir." He looked at Royce and touched his cap, then he and his helper followed Marty inside. On the stairs she told them, "We'll need an autopsy."

"Okay."

She introduced Ricky to Elizabeth Denton. He already knew Lisa. Then she left them to their tasks and went back down. Royce was standing at the edge of the driveway, fists in pockets, staring out at the woods. She remembered how lonely a father's death could make you feel. Royce turned around when he heard her footsteps.

"Hi," she said.

"Hi."

"If I can do anything, please, let me know," she said.

He shrugged. "It's over. Nobody can do anything."

"Yeah, I know. But lots of things have to be taken care of now. Lots of details."

He made an effort but not much of his old twinkle returned. "I'm a lawyer, Mrs. Hopkins. But thanks all the same."

"Yeah, that was a stupid thing for me to say. I just meant if you wanted to talk or anything. I remember when my dad died sometimes I wanted to—well, just tell somebody how he used to buy me ice cream. Stuff like that."

"Your father bought you ice cream?" They started slowly back toward the porch.

"Yeah. After Pee-Wee basketball he and Coach—I mean Sheriff Cochran—they used to take us to the Dairy Treat and we'd all talk about the game. Or sometimes my dad would take me out, just the two of us, no special reason."

"Happy memories," Royce said.

"Yeah. Mostly. Course, I got into trouble sometimes. Most kids do," she said lightly. She didn't want to talk about the scary nights when her sweet, boisterous dad would come in late with booze on his breath and throw the furniture around in a rage.

"Yeah, most kids do," Royce agreed, and suddenly kicked viciously at the lattice under the porch. A slat splintered, and he kicked again, and again, until a hole gaped in the symmetry of wood and limestone. He leaned gasping against the limestone corner of the house, staring at the hole.

Marty flinched at the first sound, then stood fast. She said, "I was mad too, when my dad died."

His tortured blue eyes turned to her and she knew she'd almost reached him. She could see him struggling for control. She said, "It's natural to be mad for a while. You'll get over—"

Royce grabbed her wrists, pulled her close, and kissed her roughly. And again, and again. He pressed her back against the cool limestone wall of his house until the flashlight and handcuffs on her belt dug into her waist, and she could feel the rage and despair and need in his taut body, the hot disorder of her own response. Boiling clouds of protest, excitement, assent, and distress formed and shredded in her mind. And fragments of thoughts: *He needs me. Chrissie loves Brad. Royce can't want me.* And from somewhere, *Choose your self.*

There was a faraway whine, a car slowing on the highway. Royce stepped back, leaving her leaning against the wall. For a long second they stood, flustered, not meeting each other's eyes. "God," he said at last, glancing at her and seeming to take strength from her confusion. "God, I didn't mean—"

"Yeah, I know, it's okay." What should she say? I'll help you through this, I'll gladly take care of you? Or maybe, don't trust me, Royce, I'm too shaky right now from packing off the last guy who needed me? She settled for asking, "Is that the doctor?"

He squinted down the driveway, smoothed back his hair, and glanced back at her. His grin was teasing again. "Yeah. Yeah, back to work, Deputy Hopkins."

Not a bad answer for now. Marty stowed her confusion and marched off to meet the approaching car.

36

WES TWISTED THE STEERING WHEEL ANGRILY AND SKIDDED AROUND the turn into the long, rough driveway. "Look, he didn't tell me what she said. All I know is that Jessup was crowing like he was sitting in a tub of butter."

Marty Hopkins had a mulish look about her jaw. "Yes, sir. I guess we'll know later if he's got anything useful."

"I don't get your attitude, Hopkins. You keep telling me she's loony, and then you turn around and believe every word she says to you, and not to him."

"Yes, sir." Face stiff, she stared out at the tangled branches and vines that came up to edge the rutted drive.

She felt disappointed, he knew, after all those trips up to this godforsaken corner of the hills to get information. But she'd better learn that this was part of the job. "Look, Hopkins, you know sometimes sources talk better for one guy than another. Can't start feeling hurt every time another cop learns something."

"No, sir. It's not that. It's that she just wouldn't have told that Jessup more than she told me."

Maybe it had been a mistake to bring Hopkins along. She'd come back from the Dentons' sooner than he'd expected, shaken up but able to give a competent, concise report of Judge Denton's death. When he said he was going to talk to Professor Wolfe, she'd offered to go, and he'd thought it might be useful to have someone who knew the terrain. But now this baffling loyalty to the loony professor made him wish she weren't along.

Wes said, "Look, Hopkins, I'm going to pull rank here.

Understand? I want to decide for myself. I want to hear what this woman says without worrying about you chiming in."

"Yes, sir."

"And if you don't like those ground rules, stay in the car."

"Yes, sir. I'll keep quiet." She spoke stiffly.

Well, what the hell, you had to keep discipline even if it meant hurt feelings now and then. Wes pulled in behind a pickup truck near the old farmhouse and climbed out to look around.

Bees, wildflowers, scrubby woods with a rampaging undergrowth of vines, a hawk circling in the hot metallic afternoon sky. This was May going on August. Wes spotted a young woman in T-shirt and jeans sitting at a table on the porch. He muttered doubtfully, "That the professor?"

"No, sir. One of her students."

"Introduce me."

Marty went halfway up the steps. The young woman said, "Hi, Martine." Wes didn't find her pretty until she smiled.

"Hi, Callie. This is Sheriff Cochran."

"Your boss. Glad to meet you, Sheriff." The smile was directed at him now. "You probably don't want to shake hands. I'm all over crayfish."

Wes saw that two dead crawdads were on the table before her, one similar to dozens Wes had caught as a boy, the other a strange slender pale one. Graph paper and shiny scientific instruments sat on the table beside them. He said, "Yeah, we can skip the handshake. Glad to meet you anyway. That white one sick or something?"

"Nope. His natural state. Listen, Professor Wolfe is real busy 'cause she has to leave so soon. But you might be able to see her. She's working over near the quarry."

"Okay, thanks. Where—"

"I know the way, sir," Marty said. "Thanks, Callie." She started for the woods and Wes followed.

"I don't promise she'll be there," Callie called after them.

A few steps into the junglelike growth and Wes was having second thoughts. It was so quiet, nothing but the whine of insects and somewhere the deeper notes of frogs. Wes liked to hear motors, radios, guys shouting hello, the comforting sounds of people. He pushed a branch out of his face and said, "What if this is a wild-goose chase?"

"Could be, sir." Disgustingly young and vigorous, Marty forged ahead. Wes had to keep ducking under the branches and vines. He was a little winded by the time they came out by the abandoned quarry, a bone-white gash in the riotous greens of early summer. Marty looked less certain now. She shielded her eyes from the glare and studied the woods, the narrow stepped ledges of the steep quarry walls, the tumbled expanse of huge blocks of waste stone at this end of the cut. Down in the bottom the turquoise waters winked, bringing back boyhood memories of skinny-dipping. This quarry was a pretty lousy swimming hole now, though, with those old cables and pieces of derrick rusting in it, and even an old car among the rushes.

"I don't see her, sir. Want me to give a shout?"

Wes scanned the terrain again. "Yeah, go ahead."

"Professor Wolfe!" she yelled. "Sheriff Cochran wants to talk to you!"

Her voice echoed faintly and then there was silence until the frogs and birds started in again. A woodpecker set up a smart clatter on a dead tree nearby. Damn place felt haunted even in the sun. The broad heaps of waste stone at this end had been invaded by cottonwoods, some of them already good-sized. Wes glimpsed gray fur moving among the limestone blocks behind them. A possum, he told himself, or a squirrel. There were red-winged blackbirds down at the water's edge. "Hell with this," he muttered. "Let's split up and go look for her."

"Wait," said Hopkins. "Sir."

He looked at her sharply and realized resentfully that she was right. If the professor was nearby she would have heard. And if she was coming, there was no sense in going away.

Only trouble was, no one was coming.

This whole setup gave him the creeps.

Hopkins seemed relaxed. Maybe that was her problem, she didn't take this professor seriously enough. Didn't realize in her gut that the woman had killed a man, failed to report a dead body to the authorities, and who knew what else. Wes realized it in his gut, all right. He found himself studying the darkness in the foliage, the shadows between the gigantic tumbled stones, many taller than a man. Dammit, he'd rather be standing in a dark Chicago alley than on this sun-baked quarry rim. His hand dropped to his holster.

"Hello, Martine."

Wes jerked around toward the sound of the husky voice but saw nothing. Hopkins said, "Hi, Professor Wolfe. This is Sheriff Wes Cochran. He's, uh, he's okay. Sir!" She showed her empty hands.

He saw it then, fifteen yards away, the silver glint of a rifle barrel thrust between two big blocks of stone, its owner invisible behind them. Not aimed at them. Not yet. Shit. He said, "Professor Wolfe, ma'am, let's put away the rifle, okay?"

He held out his hands like Marty's, palms out, fuming that she'd gotten the drop on him. A movement next to another stone yards away caught his eye for an instant. A wolf, no, a dog, stepped from the shadows, its head down. Another followed close behind. When he looked back at the rifle a woman was standing on the rock. She'd swung the rifle up to vertical, praise the Lord. She was tall, lean, in khakis and a lumpy photographer's vest. A fine-looking woman, pure somehow and serious, graceful despite the rough clothing. Hard to guess her age. Her hair was brown, caught loosely in a coil at the nape of her neck. She said, "Wesley Cochran?"

"Sheriff Cochran," said Wes. He hooked his thumbs in his belt. "We've got a few questions for you, Miss Wolfe."

"Professor Wolfe."

"Professor Wolfe." So she liked her title, too. Well, no sense getting off on the wrong foot. As if they hadn't already. He hoped she wouldn't turn out to be another of those asshole pointy-heads. He said, "See, ma'am, there are a lot of loose ends, and we think you can help."

"I've told Martine all I can."

"Look, Miss—Professor Wolfe, no offense, but I think you can do better. See, you gave Deputy Hopkins a hint about the Denton girl and the Willison thing. You're dropping more hints now about rape and revenge. And then you try and tell us you don't know anything more! And we've got the Klan involved somehow with both these cases, and two other cases that may be linked. So yeah, we think you can do better!"

"I know nothing about the Klan, Sheriff. And I've told Martine all I can."

"Professor Wolfe, you talked to the FBI yesterday. Why didn't you give us that information? Long ago?"

"Ah." Was that amusement glimmering in her dark eyes? Hard to tell from this far away. She said, "That's of no interest to Martine. She has understanding. The FBI men do not."

"What are you talking about? If you have information, you cooperate with us!"

"I've been cooperating with Martine, Sheriff."

"Look, Professor Wolfe, we've cut you a lot of slack. For instance, you're required by law to report a body to the authorities. Now, we've gone easy on you, even though you found the girl's body six years ago and didn't report it till now!"

"Sheriff, am I required to report that there are bodies in cemeteries?"

"What do you mean?"

"This body was in a coffin, placed in an underground burial chamber. If a body is properly and reverently buried, the natural assumption is that someone else took care of any required notification of authorities. The situation was unusual enough that I checked with the child's family, but you'll agree that I was not legally required to do even that much."

Shit. This one was slippery, all right. No sense bringing up the Pennsylvania case, she'd just say she hadn't been charged. Wes said forcefully, "Professor Wolfe, even supposing you've followed all the rules, we need your information. This is not a game!"

Even from this distance, the professor's dark pure eyes seemed to dig into him. "No, Sheriff, it's not a game. Not at all. Yet you're the one upset because the FBI might have scored a point. And you're the one who mentions following rules."

"Just do what's right. We all know what's right."

"Do I? Do you? I try to do what seems right to me."

Wes's shoulders tensed but he spoke mildly. "It'd be right

for you to tell us everything you know. You can start with explaining how you know Alma Willison."

"I don't know her."

"What do you—"

"I also know nothing about the Klan cards. I suspect you know much more about Klansmen than I do, Sheriff. My expertise is in biology, particularly paleobiology and evolution. Few Klansmen are enthusiastic about evolution. The only one of the bodies I knew anything about was the dead child whose burial chamber I stumbled across in the course of my biological investigations. And I told Martine about her." The dark eyes shifted from him to Hopkins. "Martine, I don't have much time. Do you have further questions?"

Hopkins said, "Uh, not really. See, Sheriff Cochran wanted to ask the questions."

"Go ahead," Wes snapped. Damn professor was baiting him, and if he didn't watch out she'd get him to show his anger. He could use a moment to plot strategy here. "Say what you've got to say, Hopkins."

She blurted, "Judge Denton died this morning."

"Died!" said Professor Wolfe. "How?"

"Convulsions," she said. "He had a seizure last night. It went on for hours and he never came out of it."

The professor nodded slowly and murmured, "So Teenia killed him after all."

"Teena?" Wes glanced at Hopkins, who looked mystified too, and back at Professor Wolfe. "Who the hell is Teena?"

A frown flickered across the professor's handsome face and she turned back to Hopkins. "Martine, it's been a pleasure knowing you. Perhaps we'll meet again. Goodbye."

Hopkins stepped toward her. "Professor Wolfe, please—"

The woman was gone. Just dropped out of sight behind the blocks of stone. Furious, Wes drew his revolver and charged toward the spot. He saw the two dogs, no, three, scrambling over some rocks and then to the right. He ran right too, to head her off in the jumble of waste blocks and cottonwoods. He clambered through a gap between two big stones. Hopkins was at his side, tugging at his sleeve now, shouting, "Sir! Sir, she won't—"

He shook her off impatiently. "Hopkins, get back to the car! Radio the state cops for reinforcements. We have to take her in for questioning."

"But, sir—"

"Do it, Hopkins!"

"Yes, sir." She was off toward the farmhouse, running too. Wes scanned the landscape of broken stones ahead and caught a glimpse of a curled fuzzy tail. He headed for it.

Damn professor needed to be taught a thing or two about the real world. Shouldn't take him long to catch up. He was glad that she'd headed for the field of broken blocks beside him rather than away from him into the woods. It wouldn't come to shooting, he thought, but if it did he wouldn't want her too far away, where that rifle became a big advantage. Close in, among the rocks, his handgun was better.

Gotta watch out for her all the same, after what she'd done to her attacker in Pennsylvania.

Shit. Better make it clear that he just wanted to finish talking. He shouted, "Professor Wolfe! Who is Teena?" God, he was puffing like a locomotive.

She wasn't. Her husky voice floated back evenly from too far ahead. "Not a Klansman, Sheriff. Goodbye."

He saw a silver glint of light on the rifle barrel, still pointing skyward, bobbing among the rocks ahead. He went full throttle, steaming over each giant block only to be faced by another. Sometimes he could squeeze between them but then the rough broken sides of the stone raked his skin and clothes. How did the damn woman move so fast? The only good thing was that at this speed she couldn't shoot. Keep her moving. Push on. Panting, he holstered his gun and used both hands to climb the next rock.

He'd hauled himself halfway up when the squeezing in his chest began. Goddammit, not now! He fumbled in his pocket for the nitroglycerin bottle and let himself slide back down the stone. He got the tablet under his tongue, but the giant fist inside his chest was clenching tighter, squeezing the cruel pain into his shoulder and down his arm. Wes leaned back against the tilted limestone block, terrified. He was sweating.

Well, why not? It was a hot day and he'd been running. Always made a guy sweat.

He wondered why he felt so cold.

Dammit, when was that nitroglycerin going to kick in? Never took this long. The pain was crushing him, taking possession of his mind, casting the real world into a kind of shadow. As though from a great distance he knew that he was resting on the warm limestone block, hearing birds and frogs, gazing at the hawks that circled in the hot sky. He knew all those things, but felt himself drifting from them, carried on an ocean of pain and fear. Was this how it ended?

Someone bent over him, touched him, opened his shirt, but he was too far away to care who it was. There was a sound, a loud sound in that distant real world, like the crack of a rifle. He was too far away to care about that either. A kind of peace began to trickle into him.

The sun beat down on the limestone.

The hawks soared.

Wes rested.

37

FROWNING, THE NIGHT-HAWK ADJUSTED THE VISOR OF HIS WHITE baseball cap against the sun and walked across the courthouse square back to his car.

There was still no new message from the Great Titan. The Night-Hawk had left a note Monday saying that Alma Willison had been carded and detained, and here it was Friday. The Great Titan always used to praise carding people. He didn't praise everything. Years ago, when he'd first joined this Province of the Klan, the Night-Hawk had been scolded for burning up a nigger's car, even though the nigger had been making eyes at someone's blond wife. But then the Great Titan had explained that it was not time yet to attract attention. It might give away the secret plan. Don't detain, don't burn anything, just watch until the moment is ripe, said the Great Titan. The Night-Hawk had been angry at first, because he'd taken care to make it look like a simple engine overheating. Mud-people didn't deserve cars anyway. But after a while he understood. When the great battle began, it had to be clear that each blow was the work of the Lord. Disguising it as overheating, without even leaving a card or a cross, was not what the Great Titan wanted, not what the Lord wanted. He that overcometh would wait for the moment of the wrath of God. *Rest yet for a little season.*

There was no note telling him to rest today.

There was no note scolding him either. He'd executed the mud-people, the Jew-boy, and the nigger, and the Great Titan hadn't scolded. That was a good sign.

The Night-Hawk drove around the corner of the square, heading back to work, thinking of what the Great Titan had told him over the years. Praise for the cardings. Cautions against premature action. Encouragement that the day was coming when whosoever was not found written in the book of life would be cast into the lake of fire. And a few weeks ago, the brief request: Alma Willison, Louisville. The Great Titan was not always clear in his instructions. But that was as it should be. *The people who walk in darkness shall see a great light.* In the end the Night-Hawk always understood.

Today there was no sign.

No message to tell him what to do.

No message to tell him what not to do.

Was that it? The Night-Hawk pulled into the service station. Was he supposed to go ahead? He'd worried that he might have been wrong about the Jew-boy and that nosy nigger, worried more now that the newspapers and television stations were talking about it. But there hadn't been any scolding from the Great Titan.

No praise.

But no blame either.

Sitting there in his car in Straub's Service, with the odor of

gasoline in the air and a hot sun blasting down on the steel
roof of his car, the Night-Hawk felt a cold thrill of excitement
run up his spine. Maybe it was time! Maybe the silence itself
was a sign! The silence of the Great Titan was a sign! Take off
the brakes. Rev up the invisible armies. Let the great battle
begin.

Tomorrow, thought the Night-Hawk. If there's no other sign
by tomorrow, it's time to become the mighty engine of the
Lord. Time to hit the gas. Floorboard it. Let 'er roll.

38

MARTY HAD RAISED THE STATE COPS AND A FLIRTATIOUS DIS-
patcher had agreed to send a couple of guys by in half an
hour. "No problem, darlin'," he said. "We know you sweet
young things from down south don't know how to bring in a
professor by yourselves."

Marty bit back a retort. She thought the sheriff was wrong,
sending her to call the state cops. Still, her job was to get this
half-wit to help. She was perched in the open driver's door
of the cruiser, on the side of the seat, one foot in the door-
frame, the other on the grass. She said coolly, "The driveway
here isn't marked except for the mailbox, and it's pretty hard
to—"

The crack of a gunshot came ringing from the woods.

Marty snapped, "Ten-forty-nine, ten-one!" and bolted from
the car. Callie was already running down the porch steps,
looking toward the quarry. Marty sprinted past her, shouting,
"Callie, I'll take care of it! Stay here! The state cops are coming
to help. Tell them how to get there!"

"More cops?" Callie shook her head. "That's a bad idea,
more cops!"

"I know," Marty yelled over her shoulder. "But it's a worse idea not to help them, right? So get back, and stay back!" She was at the edge of the woods.

"Okay, I guess."

Marty bounded along the overgrown path toward the quarry. She had a bad feeling about this, a real bad feeling. The sheriff was going at this the wrong way. And shooting was about the dumbest thing to do in any circumstances. Marty didn't kid herself for a minute—the professor might be dangerous. She was so damn prickly about her privacy, about the importance of her mysterious world. What was it she'd said about the FBI? She hadn't let them violate her. She wouldn't let Wes Cochran violate her either.

Bursting out from the woods, Marty looked around the rocky rim of the quarry. Nothing. "Sheriff?" she shouted. No answer. "Professor Wolfe?"

Still no answer.

She pulled herself up to the top of a big rock and scanned all around her. She spotted the sheriff halfway across the tumbled hill of broken waste stones. He lay very still in the bright sun.

"Sir!" Marty shouted, squinting against the glare.

No answer. No movement.

She leaped down and scrambled full-tilt across the rocks toward him, screaming, "Goddammit, Professor Wolfe, you didn't have to shoot him! You didn't!"

She swarmed up a big block of stone next to the one where the sheriff lay sprawled and dropped down to his side. Where was the blood? She didn't see any blood. His eyes were open, and when she picked up his hand the fingers moved. "Coach?" she asked urgently. "What happened?"

His pulse was feeble and his skin was pale and shiny. But his eyes focused on her and he said weakly, "Marty?"

"Help's coming, Coach. Hang in there." She inspected his legs and arms. No blood. Where the hell was he wounded? His shirt was already unbuttoned and she spread it open.

"Gotta get out. My heart—"

He was wrong, he hadn't been shot in the heart. There wasn't a scratch on his gray-haired chest and belly. She murmured, "No, sir, don't move. Not yet. You're doing fine just where you are," and spotted a piece of lined paper tucked below his left arm under his shirt. Marty pulled it out. The words were penciled clearly. "Myocardial infarction. Treated with 15 mg morphine IM, 400 mg lidocaine IM, 2:43 P.M."

Two forty-three. Marty checked her watch. That would be about ten minutes ago, just about the time she'd heard the shot. She leaned closer to the sheriff, adjusted his Stetson to shade his eyes. He looked so pale. "It's your heart, you say, Coach?"

"Yeah. Pain grabbed me like a bear hug."

"Just lie still, now. Did Professor Wolfe give you a shot?"

"A shot?"

"An injection."

He concentrated on breathing for a moment and Marty winced as she realized how very sick he was. He asked, "Before it happened?"

"No, after. I think."

"I don't— See, I was almost blacked out for a minute or two there. The pain. It's a little better now."

"Good."

"In a minute maybe I can get back—" He started to sit up.

"Coach, dammit, lie down!"

"Watch your language, kid," he said weakly.

"Coach, listen," Marty said. "You've just had a heart attack. Okay? Professor Wolfe gave you a shot of something, morphine and something else. The state cops are on their way. I don't want you to even twitch before they get you to the hospital and we know what's going on in your system."

"You're as bad as Shirl," he grumbled. But he lay still.

Marty hung on to his big hand. She was shaky, memories crowding in. Her own father full of drunken cheer one afternoon, dead the next day. At twelve she'd had trouble realizing that he was gone, really gone. The funeral had seemed unreal, her mother and Aunt Vonnie talking and crying and yelling at each other seemed unreal, the move to Bloomington months later unreal too. It didn't really happen, she kept telling herself for months. He'll come back soon and everything will be the way it was.

233

Well, he hadn't. No sense thinking about all that now. Right now, her job was to take care of this man. Her boss, her friend, her second father. Marty swiped her cuff across the dampness on her cheek.

He stirred a little. "That pain—it was like doomsday."

"Yeah."

"It's better now. I can—"

"You can lie right where you are. You're full of morphine. You can't just jump up and go trucking off across these stones."

"You're turning bossy, Hopkins."

"Damn right, sir."

He grinned weakly.

There was a crashing and cursing in the woods. Marty scrambled to the top of the stone block and waved at the state cops. One of them was dragging an aluminum-tube litter. "Over here!" she yelled. "And hurry up!"

"Goddamn, look at those stones!" said one.

They cursed some more. But they hurried.

39

CHRISSIE WOKE SCREAMING FRIDAY NIGHT, OR WAS IT SATURDAY morning? Marty ran to her bedside, Aunt Vonnie right behind her. "What's wrong, honey?"

Her big dark eyes shifted from her to Aunt Vonnie to the shadows of the room. She was sitting rigidly upright, arms straight down, fists clenching the sheets. "I don't know."

Marty hugged her. "Probably a bad dream. Do you remember what it was about?"

"No." She relaxed a hair. "A bad dream."

"Yeah. We all have bad dreams sometimes." Marty looked

at Aunt Vonnie, who was hanging on to the bedpost, her brushed satin nightgown mussed, her hair in rollers. "Hey, Aunt Vonnie, we can handle this. You go on and get your beauty sleep. You won't sell many peanut butter cookies to-morrow if you look like an old hag."

"Old hag! Least I don't frizz my hair like a used dust mop!"

"My job, it helps if I look like a witch, remember?" Marty made a ferocious face and Aunt Vonnie snorted and went back to bed. Marty turned back to her daughter. "You okay, kid?"

"Yeah. Just a bad dream. I don't remember it."

But Marty could tell she remembered the terror. She said, "Let me get my feet off this cold floor and I'll sit with you a few minutes."

She slid her feet under the covers and snuggled up to her daughter. Chrissie had warm new pajamas but that wasn't the warmth she needed now. The girl's hair smelled like flowers, some new shampoo she'd bought. Damn, why couldn't Brad hang around a little while, be a father when his kid needed him?

Or was it Marty's fault? Should she have gone with him to Alaska? She sure as shooting wasn't doing anything useful around here. Sheriff Cochran was up in the Bloomington hos-pital this very minute because Marty hadn't been able to ex-plain that Professor Wolfe did things her own way. Maybe he wouldn't have gotten himself so upset if she'd managed to explain it.

And these Klan killings. Marty shivered. The Klan was sup-posed to be done with, the violence, at least, all in the past. But these killers weren't just angry drunks. What was going on in her hometown, what ugly disease was poisoning them? Wes said the killers were isolated nutcases. He said that even the ex-Klansmen who grumbled that blacks and Jews were taking over the world were basically law-abiding. She used to agree, had happily taken on this job to keep everyone safe, to lock up the drunk and despairing until they were no longer dangerous. But these killers were beyond her understanding, turning the friendly hills she'd always loved into an unknown, fearsome wilderness.

And the Dentons. Poor Judge Denton. Who was Teenia?

Had she really killed the judge? Why had Professor Wolfe suddenly decided to mention her?

And why was Marty Hopkins getting herself all worked up in the middle of the night, snatching at every dark thought that offered itself, instead of getting some rest so that she could do something about the problems tomorrow?

She eased herself from Chrissie's bed and took an aspirin, but she got only fitful sleep the rest of the night and woke with a headache and sandy eyes.

Chrissie was looking down at the mouth, and Aunt Vonnie was dragging too as she handed around the orange juice. They all three sat staring at their muffins until the phone rang. Marty picked up. It was Chrissie's friend Janie.

"Mrs. Hopkins, can Chrissie come with us today?" She sounded bubbly and carefree. "We're going up to the White-hall Mall!"

"Your mama taking you?" Marty asked.

"Yes'm, and Daddy. They're getting a new lamp for the living room."

"Sure, she can go if she wants." Marty handed the receiver to Chrissie.

The two girls settled it. After breakfast Marty slipped five dollars to Chrissie for new earrings and dropped her off at Janie's. It was good that there'd be something to distract the kid today, to keep her mind off everything. She'd be okay, she was a tough kid, but right now she hurt.

Right now Marty hurt too.

She drove up to Monroe County to Professor Wolfe's farmhouse. The three dogs barked lazily at Marty but lay down again on the porch when a blond student Marty didn't remember came to the door. She said that Professor Wolfe was out of town for a while. Callie had driven her to Indianapolis, she said, and wouldn't be back for another hour. Marty sighed. "Okay, I'll come back later. Unless maybe you can tell me. I'm looking for someone named Teenia. Do you know who she is?"

The blonde shook her head. "Sorry."

"Professor Wolfe knows her. Maybe a student a few years ago?"

236

"I'm sorry. I never heard her mention anyone named Teenia."

Marty stopped at the Bloomington hospital, but of course they wouldn't let her see Wes Cochran. The doctor did say he was a lucky man. The shot of morphine and lidocaine was the right first aid, he told her, just what the emergency medical team would have given him. Marty was pleased and frustrated all at once. Professor Wolfe was so unpredictable, and she didn't seem to give a damn if they solved the case or not.

Driving back to headquarters, she passed the Denton place but decided not to stop. She just wasn't up to facing Royce today. Instead, she phoned when she got to her desk. But neither Royce nor Elizabeth knew a Teenia, and didn't remember Judge Denton ever mentioning her.

She pulled out Judge Denton's appointment books. Black leather bindings, pale gray pages indexed for months, small, firm handwriting. No Teenia. No Tanya, or Tonia. No Ernestine, Albertine, Celestine, Justine. No Martine. Except for Christine Stephenson, a court recorder who'd retired to Florida years ago, the only name she found in Judge Denton's notes was Tina Clay, complete with phone number. Tina turned out to be the secretary of an Indianapolis judge, a friend of Judge Denton's. Tracked down at home, Tina Clay was mystified at being telephoned on a Saturday about a man she said she'd only spoken to on the phone.

"What about a Professor Wolfe from IU? Biology department?"

"Sorry. Never heard of him."

Marty replaced the receiver glumly and turned to the last of the appointment books. Nothing. She pulled a tissue from the box, dabbed at her stinging eyes, and admitted to herself that she must be on the wrong track. But what was the right track? Why hadn't Professor Wolfe said something more? How were they ever going to find this Teenia? And if they did, would it only be to discover that she'd disappeared, like Alma Willison?

The door opened and Jessup and Manning came in. Jessup looked sour today, like a little wind-up bulldog instead of a wind-up beagle. "Good morning, Deputy Hopkins," Jessup said.

"Good morning, sir."

"Terrible news, news about Sheriff Cochran." As always, his words tumbled out too fast.

"Yes, sir. They say he's not doing too bad, but of course he can't come back to work for a while."

"Can we see him in the hospital?"

"I don't know, sir. When I left Bloomington this morning they said only his wife could visit him."

"Too bad."

"Maybe after they move him down here you can see him. Is there anything I can help with?"

Jessup glanced at Manning and then bobbed his sleek head in agreement. "We don't know what we have here," he said. "Thought maybe a local, a local point of view would help."

"Well, I can try, sir. What is it?"

"Photos. From discarded Polaroid negatives we found."

He spread half a dozen pictures onto the table before her, each carefully placed in a clear evidence bag. Marty looked at the naked subjects and frowned. "Where'd you get these?"

"We talked to a Professor Wolfe the other day. She said we'd find important, important evidence by the old firetower. Told us to look under the *Cercis canadensis*. That's a redbud, it turns out. We found the negatives there with some other trash."

"This is weird," Marty said. "Was there anything else?"

"Coke cans, Fritos bags, tissues—"

"Fritos bags."

"Yes."

"Recent?"

"Some old. Some left this past month, I think."

"And Professor Wolfe sent you there." Marty felt giddy, on the edge of laughter and shock. So that's how Professor Hart got his jollies! No wonder he'd memorized Wolfe's address! Marty had to work to keep the deadpan face she knew Coach would keep. She tapped the photo with her finger. "Did you check the view from that firetower, sir? You can see this scene?"

"Yes. The photos were taken from the top of the tower."

"Did Professor Wolfe say this evidence was connected to the Klan?"

"She said she didn't know anything about, about the Klan. But she said it was important evidence."

Marty nodded. "Well, sir, it's not for me to say, but I'd suggest going straight to the dean at IU. These young women are students, swimming on their own property. The firetower is in the national forest. This peeping Tom is using government property for his activities."

"If it's not the Klan, we shouldn't really—" Jessup looked disappointed. The little agent had probably hoped to find crosses burning at the old tower.

"You never know, sir," said Marty. She wasn't about to let Professor Hart off too easily. Secretly snapping photos of women students skinny-dipping in their own backyards was not approved behavior for professors. She suggested, "Could be blackmail, sir. Fund-raising for the Klan." She was pleased to see Jessup's face brighten. "You don't want to upset the students if there's any other way. They haven't done anything wrong. But this ought to stop. We'll handle it real careful, when you give it back to us. Of course we'll need your okay. It is a national forest."

"No, no." Jessup's appetite for the situation had returned. "We'll talk to the dean before we give it back to you." He and Manning went out. Marty shook her head. So Wolfe would have her revenge on Professor Hart. She'd sicced his own dogs on him. A dangerous woman.

But the distraction only heightened her sense of uselessness. Marty rubbed her temples and took another aspirin. She felt like such a loser. She'd messed up her family, failed the sheriff, failed to help the Dentons. She'd hoped she could at least get some information on Teenia. But the sheriff was out of commission, Professor Wolfe unavailable, Judge Denton gone forever. She'd followed every damn lead to its dead end, and now there was nowhere to go for her next move.

Shoot. She'd wanted so much to find Teenia for the sheriff.

She tried to go over her notes again in the hope that she'd missed something, but the words turned blurry because her eyes were stinging again. When Mason came back at two she grabbed a tissue, blew her nose noisily, and said in a rush, "Hay fever, sorry. Nothing much happened. Mind the phone awhile, okay? Foley will be in at four. I'll call in, got something to follow up." She ran out the door. She didn't really have anything to follow up, except that Professor Wolfe had said something about the Willisons that she'd forgotten to ask about in all the confusion. She knew she shouldn't, but right now driving to Louisville was at least doing something, even if she was supposed to liaise with the Louisville cops and hadn't, and even if what she had to ask was a dumb question, and even if she was a world-class loser who'd botched up her job and her family and her whole stupid life.

On Saturdays, the Night-Hawk worked the early shift, so by midafternoon he was already home, singing "Rock of Ages" to himself and packing his kit.

"Foul, I to Thy fountain fly," he sang. He was foul today, still black around his fingernails though he'd washed several times. He'd need to do a real scrubdown before the ceremony tonight. "Wash me, Savior, or I die," he sang, putting in the .22 and the .38 both, and two boxes of ammo. He packed some extra rags and kerosene into his bag. It looked like a doctor's bag. A doctor for the salvation of the white race. Rope too, and wire and wire cutters, and a saw. Hammer and big nails for the crucifixion. Cards, and his knives, the blued Marine knife and the small fish-gutting knife, though with the woman he wouldn't have to do the eyes. And matches. "While I draw this fleeting breath, when my eyelids close in death, when I soar to worlds unknown, see Thee on Thy judgment throne, Rock of Ages, cleft for me, let me hide myself in Thee."

All packed. He placed the black bag by the door and picked up his baseball cap. Only one more thing to do this afternoon. He'd borrowed a car for the trip to the cave tonight. Always safer to use someone else's car. It was tucked in the garage, all ready. So all he had to do was cut a couple of logs the right size. He'd do that now and take them to the cave nearer sundown. Should be easy now that the cops were gone. But even so he'd better dust over the trail they left as he dragged them into the tunnel. Blot it out. The police might be gone, but they might be back too.

He'd decided that the Great Titan himself had told the police. It was part of the invisible plan. The Great Titan was smart, brilliant even, and if the Night-Hawk was reading the signs right, it was time for things to break loose. When the great war came they'd need the newspapers and the TV and the police, and the Great Titan knew that. The reporters' interest was another sign that the time had come. The time for the great war against the mud-people, when all the secret soldiers of the invisible army would let 'er rip. Executing the woman was part of the Great Titan's design, and the police and the newspapers were part of the design. It was time, time to come out of tribulation, to have the tears wiped from his eyes.

Back when he was little Pip, no one had wiped the tears from his eyes. "Be a man, Pipsqueak! Take it like a man!" his father had roared, and little Pip had learned how to crawl out of his body and not go back until he'd built another wall in his mind and the shameful tears were safely hidden behind it. But that was before. Now he was powerful, the engine of the Lord, and it was time to come out of tribulation. He opened the Bible to the familiar page. "These are they which came out of great tribulation, and have washed their robes, and made them white in the blood of the Lamb." He would overcome. He was part of the great invisible empire that would overcome. "They shall hunger no more, neither thirst any more; neither shall the sun light on them, nor any heat. For the Lamb which is in the midst of the throne shall feed them, and shall lead them into living fountains of waters; and God shall wipe away all tears from their eyes."

The Night-Hawk changed out of his uniform and took his bag out to the borrowed car in the garage, locking the kitchen door behind him. He'd left his front-door key somewhere. No big problem, but he should remember to check around at work and see if it might be there. He backed out past his own car in the driveway and closed the garage door, and set out to do the work of the Lord.

40

MIDAFTERNOON ON A MAY DAY IN LIMESTONE COUNTRY. THE Night-Hawk's borrowed car rolls smoothly toward the woods, seeking the wrath of the Lord. Somewhere far below the roads Alma Willison crouches in the dark, sawing at a steel chain with a front door key and a prayer. North of town, an ambulance speeds down the highway from Bloomington toward Nichols County, carrying a paramedic minding his monitors and, attached to those monitors, a dozing Sheriff Wes Cochran. And south of town, a sheriff's department cruiser tears along the highway toward Louisville, its wheel gripped by white-knuckled Deputy Hopkins, who is swallowing tears and running on despair.

Far above them all, a jet plane climbs to its appointed altitude, thundering south from the Indianapolis airport. A lone, lanky woman in one of the window seats pulls a laptop computer from under the seat ahead and places it on her lap, but before opening it she pauses to look at the scene below. The woman sees highways and towns, flat farmland yielding to wooded hills, *Acer* and *Cercis* and *Diospyros*. Beneath the vegetation she sees a karst landscape of sinkholes, springs, disappearing streams, caves. She sees further. She sees a vast tropical sea alive with tiny shelled creatures who build their carbonate shells, reproduce, die, and sink in ever-thickening layers to the sea bottom, while beyond the sea continents collide and mountains rise and erode away. She sees glaciers slide down from the north and retreat again, leaving scoured and flattened land and outwash plains, and she sees vigorous life-forms colonizing the forbidding new environments. She

242

sees great extinctions and great flowerings of species, life changing the earth and being changed by the earth.

The woman sees the frail web of asphalt flung across the hills by one of the more recent species, and she sees that those thin threads of hydrocarbons will succumb to the earth's cycling waters and rambunctious life. She sees the tiny steel capsules rolling atop the asphalt strands, carrying members of that busy species, humanity. Humanity, that along with its cultivated crops, its livestock, its parasites, and its symbionts has already increased the carbon cycle by 20 percent, the sulfur cycle by 100 percent. She sees a new age of massive extinctions already commencing, and she sees beyond to an earth crowded with new post-human species.

She sees life feeding on life and on death, and respects it.

She sees a chain of quarries below, gashes struck through the shallow teeming topsoil deep into the once-living bedrock, and she sees the shine of Brother Sun's light bouncing from the life-giving water in those depths.

She is at one with the reflected light, with the earth, with the cycling dance of death and life.

Does she think about Martine LaForte Hopkins, about Wesley Cochran, about Alma Willison, about the Ku Klux Klan? Perhaps not, because when at last she turns from the window she opens the case of the laptop computer, pulls some notes from her pocket, and begins respectfully to record her scholalry observations of evolutionary adaptation in the pale, blind creatures who thrive in the dark wildernesses within mammals and within limestone caves.

41

WES WOKE UP TO A WHITE CONFUSION. OH YEAH, HOSPITAL.
Too damn much light. And not the room he knew. Oh yeah,
they'd moved him. Home, the Bloomington doctors said,
you're going home. But they meant this place. Well, at least
he was off those damn IVs. He flexed his arms. Felt good.

Shirley was dozing in the chair by his bed. She looked exhausted, her face relaxed into sags, her bouncy blond hairdo
drooping around her forehead and ears, showing the gray.
He was suddenly awash with love and gratitude for this tired
woman who had chosen him. In sickness and in health, they'd
pledged each other as green kids, almost without thinking
because it was so irrelevant back then. Sickness then meant a
cold or a sprained ankle. Now suddenly the fact that Shirl
was willing to abide by that long-ago contract was his greatest
treasure.

Cut it out, old man, he scolded himself. Don't get sappy.

He owed other people too. Marty Hopkins, for one. And
that crazy professor who'd shot him full of the right stuff,
fired a rifle to get attention, and run back to the house for a
litter, they'd told him. Of course when she heard the state
cops coming she'd melted away like a wild thing into the
woods, and who knew where she was now? Not doing her
civic duty by telling them about the case, that's for sure.

Dr. Hendricks bustled in, white-haired and lively. Shirley
stirred in the chair and pushed back her droopy hair with both
hands. "Oh, hi, Doc," she said.

"Hi, Shirley." Doc picked up the charts at the foot of the
bed and then looked up at Wes. "How ya doing, Champ?"

"Glad to see your lumpy old face, Doc," Wes said. "Up in

244

that Bloomington hospital, they treated me like a broken radio or something. Testing all my circuits."

"Well, your circuits are doing better, but you better sit down with me pretty soon and figure out how to take the weight of the universe off your shoulders or they're going to kick out on you again."

"Yeah, okay. Shirley here tells me I have to eat different, too."

"And walk to work," Shirley said firmly.

"We've both been telling you that for four years, Sheriff," said Doc.

"Yeah, yeah, I know, don't rub it in."

"This time you do it," Shirley said. "I can't take many more days like these."

Wes squeezed her hand. "I promise, boss. Listen, Doc, is there any news? We've got a major case, and—"

"Wesley Cochran! You're in a hospital!" Shirley exclaimed.

"Shirl, honey, I just can't keep from fretting about this one. You could lock me in a closet and I'd still stew about it."

Doc said, "You need another sedative, Champ. But Art Pfann's out there. He's been waiting a couple of hours."

"Good! Send him in! Can I sit up any straighter here?" He scrabbled at the sheets, trying to lift his shoulders.

"Wait, idiot!" Shirley hit a button and the head of the bed rose, pushing him into a sitting position.

Doc went out into the hall. Wes heard him say, "Ten minutes."

The prosecuting attorney, followed by Special Agent Jessup's assistant, Manning, came in. "Sorry to bother you, Sheriff," he said. "How's it going?"

"Well, Art, Shirley thinks I don't lack too much of being sick," Wes said. "But I'm okay. What've you got?"

"FBI sent a match on some fingerprints," Pfann said. "Jessup had to go to Bloomington to check something out, but Manning here got the stuff. Can we talk?" He glanced at Shirley.

"I'll be back in a minute," Shirley warned, and left.

Pfann said, "Looks interesting. Tell him, Manning."

"Guy named Hardy Packer," Manning said. "Supposed to

be involved in those Klan bombings a few years ago up in Whitecastle."

Wes felt s surge of adrenaline despite the calming drugs. "Could be our man," he said. "Where were the prints? At Goldstein's?"

"No, we couldn't raise any there. Guy was real careful. Same thing at Sears's—clean as a whistle. But we found prints a couple of places in that cave. The coffin lid."

"The coffin lid! He didn't wipe that?"

"He did. Nothing on most of it except your deputy's prints," Manning explained. "But way in the back corner we got lucky. He missed a spot."

"So what do we know about this guy?"

"The Bureau is sending more stuff to Agent Jessup. Right now we've just got the name, and some information that he was raised in these parts, over near Campbellsburg. Quiet fellow, they say in Whitecastle, but real good with guns and explosives. He dropped out of sight when the Whitecastle cops started closing in."

"Packer," said Wes. "I remember a Packer from when I was a kid. Old man lived on a farm down there. Wife ran off, didn't she?"

"I don't remember," Art Pfann said.

Manning said, "Right, and a few years later he lost his place and took his boys to Terre Haute. Older boy joined the Marines, killed in Nam. But after junior high in Terre Haute there's no trace of the younger one until the Whitecastle killings started."

"I recollect that the old Packer place wasn't too far from that cave. Five miles, maybe." Wes shook his head. "But there's nobody by that name around now."

"There's a photo. Lousy, but something," said Manning. He took it from the envelope. "Packer's the second from the right."

Wes squinted at it. Five men, four in white robes, the second from the right in a black one. Figured. He had a beard. Wes covered the beard, focusing on the nose and eyes. Goddammit, there was something familiar there. What? What?

"You don't know him?" Manning was clearly disappointed.

"I know him. Just can't place him. Art?" He thrust the photo at Pfann but he shook his head too.

"I guess he doesn't wear a beard like that now," he said.

Wes leaned his head back on the pillows. Who was it? Dammit, he was getting old. Didn't even know his own county.

The nurse came in, followed by Shirley. "I'm sorry, sir, ten minutes are over."

"Yeah. Okay." Pfann handed the photo back to Manning. "Well, Sheriff, contact us if you think of anything. Take care of yourself, now."

"Okay. Sorry." He watched Pfann and Manning heading for the door and suddenly heard himself add, "You said the prints were two places in the cave."

"Yes, sir."

"Was the other place the oil spout?"

Pfann turned back. "Yes, it was."

"Lemme see that photo again!"

"Mr. Cochran, you must rest. Doctor's orders," the nurse chided. She held up a hypodermic to the light.

"Hey, you trying to make me mad?" He couldn't manage a very convincing roar, but it was enough to widen the nurse's eyes.

Manning handed him the photo again. Wes said, "Newton. Gil Newton. Goddamn."

"Newton?" Manning pulled out his notebook.

Wes showed the photo to Shirley. "What do you say, Shirl? The guy in the black?"

She nodded slowly. "My God, Wes. You mean he's the one—?"

Pfann, peering over her shoulder, was nodding too. Wes handed Manning the photo and pushed back his covers. "Gil Newton. Goes to our church, the son of a bitch. Moved here five or six years ago and old man Straub gave him a job at his service station."

"Straub was Great Titan of the Klan back then?" Pfann asked.

Wes nodded. "Your daddy and I and everybody else needed his help to get elected, until the Hines beating."

Manning's eyelid twitched but he said only, "Home address?"

"Out on the Dodd Road, near Guthrie Creek." The nurse moved in with the needle but Wes shook her off impatiently. "Shit, he may have that Willison woman from Louisville! Description of the kidnapper was vague but it matches Newton as far as it goes. Don't let people go storming in there, Art. There's a chance she's still alive. Maybe—maybe I'll use Hopkins. She's good at talking to people. We can . . ." He started to swing his legs out.

The nurse pushed him back, clucking, and lowered the head of the bed. Shirley said, "Hey, Champ, the prosecuting attorney will call the right people."

"Listen, I know this case! I've gotta get out of here!"

"No way!" Shirley exclaimed. "I'll have them put you in a straitjacket before I let you go!"

Art Pfann was backing toward the door. "Take it easy, Sheriff. We'll do it right. We'll—"

"Goddammit!" Wes struggled up and swung his legs over the edge of the bed again.

"Champ, stop it!" Shirley grabbed his arm. The nurse grabbed the other.

Pfann said, "Hey, we'll be back when Jessup gets here," and hustled from the room, Manning hard on his heels.

"Shirl, get out of the way! I've got to get to a phone!" Wes said. Damn women had no idea what was important.

"No, Champ. And I'm not going to let anyone else in here if you don't lie back down right now!"

"Goddammit, Shirl!" The trouble was, he felt about as strong as a wet noodle. If he stood up now and fell down—

"I'm not kidding, Champ."

She wasn't kidding. He could tell. He sighed and said, "How 'bout a deal? Get me a phone in here."

The nurse frowned but Shirley said, "Done."

"And none of that sissy sedative stuff!" he growled, pointing at the hypodermic.

The nurse said, "But Dr. Hendricks—"

"Nah. Doc Hendricks knows it's against my religion. I'll take care of Doc Hendricks."

Shirley took the nurse by the arm. "Let's go get the doctor. Maybe he can talk him into it. And we'll get the phone connected too." But she waited till Wes was lying back on his pillows before she steered the nurse from the room.

Good ol' Shirl always saw reason in the end. Tired or not, he couldn't rest now. He knew as much about Newton as anyone in the county. They'd need him. Wes yawned. And when he got his phone he'd alert Foley and Hopkins and . . .

When Doc Hendricks and Shirley returned a few minutes later, Wes was asleep.

42

WAYNE WILLISON WAS IN THE FRONT YARD WHEN MARTY PULLED up. He was wearing a short-sleeved tan polo shirt and was pulling weeds from under the hedge. He straightened as she cut the ignition and climbed out.

"Howdy," he said, looking at her with a mixture of hope and dread. "You're the one from Indiana."

"Yes, sir, I'm Deputy Hopkins, Mr. Willison. No news yet, I'm afraid. But I have a couple more questions."

"Sure. Whatever." He rubbed his hands against his khakis. He seemed older than on her last visit. Marty wondered if he'd slept at all since his wife disappeared.

"Is Milly around?" she asked.

"Up the street." He gestured toward a small group of children running around a yard at the corner. "I hate to let her out of my sight these days. But I don't want to lock her up like a prisoner. So I compromise and work in the yard a lot." He glanced around the tidy lawn and tried to grin. "Going to be the neatest front yard in fifty states before long."

"Yes, sir. You're wise to keep an eye on her."

"The police send a car by every couple of hours, too."

"Good."

"Now, do you want me to call Milly?"

"No. No, sir, the questions are for you. I'd like to ask you about Milly's birthday."

Suddenly there was caution in his blue eyes and Marty's spine tightened. Something important here. He said too casually, "Alma usually has a party for her, a few little friends."

"Yes, sir." Marty was thinking fast. Wolfe wouldn't have been interested in a kid's party. But a celebration of a birth— She said, "You're her grandparents, right? Who are the parents? Your son, or daughter?"

"What does this have to do with my wife missing?"

"We don't know, sir. We're just trying to get a complete picture. It all helps."

"I wish Alma was here."

"You mean the parents are her secret, something like that?"

"She knows more about it. Look, Deputy Hopkins, I don't see how it can help find her, but I do see how it could hurt Milly."

"We won't hurt Milly, believe me. We're not in the business of telling secrets, Mr. Willison. But really, it may help us find your wife."

"You really think so? Well—yeah—"

"The thing is, it might tie in with other information we have," Marty explained. "Mr. Willison, who are the parents?"

"I don't know." Wayne Willison rubbed the back of his neck. "See, we only had one child, Alma and I. Little girl who died of leukemia when she was only five years old. But then seven years ago someone asked Alma to take care of a baby awhile. Alma was on this church committee that helped poor families and it was connected to that. And Milly was such a sweet baby. I got to loving her right away. And Alma was so happy. Pretty soon I didn't want the family to come back for her, ever."

"Did she say anything more about the person who wanted her to take care of Milly?" A hunch was nibbling at Marty's mind.

"Not for a long time, then she said the mother was dead. By then I didn't care. I wanted the kid forever."

"So you adopted Milly?"

"Well, that was another thing. I suggested it, of course, but Alma wouldn't hear of it. She didn't want to adopt her." He looked anxiously at Marty. "Do you really think it's connected? Maybe the father tracked us down? Thinks he should take revenge?"

Marty nodded slowly. She didn't like that possibility either. Suppose Milly's father had been a Klansman, a violent fellow. Maybe in jail for a while. He got out, he started taking revenge on the folks who he imagined had done him wrong, including the woman who had cared for his little girl for years.

Willison asked timidly, "Could the father take her away from us?"

"Not if I have anything to say about it."

He asked more belligerently, "You work for government. Government takes children away sometimes."

"Sir, really, I'm just trying to get your wife back." But another possibility was needling at her. She could imagine a woman mourning for a dead daughter, mourning for years, finally snapping and kidnapping a baby, pretending its mother was dead and its family didn't care. She asked, "Mr. Willison, another question. Is Milly's real name Teenia? Tina, Tanya, anything like that?"

"No. Her real name is Camille."

"Did your wife ever mention a Teenia? Or do you know of a Teenia?"

"Not that I remember."

"Could it have been Milly's mother's name?"

"I just don't know."

Marty sighed. "Okay. Is there anything else? Anything that might help us identify her family?"

He hesitated and Marty knew there was more. She coaxed, "Mr. Willison, sir, I know you're torn up about this, not knowing if it's really helping your wife. But it's useful, really, if we have as many facts as possible."

"Yeah. Well, I've already said too much, or else not enough. Might as well go all the way. Alma's been keeping a little box for Milly, something from her mother."

"May I see it, sir?"

He glanced up the street doubtfully. Marty added, "I'll

251

keep an eye on Milly if you want to go get it yourself. Really, it might help us figure out where to look for your wife."

Willison said, "Be right back," and bounded into the house. Up the street, ponytailed Milly heard the door slam and stopped chasing a neighbor boy. She stood stock-still on the sidewalk, staring at her house. Marty waved and smiled reassuringly but the child waited, rigid, until the door opened again and Willison emerged. Then Milly gave a shout and started after her little friend again.

Marty thought of Chrissie, of how she'd worried that Marty would leave too, like Brad. Little Milly had lost a father too, and two mothers. God, life was hard on little kids.

But looking at Wayne Willison's haggard face as he approached, she decided life wasn't real easy on grown-ups either.

He held a small cardboard box with a bouquet design on the lid and script letters, "Floral Note Cards." "This is it," he said. "All I know about her before she came to us."

He handed the box to Marty and she removed the lid. Inside was a blue note card that said simply, "Kentucky State Archives, Birth Records, Book 733, page 514."

Her birth record. Milly's birth record. The parents would be on it! But shoot, this late on a Saturday offices were closed. Plus, this one was way down in Frankfort. There'd be no hope of getting in. She'd have to wait till Monday, unless she could convince some higher-up that it was worth dragging an archivist in from home. Maybe the Louisville cops could do it. This was a big case, after all, and this information might help explain why Alma Willison had disappeared, and might give them a man's name.

She started to reach for her notebook to write down the information and felt a little shift in the box. There was something else in it. She lifted out the blue note card. Underneath, a tissue was folded around something lumpy. Gently, Marty pushed the tissue off, and whispered, "Oh, God."

It was a necklace, a gold necklace, expensive and lovely. It was worked in a rhythmic repeating design of leaves and

252

Marty knew its pattern too well. It matched the bracelet on the little skeleton in the cave. It was the necklace painted in the portrait in the Dentons' front hall.

The little victory of a hunch confirmed didn't stop the nausea that swelled in her throat.

"What is it?" Wayne Willison asked sharply.

Marty swallowed. "It's okay, Mr. Willison. This turns out to be a real good lead. Let me give you a—" Whoops. She couldn't take it as evidence and give him a receipt. She was way out of her jurisdiction. Hopkins the loser blows it again. She said, "No, on second thought, call the police here. They're in charge of this end of the case. I know what to follow up on the Indiana side. Get the box to them as fast as you can, okay?"

"Okay."

"Tell me, did your wife have any friends called Denton? A girl, Phyllis Denton? Maybe Elizabeth Denton? Judge Harold Denton?" He was shaking his head, but she went on, "Hal Denton, Junior? Royce Denton?"

"No. You asked me about these people last time. Hal Denton—it seems I've heard that name, but I don't think it was from Alma."

"What about a woman called Wolfe? Professor at Indiana University?"

"No. I never heard of any of them, except maybe Hal Denton, and I'm not sure of that."

"Okay. But there's got to be a connection. Well, tell the police here to take real good care of Milly's box. Be sure they give you a receipt. I'll get to work on our end of it."

"Do you know where Alma is?"

"Not yet, sir, I'm sorry. But this gives me something good to work on. I'll get back to you real soon."

She hurried back to the cruiser, drove slowly past the kids playing at the end of the block, and then peeled out of there. She'd call in when she crossed the river, and then head for the Dentons' to break some more bad news.

The shadowy man she was chasing suddenly seemed more real. Not just violent, not just crazy, not just an anony-

253

mous Klansman filled with hatred. Now there was a sense of a personality too: a guy who hated women, or feared them, she figured, if he was attracted to a girl, to a pretty blue-eyed judge's child— Marty felt nauseous again. Time to put this guy away. She sped back toward her home and her daughter.

43

"GO ON OUT, SHIRL, JUST FOR A MINUTE. WE GOTTA TALK," WES coaxed.

Prosecuting Attorney Pfann had returned with Special Agents Jessup and Manning, who were standing uncomfortably by the hospital bed. Arms crossed, Shirley eyed them all suspiciously.

Wes said, "I won't get overexcited. Cross my heart."

"And hope to die!" Shirl reminded him sharply. "Remember that. I'll be back in ten minutes." She marched from the room and closed the door. Wes considered himself lucky that she hadn't slammed it.

Art Pfann cleared his throat uneasily and rumbled, "We'll be quick, Wes."

"I'm okay, dammit. It's my heart, not my brain." Wes glared at the prosecuting attorney. Young whippersnapper. "So what are we doing about Newton?"

Pfann said, "We're getting a warrant to search his house. I dropped by Straub's Service but he's off till tomorrow morning. So we'll take him at home."

Agent Jessup said, "But we don't just walk up, walk up and knock on the door. This fellow Hardy Packer—what's he calling himself here? Gil Newton?—he's no pushover."

"Tell us about him," Wes said.

"Okay." The little man flipped the crisp pages of his report.

"Ten years ago in Whitecastle they had some problems. A synagogue was bombed, a Jewish doctor's, doctor's house, a black man's car." He always sounded like a tightly wound toy, in a big hurry to get nowhere, Wes thought. But this was important. "Worst was a black man, beaten, fingers chopped off, shot. Fingers were jammed in his mouth when they found the body hidden in an old oil drum, cross smoked on the side. Packer was picked up with a batch, a batch of other guys. They questioned him and released him when someone alibied him. A week later the alibi was shot full of holes, but when they went to find him he'd disappeared. Never found a trace of him till now. They finally charged five other men, and three of them claimed they'd only roughed up the black man. Said Packer was the one who'd pulled the trigger, hidden the body, set the bombs. He was expert, he was cool, he followed orders. None of his buddies claimed, claimed to be very friendly with him. They said he kept to himself, wouldn't talk about much of anything except mechanical stuff."

Wes nodded. "That fits Newton, all right. Son of a bitch hardly opens his mouth except about transmissions and oil changes. Still—I can't see the guy plotting a murder campaign."

"He didn't in Whitecastle either. Packer was what they called the Night-Hawk of the organization." Wes nodded. The black robe had told him as much. "He took care of the fiery cross and of violence. But basically he took orders. The other guys were in charge."

Wes shifted on the bed. "There's someone in charge here too. Newton's not the leader type."

"Okay. Who?" asked Jessup.

Wes shrugged. "Lots of possibilities in this county. There's plenty of sympathy for Klan ideas, except for the violence, and I guess a handful even agree with that. But the turkey behind Newton is keeping himself pretty well hid."

"Well," said Art Pfann, "maybe when we pick up Newton he'll tell us about his boss."

Wes grunted. Newton wouldn't tell, he was sure. If quiet Gil Newton had a streak crazy enough to do those crucifixions, he'd be crazy enough to keep his mouth shut about his bosses. Damn, soon as Doc Hendricks let him out of this hospital he'd better have another talk with old Lester. Lester's chief was Newton's chief too. Had to be.

Wes said, "I was wondering. That Professor Wolfe sent you to look for some evidence. How did that fit in?"

Jessup snorted. "Didn't. Different problem. Some peeping Tom was taking Polaroid snapshots of coeds swimming."

Art Pfann chuckled. "Do-it-yourself *Playboy?*"

"Right. A couple of them are real lookers. Anyway, the peeper turned out to be another IU professor. I met him, in fact, guy named Hart. We ran a check and there's nothing to connect him to the Klan or to any of the killings. But his dean was furious, plans to bring him up for censure."

"Yeah, IU tries to look out for its coeds," Wes said. He was secretly delighted that Jessup had been sent on a wild-goose chase, and secretly chagrined that he himself had been taken in too, had gone charging across those goddamned mankiller rocks for the sake of the same wild goose. Hopkins had read the professor right. Should have trusted her judgment.

Jessup asked, "Anybody know what Packer's house looks like?"

Art Pfann shook his head. "Newton's? Never been there."

"Bert Mackay works with him at the service station. He might have visited," Wes said. "But I wouldn't be surprised if he's never been there either. Newton keeps to himself. Hardly even says hi after church. About the house—why don't we have Sims or Hopkins drive by, real casual, give it a close look without stopping?"

Jessup frowned. "We don't want to tell a lot of people about this. How do we know for sure where their loyalties lie?"

The little shit was accusing his department of a Klan connection. Wes said mildly, "Well, I s'pose we could get a couple of you feds in a big armored truck to cruise by pretending to take vacation snapshots. You think that'll fool him?"

"Hey, Wes, simmer down," Art Pfann said nervously. "You promised Shirley. Mr. Jessup, the sheriff is right. An unfamiliar vehicle on that lonely road would draw this fellow's attention. Spook him. But Sheriff Cochran's cruisers do go by from time to time just in the normal course of things."

"Sims's uncle went to that Klan rally," Jessup pointed out stubbornly.

GRAVESTONE

"Okay, how 'bout this," Wes offered. "One of your agents goes with—say, Mason, he's on now. Don't even tell him which house we're looking at. We just drive by, no slowing down."

"Sounds good to me," Art Pfann said, and Jessup nodded slowly.

Wes went on, "There's likely a hostage, too. We could get— Well, Hopkins is good at talking guys down."

"We've got hostage negotiators," Jessup said stiffly. "Trained."

Wes shrugged, unwilling to argue this one. He'd be just as glad if Marty Hopkins didn't have to go up against a man as desperate and vicious as this Packer seemed to be. Goddammit, hard to believe that quiet Gil Newton was the one they were talking about. He said, "Well, get your boys here, whoever you need. And try not to get the county grapevines going about lots of feds parachuting in, or he'll be gone. Also—" He frowned. "How about you stake it out and wait for him to leave the house? One team can follow him, another can go in the house and get the hostage. Might save some shooting."

Art Pfann said, "Makes sense to me."

Jessup started to mutter something but there was a crisp rap on the door and Shirley stuck her head in. "Ten minutes are up," she said.

"Yes, ma'am, we're just leaving," Jessup said almost eagerly.

"Anything else, Wes?" Pfann asked.

He sighed. "Yeah. I really want to see this turkey locked up. So don't blow it, okay?"

Pfann gave his shoulder a squeeze. "We'll do our best." He followed Jessup, who seemed to be greeting someone in the hall. Then Pfann's booming voice joined in. "Hal! How you doing? God, I was so sorry—"

"Yeah, thanks, Art," said Hal Denton's voice. "We're pretty much okay, considering."

"Your mother?"

"Exhausted, of course. Royce is doing what he can for her. You just saw the sheriff? How's he doing?"

"Coming along pretty good."

"I'll just say hello while I'm here. See you later, Art." And then Hal was in the doorway, in shirtsleeves with expensive suit trousers, the knot of his tie loosened a little. He smiled at Shirley. "Hi, Mrs. Cochran."

"Hi, Hal. Sorry to hear about your father. Tell your mother I'll be by to see her soon as I'm through here."

"Yeah. How's your patient?"

Wes saw her melt a little at his high-powered grin. "Could be worse," she said, then added as severely as she could, "Dumb ox keeps trying to run the county. Gets himself worked up."

"Yeah, some of us got no sense." Hal stepped to the bedside and shook Wes's hand. "You listen to her, now, Sheriff."

"Got no choice," Wes said. "Hey, Hal, sorry about your daddy."

"Yeah." Hal's mouth tightened and Wes saw the weariness and sorrow in his face. "That's why I'm out here at the hospital. Dr. Sidhu, you know, the guy who did the autopsy, he found something odd about those little tumors. Cysts, he called them, and said they didn't look like cancer to him. Doc Hendricks says maybe they're related to that stomach problem Dad had a few years ago. Wants to send to Indianapolis for more tests. I'm here to sign the papers."

"Not cancer?" Wes asked sharply. "You mean he might have been right? Someone was trying to kill him?"

Hal shook his head. "No, no, it's definitely natural causes. Either way." He smiled sadly. "You can stop worrying about it, Sheriff. Dad had me going there with his talk about somebody killing him. That's why I called you in. But he was hallucinating. Doc said that was no surprise. He had dozens of those cysts in his brain. In his muscles too, it turns out."

Wes shook his head, remembering the gaunt creature in the sickbed. "Poor guy. I'm sorry to hear that. Hal, I wanted to ask, do you know anybody named Teenia? Might be connected with your father?"

Hal shook his head. "No. Your deputy called Royce this morning and asked that too. How come?"

"Just checking out a rumor. Nothing important." Especially since it had been natural causes.

Hal held out his hand. "Yeah. Listen, Sheriff, take care of yourself, okay? I have to go help Mother and Royce now.

They're sorting through his things. Big job—you know, old files and cardboard boxes, some from when he was a kid."

"Yeah. Thanks for stopping by, Hal."

When he'd left, Wes saw that Shirley was dabbing at her eyes. He said, "Poor Dentons have a lot to cope with."

"Yeah." She glared at him with brimming eyes. "But I'm not crying for them as much as for me."

"For you?"

"Wes, you were that close!" Her fingers pinched the air, not quite touching. "Do you even realize how close it was?"

"Come on, Shirl, you think I'll ever forget lying on that godforsaken stone, watching the hawks, with what felt like a sixteen-wheeler parked on my chest?"

"Well then, why won't you quit for a while? I saw how you perked up when you thought Judge Denton might have been murdered!" Scowling, she stepped closer to his bed. "Why can't you let Grady Sims and Art Pfann take care of things?"

"The Good Lord spared me for something, Shirl. And it just might be this case. I was the one who recognized him, right? And somebody's got to stop the bastard." He took her hand. "If we're lucky, they'll collar Newton and—"

The phone rang. His hand hit the receiver just before hers, and for a second she resisted, trying to keep him from picking it up. Then, with an exasperated sigh, she flopped down into the chair again.

It was Marty Hopkins. "Hello, sir. Foley gave me your number there. How're you doing?"

"Okay, but Doc Hendricks and my wife are in cahoots. Won't let me out of here. Uh, Hopkins . . ." He hesitated, then decided to tell her. "Got some news for you."

"News, sir?"

"For you. Not for Foley or Mason or Sims or anybody else. FBI's real touchy about spreading the word to all us Kluxers."

"Yes, sir, FBI sure knows its way around these parts, sir."

Wes snorted with laughter. "Settle down, Hopkins, we're playing this by the rules. The news is we've spotted our man. They're picking him up this afternoon."

"Hot damn! What's my assignment, sir?"

"Your assignment is to stay out of Mr. Agent Fucking Jessup's way."

"Sir?" He could hear her disappointment and disbelief.

"Same as everybody else's assignment. I'm not authorized to tell you any of this, by the way."

"Yes, sir, thank you. I bet you're not authorized to tell me who it is, either."

"No, I'm not. It's Gil Newton."

"Newton! Shoot, he couldn't— Well, he could follow orders maybe. He's a real good mechanic. But there must be someone else planning it!"

"Yeah, I told them that." He sketched the evidence against Newton for her, the prints and the photo of the Whitecastle Night-Hawk. "They say his real name's Hardy Packer. Lived over near Campbellsburg when he was a little tyke."

"Packer. Seems I've heard of them."

"Could be. They moved to Terre Haute after the mother left."

"Think he's got Alma Willison, sir?"

"They're assuming he's got a hostage."

"Good. Shoot, I wish I could be in on it, sir!"

"You can make sure we got an empty jail cell. Don't want the boys doing the usual Saturday night round-up and filling it up with drunks."

"Uh, yes, sir, I'll do that when I get back. This is kind of a long-distance call."

"Hopkins?" he asked sharply. "Where are you?"

"Well, sir, I, uh, I went to Louisville. Found something."

"What?"

"On the Denton case."

"Not much of a case anymore, Hopkins. The judge's autopsy showed natural causes."

"There's still Phyllis Denton, sir. And Alma Willison."

"You've got something about Willison?"

"Yes, sir. You know they've got that little kid Milly?"

"The granddaughter, yeah."

"Sir, I believe Phyllis Denton was Milly's mother."

"Phyllis Den— You're kidding, Hopkins! Phyllis was what, twelve?"

"Yes, sir. Mr. Willison said his wife was real secretive about where Milly came from. But he showed me a box she was saving for the kid with stuff from her real mother. There was a necklace inside. Matched the bracelet on Phyllis's skeleton."

"Christ! So how did the Willisons end up with her? You think Alma did something to Phyllis and stole the baby?"

"Yeah, I've thought about that. Or maybe Phyllis was running from the father when she died, and he just now found out where the baby was. Kidnapped Mrs. Willison for revenge."

"Willison didn't tell you who the father was?"

"Willison said he didn't know, and I believe him, sir. He was real open about the other things. There's a note in the box that says there's a record of the birth in the Kentucky state records in Frankfort. That might say. But they aren't open till Monday."

"The Louisville police can get in there, can't they?"

"Uh, yes, sir, uh, when they're brought up to date."

"You didn't tell them yet, Hopkins?"

"I told Mr. Willison to call them."

Yeah, they'd be touchy about her invading their turf. He said, "Well, watch it, Hopkins. Too much unauthorized stuff going on these days."

"Yes, sir. I thought I'd talk to the Dentons again, see if they had any idea about who the boyfriend was. I'll break it to them gently."

"Good. Do that first, then make sure there's a cell waiting in the jail for our boy Newton. But don't tell Foley or the others why."

"Yes, sir. See you soon, sir."

Wes replaced the receiver and leaned back, suddenly exhausted. Shirley's lips tightened and she lowered the bed for him. When he frowned at her she said, "I'll wake you if anything important happens, Champ. I promise."

Well, a man had to trust somebody in this life. Wes closed his eyes.

44

MARTY LEFT THE PHONE BOOTH AND TURNED THE CRUISER toward home. So the case was breaking at last. Dead ends suddenly opening up. She ought to feel happier. They knew who had done the killings now. Gil Newton, really Hardy Packer, involved in those Whitecastle bombings—okay, she could believe that. It was the big break they'd been waiting for. So why was there so much disappointment mixed in with her rejoicing?

Maybe it was that she sensed there was more to it. Gil Newton was such a strange, quiet type—someone else must be working with him. The end was not as close as the FBI thought. And maybe she was disappointed also because she wouldn't be in on the capture. Nor would Wes Cochran. It was like helping your team earn a shot at the state championships, and then getting benched right before the big game. The FBI would roll off with all the glory, and Coach would lose his treasured reputation for solving Nichols County problems without pulling in outsiders.

She reached Paoli and turned north. His heart—that was another thing. She couldn't kick her guilty feelings about that. Why hadn't she been able to explain that Professor Wolfe did things her own way? If she'd just been able to get that across . . . But she hadn't, and now he lay in a hospital bed.

Even her little personal triumph weighted down her soul. She'd found some new information about poor Phyllis Denton, but it was hard to rejoice. It would just add one more heartbreak to that overburdened family. She dreaded seeing them again, dreaded the brutal questions she would have to ask. But that was her job. And much as it would hurt, she knew they too wanted to know what had happened to Phyllis, to catch and punish her seducer and killer.

But Marty still dreaded the interview.

She rounded a bend and saw the intersection with County 860. A few miles east and a couple of miles north on Donaldson would bring her to Phyllis's cave. But why bother? They'd already found all there was to find there. They'd searched, the state crime technicians had searched, the FBI had searched.

So why had Professor Wolfe said she wished she'd had time to check it again?

Marty was turning the cruiser toward the cave even as she told herself it was pointless. It would be dark in there, now that the state cops had removed their generator and lights. She still had the caver's helmet in the trunk—ought to get that back to Floyd Russell soon—but she shouldn't go in there alone, according to Floyd. And there wouldn't be anything to find anyway.

So why was she parking, taking the helmet from among the emergency flares and bolt cutters and jump cables in the trunk, tying up her hair so the helmet would fit better, sticking spare bottles of fuel and water for the lamp into her belt? Because she didn't want to face the Dentons, she admitted to herself. Put it off for another few minutes. Hopkins the scaredy-cat.

Feeling silly, Marty headed up the hill to the cave entrance.

Gary Trent was a SWAT commander for the Indiana state police. He knew that Special Agent Jessup was frustrated because on such short notice he'd only been able to muster eight men. There were thick tangled woods in this part of the state, a lot of ravines and old barns, and Jessup was fretting about what would happen if Packer slipped past them as they tried to close in. But before joining the state police, Trent had served two tours of jungle firefights chasing wily, well-motivated enemies on their home turf, and he was confident. "These are eight stand-up guys," he said. "We'll place six in the woods surrounding the place, send two to the door with a UPS package. You'll stay back. Getting the overall picture," he added diplomatically.

"Right," Jessup said. He seemed to view himself as a sort of general, plotting the campaign. Commander Trent viewed him as a rear-echelon motherfucker. Jessup said, "Now, half an hour ago, we had a sheriff's cruiser drive by. He was at home."

"They saw him there?"

"His car was in the driveway. It's an isolated area, can't go anywhere without a car."

Trent knew Wes Cochran slightly and would have preferred working with him. Like Trent, Cochran knew that people could be away from home even when their cars were in the driveway. Like Trent, he knew that people sometimes went hunting, or fishing, or hiking, or murdering, without their cars. But Trent had survived Vietnam by focusing on reality instead of what higher-ups fantasized, so he said to Jessup, "Let's look at the map again."

They were talking scrubby woods here, knolls and hills, lots of undergrowth at this time of year. They'd drop the backup men on a nearby back road to hike three miles through the woods in hard armor and surround Packer's house. When the backup was in place, two men in a UPS truck would arrive with a big package. Under the too-loose UPS uniforms, they'd wear lightweight armor and carry the latest automatics. In the box would be a sledgehammer in case nobody was polite enough to answer the door and they had to invite themselves in.

Trent inspected the mapped terrain, decided how to deploy his men, and said tersely, "Let's move."

Marty Hopkins looked carefully at the chamber where Phyllis Denton's coffin had been. Except for the cross smoked onto the buff wall, there was nothing to see now. Even the long-ago pop bottles left by long-ago picnickers—a young Royce, maybe?—had been removed to the labs. She started back toward the outside, but paused when she reached the entrance to the crawlway that led to the blindfish cavern.

No need to look there.

But Professor Wolfe would have looked there.

With an exasperated sigh, Marty plunged into the tunnel. Professor Wolfe was as tough a boss as Wes Cochran. Got inside her somehow, and issued commands that were hard to ignore.

Anyway, this shouldn't take long. She didn't much like this part of the cave, the closeness after the larger cavern, the way things skittered away at the edge of the light, the way she felt like an invader in a pure wild world. She tucked her flashlight up her sleeve so she'd be sure it didn't get scraped off in the tight part. And here it came—the ceiling ever lower, pressing her down onto her stomach on the muddy floor. Like being the filling in a monstrous stone sandwich. Bacon lettuce and Hopkins on stone. She belly-crawled and at last squirmed out into the cavern where the slow, pale fish swam in the clear stream.

There was nothing here. At the far end next to the rock pile where the river disappeared was the vertical slot. It was the entrance to that twisting tunnel that led to the cavern with the iron ring. Across the shallow river, the water-worn tan boulders were piled high, the remains of a long-ago ceiling breakdown, Floyd Russell had said. Up near the top, he'd said, was a passage too small for adults.

Wolfe, though, had said there was a back way into this cave. Through the breakdown pile. Could that be it?

Marty knew she shouldn't try anything like that by herself. But maybe she'd just take a peek, as long as she was here. She stepped out to a rock in the middle of the stream and then jumped to the far side. About five feet up in the pile of boulders she saw it—a thirty-inch-high opening larger than the muddy crawlway she'd just come through. She was staring into the opening when she heard a faint cough.

Her body reacted faster than her mind. She found herself crouched behind a larger boulder, heart pounding, ears straining, gun in her hand. In a moment it came again—a throat-clearing, far away, just audible over the gurgle of the water.

It came from just across the stream, from the entrance to the jagged tunnel that led to the iron-ring chamber.

Okay, Hopkins, steady now. Coach said the FBI was picking

up Newton. Plus, it's Saturday. This is most likely just some kid exploring the cave, now that it's open again.

She crossed the creek again as quickly as she could and entered the slot in the rock.

Hard to be silent here, walking stooped over like this. She was very aware of the padding of her feet against the stone as the stream sounds receded behind her, very aware of the blazing glare of her headlamp. Here came a turn. The cougher would know she was coming because of the light. So use some misdirection, Hopkins. She paused, removed the lamp from the hat, and held it in her left hand at head height, her gun ready in her right hand. Drop to a squat, light still held high. Push it around the corner, aimed into the next part of the passage. If nobody shoots, peek around behind it, head low, keeping tight in the shadows behind the light, and if the coast is clear move around the corner.

Okay. No problem in this next section.

No noises, either. She hoped her quarry hadn't slipped away from her somehow. Although she had to admit she also hoped he had.

One more turn, or two? She couldn't remember. Her arm was getting tired of holding up the lamp. All she needed was a pedestal and she'd be the Statue of Liberty. A weary Statue of Liberty. So get it over with, Hopkins. She pushed the head-lamp around the next corner.

No shots.

Scrunched low in the shadows, gun ready, Marty edged around the corner.

There was the blond-walled chamber. And a heap of muddy rags in the middle. And movement among the rags—a hand shading eyes that were squinting against her light.

A voice said uncertainly, "Hello." A kid, or a woman. It said, "Did you bring something from McDonald's?"

"No, I didn't."

At the sound of Marty's voice, the figure gasped and jerked back with a clinking sound. The blanket fell aside and Marty saw a disheveled woman. There was a metal cuff on the leg she could see, a chain. Fear twisted the woman's mud-streaked face.

Marty turned the headlamp to shine on her own face and said, "Ma'am, I'm Deputy Hopkins. Are you—"

"Oh, God! Oh, thank God! Get me out, please, please get me out!" The woman began to sob.

Marty didn't see any signs of a weapon. She holstered her gun. "Yes, ma'am. I'll just put my hat on, and show you the way out. You've got a chain on?"

"Yes. Oh, God, hurry, he might come! Did you—" something. Marty couldn't understand for the sobs.

"Take it easy, ma'am. Are you Mrs. Willison?"

"Yes. Yes. Did you catch him?"

"The others are picking him up right about now, I expect. Can I look at that chain, ma'am?"

"Oh, hurry, please hurry!"

Marty tried her handcuff key, but it didn't work. "Mrs. Willison, I'm sorry. I'll have to go get the bolt cutters."

"Don't leave me!" Alma Willison shrieked, clawing at Marty's sleeve. "Get me out! Don't leave me!" She began coughing and sobbing.

"Take it easy, ma'am. I'll be right back. Here, have some water." She pulled her spare bottle of water from her belt and handed it to Alma Willison, who drank thirstily. Marty handed her her flashlight too. "Here, at least you won't have to wait in the dark. I'll only be a minute."

"Don't make him angry! He knows I'm a white Christian woman. But he has guns—oh, God, he won't let you come back! He'll kill me!"

"The others are picking him up," Marty soothed, although prickles of uneasiness were running across her skin. "I'll be right back, honest."

"Don't leave! Oh, God, don't leave!" Alma Willison's sobs intensified.

Marty hurried through the tunnel, spurred on by the weeping behind her. When she forgot to stoop and cracked her helmet against the low ceiling she slowed a little, remembering Floyd Russell's warnings about damaging her lamp, about getting hit on the head.

She hurried along the water's edge to the horizontal slit that was the end of the crawl tunnel and squeezed in. Soon she was crawling rapidly, racing through the passage. Not that different from a tricycle race, she decided, lots of hard effort in a cramped position. Give her a good basketball game any day.

She reached the main cavern, sprinted for the opening, and swarmed up the piled rocks. The cruiser was parked halfway up the hill. She opened the trunk, scrambled through the flares and blankets and other emergency equipment to pull out the bolt cutters, and hurried back into the cave.

Loping through the spacious entrance chamber, glancing at the freshly cleaned corner where the pop bottles and oil spout had been, the memory that had been nudging at her mind ever since she spoke to the sheriff finally surfaced. It was Elizabeth Denton's voice talking about long-ago trespassers in the cave, about "the Packer boy who left his name." Royce and Hal, Jr., had cleaned off the graffiti. Erased the name.

Had the Denton boys known Hardy Packer?

Marty pushed the bolt cutters, over two feet long and heavy, into the crawl passage ahead of her. So it wasn't only Alma Willison she'd want to talk to. She had a whole bunch of new questions for the Dentons, as soon as she got that poor woman out of here.

45

THE NIGHT-HAWK HAD CUT THE TWO LOGS HE NEEDED FOR THE cross, from a dead dry tree that would make a good blaze. He loaded them into the car he'd borrowed from Johnny Peters. Johnny was having new shocks put in, and it would be ready for him Monday morning, clean as a whistle and riding smooth. But right now it had been requisitioned for the great war. Of course he couldn't tell Johnny, but Johnny wouldn't mind. He'd been hurt bad by the mud-people too. It only took a couple of beers to start Johnny mouthing off about the Jew lawyer who was forcing him to pay so much support for the kids his no-good wife had taken with her when she ran off. And just because he tried to keep them in line. The Night-Hawk couldn't figure it. Everybody knew you had to whip kids sometimes, or they wouldn't grow up right-thinking. He could remember plenty of whippings himself. But there was that Jew lawyer siding with the wife. Wouldn't let Johnny even see his own kids, but forced him to pay anyway. Yes, Johnny would be pleased to know he was contributing to the cause.

He drove Johnny's car from the highway onto a graveled farm road, closing the gate behind him, and then past a couple of fields to a dirt track that wound its way into the wooded hills. He parked under a big hickory in a dense part of the woods and took the logs and his kit from the back. Quietly he carried the logs along the trail. It would be sundown in another couple of hours, but right now he could still be seen from the road below if he wasn't careful. He reached the edge of the trees and froze.

A sheriff's cruiser was parked partway up the hill.

Fury and terror came bubbling up together, but the Night-Hawk capped it and sank slowly to a squat to think things out. The sheriff—no, he'd heard this morning at work that the sheriff was in the hospital. The Lord had struck the sheriff down already. This would be a deputy, then, a deputy in the cave. Why? They'd already taken away the saint in her coffin and everything around her. Most likely they were desperate, just looking it over again, hoping to see something they'd missed.

They wouldn't go very far in. They never had before. They wouldn't go to the blindfish river. Would they?

What if, somehow, they'd learned something about the woman? He couldn't think how, but what if they had?

Wouldn't make any difference. Either way, he'd better check. He took the .38 and his brother's Marine knife from his kit, then tucked the bag out of sight behind a rock. He left the two logs lying innocently at the foot of a tree. Quietly, he made his way to the mouth of the cave, and lay among the rocks, hidden from the road, listening.

Nothing.

The Night-Hawk slid into the cave and, without lighting his lamp, descended the well-known route to the cave floor. Still no noise, no light. He ran through the big cavern, fingers trailing along the wall, to the chamber where the saint's coffin had been.

No one was there.

He hurried back until he reached the opening to the crawl-way that led to the blindfish cavern. Couldn't hear anybody there either. But the pebble he left on the crawlway floor had been moved. So that's where the deputy had to be. And suddenly the Night-Hawk understood, and rejoiced.

The Lord was smiting the sheriff's department.

And the Night-Hawk was one of His chosen instruments.

Chosen for more than just Alma Willison. Chosen to attack the law itself, the law of the mud-people.

He needed a plan. He didn't know how many deputies there would be. But on a Saturday, and with Sheriff Cochran in the hospital, it was most likely there'd be only one or two. It would be worthwhile to take out their vehicle, to cut off escape and avoid curious eyes. Like Willie Sears's eyes. He crept back to the cave entrance, checked the lonely road for passing motorists, and then slipped from the cave and down to the cruiser. It took only a moment to hot-wire the engine. He drove it down to the road and then up the back way he'd come before. He parked it under the hickory, next to Johnny's car, and removed the distributor cap so that no one could drive it away. Then he zipped up his black sweatshirt and returned to the cave.

"You came back!"

"Yes, ma'am, of course I came back." Marty was pleased that Alma Willison seemed a little less panicked. In a calm, businesslike voice, she told Alma, "Here, hold your feet apart a little. You'll have to wear those cuffs until we get a key that fits. But we can get the chain off."

"I was sawing the chain. See?" She pointed at a rusty link.

There was a groove in it, right enough. Marty said, "Yes, ma'am."

"Hours and hours, I sawed on it."

"Yes, ma'am." Marty had the link next to the left legband in the jaws of the bolt cutter. She braced herself and pressed the long handles, grunting. The link snapped.

"Oh, God! Oh, thank you, thank you!" Alma Willison began to cry.

"It's okay. Now, ma'am, let's have the other foot."

Still weeping, Alma Willison held out the other foot. Again Marty bore down on the handles and clipped the chain from the leg cuff. "There we go," she said.

Alma half-ran, half-crawled to the opening, then lurched to a sudden stop and whispered, "Is he out there?"

"No, ma'am."

"You don't know him. He comes in secret. He'll kill me. We have to do what he wants or he'll kill me. You too." Her terror thickened the air.

Marty asked gently, "You want me to go first, Mrs. Willison?"

"You don't know what he wants! You might make him mad!"

Marty sighed. Why was it so damn hard to rescue people? *You're lucky if you can rescue your self,* Professor Wolfe had said. Still, she could sympathize with Alma Willison, if she'd been in this guy's power for so long, in the dark so long. And it wasn't a pointless fear—there was always the chance he really would show, even though the FBI had probably picked him up by now, along with all the glory.

"Okay, look, Mrs. Willison. I'll go first. If you get worried about anything you can come right back here and do whatever you think is best."

"I don't want to come back!"

"Let's go, then." Marty stooped and plunged into the opening, and in a moment she heard Alma Willison's hesitant footsteps behind her, then Alma's hand on her back.

"Am I going too fast for you?"

"No," Alma whispered.

"Okay, in a minute we'll come to a wider place, with a little river in it. Can you hear the river?"

"Yes."

"We'll go along the edge of the river a short way and then comes the hardest part. We have to crawl on our stomachs a little ways through a low tunnel. It gets bigger pretty soon but we still have to crawl. Do you remember that coming in?"

"No. He knocked me out, I think. I woke up back there in that dark place."

"I see. Well, after we get through that crawlway, we can pretty much walk the rest of the way out of the cave." Marty was thinking of the strength it must have taken to pull an unconscious woman through that crawl space. Gil Newton wasn't a big guy. Then she remembered seeing him move that engine aside. Four hundred pounds, and he'd pivoted it as easy as moving a footstool. "Just a little farther, now," she said to encourage herself as much as Alma. She turned the last corner. Only a few feet from the opening into the blindfish chamber. She saw the light from her headlamp sparkling on the stream.

A guncrack. Thundering echoes brawled from wall to cavern wall.

Quicker than thought, she was back around the corner, ears ringing, her gun in her hand.

A shot. Someone was shooting at her. Muzzle flash—yes, there had been a muzzle flash, from the tiny entrance of the belly-crawl forty yards across the chamber. So he was blocking her way out. She tightened her grip so the gun wouldn't shake so bad in her sweaty hand. She hadn't been hurt—the bullet had hit the limestone next to her. Was Alma Willison okay?

Better than okay. As the roaring in her ears faded, Marty heard the hurried retreat of Alma's footsteps back to the chamber. Thank the Lord for that.

Who was it? Not a cop. Even the feds identified themselves before shooting. Had to be Alma's captor. Had to be Newton. A man who had killed and mutilated Goldstein and Sears, who had kidnapped Alma Willison. And Judge Denton's daughter? She'd been in this cave. Maybe this guy had—

Didn't matter now. What mattered now was his gun.

A single shot. Probably not an automatic, probably a .38 like her own. They were matched on that score.

He wasn't using a light. Maybe he'd just extinguished it briefly, but there was no doubt he could get around here in the dark better than she could. Hardy Packer, a little boy playing in this cave, writing his name on the wall, building a shrine to Phyllis complete with Klan card and smoked cross, hiding the kidnapped Alma here—even while the cops were watching it, she realized—yes, this man knew the cave a hell of a lot better than she did.

If Alma Willison had been Grady Sims or a caver like Floyd Russell—or if she'd even been in a normal state of mind—she might have been some help to Marty. But Alma was too shook up to be dependable now, just as likely to do something to help Newton as to help her. Thank the Lord she'd run back. But it would be better to get the action away from her. Didn't need Alma coming up behind her, snatching at her gun arm, shrieking, "Don't shoot, you'll make him mad!"

The bolt cutters lay at her feet. She'd dropped them when she grabbed for her gun. They gave her an idea. She said, "Grady, guard this passage, okay? Light off so you can see his muzzle flash." She kept her voice low, as though talking to someone a few feet away, but she figured both Newton and Alma Willison could hear most of it. "I'll take care of that turkey with the gun and bring back the bolt cutters so we can get her out of here." She then muttered a couple of syllables low in her throat and added in her own voice, "Okay. See you in a minute."

Enough talk. If she was lucky, Alma was scared enough to sit tight and Newton would figure he was up against two deputies. Now for the second act. Use her hairband to strap the light to the end of the bolt cutters, hold it out sideways and up. Crouch down, hugging the wall. As she worked she called out, "Gil, take it easy, now. We don't want to hurt anybody here, okay?"

No answer.

"Let's talk this over, Gil, okay?"

No answer.

She took a deep breath and eased the hat out along the far wall.

Shots erupted again, a tidal wave of sound swamping the cavern. Two racketed against the wall above her head, and one glanced off the bolt cutters and sent shock waves along her arm. Marty counted shots because it was important. Four shots, five with the first one. One more coming. She shouted, "Drop the gun! You're under arrest!"

No answer.

The muzzle flashes told her he was still across the cavern at the end of the belly-crawl. But she didn't want to shoot back yet. That would reveal her position five feet away from her light.

She wriggled around the edge of the tunnel into the stream chamber, careful to stay in the black shadows, careful to keep the bolt cutters with their perched light well away from her, although her arm was about to drop off with the effort. She stepped into the middle of the stream just as the sixth shot blasted past.

"Goddammit, I'm hurt!" Marty screamed. It wasn't true but it allowed her to dip the lamp on the bolt cutters near the stream surface, to rest her arm. She gained the far side and started up the breakdown pile. She dragged the light behind her as she clambered into the pile of boulders. Laboriously she tugged the hat along, made it disappear behind the first boulder. Laboriously she turned it so it was shining out across the stream toward the entrance of Alma Willison's prison to make sure he couldn't sneak in there. As her ears stopped ringing from the gunshots she heard the metallic snicking sounds of Newton reloading.

She was safe here behind the boulders, but only for a moment. Marty drew her handgun, rested the bolt cutters so that she could reach them from higher up, and climbed above the level of her light. Pointing her gun in the general direction of the crawlway where she'd seen the muzzle flashes, she pulled up the hat, left-handed, to ankle level, and aimed it toward the entrance to the crawlway.

Nothing.

Had he run?

Then two shots hit the boulder near the lamp at her feet, spitting chips of stone at her. She jerked her gun toward the muzzle flashes, fired twice, and dropped behind the boulders again.

He'd left the crawlway at the other end of the cavern. He was crossing the stream in the dark, she realized. On this side of the stream he'd be shielded from her gun by the same boulders that protected her from him. She needed to get higher.

The crevice up there. He couldn't get behind her there. That would be safest. She swung the light up in an arc to sight on the cleft, and drew two more shots. But on the downswing she glimpsed a dark hunched figure leaping sideways away from the brightness. Should she leave the light out here to— Nah. No way was she going to give up the light. She scrambled up the rocks and into the crevice.

It wasn't as tight as the other crawlway. This one was maybe four feet wide and thirty inches high. She scurried along on hands and knees, dragging the light behind her on the opposite side. Didn't want to go too far—Alma Willison would be in danger if he thought Marty was too far away or too seriously wounded to come out again. She rounded a sharp right in the tunnel and turned around. She set the lamp high in the corner to shine back at the entrance— No, Hopkins, lure him in! She adjusted it so there was darkness on the far side of the tunnel.

Gun cocked, Marty waited.

46

THE NIGHT-HAWK WAS REJOICING. THE LORD HAD SENT WORTHY opponents after all. He'd been disappointed at first when he heard the puppet's voice. Brad Hopkins's wife, where was the glory in victory over her? But he'd overheard her speaking to Grady Sims, telling Sims to guard the cavern where the hostage was. So the real battle would be with Sims. Still, he'd better get rid of the Hopkins woman first. She'd turned out to be tougher than he thought. Screamed when he shot her, but even though her movements were strange and lurching now, she'd succeeded in reaching cover among the boulders of the breakdown pile. And smart. She'd figured out where he was. One of her bullets had smashed the cave wall inches away from his shoulder. So the Lord needed his skill and strategy to take her out.

The best thing to do would be to crowd her into the cleft, he decided. The boulders in front of it would shield him from Sims's bullets, although Sims wasn't firing yet. Maybe he'd gone back where the captive was. The cleft in the boulders led to an easy crawl for eight feet, a right-angle left turn for six more, then a right-angle right turn that squeezed down rapidly to become impassable—a tight V-shaped tube two feet wide at the top but sloping in rapidly on each side so the walls were only inches apart at the bottom. And nothing else. The floor had long since crumbled into the other cavern below it, leaving only a long jagged gash four to eight inches wide. If you directed a light down there you could see the cavern below, with a stream like the one in the blindfish cavern. Once little Pip had gone through the V-shaped tube, bracing himself against the walls so as not to slide down and get jammed in

276

the open crack; but Chip had already grown too big to follow and had called to him impatiently to come on back, he was leaving. Pip had hurried but his brother was far ahead when he got back through the tube, and he'd crawled as fast as he could in the dark, crying, bumping his head because Chip had the flashlight, terrified until he saw the far-off glimmer of his brother's light. And afterward his father had noticed his tear-streaked face and bellowed, "Been crying again, Pipsqueak? When you gonna be a man?" and began unbuckling his belt, and Chip had run out of the room, and—

The Night-Hawk shook his head. He'd learned not to cry. It had all been for the best, all meant to form him into a powerful engine of the Lord. And now the Lord was testing him again, sending him these deputies, these wily puppets of the mud-people, because it was time to smite the mud-people's law. The Great Titan would be proud of him.

He heard movement high in the breakdown pile, saw the light behind the rocks bobbing up and disappearing into the cleft. Good, crowd the puppet in. Wouldn't be long now. She'd have to reload soon. He'd wait till her light disappeared around the next corner, and—

The light had already stopped moving. The puppet had turned around too soon.

Only half the passageway was lit. He could drive hard along the dark side—but no, that could be a trap, just what the puppets wanted. Well, there were other ways of fighting. He stripped off his dark sweatshirt and knotted each sleeve at the cuff. In the light spilling from the cleft he saw a thin rock on the breakdown pile, about sixteen inches long. Perfect. He snatched it from the light and dodged back, alert for Sims as well as the woman puppet, then pulled the sweatshirt over the rock so it lodged in the two armholes. Crouching next to the cleft, ready to roll, the engine of the Lord heaved the sweatshirt-laden rock into the crevice. When the guncrack came he launched himself into the cleft, legs like pistons, driving toward the light.

But the light was fading. In the dark he cracked a knee against the end of his sweatshirt-clad rock and realized that the puppet wasn't reloading just around the bend where he expected. The puppet was running, maybe anticipating his attack. Smart—but not smart enough. He rounded the corner and fired quickly, but the light was disappearing around the next corner.

Good. Crowd the puppet back, push her into the V-shaped tube, kill her where the cave squeezes tight. Don't let her stop to reload. She was wily, this puppet, but she couldn't reload while crawling. She would have to stop for that. And if he could press her into the tight part, where she couldn't turn around, she couldn't shoot real well even if she did reload. He'd have all the time in the world to destroy her. Push her deeper, deeper, until the rock itself squeezed her to a stop.

Marty could tell the rock was pressing tighter. As she rounded the second bend the bolt cutters jammed. They were useless now because there was no room to hold the light away from her. Quickly she unfastened the lamp and clipped it to her helmet, then wedged the bolt cutters upright behind her. Might slow him down long enough for her to set an ambush. Although this tunnel was getting too tight for much action. She hurried around the next corner, fumbling at her gun belt, found her ammo, paused to chamber two rounds, cocked the gun.

And couldn't turn around.

Behind her she heard a thud and a grunt. He'd hit the jammed bolt cutters, and she had an instant of advantage while he figured out what had happened. She backed into the corner she'd just left, bouncing sideways so she could turn her gun and light on him at once. She squeezed the trigger once and lunged back to safety. He was shooting now too. Something stung her leg but she ignored it and surged forward. Damn, it was getting tight. About ten feet ahead she could see what looked like a bigger space. She shoved herself forward, squirming between the tight walls. Get to the bigger cavern, turn, shoot him as he came through. And get there quick, Hopkins, if you don't want your rump full of lead.

Her shoulder crunched painfully against the stone. Damn! But her light showed more space above in the small V-shaped tube. She wriggled upward, arms and legs braced against the sloping walls, and moved forward again.

She realized suddenly that she hadn't heard him for a minute.

Don't stop, Hopkins. Move! But listen.

She heard a whisper, like the stream in the blindfish cavern. And then she heard a ripping sound.

She forced herself forward again, holding herself high in the tunnel by bracing her legs and forearms against the walls, not knowing what the sound meant except that it wasn't friendly. It was tight here, a narrow mucky-looking floor about a foot below her, and even up here at the widest she only had an inch or two of wiggle room. Her helmet scraped the roof. She moved by shoving her left side ahead, shoulder and hip together, then her right, then left, then—

Then her foot slipped down and jammed.

She pulled hard but it was wedged somehow below her. She couldn't see in this cramped space. She'd have to reach back and feel for the problem with her right hand. But let go of the gun, Hopkins, or you'll have your own bullet in your fool foot.

She set the gun carefully on a bulge in the rock and started to wriggle her arm under her so that she could reach back to the jammed leg. She listened intently for Newton behind her but heard nothing. Coach had said bombs. Did bombs make ripping sounds? Had he set one and run away? She twisted to free up her arm and her hat brushed against her revolver. The gun slid down the sloping wall toward the dark floor below. It disappeared.

There was a splash.

Marty froze, and for the first time swung her headlamp down to inspect the narrow muddy floor below her. And saw that there was no floor.

The blackness was not muck. It was vacancy.

She'd squeezed herself into the top of a V-shaped tunnel with no floor. Only a long, four-inch-wide gash opening down to another, lower cavern. Through the slot her light revealed, ten feet below her, a stream running smoothly over limestone.

And over her gun. There it was in the stream, dark against the pebbles.

And her foot was stuck in the gash.

And behind her she heard a quiet thump. Newton was moving again.

"Aw, shit," whispered Marty Hopkins.

47

THE NIGHT-HAWK TESTED HIMSELF: STRETCH RIGHT LEG, LEFT leg, right arm, left arm—yes, there was more pain in his shoulder when he did that, but nothing disabling. His fingers were strong, his movements only a little slowed by the bandage he'd ripped from his shirt and tied firmly around his shoulder. He'd been bleeding some but that had stopped with the pressure of the bandage. He was proud to be wounded for the Lord.

He debated turning on his light. "They need no candle, neither the light of the sun, for the Lord God giveth them light and they shall reign for ever and ever." On the other hand, he didn't know this part of the cave as well as the rest. After little Pip had been left in the dark he hadn't liked it here much.

But it was an advantage to work without a light, a shadow among shadows, especially now that he had the puppet deputy on the run. The puppet was scared to have things coming out of the dark at her. The only problem was if she did something unexpected. Like wedging those bolt cutters in the passage. He'd rammed right into them and it had taken him a few seconds of groping to figure out what was going on. And in those seconds she'd suddenly appeared at the turn, light blazing, dazzling him, and before he got his gun up she'd winged him in the shoulder and disappeared.

But the wound wasn't bad, hadn't hit bone.

He probed the bandage and recited to keep down the pain. " 'And lo, a great multitude, which no man could number, of all nations, and kindreds, and people, and tongues, stood before the throne, and before the Lamb, clothed with white robes, and—' " No. That couldn't be right. Not all nations and kindreds. White nations. White robes, white people. All nations and kindreds—that couldn't be right. Could it?

No. But it made him feel shaky.

No reason to feel shaky. The wound wasn't bad. And the Hopkins deputy would get stuck up ahead and panic. Time was on his side, so he didn't have to rush. He went back around the corner and felt for his sweatshirt, still lying where he'd thrown it to draw her fire. He unknotted the cuffs and took out the stone. His bandage was firmly tied and didn't interfere much with his movement as he eased the sweatshirt on. Of course there were a few twinges but he'd always known there would be tribulation. The *Vanguard,* the *Crusader,* the *National Alliance Bulletin,* the Bible—all said there would be tribulation before victory.

They shall reign for ever and ever.

The Night-Hawk breathed in the cool clean air, breathed out, breathed in. A well-tuned machine, problems no worse than a dent in its side. Gun in his right hand, he rolled forward again, tracking the puppet of the mud-people, driving for victory.

Above the soft gurgle of the stream below her, Marty heard the muffled sounds start up behind her. He was on his way again. Well, look on the bright side, Hopkins. If he's still hanging around it probably means he didn't set a bomb. She wriggled her leg but succeeded only in getting her shoe stuck more firmly. Oh boy. *Mommy, you're such a klutz,* Chrissie would say. If she ever saw Chrissie again.

She jerked her leg angrily and suddenly her heel slid within the jammed shoe. One more pull and her foot was free. Bare, but free. She pushed herself up toward the wider top of the tube and squirmed forward again. She shoved herself through the tube, not looking down toward the gurgling water below, hoping that the larger cavern ahead had a floor. The stone seemed to grip her in a tight fist. Dammit, Professor Wolfe, were you lying about a way out? She thought for a moment, exhaled, shoved hard with both feet, and suddenly her head was out, one arm, one shoulder. Yes, there was a floor here, and space. Glorious space, about four feet high. Both shoulders through. Hips jammed. Marty grunted with effort. She heard a click as he cocked his gun behind her. Violently, she twisted her hips sideways to get the benefit of the height of the V-shaped tube and with a wriggle she was through and rolling aside. The gun behind her blasted but the bullet hit the far wall of the cavern.

Which way now?

A hasty sweep with her light showed that the cavern ran at right angles to the V-shaped tube. To the right it narrowed to a tunnel only a little larger than the tube she'd just escaped. A steep pile of rocks on the left had spilled from a hole in the ceiling. Well, up was better than down. Marty scrambled up the rockslide ten feet or so and found herself at the end of a passage six feet high. She stood up for the first time in much too long, noticing how much her leg ached, how cold the stone floor was on her bare foot, how good it felt to move forward quickly even limping. She felt her calf. Her pants leg was wet, and when she held her fingers in her light they were red. Shit! Shit, she'd been hit!

Easy, Hopkins, worry about that later. Get out first. Get to the cruiser. Radio for backup. But several feet along the passage, she had to pause. Another passage led off to the left. Which way? She couldn't tell from here if one passage led higher than the other.

Pulling her lipstick from her pocket, she marked a C on the main passage wall and just around the corner of the side passage, an X. The letters looked thin, and she wondered if she could make them out if she had to come back. Well, her pursuer couldn't see them too well either. It would take him a minute to get through that tube, although he probably wouldn't be stupid enough to get his shoe caught. And once he was through he'd be faster than she was with her damn bleeding leg.

She hurried down the tunnel she'd marked C. For Chrissie.

The Night-Hawk was surprised. How had the puppet gotten through the tube? He'd wasted a shot in his frustration, seeing her dark silhouette in the tube suddenly twist and roll away. How had she done it? Then, as her light swept the cavern walls beyond the tube, he saw that the far end was a little wider than it had been. Sometime in the last fifteen years a rock had split off from one wall and rolled down across the gash in the floor.

It made him angry. He launched himself at that narrow tube, furious that his trap hadn't worked. But he'd soon kill this annoying puppet. Kill her, and— *If thine eye offend thee pluck it out.* He'd kill her, cut off her trigger finger, stuff it in her mouth. Or up her asshole. The thought excited him. The Great Titan would be proud.

This tight part of the cave was slow going but he'd get through more quickly than she had. He focused on his power, the Lord's power, in the bunched muscles of arms and legs, in his strong back. He lifted his shoulders into the wider top of the triangle. The Lord was testing him, but he would pass the test and kill the puppet. He would overcome. He moved his arms and shoulders, left, right, left, ratcheting himself along the tunnel. Far below, he could hear the gurgling of the stream.

It was still a tight tunnel.

But now that the rock had fallen it wouldn't be so hard to get through. The puppet had gone right through.

She might turn around, try to shoot him in this tunnel. He edged along cautiously, gun aimed at the V-shaped glow of her light on the blond walls of the chamber ahead, ready to shoot the instant her silhouette reappeared.

Then her light became faint. She was leaving the chamber. Good, she was still on the run. He didn't want her waiting to shoot him, didn't want to do that final squeeze out of this tube with her gun on him. He kept his right arm forward so that his gun would emerge as soon as he did. A couple of feet more, then he'd be able to shoot easily even if she returned soon. He reached out with his arms and shoved with powerful legs. Good. Now once—

His left shoulder slipped down.

What was wrong? He backed up an inch or two and reached across with his gun hand to see what was wrong. His fingers touched wetness. Water in this tube? Usually water dripped from above, but the ceiling was dry.

Ahead, everything was black. She was gone.

The Night-Hawk shoved his gun into his sweatshirt, cupped his hand over his lamp, and spun the wheel. In a moment the flame blazed out and he had to squint against the brilliance.

Tight stone walls holding him. Black gash for a floor, revealing the stream burbling along below. A shoe stuck in the gash, covered with blood. He almost laughed out loud. So the puppet had lost a shoe! And she was bleeding! That would make it easier to—

The blood was still dripping.

And it came from above, trickling down the wall past the shoe and into the river below.

The Night-Hawk twisted his head to shine his light to the left and saw that the arm of his black sweatshirt had turned red and spongy with blood. No wonder it slipped on the wall. He'd put plenty of padding against the wound, and tied it tightly, but the bandage must have slipped while he was straining to get through this tunnel. Blond stone tunnel, his hand white against it, his sleeve now a lustrous dark red. He stared, amazed. Another drop slid down from his elbow and his heart fluttered stupidly.

Then his father's voice said, "Be a man, Pipsqueak!" The walls in his mind glowed danger and the Night-Hawk snapped back to attention.

He could go back, but there was a good chance the puppet would follow and attack him as he sat trying to dress his wound. Slippery or no, forward was better. He'd kill her first, then fix the bandage. He'd come out of tribulation to victory. But he'd better put on some steam. Time was no longer on his side.

He breathed in deeply, out again, in again. Ahead his light

glared on the sharp-sloping walls of the tube, and reflected more gently on the buff of the cavern beyond. Only a few more feet. The Night-Hawk put himself in gear and pushed ahead.

Commander Gary Trent joined Special Agent Jessup in Hardy Packer/Gil Newton's living room.

"Man's gone," Trent said.

Jessup couldn't keep the bitter disappointment from his voice. "Place looks clean."

Clean wasn't the half of it. Trent had noticed a faint smell when he first led Jessup through the splintered front door. Once Trent had finished reassuring the little agent that yes, they'd remembered to look in the bedrooms and closets and cellar and attic, and no, the team members in the woods hadn't seen anyone escaping, he'd had time to note that the odor was chlorine. The whole place had been bleached recently, and not for the first time. Pale scrubbed wood, a table with a couple of blond chairs in the kitchen, a narrow mattress in the bedroom made up with white sheets and coverlet. The living room had a single stuffed chair aimed at an old television in the corner, a Sears Roebuck home gym, a white bookcase filled with stacks of hate tracts and newspapers—*Vanguards, Crusaders*—and three or four Bibles. There were only a couple of pictures on the wall, one of them a blurry snapshot of a grim-faced man standing behind two rigid boys maybe nine and twelve years old, the other an Easter picture of a dazzling white angel before an empty tomb.

No dust under the bed, no grease in the sink, no ring around the tub. They'd analyze the traps for the sinks, tub, and washing machine, and they'd analyze whatever the technicians could vacuum up, but this fellow was clean and careful. Just like Jessup, Trent thought.

"Want to look in the bedroom?" Trent asked.

"Okay." Jessup followed him into the neat room. Trent opened the closet door and showed him the two robes and two hoods stored neatly on the shelf. One was white, one was coal black. Both bore the Klan blood-drop insignia on the breast. A couple of spare service-station uniforms hung there too. Jessup said, "One-track mind. No hobbies, I guess."

Trent nodded. Klan robes, Klan tracts, Bibles, guns. Lots of guns. Guy could outfit a platoon from his front closet. But that was it, except for the gym and the TV. There was no alcohol in the kitchen, no cigarettes or other drugs, not even a girlie magazine. Guy was pure as the driven snow.

And where was he? Hunting, maybe. Or maybe he'd found other transportation and was far away.

They settled in to search.

It was two hours later when one of Trent's team opened an old issue of the *Vanguard* and found the slips of paper, once scrolled but now carefully flattened between the pages. There were about twenty of them, handprinted with small, firm letters, undated. Many said, "Watch until the time is ripe," or, "Patience. It is not yet the moment to attract attention." But one of them said "Miscegenation, Lawrence Road?" and another said, "Alma Willison, Louisville KY."

Jessup had photos made before he sent the papers to the lab for analysis.

Marty had been crawling through the dark forever. No, probably only half an hour. At each intersection she marked the branches, and twice when her chosen trail had dead-ended she'd crawled back and changed the marks so she'd know which paths were useless.

She was shivering. For a while the adrenaline and violent effort had kept her plenty warm, but it was wearing off and her light summer uniform wasn't meant for temperatures in the midfifties. Plus, she'd managed to tear it squeezing through the stone, long rips on her left thigh and back, and of course on her calf where the bullet had ripped flesh and fabric. There was a slow breeze in the cave that didn't help.

She came to another intersection, inspected each tunnel, decided the left led upward, and then saw she'd already marked it.

What the hell?

Okay, Hopkins, don't panic. Figure it out. Last time she'd marked an intersection, she'd gone left, crawling uphill. Then the passage had turned left again, downhill. Definitely down-hill, but there were no uphill options. Then it turned left again and stayed level to this intersection.

Okay, that made sense. She'd circled back to the same tun-nel. If she went left again, uphill, she'd be back where she started this loop. Change the letters, and move on.

But still she hesitated. Was this really the best strategy? She'd lost her weapon and had been fleeing frantically ever since. Find the back entrance Wolfe had mentioned, get out, get to the cruiser, radio for backup. Not a bad strategy if she really could get out that way. But it could take hours if she had to explore every damn branch of the cave.

It could take more than hours. It could take forever.

Would it be better to go back the way she knew?

He'd shoot her. But was there some way to outfox him? Leave her light somewhere, hide in a side branch in the dark, and when he came along and shot at it, maybe jump him from behind?

Naw. He was too damn strong. Hand-to-hand was not the answer even if he had no gun.

Maybe wait till he passed her, then run back the way she knew? But how would she find her way if she left her light behind?

Marty stared at the two tunnels, inspecting one unworkable option after another.

Alma Willison huddled in her blanket. For a while there had been gunshots, two or three blasts, then a pause, then two or three more, all thundering and echoing. The last ones had seemed far away. But for a while now there had been nothing at all. He'd killed that deputy. He'd come back for her soon, she knew. She'd have to start all over, soothing him. She'd already hidden the telltale flashlight and the water bottle under the McDonald's cartons. If he found them he'd kill her. She'd also hooked the cut links of chain back onto her leg cuffs. If he noticed they were cut he'd kill her too.

That young deputy had been stupid to think she could help. She'd damaged all of Alma's careful work. Have to start all over.

He'd be back for her soon. Alma pulled the blanket tighter and waited.

Hard work getting through this tube. The Night-Hawk pushed forward, keeping high in the wider part, but after a while his shoulder jammed painfully and he was still four feet from the end. Maybe he should peel off the sweatshirt. It was bulky. Carefully, he unzipped the sweatshirt and writhed out of it. Awkward in this narrow space, when he had to hang on to his gun and keep his knees and elbows braced against the sides so he wouldn't slide down and get stuck in the narrow part. Then, gun in his right hand and sweatshirt in his left, he pushed ahead again.

This time he progressed to two feet from the end before he jammed.

He was panting from the effort, and his heart was fluttering again. Was he wrong? Had he grown too large to get through, even though the passage was larger than when he'd been a boy? Even though the puppet deputy had gotten through?

He rested a moment, thinking.

Should he go back?

"Be a man, Pipsqueak," said the voice. "I'll show you what a real man is."

No, no! Listen! In panic, the Night-Hawk collected his arguments. If he went back, he could kill the deputy guarding the captive. The Hopkins deputy was long gone. She'd probably lost herself in the cave already. Deputy Sims, who was waiting with the captive, might come looking for him if he waited too long. Sims was a man, the main assignment, and right now he'd be easy to take by surprise. The Great Titan would be pleased. The Lord would be pleased. The Night-Hawk began to back up.

His knee skidded down the blood-slick left wall and jammed in the crevice.

Easy now. Pull it out—no, too much pain that way, don't hurt the machine. Try another way.

Be a man, Pipsqueak!

Enraged, he pulled like a man. He was panting. Fleeting breath. *Rock of Ages, cleft for me.* He got the knee out and braced it on rock. *Let me hide myself in Thee.* His lamp glinted on the reddened wall, on the pale rock ahead. A voice was saying, "Be a man, Pipsqueak!"

It was on a throne, the voice was on a throne. *While I draw this fleeting breath, when my eyelids close in—* No, no! Be a man! The Night-Hawk wriggled forward. But his legs wouldn't move. He saw the tunnel growing longer and narrower, like a rifle barrel. *When I soar to worlds unknown, see Thee on Thy judgment throne—*

The voice on the throne said to him, "These are they which came out of great tribulation, and have washed their robes, and made them white in the blood of the Lamb. Therefore are they before the throne of God, and serve Him day and night in His temple."

The figure on the judgment throne dazzled him. He was made of light, beaming in every direction. The figure said, "Been crying again, Pipsqueak?"

It was true, Pip knew. He was full of rage and helplessness, and he'd been crying. He could feel the warm tears on his cheek even now. When he tried to brush them off, his wounded shoulder slid down and wedged in the cleft.

"Be a man, Pip!" The figure was huge and made of light. The protective walls in Pip's mind were melting in the light. The figure unbuckled his belt. "I'll show you what a real man is!"

The erection was enormous, red, glowing. The figure said, "Take it like a man, Pip!"

Obediently, little Pip opened his mouth.

"They shall hunger no more, neither thirst any more," intoned the figure. "Neither shall the sun light on them, nor any heat. For the Lamb which is in the midst of the throne shall feed them, and shall lead them into living fountains of waters: and God shall wipe . . ."

The voice faded, and the light, and the whisper of the stream, and the drip, drip of little Pip's tears and the Night-Hawk's blood joining the waters below.

48

HEADLAMP OFF, MARTY CROUCHED IN THE DARK, PRESSING HER-
self into a narrow indentation in the cave wall, watching.

She knew where she was. She'd decided to go back, hoping
to bypass him in the maze, and was now almost back to that
tight V-shaped tube where she'd lost her shoe and her gun.
From her hiding place she could see the top of the rock pile
she'd climbed right after she'd squeezed out of the tube. She
could see it because there was light somewhere below it. Her
first terrified thought had been that Gil Newton was on his
way, so she'd backed into this crevice, dousing her light, ex-
pecting him to appear any minute. She was clutching stones
in each fist, a pitiful substitute for the handgun she'd lost.
She hoped that he'd pass her by and she could scurry down
the rock pile, through the tube, and out of the cave while he
took his turn in the tunnels. If he didn't pass her by—if he
saw her—it would be the end. Still, maybe her stones could
do a little damage before she fell.

But she'd been watching for twenty minutes, and he hadn't
come yet.

Stranger still, the light hadn't moved. Even sitting still, people moved their heads sometimes. Maybe he'd taken off the
helmet and propped it somewhere to mislead her.

Okay, Hopkins, what are your options?

She could resume her hunt for the back way out—but the
chances of success there were very slim. She could stay where
she was and wait for someone to notice the cruiser she'd left
near the cave entrance and come to her aid—but that could
be many, many hours, and even if Newton didn't find her
first she'd be dead of thirst and cold by then. Already she had

to clench her teeth to keep them from chattering and giving her away, and her calf was throbbing where his bullet had hit. And poor Alma Willison, already off her head with terror, might do something foolish. It was a little miracle that she was still alive, but she wouldn't stay that way when Newton discovered she'd been freed.

Maybe he'd already caught Alma. Left one of his lights in the tube to keep Marty at bay, gone back to kill Alma and make his escape. And Marty had fallen right into the trap.

If that was what had happened. There were other possibilities. Maybe he was right there below, sitting next to his helmet, happily drinking a Thermos of hot coffee and waiting for her to pop out so he could shoot her.

She could also die waiting in this tunnel. She'd better check.

She took a deep breath, firmed her grip on her stones, and tiptoed to the opening, staying in the blackness next to the rays that beamed up from below. Holding the stones ready, she edged her head out to see where the light was coming from.

And ducked back instantly. She couldn't see the lamp itself, but the light was coming from inside the V-shaped tube, and shone clearly on a hand holding a gun.

But no shots followed.

What was he doing?

If the light was on his helmet, he was too far back in the tube to see her. If this was an ambush, why didn't he come on through the tube? She'd had trouble getting through, true. But Newton was tough, knowledgeable about this cave, stronger. And larger.

But not that much larger. Was he—good Lord, could the man be stuck?

Marty peeked down the rock pile again. The hand didn't move. The light didn't move. A black mass next to the hand didn't move.

Even if he suddenly came out of the tunnel, it would take him a minute to squeeze through.

If she stayed well to the right, she'd be in shadow, never in sight of eyes back in that tunnel.

Okay, Hopkins, you'll never have better odds. Go!

She slid quickly down the rock pile, staying in the shadow to its right. A rock came loose and bounced left and she tensed against the wall, waiting for the shot, but none came.

The hand still hadn't moved.

Marty traded her stones for a heavy rock not quite as big as a basketball, crabstepped along the shadowed wall until she was next to the little V-shaped opening, and smashed the rock down against the wrist. The gun clattered down from the white fingers, but his body blocked the crevice where her own gun had disappeared. She reached in and snatched out his gun, jumping back into combat stance, pointing it into the tube. "You're under arrest!" she gasped.

Nothing moved. The white hand didn't move. It was at a weird angle now.

"Gil, do you need help?" she asked.

No answer.

She couldn't hear any breathing, only the faint sound of the trickling stream far below.

It might be a trick. He might have another gun. Marty sidled around to the shadowed wall, out of his sight. She spun the wheel to light her headlamp. It seemed to take forever, maybe because she didn't dare take her eyes from the hand that still lay against the sloping stone of the tube, at that odd angle now, but not bleeding. Finally there was a pop and her own light shone out again. She steadied the gun and moved cautiously to peer into the tunnel.

The black mass was a sweatshirt. She pushed it out of the way with her left hand.

Gil was in ragged shirtsleeves. One shoulder, bare except for a red rag, had slipped down into the crack at the bottom of the V, and his head lolled sideways a little, held up by the steep slope of the wall. His face was pale, the mouth open, and the eyes wide in sightless terror. She could see the streaks of tears on his cheeks.

"Gil!" she exclaimed. Keeping the gun in her right hand, she grabbed the smashed wrist with her left.

There was no pulse.

From here, she could see blood on his shoulder, blood

soaked into the rag he'd tied around it, blood running down the cave wall.

Cautiously, she pushed aside the sodden rag. The wound was a tiny hole. Hard to believe that much blood could come from it. But there would be an exit wound too, more ragged, where the bullet had exited.

Where *her* bullet had exited.

She'd hit him. One of her bullets had hit him.

She'd killed him.

Nausea rocked Marty back on her heels. Nausea and— Face it, Hopkins, relief. You won the big one.

She swallowed and took longer than strictly necessary to holster the gun. Then she gritted her teeth, grabbed his arm in both hands, and tugged. He didn't budge. She tried pushing, grunting with the effort. She tried to lift him but he was wedged tight. She grabbed his arm again and jerked.

Nothing worked.

Marty leaned forward and shouted into the tube, "Mrs. Willison?" Her voice bounced and echoed back at her.

There was no response.

"Mrs. Willison, it's okay! Can you come to the rock pile, next to the stream?"

Still nothing. Probably she couldn't hear her. The passage that connected the little V-shaped tube to the blindfish cavern right-angled twice. Maybe voices couldn't carry.

Or maybe Alma Willison had already escaped. Or maybe Alma Willison had died of fright. Something—Marty knew it wasn't real, it was in her mind—passed through the shadows with great soft wings.

Marty shouted again. She shouted till she was hoarse, but there was no response. She leaned back, panting and shivering. Cold, she was cold. Gil Newton's sightless eyes were still fixed on her with that look of terror. Gently, she reached in and closed the staring eyes, and with the back of her fingers wiped the streaks from his face. Then she picked up the black sweatshirt, still sticky with blood, and draped it over her shuddering shoulders.

She'd killed a man. Later, she'd deal with that.

Right now the problem was that his death might kill her too. His unbudging body plugged the only exit she knew.

Don't think about your chances, Coach used to remind them when the game got tense. Think about moving that ball. So go, Hopkins. Hunt the other way out.

Marty started up the pile of rocks to the maze of passages above, wearing a dead man's sweatshirt.

It had been a long time since she heard that last shot, and Alma was getting hungry. She never knew when he was going to bring her dinner. Maybe that stupid deputy had made him forget.

Should she try to leave?

It wasn't safe to leave. He'd kill her. He was out there.

But then why hadn't he come?

Alma closed her eyes and prayed. She remembered that once she'd been a bookkeeper, logical and orderly. She remembered that the stupid deputy had cut the chain for her. She remembered that once she'd wanted it cut. She'd sawed at it herself for hours.

She remembered Wayne, and she remembered Milly.

Silently, Alma unhooked her chains again. She tiptoed to the stacked McDonald's containers and pulled the deputy's flashlight from under them. Then, cautiously, she left the chamber.

The hardest part was where she'd heard the shots before. She whispered another prayer and tiptoed around that corner. When nothing happened she felt the rush of joy.

The deputy had said something about following the river and then crawling through a low tunnel. It took a while to find the entry, just a horizontal slit in the rock. She might have missed it completely except that her flashlight picked out the brassy glint of spent cartridges inside the tunnel. She tried not to think about what might lurk there and squeezed into the passage, moving as fast as she could in a belly-crawl. Soon it enlarged and she was able to rise to hands and knees. Crawling with the flashlight in her hand made the circle of light jerk like a drunken Tinker Bell. Alma giggled. Milly would like that.

She emerged into a huge cavern. The flashlight beam showed a seven-foot ceiling. She remembered the deputy saying that from here you could walk out of the cave. But which way? Left or right? Right or left? She sat frozen, unable to decide, and finally thought to pray again. Then she remembered that she was logical and orderly. Try left, and if that didn't work, try right. She started off, following the wall so she wouldn't lose track.

Around the second bend she saw, high up, a small opening above a heap of boulders. Through it came the glow of dusky sky.

Alma scrambled up the rocks like a bunny, and giggled again. In the twilight she could see a road below. But she slowed as she made her way down the unfamiliar hill.

This was his territory. He was powerful. He'd catch her again. He'd stopped the deputy somehow. She mustn't let him catch her.

Shivering, Alma's anxious eyes swept the horizon. And off to the left, saw a church spire against the twilit sky.

Breathing a prayer of thanks, she hurried toward it. Twice cars passed on the road, and each time she dived into the brush so he wouldn't see her. God was with her. Music was coming from the church, "Amazing Grace" on the organ. But when Alma crept inside, it was dark except for the organist's light. She sat down at the end of a pew.

The organist was a brown-haired woman in her forties. She finished the piece and looked around inquiringly. "Eula? Is that you?" When she spotted Alma she gasped. "Lord, honey, you're a sight! Who are you? What happened to you?"

"I want to go home." Alma's fingers dug into the thin pew cushion. "Please."

The organist stood up uncertainly. "I'm Betty Strathman. What's your name?"

"Alma. Please, I want to go home."

"Where's home?"

"Madison Road."

"Madison Road?"

"Louisville."

295

"Lord, honey, you're a long way from home! Where's your car?"

"I—I don't know."

Betty Strathman frowned. "What happened? You're all muddy. Did someone hurt you?"

"No, please!" Panic swamped Alma. Don't let anyone know, or they'll tell, and he'll find me! She said, "I fell. It was all my fault!"

Betty said gently, "Are you sick, honey?"

Alma snatched at the idea. She said humbly, "Just my nerves. I'm better now. Sometimes I have these spells and leave home."

"You're sure you're better? You want a doctor?"

"I have one at home. Please."

"Well, I'll call the sheriff, and—"

"No, no!" Alma's terror stopped Betty Strathman in midsentence. The sheriff had no power over him, she knew. How could she keep the woman from giving her away? "Please, they'll take me to—to a hospital!"

Betty Strathman nodded slowly. "I know, honey. My own auntie got put in a nursing home a few years ago. Hated it. Kept running away. You sure Louisville is where you want to go?"

"Yes, please. My husband will be worried."

The mention of a husband smoothed away Betty's frown. "Well, come on back to our ladies' room and freshen up. I can take you as far as the cafe at Paoli, and I bet one of the girls on night shift down at the Louisville cannery will take you on from there."

So Alma Willison, face scrubbed but clothes still grubby, was delivered into Wayne's arms shortly before the ten-to-six shift at the cannery began. She began to weep uncontrollably, great shuddering sobs that set Milly to crying too. Wayne, in a delirium of relief and worry, took her to the hospital and got her admitted for observation. It wasn't till after midnight, when Alma had dropped into a heavily sedated sleep, that Wayne thought to call the Louisville police.

"She's asleep now, sir?" the dispatcher asked.

"Yes. Doctor says she needs a lot of rest now."

"Okay, then, we'll talk to her tomorrow. She's back safe, so there's no rush, is there?"

Marty didn't know how long she'd been limping and crawling through the cave.

Long enough for the thought with black dusty wings to flap by several times.

Long enough for the stickiness in Gil's sweatshirt to stiffen up.

Aunt Vonnie would be shocked. "Lordie, girl, you've got the fashion sense of a toad!" Chrissie would say, "Gross!" But she'd also brag about it all week at school.

Marty was still exploring the tunnels she'd skipped the first time. This passage, after some twists and turns, ended in a rock pile. She climbed up a short way, remembering the collapsed ceiling back near Gil Newton's body. But this rock pile was larger and there was no route through, even though she tried moving some of the stones near the top. When a rock the size of a suitcase dislodged and careened down the pile, just missing her left leg, she quit. Wolfe couldn't have meant this way.

This was hopeless. Shoot, might as well sit down, rest her poor leg, die comfortably instead of rushing around like a trapped rabbit.

But she'd promised to stick with Chrissie.

Okay, Hopkins, up you go. Plod on.

She returned to the intersection, marked a red X, and went on to the next unexplored branch passage.

This one was pretty big, five feet high, okay to walk at a stoop. She bent over and started through.

Her light seemed dim.

Hold your head up, Hopkins. Keep it straight.

But it didn't get any brighter.

How long had she been in here? Marty squatted, took her lamp from the bracket, and saw that her fuel was low. Carefully, she removed the spare bottle of carbide from her pocket and got things arranged before extinguishing her light, emptying the ash onto the cave floor, and refilling the lamp by touch. Thank the Lord she'd brought along the extra.

She spun the wheel and the light popped back to life. She returned the lamp to her helmet and slogged on.

It sure was dim.

What was wrong?

She took off the lamp and squinted at it, and suddenly felt clammy all over. The water was nearly gone. Water dripping on the carbide produced the fuel gas.

When the water was gone, the light was gone.

And she'd given her spare water bottle to Alma Willison.

Wait a minute! There were streams in this cave. The blind-fish stream, and the one she'd dropped her gun into.

But a corpse blocked the way to both.

Maybe one of the lower passages she'd rejected led to a stream.

And maybe not.

Find a way out, Hopkins. Move!

She hobbled quickly along the passage. In the feeble light she saw that it was growing narrower. Another impassable trail. She rushed back to the intersection, marked another red X to show that both were dead ends—but why bother, Hopkins, you won't be able to see it when the light's gone—and headed for the next branch at a near run.

But the failing light lasted only a few yards more. Before she got to the intersection it blinked out.

She reached out to touch the wall, its rough chill disheartening yet somehow comforting, somehow keeping the great black wings at bay. She leaned her back against the stone as she sank slowly to sit on the floor.

Marty had never, ever known darkness as black as this.

49

"SO NEWTON WASN'T HOME, HUH?" WES SAID TO ART PFANN.
"Well, hell, it's Saturday night, what do those G-men expect?"

The prosecuting attorney shook his head. "His car was
there. He must be with a friend."

"Didn't know he had any." But if you were willing to do
things for the Klan, you automatically had friends, Wes knew.

"Here." Art handed him an envelope. "Found these notes
at Newton's house. The originals are on their way to the FBI
labs. I got you a set of photos."

Wes grunted and glanced at the top two. "Signed GT. I bet
Jessup's combing the phone book."

"Yeah."

"GT. Doesn't mean much to me either. But I'll think on it.
Tell you what. Hopkins has been working hard on this. Foley
says she's running late, not back yet. But when she gets in
I'll give her a look at these."

Art Pfann nodded. He looked older, Wes thought. Nothing
like losing a killer to bring on the gray hairs.

He and Art riffled through the nineteen photos of the notes
found in Gil Newton's home. They were able to make a rough
chronology of a few. Goldstein must be recent, because he'd
moved to the county only four months ago. This other note,
to card Horace Thomas, was probably from four years ago.
Horace Thomas was a black man who'd worked for a while
at Andy Ragg's trucking business and then suddenly packed
up his family and moved away. Andy, an easygoing fellow,
had complained, "Didn't think Horace was gonna turn out
shiftless like them others."

There were a few notes with names Wes didn't recognize.

Of course he knew Alma Willison—that was probably recent. But most of the instructions called for patience, for waiting on the Lord.

Art shook his head. "This stuff is pretty terse. We'll need a lot of other evidence to build a case."

"Let's catch him first," Wes said. "One more thing. Our man fixes cars. Why don't you roust out Bert Mackay, find out which cars are supposed to be at the station for servicing, and see if one is missing?"

"Hey, right! I'll get right on it!" Rejuvenated, Pfann hurried from the room.

Wes didn't feel rejuvenated. He felt like it was past his bedtime. So when Shirley returned and said it was time to swallow his pills and get tucked in, he didn't grumble too much. He'd just have a little snooze. Art would wake him if anything happened.

He did kind of wonder what was taking Hopkins so long.

Marty stared into depths upon depths of blackness. Those great cloudy fears flapped seductively about her. Mustn't let them get too close. Think, Hopkins. Think!

Okay. What are the options?

Shriek! Pound on the walls! Scream for Mama!

Easy now, Hopkins. Agreed, it ain't good.

Marty pulled her knees closer to her chest and hugged them. Funny how darkness made sounds sharper—the rustle of her uniform trousers, the rasp of her one shoe on the cave floor, even the sound of her own breathing. Her eyes were stretched wide open, shifting about anxiously, as though the inkiness might recede if she only looked hard enough. But Wolfe had said no light had hit this rock since it was living sea creatures, 350 million years ago.

Don't get distracted, Hopkins. Think!

Okay. Three options. One, keep hunting a way out, feeling along the cave walls. That would take a long time. Two, go back to where Gil Newton lay caught in the stone, wait for the sounds of a rescue party—that would take a long time too. Three, sit here and die.

Nah, that'd make Chrissie mad. Scratch three.

Marty got back on her feet and started groping along, one hand in front to feel for upcoming obstructions, the other trailing along the wall to keep her oriented.

Hunt for a way out, or go back to Newton to wait?

Well, in the dark they weren't really two options, she realized. Without being able to see the marks on the intersections she couldn't find her way back to Newton anyway. What systems she'd been able to use so far in her explorations had all been wasted. She couldn't tell the passages she'd checked from the ones she hadn't. Panic pulsed through her. Come on, Hopkins, get a grip. At least nobody's shooting at you anymore.

Yeah, big deal. Death by starvation is just as sure, and not much more comfortable.

She remembered the look of horror in Gil Newton's dead eyes.

Her mother's look had been of peace. She'd been in pain for months, but at the end she seemed more peaceful. But of course Aunt Vonnie had been there to help, and finally to close her eyes.

Who would close Marty's?

Get a grip, Hopkins!

She came to an intersection. What now? Okay, the main thing was not getting lost. Keep a hand on the wall, to avoid repeating the route by mistake. She groped her way into the new passage.

Would she end up like Phyllis Denton, a skeleton to be discovered in the distant future by some horrified caver?

And to be discovered in the immediate future by those creepy things Professor Wolfe studied? Food for cave creatures. A CARE package from the surface. Hopkins on stone, yum yum.

She remembered Professor Wolfe talking about being high on a mountain or deep in a cave. "You know you are alone," the husky voice had said. "All you have is your self. You know you will die. Your own mortality becomes a fact of life, like gravity."

Yep.

Her groping fingers felt the cold walls. Made of corpses.

Other creatures that had once loved the sun, and now were buried with her. Tiny dead companions. "Hey, guys," Marty said to them, "what's it like? Being dead?"

There was no answer. *You gotta walk that lonesome valley, you gotta walk it all by yourself.* She groped on.

Funny how you never thought much about death before it happened. She'd always thought that someday in the distant future she might die like her mother, with a dimly imagined grown-up Chrissie tending her.

Chrissie, Chrissie. I'm sorry, kid.

Her bare foot stepped into nothingness and she lurched back, arms flailing. Gravity's a fact of life too, Hopkins! When she had her balance again she knelt carefully and patted the cave floor ahead of her with both hands. A cave-in, she decided, big enough to climb down to a lower level, maybe. But how far down? And did she even want a lower level? She listened hard but heard no trickling water. And if she went back down there in the dark, she might not be able to get back up to this level. Better give up on this tunnel for a while. She turned and hobbled back.

She was exhausted. Not very dramatic, this death. Not very glamorous. People always said they wanted to die with dignity, but there was no dignity here. Terror, yes. The look on poor Gil Newton's face— Don't think about that, Hopkins. Think about Professor Wolfe's hypnotic voice. "All you have is your self." That sounded dignified. But hey, Prof, what if your self is lost, and scared, and hungry, and thirsty, and exhausted, and has a sore leg, and has to pee? Shoot, no dignity left at all.

Well, she could fix that last problem. No one could see her here, that was for sure. Total privacy. She could squat right here and—

Oh God.

It wouldn't work. Would it? The chemicals or something would be wrong. Wouldn't they?

But she couldn't be much worse off than she was already.

Marty unbuckled, pushed down her pants, removed the lamp from her helmet. She flipped open the top of the water container and very carefully peed into the small hole in the top. It was a sloppy business finding the stream in the dark but she was soon rewarded with the satisfying sound of a container filling. When it was done she replaced the lid, wiped everything off as best she could, cupped her hand over the lamp, and spun the wheel.

On the fourth try, a blaze of light filled the tunnel.

"Whoopee! Whoopee!" Marty jumped up and down and almost tripped on the pants still hanging around her ankles. She pulled them up again, buckled, clipped the headlamp back onto her helmet, and started almost jauntily back to the intersection. She marked it and set off to check the next branch. "You gotta walk it all by yourself," sang Marty.

Her elation did not last long. The light was glorious—but temporary, she knew. Her damaged leg throbbed with pain. Hunger came and went, but thirst was a constant now.

And she ran into dead end after dead end. Some passages pinched down, too narrow to continue. Others were blocked by piles of rock from ceiling breakdowns.

She'd have to sleep eventually. Fatigue twined around her like heavy chains, making every step a struggle, every thought hard to hold. And even with all the effort, even with the sweatshirt, she was shivering again.

Marty limped down the passage to the next intersection. She knew she was going deeper. Was that a bad sign? Hard to decide. If only she wasn't so tired. *Think, Hopkins!* She groped for a thought. She was not as far down as the stream caverns. Okay. Maybe she should check this level until she got back to the tunnel where Newton lay, then try the deeper places. She stumbled forward. This passage was long. Smelled muddy, too. Seven feet high, rounded by a long-ago river. Mud on the floor—maybe not so long ago after all. It pinched down soon to a low belly-crawl but she thought she could see a larger room beyond. She wormed her way through the mud and stuck her head out. Big, but probably another dead end. She dragged herself out anyway. Here the head-high passage sloped up steeply but it was hard to walk because of the mud and debris on the floor and because of her aching leg and because she was exhausted. Her light shone on a huge pile of rock and debris that blocked the passage at the end. Marty sighed, stretched, and turned around to crawl back.

Hey, Hopkins, what do you mean, debris?

She looked back. Something white among the boulders.

She limped through the muck toward it, then recoiled. A bone! God, this cave was full of death! She turned her face away.

Hey, Hopkins. Do the job.

She looked back again. A big bone, over a foot long—yeah, you're not talking squirrel here. And more glimmers of white farther up among the boulders, obscured by something.

Marty made her way closer, peering at the rock pile. The remainder of the skeleton rested about five feet up from the floor. Huge pelvis, a pile of ribs, a few scattered vertebrae as big as baseballs. The skull was there, long and jagged among the twigs. A cow!

A cow, Hopkins?

"A cow," Marty muttered. "And twigs. Dead bushes. How did—" She limped closer, looking up at the ceiling. The pile of rock didn't quite plug the hole it had left when it fell to the cavern floor. When Marty climbed a few steps among the stones and looked straight up she could see a long, long way. She could see a ragged moonlit cloud.

Cloud. Moon. Sky.

Sky!

There was only a small space left among the collapsed stones, but by gum, if a cow could get through, so could she. Marty scrambled up to the top of the rock pile, where a few leggy vines were trying to grow.

She was at the bottom of a sinkhole. A pit, really, fifteen feet at the widest point and twenty feet up to the rim, most of it vertical rock. One side was overhung by a ledge. A couple of bushes had found toeholds partway up, but when she jumped and grabbed them they came loose, pelting her with clumps of clay.

That cow had had a big advantage. It was going down, not up.

How to get out?

There was a dead sapling that had fallen to the floor of the sinkhole. She propped it against the side of the pit and crawled up it, but she could only get about five feet higher. After that the branches snapped under her feet.

She needed a better ladder. Or a rope. Or a helicopter. Or a derrick. She needed the whole damn fire department.

So get it, Hopkins.

Marty laid the sapling down again and began to collect dead bushes and every twig she could find. She stuck them among the branches of the sapling, binding them loosely with vines. Then, grunting, she maneuvered the slim trunk upright against the pit wall again, brushy end up. It didn't reach the top, but it was as good as she'd get. She picked up a dead branch, lit one end with her headlamp flame, and held it up to her bundled brush.

It took a minute, but most of the twigs were dead and dry and eventually flames caught, making a giant torch in the night. There was still some ammo in Gil Newton's gun, and she fired a round every few minutes and shouted, "Help!" or "Fire!"

Nothing happened.

After a while the flames died down, leaving only the charred sapling and the ragged clouds in the sky.

"Help!" Marty shouted again hopelessly. "Fire!"

"Fire's pretty well out, miss." A man's voice.

"Oh God! Help! Please, sir, help me!"

"Where are you?" A flashlight beam whisked along the bushes at the rim.

"Down in the sinkhole. Do you have a rope or anything?"

The beam found her face and made Marty blink. He said, "I'll fetch one. You fall down there?"

The voice was familiar. Marty said, "Bud? Bud Hickman?"

"Yeah. Marty Hopkins?"

"Yeah."

"Lordie, Marty! You hurt?"

"Not too bad. But listen, if you'll be anywhere near a phone, call the sheriff's department, okay? I've got to talk to the sheriff's department."

"Sure thing, Marty. Be back quick as I can."

Bud and his flashlight went away. Marty sank onto a boulder by the rock wall and leaned back to wait. She'd see Chrissie again after all! Her eyes sought the veiled moon in thanksgiving.

That was her last clear memory for a while.

50

"SIR!"

Wes looked up from the photos of the notes found in Newton's house. Marty Hopkins was struggling into his room, wearing a hospital gown. Wes was pleased. Doc Hendricks had told him she was in no shape to talk when they'd brought her in late last night. Today she was limping, one leg swathed in bandages, but still was managing to keep ahead of Chrissie and Vonnie. They pushed in behind her, wearing their Sunday best. Vonnie was hollering, "Marty, you're supposed to be in bed! And don't bother Wes, he's—"

Hopkins ignored her and blurted, "Sir! Alma Willison! She's in the cave! The one where we found Phyllis Denton's body!"

"Marty! Come back here!" Vonnie wailed, and turned to Shirley, who was sitting in the bedside chair. "Shirley, I'm sorry, she's just—"

"Well, Hopkins," Wes said, putting the photos down beside him on the bed, "you don't look ready for church yet. But you're not half as bad off as they told me you were."

"Sir. Alma Willison!"

"Alma Willison is in Louisville," he told her. "Turned up at home last night, out of the blue."

"Oh, thank the Lord!" Hopkins leaned against the foot of

his bed, and for the first time Wes saw her exhaustion. Gutsy kid, that one.

Vonnie smoothed her pink-flowered dress and apologized. "Shirley, I don't know what to do with her! As soon as they took out her IV tube, she went running down the hall to bother Wes!"

Chrissie, her little face worried, was tugging at her mother's gown. "Mommy, come on!" Marty patted the girl's head but her eyes stayed on Wes.

Wes said, "Yeah. Let's talk, Hopkins."

Shirley sighed and stood up. "Give up, Vonnie. They'll never mend if we don't let them gossip."

"But the doctor said she was supposed to stay in bed!" Chrissie said.

Shirley bent down to her. "Honey, these two have important work to do. And if they can't do it they fret and get worse instead of better. Now, your mama can sit down right here and take it easy, and we'll let them talk for five minutes. Then they can both get some rest. Okay?"

Chrissie looked up at her mother with those big dark worried eyes, and Marty kissed her on the forehead. "Chrissie, honey, Mrs. Cochran is right. I'm going to be fine."

"Don't try to be so tough!" Chrissie objected in a tone that sounded so much like Marty that Wes repressed a smile.

"Sure I'm tough! Tough as you, anyway," Marty said. "Honey, I'm sorry I gave you a scare. But see, it's not your job to take care of me. I'm the grown-up and you're the kid, remember? Go on to church with Aunt Vonnie, now, and let me talk to the sheriff."

Shirley steered Vonnie and Chrissie firmly out the door, and Hopkins hobbled over to the chair and sat down. "Is Alma Willison okay?"

"More or less," Wes said. "I don't have any details. Foley got a call from Louisville, and they said she was in the hospital for observation. Hysterical when she got there so they popped her full of drugs and she's out like a light now. Louisville hasn't talked to her yet. But listen." He shifted on the bed. "The main thing is Gil Newton. The feds lost him. Slipped right through their little manicured fingers."

"You're telling me!" She gestured at her leg. "He's the one who shot me!"

"What?" Wes straightened with a jerk. Damn Doc Hendricks, he should have let them talk to Hopkins earlier! "Where was he?" He reached for the phone.

"In the cave. He's dead."

"Dead?"

"Yes, sir."

His hand still hovered over the receiver. "You're sure?"

"Yes, sir."

"Okay." Wes scrutinized her tired face and leaned back against his pillows. "How about you start at the beginning, Hopkins?"

"Yes, sir." She took a deep breath. "I was coming back from Louisville and the turnoff for the cave is right there, so I stopped to look at it one more time."

"How come?"

"No good reason, sir. It was just, uh, Professor Wolfe said she wished she had time to look at it again."

Wes snorted. "Wolfe! Why'd she say that? The lady who doesn't know anything about the Klan?"

"Yes, sir. Maybe that's the truth. Maybe that's why she wanted to look, because I told her there was a Klan card with Phyllis and she hadn't noticed it. So anyway, I went in, and found Mrs. Willison."

"She couldn't have been there the whole time, though. The state cops were guarding the place."

"Yes, sir, but they didn't start round the clock till Tuesday, after we found the Klan card. Mrs. Willison was kidnapped Monday. And he'd taken her back away from the front part of the cave. The cops up front couldn't have heard anything."

"Okay. You better draw me a map later. So you found her."

"Yes, sir, chained to the wall. I cut her loose and started to bring her out, but before we got very far Newton turned up and took a shot at us. She ran back and I went out to try to get him away from her." Her face was white, and she licked her lips. "He, uh, chased me into this other little tunnel. We were shooting at each other. I squeezed through a real tight place and got away into a different part of the cave. Later I came back and Gil was lying there dead, stuck in that tight place. I guess he bled to death. I guess I hit him. I couldn't—

couldn't move him." She fell silent. There was moisture on her pale forehead.

Wes thought about being in that cave, thought about bullets in those tunnels, thought about a passage so small a man could get trapped in it. He said, "Take it easy, Hopkins. You got out. It's over."

"Yes, sir. I'm okay." She didn't look okay. She took a deep breath and said, "It's just—I wanted to bring him in. I didn't like shooting him, Coach, and—and—"

"It was him or you, right?"

"Yes, sir, but—"

"Hopkins, I don't know anybody likes to kill people. Except maybe Gil Newton, and we're rid of him now. I'm glad you did it, and I'm glad you feel bad about it. Okay?"

"Yes, sir."

"Now." He shifted his weight. Had to be businesslike here. If the whole damn department was going to end up here, they oughta have these hospital nighties done up in official tan. He said, "We gotta pick up the body. Where is it?"

"Still in the cave. Stuck, like I said, sir."

Wes picked up the phone and dialed the prosecuting attorney at home. "Hey, Art!" he said. "Wes Cochran here. Glad I caught you before church. We've got Newton for you. Dead."

"Newton? Dead?" Art Pfann's voice boomed over the line. "Are you kidding? Where are you?"

"Still in sick bay. Newton's out in that cave where—"

"You're hallucinating!"

"Why? You got him somewhere?"

"No. What do you mean, cave?"

"Just listen a minute, Art. Hopkins caught him in that cave, shot him dead. You guys can pick him up if you're interested." There was silence on the line. Art Pfann speechless, that was a new one. Wes added, "Or you can let him lay. Hell, Art, I don't care."

"Is, uh, is Hopkins there?"

"Think the old man's raving, do you? Here she is." Wes handed the receiver to her with a wink. The old team had done okay.

"Yes, sir, Mr. Pfann," Hopkins said, sitting up straight, as though Pfann were in the room. "No, I'm okay, only they don't want to let me out till tonight. But you can get hold of Floyd Russell. He's a cave naturalist at Spring Mill State Park. Tell him Newton is in that tight place past the blindfish cavern. Not the place with the iron ring, the tight place. He'll know . . . Yes, sir, that's right. . . . Yes, sir, here he is." She handed the receiver to Wes and sagged back in the chair.

"Got all that, Art?" Wes asked.

"Yeah. But you don't have to sound so smug, you son of a bitch."

"Call me when you find him, Art."

"Natch."

Wes hung up, looked at Hopkins, and stopped smirking. "What else?" he asked gently.

"Sir?" Her eyes jerked up. She'd been staring at the arm of the chair.

"Hey." Wes held out his hand, and she hesitated, then touched it shakily. He gave her hand a squeeze. "I killed some guys in Korea, Marty. Them or me, same thing. But still—this one guy especially. I remember his face, he was so young. He stays with me. Still have dreams about him."

"I didn't know."

"Well, hell, you have to go on, baggage and all."

"Yeah." She nodded. "Yeah."

"Was there more? After you found out you'd killed him?"

"Not really. It was just—he was in the way, stuck. I couldn't move him. I couldn't get out. I had to hunt for another way out."

Wes whistled. "Lord, Hopkins, I think I'd rather get shot at! You know Bud Hickman found you two miles away in a sinkhole."

"Two miles," she said wonderingly. "Is that all?"

"You'll be okay. You did great."

"Thanks, but . . ." She tried to smile. "But maybe I better borrow Chrissie's nightlight for a few days."

"Hell, Hopkins, buy one of your very own! Get an angel, a Donald Duck—any style you want. The department'll cover it."

That brought a chuckle. "I'll ask Foley for the nightlight requisition form, sir."

"Do that."

She sat up straighter, trying to be official again. "Did anything else happen?"

"They found a bunch of Klan stuff at Newton's house, and a gun collection."

"Yeah, figures."

"Yeah. They found these too. Photographed them before they sent them to the lab. Little notes." He spread the photos beside him on the bed, and she stood up to inspect them curiously. When she didn't comment he said, "Could be Newton's chief. But these sure don't give much away."

"No, sir. Careful guy." She frowned at the photos.

"Jessup thinks Newton might've written them himself."

"Could be. I don't know, there's something about them but I can't get hold of it." She shook her head. "I'm sorry, sir."

"Well, get some rest," Wes advised. "Let me know if you think of anything."

"Yes, sir. You get some rest too."

"Don't fuss over me, now. I'm the grown-up, remember?"

He was teasing but she looked at him with bleak eyes. "So'm I, sir."

"Course you are. You did real good, Hopkins."

She shrugged, frowned one last time at the photos of the notes, and limped out the door.

51

THE ATLANTIC OCEAN LOOKS ETERNAL TO QUICK-LIVED HUmans, but it's not as old as Indiana limestone. It was born more recently, while the dinosaurs roamed. Its life-rich waters spread from the icy north across the warm tropics and on to the icy south. On the North American continental shelf down around the Bahamas, it is a shallow tropical sea, rolling gently against the beaches, nurturing fantastic and beautiful life-forms.

A rangy woman in scuba gear was gliding among the vivid fish and branching coral forests. She was enjoying the splendor of this bright watery wilderness, but her interest was focused on its tinier denizens. She was not thinking about a message from her students in Indiana that had been delivered to her rented cottage back on shore. The message summarized several local newspaper articles: their acquaintance Deputy Hopkins had killed a Klan man in a shootout in a cave; a hostage, Alma Willison, had escaped alive; the Nichols County sheriff was still hospitalized but doing well; and the IU dean had requested and obtained a letter of resignation from Professor Hart, who had demonstrated an unseemly voyeuristic preoccupation with certain female students. Professor Wolfe had nodded in satisfaction, wondering idly what the trustworthy gray-eyed warrior Martine would decide about Phyllis Denton. But she'd set aside the message from Indiana and turned back to the fascinating struggles and harmonies of life in this tropical sea. Now, as she made her way through the sunlit waters, she was carefully and respectfully collecting samples of foraminifera, little one-celled creatures that grew and reproduced and built tiny calcium carbonate shells and died, sinking to the sea floor by the millions to form an ever-thickening calcium carbonate mud.

Professor Wolfe had not thought long on Indiana's fleeting problems because she had more important things to observe. She was watching the limestone form.

52

MARTY WOKE UP MONDAY MORNING IN HER OWN BED, TO THE familiar slant of the early sun through the venetian blinds, the familiar noises of Aunt Vonnie running water in the kitchen. Familiar, and yet strange, removed. Was it really only one night she'd been away? She climbed cautiously out of bed, stretching with care, testing her joints and muscles. Her bandaged calf still ached but otherwise she didn't feel bad. Older, yes. Ancient.

She knew who had written the notes to Gil Newton. Strange, there was no sense of "Aha! That's it," just a sad recognition of something she'd almost known for a long time now. The question was what to do about it. She picked up her uniform and underthings and started for the bathroom, yelling, "Chrissie! Get up!" at the closed door. The girl's answering grunt sent a wave of astounded gratitude through her. She wanted to run in, hug her, feel the skin-to-skin aliveness of Chrissie, of herself. But when she opened the door Chrissie was stroking her Manhattan T-shirt sadly. She thrust it guiltily behind her and wailed, "Mommy, you're supposed to knock!"

"Sorry, honey. You're right." Marty closed the door and continued down the hall. Her daughter, flesh of her flesh. Of Brad's too. Trying to love her dad, to value what he valued, to get along without him. Marty ached with wanting to help her. But how?

Better think about that a little later. There was work to do today. When she'd showered she called Wes Cochran and talked things over.

After breakfast she drove Chrissie to Janie's so they could

catch the school bus together, and then headed for the Dentons'. Turning into the drive she noted the mist in the same hollows, the gleam of the same dogwoods back in the woods, the same cars parked in the turnaround. Her tires crunched on the gravel, and off behind the house the coonhounds bayed. It was like revisiting a childhood scene, all the same and all different.

Hopkins, you sentimental fool, do the job. She parked next to Hal, Jr.'s car and limped up the limestone steps to the dark door.

Elizabeth Denton answered, dressed in a maroon tunic dress with neat white piping at the collar and cuffs. "Oh! Come in, please," she said.

"Sorry to bother you, Mrs. Denton. I was hoping to talk to your sons before they had to leave for the day. Hope I'm not disturbing your breakfast."

"Oh, no, not at all, we're all finished. They're out back feeding the dogs. Please, make yourself at home, I'll go call them." She hurried off as though she were the maid.

Marty walked into the library, glancing at the big old rolltop desk, the armchairs and oak table, the shelves of books. She wandered around the room, scanning the titles. Law books, best-sellers, hunting books, history books. She paused and pulled one from the shelf. She'd seen this cover before, the strange eyeless head, the hooks around the mouth. An Indiana University Library book. Inside, small print, some photos, a lengthy index. Marty found what she was looking for, turned to the pages indicated, and read the section carefully before replacing the book. It almost fit. Almost.

"Deputy Hopkins!" Royce bounced into the room, a playful twinkle in his eye. "Our national heroine! Well, county heroine, at least."

Hal, Jr., was right behind him. "Outstanding, what you did," he exclaimed earnestly. "Art Pfann called yesterday, after they recovered the body from the cave. Gil Newton! Who would have guessed? We always stopped at that station ourselves! Anyway, it was outstanding."

"Just doing the job," Marty said stiffly. Who the hell was Hal to say *outstanding*? What did he know about total blackness, about absolute loneliness, about killing someone in a horrible blood-smeared tube, someone you thought you knew? Then she felt guilty. He'd lived a nightmare too, his father's body and mind wasting away before him from those horrible cysts. She couldn't know his pain, just as he couldn't know hers. She shelved her guilt and sympathy and anger and said, "I have a couple of questions for you. The sheriff figured you'd still be here, 'cause you had to go through your father's things."

"Sure." Hal, Jr., glanced at his watch and leaned back against the desk. "We have to leave in a couple of minutes, but ask away."

"Your father used to be a Klan member," Marty said.

Hal stiffened but Royce said easily, "I remember when I was small he used to go out. And we found his robe in the attic. Classy red job. But he'd pretty much quit even before I left for college. Wasn't involved in that mess fifteen years ago."

Marty looked across at Elizabeth Denton, who was sitting on the edge of a chair by the window, a little apart from them. "Mrs. Denton? Did he go to any Klan meetings the last couple of years?"

"Yes."

"Mother!" Hal protested, straightening.

"Hal, the excellent Deputy Hopkins is not trying to besmirch your campaign," Royce said. "Just getting the facts. Right, Deputy Hopkins?"

"But are they facts?" Hal asked hotly. "I don't believe there were meetings! Did you have any evidence, Mother?"

"Someone had to wash and iron the robe, and mend it," Elizabeth said. "He was a Great Titan. Had to look smart."

"Smart!" Hal exclaimed. "God, Mother, why didn't you—"

Royce said, "Hal, a more interesting question is why Deputy Hopkins knew to ask about the Klan."

"The FBI found the notes telling Gil Newton what to do," Marty explained. "It was your father's handwriting."

"My God!" Hal's scowl faded to dismay and he ran his hand through his sun-streaked hair. "How can that be? Are you sure?"

315

"They're having an expert look at it. But I'm sure, yes. I know his writing. I spent hours studying his date books. And also, the notes were signed GT."

"Great Titan," said Royce. He looked as shaken as Hal now. "You don't mean he ordered up those murders!"

"He couldn't have!" Hal insisted. "He wouldn't! And he was sick! He couldn't write, couldn't telephone—and anyway, he couldn't think straight half the time!"

"What are you saying?" Royce asked. "He went crazy and asked for an old-style murder? And Newton gave him one?"

"I'm still trying to get a time frame," Marty explained. "See, he wrote a lot of notes saying be patient, it's not time. But there's one about Goldstein. 'Miscegenation on Lawrence Road.' That had to be recent because Goldstein just moved there two months ago. Your father became ill six months ago, right?"

"That's right!" Hal exclaimed eagerly.

But Royce shook his head. "It was progressive," he said. "He couldn't work, but he was still getting around those first few months. If he woke up feeling okay, he'd drive down to the courthouse or somewhere."

"Mrs. Denton?" Marty asked.

"Yes, that's right. Two months ago the convulsions got more frequent and the doctor prescribed more drugs so he had to stay in bed. Before that—well, he wasn't supposed to drive but sometimes on good days he would. He even went out a couple of times after he was on the sedatives."

"Almost ditched the car the second time," Royce said. "That's when I decided to move back and give Mother and Lisa a hand."

"Where did he go the last time?" Marty asked.

"To—" Elizabeth Denton's eyes widened and she raised her fingers slowly to her lips. "I didn't realize—he went to the service station."

"Mother, how can you be sure?"

"Because afterward he was complaining about Bert Mackay. That idiot Mackay, he kept saying. Oh, I didn't realize!"

Marty frowned. What had Bert Mackay told her? Could tell the judge was failing, he'd said. Had a fit, was shaking his fists and could hardly drive away, after he gave Bert a note for the mechanic, and all it said was—it said, Not yet time. So Bert had thrown it away. Marty swallowed. Goldstein had been killed because that note hadn't reached Gil Newton. Judge Denton had told his violent Night-Hawk to notice Goldstein, and then had not been able to call him off.

So Goldstein had been murdered, and the witness, Willie Sears.

Hal said miserably, "Is there any way to keep this quiet?"

Marty steeled herself. "I'm sorry, Mr. Denton. There's more."

"How can there be more? My God, if you accuse him of directing that Klan killer—"

"We can prove it, sir. The other thing is about your sister Phyllis. The thing is, Phyllis had a baby."

Royce and Hal, Jr., spoke at the same time. "What?" "You're kidding! She was twelve, for God's sake!" But Marty was watching Elizabeth Denton, sitting by the window in her neatly piped tunic dress, hands clasped, head bowed, unmoving.

"Mrs. Denton," Marty said gently. When Elizabeth raised her head, dry-eyed, Marty said, "You knew, didn't you? About Phyllis's baby? You tried to take care of them."

"I took her out of the state," Elizabeth said. The two men moved closer to each other, staring at their mother. "There's a home in Louisville for girls in difficulty. I drove her there on back roads. It had to be secret. When everyone started searching for her it was hard. Sometimes I could pretend to be searching somewhere and go visit her instead. I mailed two letters from her. I even bought her a leather jacket and took a snapshot of her next to a motorcycle, to throw off the sheriff."

"You did that?" Hal exclaimed. "Mother, why? And why didn't you tell us?"

"I didn't want your father to know. You would have told him, you know that. He was the strong one, you sided with him. So I didn't dare tell anyone."

"Why not?" Hal demanded. Marty raised her hand a little in warning but he stormed over to Elizabeth, towering over his mother with clenched fists. "My God, Mother, for years we've been looking! For years we've thought she ran away!

But this— And who did it to Phyllis? My God, I'll crucify him!"

Elizabeth looked up at him with dead brown eyes. "Your father was the baby's father."

Hal stared at her, uncomprehending. But Royce turned away from them, swinging, crashing his fist into the closed rolltop of his father's desk. Two of the oak slats cracked. At the sound Hal seemed to crumple. He moaned, "My God," and slumped into one of the leather wing chairs.

Royce had pulled himself together a little, but his voice was shaky as he asked, "You have proof of this blot on the family honor, Deputy Hopkins?"

"There are records in Kentucky." Marty shifted her weight. Her leg ached but sitting down didn't seem right. "The information was recorded officially."

"I wanted to be sure the baby could claim her inheritance," Elizabeth said. "And after Phyllis committed suicide—"

"Suicide?" Hal asked.

"She got to feeling so blue after the birth." A tear glinted on Elizabeth's cheek but she went on steadily. "I couldn't be with her much because by then your father and the sheriff had taken over the search and always wanted me home by the telephone in case the kidnapper called. And of course if I went out without permission your father would—he'd be very angry. I did manage to get away to take the baby to a church group there in Louisville, and asked them to find someone to care for her. I thought when Phyllis was better she could sign adoption papers. But Phyllis took those pills and—and died." Elizabeth looked away for a moment, head bowed. "And then I thought—the baby is his daughter too. The baby is in his will."

"His will." Royce was sucking on his bloodied knuckles but laughed suddenly, harshly. " 'To be divided equally among my surviving children.' What a joke on the old man!"

Marty asked, "Did you bury Phyllis in the cave, Mrs. Denton?"

"I stole money from his wallet one night, and hired a couple of Louisville men to help. I told the funeral home we were bringing her back to a family graveyard. That was true in a way. So they released her to me, and after we put her in the cave we dynamited the entrance. I didn't think people could still get in."

"Not many could," Marty said soothingly. So Professor Wolfe had seen the coffin as Elizabeth Denton had left it, and later Gil Newton had found it, and for strange reasons of his own had left the Klan card.

"But, Mother, why didn't you tell us?" Hal asked again. "We could have helped poor Phyllis. And the baby—"

"No!" Elizabeth was suddenly so fierce that Marty felt a chill. "You always sided with him. I didn't want the same thing to happen to the baby that happened to Phyllis! And to me!"

"To you? Mother, of course Dad had a temper, but he always said you drove him to it," Hal protested.

"Mr. Denton," Marty said firmly, "look at the facts. Judge Denton beat his wife. He beat and raped his daughter. Probably beat you and your brother too." Royce's raw-knuckled hands clenched on the chair back, and she knew she was right. "Those things are against the law, okay? Maybe he was a judge but he was a criminal too." She turned to Elizabeth. "Mrs. Denton, why didn't you report him to us?"

Three pairs of Denton eyes looked at Marty in disbelief. Elizabeth said gently, "It wouldn't have helped. His friends run the county. They wouldn't believe it, or if they did they wouldn't care, and he would have hurt us worse than ever." Royce and Hal, Jr., were nodding. "And suppose somebody did believe me, and did put him in jail. What was I supposed to do? He didn't let me have money of my own. He took what my parents left me. He didn't even let me write checks. No money, no job, three children to raise . . ."

Marty nodded slowly. She wanted to think she would have chosen differently. But she remembered how hard it had been for Mary Sue Peters to get a judgment against Johnny, when everyone knew Johnny was a drunk and their kids kept showing up in school with black eyes. And Johnny didn't have half of Judge Denton's power and reputation. *Poor judge, his wife's gone crazy to say things like that,* everyone would think.

Marty would have thought that too, back then.

Hal still sat miserably in the leather wing chair, his face in his hands. "Surely all this doesn't have to come out? He's dead now. What good would it do? It wouldn't help anyone!"

"Well, sir, of course we have to report to Prosecuting Attorney Pfann."

Hal looked up, hope in his eyes. "Yes. Art Pfann is in charge, isn't he? I can talk to him. Maybe come to an understanding."

Royce had moved nearer his mother. Marty said, "It seems to me, sir, we ought to come to an understanding about the little girl."

Elizabeth whispered, "Yes."

"What do you mean?" Hal asked.

"See, the thing is, she's got a nice foster family now. I'd sure hate to see that broken up. And she's got an inheritance coming too, right?"

"A third of the estate," Royce said.

"We're the executors, Royce," Hal said hopefully. "We can get the kid here. Or we could—"

"No!" Elizabeth gasped.

"You're not an executor, Mother," Royce said quietly. His hand clenched on his mother's shoulder and Elizabeth winced. Marty remembered the violence of that unexpected kiss, how it had shut her up, how it had put Royce back in charge of the moment. Dentons didn't love, they controlled.

She said coldly, "Mr. Denton, sir, let me finish. When I spoke to Sheriff Cochran this morning we agreed that we had to report to Prosecuting Attorney Pfann. But we hadn't decided yet whether to report to Special Agent Jessup."

For a moment the silence crackled.

Then Hal sighed. "The feds. Okay, look, the little girl can stay where she is. And get her inheritance. It's the right thing to do. And we don't want the girl's guardians to publicize all this by going to court. We won't contest it, right, Royce?"

"Is that your price, Deputy Hopkins?" Royce asked.

For an instant Marty was too angry to answer. Hal said quickly, "Don't say that, Royce; she's trying to help."

"My oh my, big brother, we certainly want to keep things

hushed up. We certainly want to be a congressman, don't we?"

Hal said crossly, "Come off it, Royce. Number one, it's the right thing to do. We want to save Dad's reputation. And Phyllis—my God, we owe it to her! It's the right thing to do. Number two, if it gets into court, none of us will get anything for a long time. And number three, your career won't be worth much either if all this comes out." He glanced at his watch. "Royce, I've got to get on the road or I'll miss my speech. Can you get the papers drawn up about this child's inheritance? I'll be back by three to sign them. Let's get all this behind us." At Royce's nod he hurried out.

Royce looked after him. "Hasn't sunk in yet. Poor Hal. I see a lifetime ahead of us, pretending, hoping no one will find out the truth—"

Elizabeth murmured, "That's not very different from the life we've had."

"But it used to be all in the family. Now Art Pfann and these delightful folks at the sheriff's department can make us dance to their tune." Royce clicked his heels and bowed to Marty. "Deputy Hopkins, I'm going to go start the official paperwork you require. May I walk you to your official car?"

"Thank you, Mr. Denton," Marty said coolly. "But I have a couple more medical questions about Phyllis. Maybe your mother would find it more comfortable if you weren't here."

Royce saluted. "Your wish is my command." But Marty caught the bitter edge in his playful words, and watched him out with regrets.

53

MARTY WAITED UNTIL THE CRUNCH OF THE BROTHERS' TIRES ON the driveway faded before she turned back to Elizabeth Denton. "Mrs. Denton, I do have a couple of questions, but they're not about Phyllis. They're about how your husband died."

Elizabeth's eyes, suddenly alive, searched Marty's.

"I mean, we know what killed him. They told us at the hospital it wasn't cancer, it was cysts in his brain. *Cysticercosis.*" She pulled the gray book from the shelf again, opened to the section she'd found before, and read, " 'The life cycle of *Taenia solium*, the pork tapeworm, depends on two hosts. The adult worm sheds egg-bearing segments called proglottids. When these proglottids are ingested by a hog, the eggs hatch in the animal's intestine, pass through the intestinal walls into the bloodstream, and are carried to the animal's muscles. There the larvae enclose themselves in cysts. When the muscle is ingested by a human as pork that has not been cooked well enough to kill the larvae, the larval forms emerge from the cysts and attach themselves to the human intestinal wall. In this nutritious, though dark and acid environment, the larvae grow into adult tapeworms up to ten feet in length. The adults consist of an eyeless head (scolex) attached to the intestinal wall and about one thousand egg-bearing proglottids. As they ripen, the proglottids are shed in human feces. If the proglottids are ingested by a hog, the cycle begins again. The human host may feel abdominal pain, weakness, or increase in appetite, but often there are no symptoms and diagnosis is based on seeing the proglottids in the feces.' "

Marty kept her finger on her place and looked up at Elizabeth. "Dr. Hendricks says your husband had tapeworm six years ago."

"Yes," Elizabeth said.

"It was a few months after your daughter disappeared."

"Closer to a year," Elizabeth said reluctantly.

"Is this book why you told me to talk to Professor Wolfe?"

"I knew you would find out soon. I thought she could help you understand."

"Did Professor Wolfe tell you what to do?"

"No. No, I only met her once."

"Only once?"

"One night I was out in the garden alone and she came up behind me. I was frightened at first, but she was gentle and understanding. She said she'd found a coffin in a cave, and she handed me the card I'd left with Phyllis's name. She— somehow she gets you to talk about important things."

"I know."

"I told her how unhappy I was. And she said: 'You are angry, too, Elizabeth.' And I'd never known that! I'd never dared be angry! I knew I was unhappy, yes. I knew I was helpless and guilty because I hadn't saved my daughter. But I didn't know I was so angry. I told her the story, all about Phyllis, and her father, and the baby, and Alma Willison. And I got angrier and angrier. I told her I wanted him to understand what he'd done. Really understand. I wanted him to despair the way Phyllis despaired. I wanted to invade his body as he'd invaded Phyllis's. I wanted to kill him from within, as he'd killed her." The chilling fierceness was back in Elizabeth's voice and posture. "I asked Professor Wolfe what to do."

"What did she say?"

"She said I must choose my self."

Yeah, thought Marty, that's what she'd say, all right. "Did she tell you about this book she wrote?"

"No. But when she first told me she'd seen Phyllis, of course I was distressed. I didn't want him to find out. I asked her how she happened to be in that cave, and she explained that she was an evolutionary biologist, studying animals that had adapted to life in darkness."

Like *Taenia*, thought Marty, and the ghostly blindfish. Like Elizabeth Denton. Like Gil Newton.

Like Marty Hopkins?

Nah, Hopkins, you sure didn't adapt very well to darkness.

Elizabeth went on, "A week later my husband had to give a speech at IU. I went with him to the luncheon, then he was invited for a drink with his important friends and I waited for him at the library. I looked for Professor Wolfe's books. And there was the pork tapeworm, like a gift. I'm afraid I stole the book. I put it in my purse, and went to the medical section, and tore out some pages with pictures of contaminated pork, so I knew what it looked like."

She paused. Marty decided against reading her her rights. She didn't want to interrupt now, and wasn't sure if she wanted all this to be official anyway. So she said, "And you bought some, and made sure his portion wasn't cooked very well?"

"It was easy. He loved homemade sausage. He developed a tapeworm nine feet long, Doc Hendricks said. But you know, it didn't bother him much. No real symptoms. It was disgust that sent him to the doctor. I could find proglottid segments wiggling in his soiled underwear."

Marty repressed a shudder and moved on. "Okay, no symptoms. There's another step, isn't there? Let me read a little more here, to make sure I understand. 'There are seldom lasting effects to humans from the harboring of adult *Taenia solium*. However, harboring the larval stage can cause problems. If a human ingests proglottids ripe with eggs, from unsanitary food or contaminated hands or clothing, the human rather than a hog becomes the intermediate host. The eggs hatch and the tiny larvae migrate to the human host's muscles and brain, where they form cysts just as they do in pork. There are usually few symptoms at first, but after a few years the encysted larvae die and decompose. The toxins from the decomposing larvae poison the surrounding host tissues of muscle or brain, and neurological symptoms including epileptic seizures are common. Particularly heavy infestations of larvae may cause death in the host.' "

Elizabeth bowed her head.

Marty remembered her in her kitchen, dropping chunks of meat—and what else?—into the grinder, watching the thick ribbon of ground meat piling into the bowl. Nausea rolled in her stomach and she took a deep breath and closed the book. "So, somehow or other Judge Denton swallowed some of those proglottids. And six years later they started dying and poisoning his brain. And you knew what was happening, but you didn't tell the doctor."

"Dr. Hendricks didn't make the connection. I guess it's pretty rare. And there was nothing a doctor could do anyway. He gave him antitumor medicine, but it probably just killed the larvae faster."

"Yeah. Now—by the end, he knew. He could barely communicate, but he talked about his daughter killing him. About Professor Wolfe."

"Yes. My plan was to tell him when he—if he got very sick. And a couple of months ago, when he started having seizures every day, the doctor gave him more sedatives and told him to stay in bed. He obeyed orders. He was really frightened about his health. And so I thought he'd stay in bed when I told him that Phyllis had left because she was pregnant. He didn't believe me at first. He said I was lying, she was too young, and threatened me. Lying there in his bed, he threatened me. I mentioned Alma Willison so he'd know there was a real person. And—I couldn't believe it, but sick as he was, he got out of bed and slugged me with a chair and lurched out of the house and drove off to the courthouse. But he needed his sedatives so he came right back, and nothing ever came of that trip. Unless . . ." she added anxiously.

"Yeah." Marty nodded. "I think something came of that trip. I think he left the note for Gil Newton about Alma Willison. And Newton found her, and waited for more instructions, and when none came he kidnapped her." And would have killed her next. The search team had found the kit with the rags and kerosene, and the logs cut to size for a cross.

"Oh, God." Elizabeth dropped her face onto her hand with the first remorse Marty had seen. "I was so frightened when you said there was a Klan card in her coffin. I thought he'd found her. I was afraid he'd find the baby too, even though

I'd hidden her in Kentucky. I thought I'd made him helpless but I was wrong. I thought he'd never talk about it—but with those people he didn't have to give a reason, did he? He could just command them."

"Yes."

In a moment Elizabeth went on, "Well, I didn't tell him any more for a while. He felt good some days, and beat me, but I wouldn't tell him any more. Finally he was bad enough that the doctor instructed us to tie him down. I waited for his good spells—by then there weren't very many. And I told him about the worms in the cysts, and what Professor Wolfe said. And I told him Phyllis was dead, and that he'd killed her. He couldn't talk much sense then. But he understood. At the end he understood why he was dying."

"He sure did," said Marty. She shifted her sore leg. "Mrs. Denton, ma'am, I'll have to take you in. You know that."

"Yes. What will happen?"

"You'll want a lawyer. Maybe your son?" Elizabeth shook her head firmly and Marty continued, "We'll read you your rights and take an official statement, and Art Pfann will decide what to do."

"It doesn't matter anymore. If that baby is safe, it doesn't matter. You'll watch out for Phyllis's baby, won't you?"

"Yes, ma'am. I don't think your sons want trouble, but I'll watch."

"Good. Will I go to prison?"

"Maybe not." Marty held the door for her and they stepped onto the broad porch. "Depends on the lawyers. But what can Art Pfann charge you with? Serving undercooked breakfasts?"

Elizabeth Denton didn't smile. She said, "When he killed Phyllis, he killed me too. So it really doesn't matter anymore." She gave one unregretful glance at the great limestone house and climbed into the cruiser.

54

CHRISSIE PUSHED OPEN THE GLASS DOOR AND BOUNCED OUT INTO the bright July sun. Wind whipped her dark hair and molded her raspberry-colored T-shirt to her ribs. Marty, right behind her, had to raise her hand to keep her curls from blowing into her eyes. She followed her daughter to the edge of the deck, where Chrissie was touching the protective mesh that rose from the stone parapet. "What's all this wire for, Mommy?"

"To make sure nobody falls."

The girl looked down eighty-six stories to the cars rolling along the streets below. "Gross," she said. "Hey, is that the World Trade Center?"

"It sure is."

"Oh, God, Janie will never believe it! And where's the Chrysler Building?"

"Other direction. Past that fat man, see?"

Chrissie wriggled her way among the other tourists to claim a section of the northern parapet. Marty followed more slowly, looking down at the roofs of buildings, at the hot streets, at the broad flat river. Across the river was more city, lots of city, disappearing into a line of haze. Beyond the haze was a line of blue hills, hazy too. Beyond the hills, far beyond, was Indiana. Home to her, and to this great building.

Chrissie was looking at the tall structures to the north around the silvery Chrysler Building, her eyes shining. "Daddy's right," she said. "It's a magical city."

"Yeah."

"Someday maybe I can see it with him, too."

"Yeah, probably."

"But I'm glad I saw it for myself."

327

Marty knew then that it had been worth it, blowing the last of the house-painting money for this three-day weekend in the magical but very expensive city. She said, "That's right, Chrissie. We don't have to wait for anybody. We'll just do things for ourselves."

"Yeah. Hey, this stone came from home, didn't it?"

"From the Empire State Quarry. Your own granddad helped dig it up."

"Neat. Look, Mommy, is that a sea-lily fossil?"

Marty peered over the small raspberry-colored shoulder at the limestone block, cut smooth but weathered a little now. She could see a sparkling sea floor from long ago, strewn with tiny latticed fans and cords, and—yes, there it was, a disk like a shirt button. A sea-lily stem. This great magical building was a monument to life.

"You're right, Chrissie," she said, running her fingers over the stone.

Seashells in the sky.